A Note from Winterbottom

By W J Brown

Text copyright © 2015 William Joseph Venning Brown
All rights reserved

The characters and events in this book are fictitious. Any similarity to real persons, living or dead, is coincidental and not intended by the author.

For Philippa

Table of Contents

Chapter 1   5

June 5   A tall man   A journalist   Johnson   5

June 23   The tall man   A drunk   15

June 26   Sir Richard   Henry   Dame Jennifer   Carol   Jane   19

Chapter 2   30

August 2   Anthony   Peter   Emily   30

Chapter 3   48

July 29   Anthony   A Scandinavian   Smith   Brown   Helen   Walter   48

Chapter 4   80

July 29   Anthony   Paul and Anne Baxter   80

July 29   Anthony   Maurice   90

Chapter 5   101

Previously   Maurice   Patricia and Christopher   101

Chapter 6   115

July 30   Maurice   Anthony   Henry   An Aide   Senior Policemen   115

Chapter 7   134

July 31   Anthony   Helen   Walter   134

Chapter 8   142

August 2   Anthony   David   Frieda   Hank Edwards
Emily and Peter Williams   Andrew Bond   *142*

Chapter 9   191

June 26, evening   Henry   Jennifer   *191*

June 28   A security officer   Jane   Jennifer   Sophia Adeleke   *199*

June 30   Henry   Jennifer   Charles   David   *213*

Chapter 10   232

July 3   Jane   Harriet   *232*

July 3   David   *241*

July 10   Jane   David   Alan   *246*

Chapter 11   252

July 17   Armstrong   Jane   Danny   *252*

Chapter 12   271

July 22   Jane   Lucy   *271*

July 23   Jane   *279*

July 24   Lucy   Jane   Axel   *281*

Chapter 13   296

July 30   Maurice   Alan   Jane   *296*

Chapter 14   305

July 31   Maurice   Jennifer   Charles   Armstrong   Alice
Danny   *305*

August 2 Jane Maurice	*316*
August 4 David Jane	*328*

Chapter 15   332

August 3-7 Anthony Helen Walter	*332*
Monday August 7 Anthony Jane	*341*

Chapter 16   343

Monday August 7 Henry Richard	*343*
Monday August 7 David Jennifer Jane	*350*
August 7 Afternoon Henry Alan	*360*
August 7 Late afternoon David Jane	*363*

Chapter 17   367

Tuesday August 8 Jane Axel Anthony Frieda Alison	*367*
Wednesday August 9 Tall man Johnson	*382*

Chapter 18   387

Thursday August 10 Richard The Prime Minister Armstrong	*387*

Chapter 19   391

Wednesday August 9 Alan various police a criminal	*391*
Thursday August 10 Henry Alan Jennifer, David and Jane (off stage)	*398*
Thursday August 10 Bruno Tall man	*401*

Chapter 20   404

Friday August 11   David   Jennifer   Jane   Charles   Anthony   Henry 404

Saturday August 12   Frieda   Anthony   Patricia and Christopher   Maurice 412

Chapter 21   423

Monday August 14   Patricia and Christopher   Frieda   Maurice   Anthony 423

Tuesday August 15   Frieda   Maurice   Anthony   Patricia and Christopher   Henry (Hank) Edwards   Emily and Peter Williams 430

Chapter 22   451

Tuesday August 15   Jane   David   All the politicians and senior civil servants 451

Chapter 23   464

Tuesday August 15   David   Jane   Alan   Armstrong   various Senior Persons 464

August 15 Afternoon   Lucy   Axel   Johnson 473

August 15   Axel   Edwards   Rembrandt 488

August 15   David   Alan   Jane 501

Chapter 24   508

August 15   The Cast, excepting only the Great People in London 508

The following year 526

Acknowledgements   530

Chapter 1

June 5   A tall man   A journalist   Johnson

Summer days in London are not hot, by most countries' standards. But the sun can be tiresome, there is little shade, and the dusty pavements feel hard on the feet. On such a day two men met in a basement on Broadwick Street in Soho. The Englishman would have preferred a bench in the park, by the Serpentine, in the shade cast by the Indian bean trees, but the foreigner, tall and fair, his light cashmere coat draped over one shoulder, had insisted on this seedy rendezvous. The area windows were shuttered, the illumination, such as there was, artificial. There was a smell of mould and old alcohol, and an intimation of venery.

"This is – this is – " the Englishman, frowning, looks carefully at his companion, " – quite unpleasant."

"Is it particularly bad? I was told that it would be suitable. Neither of us is likely to be recognised here, surely?"

"You can say that again." The Englishman swallows some of the champagne in his glass, purses his lips in distaste, and explains to the foreigner, "We call this sort of bar a clip joint. Soho has many of them. They come and go, they change their names, sometimes they change the girls – "

"But not the carpets?" says the foreigner, who has just folded his legs and felt a hint of reluctance as his foot left the floor.

"Not the carpets, not the curtains, not the furniture, nothing to speak of. I mean, you can't actually *see* anything, can you?"

He is a man in late middle age, dressed fairly fashionably yet with an air of scruffiness. He has lived in London all his life, except for a short spell in the Midlands at the start of his career.

"There used to be an Italian grocer just round the corner in Bridle Lane, best cheese and coffee in London."

He is a cynical man, as are almost all of his profession, and has found that as he grows older it has become more difficult to maintain even an appearance of good will and enthusiasm. He knows that the public believe journalists tell lies. He, on the other hand, has never interviewed a member of the public who has told him the plain truth; on the whole, he thinks, people just make things up.

He continues, "This wine's diabolical. And look at that girl – have you ever seen a fat pole dancer before? I hope you're not expecting me to pay for all this."

The foreigner's expression does not change. "I think you will find my information compensates for the inadequacy of the rendezvous. She seems pleasantly rounded to me."

He takes a sheet of paper from his briefcase and runs his eyes over it for a second or two.

"We understand that your proprietor harbours deep suspicions concerning the honesty, the loyalty, of a certain important member of the British Government."

"Do you? Who is 'we'?"

"A group of concerned business men, of several nationalities, who share your proprietor's views concerning, ah, the benefits of unhindered international trade."

"My proprietor's views do not influence the editorial policy of the newspaper."

"Of course not, he has often made speeches to that effect."

The journalist gulps down some more of his nasty champagne.

"Well, which important member of the government?"

"Armstrong. We have received information that he has taken corrupt payments in respect of contracts for the supply of certain matériel to your Defence Department."

The journalist hopes that the tall man has noticed nothing unexpected in the manner in which his statement was received. The light is low and in any case he has, as far as he knows, shown no expression other than an appropriate amount of interest combined with a deal of disbelief. The tall man has not, in fact, given much thought to the way in which the journalist might try and disguise his reaction.

The journalist replies. "Oh yes. Are you sure it's not satanic rituals? Drug trafficking perhaps; underage sex?"

He smiles.

"I understand your scepticism. We shall provide documented evidence. In the meantime, you might look over an outline which I have prepared for you of the manner in which this fraud was perpetrated." He hands the sheet of paper to the journalist, who scans its contents carefully, absentmindedly pouring himself and drinking another large glass of the dyspeptic wine. He waves away the tubby pole dancer who has come to ask the gentlemen if either of them would like a private entertainment.

"Why my paper, why me?"

"Your paper because it is widely respected, yourself because you are well known to be a fearless investigative journalist."

"Bollocks."

"Perhaps I might add that I am not myself a person who enjoys the enormous wealth of my associates. I am more what you might term a consultant, a distinctly peripheral member of the consortium."

"Got it. If this doesn't turn out to be a load of cobblers, how much are you going to want?"

"I think maybe one hundred and fifty."

"Don't be daft. We've never paid that, not even for one of the Diana stories."

"But this is bigger, certainly more important."

"When will you have the proof?"

"In about four weeks, so I am told by the CEO of the firm concerned."

"The firm concerned? What do you mean?"

"Naturally, an honest competitor of the company whose bid succeeded."

"Let's have another squint at that bit of paper you've got there. This would be an exclusive?"

"Yes, of course, an exclusive. I would rather not leave this note with you; maybe you would like to study it now."

The journalist peers at the paper again, finding it difficult to read properly in the alternately red and orange light of the spots illuminating the dancer.

"It doesn't give the name of this firm of yours. Shall we drop the 'consortium' crap?"

The tall man smiled. "How perceptive you are. Names and, ah, *pack drill* in four weeks?"

"That's not good enough. I need to know which contract you're talking about, what the stuff – the matériel – was, and when it happened."

The other man leaned over closer to the journalist, and whispered a name. "The matériel was a metal used for the tips of armour piercing shells. The contract was concluded eight months ago."

"You mean depleted uranium?"

"Do not, ah, *vault the cannon*? You shall have complete information in a month, I promise you. In the meantime, you must negotiate my payment with your employer. I think perhaps a hundred and twenty five; do you think that more reasonable?"

"Still too much. Unless it's watertight. We'll see. How shall I get in touch?"

"Here is my card, and the number of my cell."

The journalist laughs. "In English that means somewhere in Pentonville. What are you, German?"

For a moment the other man appears disconcerted.

"I apologise, I should have said 'mobile'. Now, shall I pay for our drinks?"

"Why not? You'll be getting a fat envelope in a month, won't you?"

The tall foreigner raised his finger, and despite the gloom, only intermittently punctured by the remnants of the spot illuminating the languidly gyrating dancer, who was wondering whether it was really worth taking her thong off for the two blokes who seemed about as fascinated by her as she was by them, the barman was at the table in a shot.

"Another bottle, gentlemen?"

"No," said the foreigner, who handed him a couple of notes.

"Don't you want a receipt?" asked the journalist.

"I do not. Our accountants do not query my claims."

"Lucky you. Is that it, then?"

"I think I may stay on a while. I have no particular objection to plumpness."

"Chacun et cetera. By the way, you got the metaphor wrong, jump the gun means a false start in a race, setting off before the starting gun, it's nothing to do with battles."

The tall man frowned, understood, nodded.

"Best of luck, then, mate," said the journalist. "I'll be in touch."

*****

The tall man did not, in fact, stay more than a minute or two after the journalist had left. He set off south, to walk down Lexington Street towards the National Gallery, where he had arranged another meeting, underneath Bacchus and Ariadne, at five o'clock. The commercial attaché from the embassy of a small, corrupt and oil-rich African kingdom kept him waiting for a few minutes, and then gave him a lecture on the colour palette favoured by the painter Titian. The tall man endured this orotund disquisition patiently, then suggested, "Shall we go back to the cloakroom? I've left my briefcase there."

"With the...?"

"Of course. You'll want to examine it, naturally. I think perhaps the members' room in the Royal Academy?"

A short walk only. They threaded their way through the exhibition queue.

"Extraordinary. And tell me again, how did you come by it?"

The diplomat was now holding a cartridge paper folder, opened flat, inside which, protected by sheets of tissue, lay a pen and ink drawing, about the size of a sheet of foolscap. It was hardly foxed, maybe a couple of brown specks on the margin. It showed beams of light illuminating a swirl of bodies and winding sheets, tumbled together in a great chasm which had been revealed by the shattering of the marble slab which had capped it. Some of the topmost bodies were showing signs of life; they seemed to be heaving themselves up, on elbows or straightened arms, and their mouths were open as if singing, or shouting.

"Look on the back," said the tall man, and the attaché, without touching the drawing, carefully eased it over with the tissue paper. He read, written in a different ink which had by now faded to an almost illegible sepia, the words 'The opening of the fifth seal, Wm Blake, 1798'.

The tall man explained that it must have been a preliminary drawing for a series based on the seven seals in the Book of Revelation. It had been found in a cardboard file with two drawings of horses, which had not been titled or signed, which might, he said, have been sketches for the opening of the first and second seals. This folder had been lying in the attic of the great niece of the builder who had demolished Blake's house in Lambeth at the end of the Great War. This lady had recently died, in her middle nineties, and her grandson had found them when he was preparing an inventory. Sensibly, however, he had not reported his find to the Estate Duty office of the Inland Revenue.

"Is that not illegal?" asked the attaché.

"Come off it," he replied.

"I do apologise. It was an attempt at irony. You explained that you have a note, from an expert in the work of the artist William Blake?"

"Oh yes, here it is, Sir Benedict Nallmarist." Who had been an expert before his stroke, but would sign anything for a monkey, the tall man might have added.

"I believe, that is, the Prince's new wife has told me, that this Revelation book is part of the Bible?"

"Yes. Quite dramatic, if rather far-fetched."

"I avoided the missionary schools myself. I found voodoo a much less threatening religion."

The tall man found the attaché's manner, and sense of humour if that is what it was, rather trying, although it was partly explained by the tie which he was wearing, which suggested that he had attended, or wished those people who knew about that sort of thing to think that he had attended, Balliol College at Oxford. However, he paid over the amount they had agreed, and asked about the other two drawings; the tall man prevaricated, but said that he would put out feelers.

"Please do. The Prince's passion for religious art may wane when his affections are captured by a less pious consort."

The tall man left the diplomat in the Royal Academy admiring a collection of Hogarth prostitutes and made his way to an address in Mayfair. He was recognised by the security staff and escorted to the inner hall, where he ascended unaccompanied to the only floor at which the lift which he had chosen stopped. Met at the door by a secretary, he was taken to a room furnished with chairs and table in the Chinese Chippendale style, ginger jars and dark fretwork jardinières, where he was offered coffee, which he refused, or a glass of wine, which he accepted. Shortly afterwards he was joined by another, whose attitude exhibited the slightly unwarranted self-assurance of those who have retired early after reaching a middling rank in one of the uniformed services. This man waved him to a chair and asked him how things were progressing, to which question he gave a comprehensive answer in tones which would have satisfied Lord Reith. The man then asked him if he thought that the journalist would immediately try to follow up the lead which they had given him – a lead with a dead end, a complete fabrication – or whether he would continue his present inconvenient, not to say potentially disastrous, enquiries. He was angry, self-righteously angry, about the way in which the journalist's activities were endangering one of their most rewarding projects.

He expressed himself forcefully, crudely, and at some length; the gist of his tirade was that the present operation, which was now at risk, might have been started as a sideshow, but had become their most profitable activity in terms of the ratio of profits to risks – bleedin' little goldmine – and although involving some extra arrangements, these were considerably less onerous than the organisation – especially the human resources implications – of the more conventional businesses in which they were partners. He ended by asking the tall man how long he thought their ruse would keep the fucking journalist off their backs.

"I'm afraid I can't say. I've done my best for the moment. It should give us a breathing space, but obviously it's not a long term solution. And it's not just Winterbottom; there are rumours: Rembrandt's made one or two mistakes. That Bradley he did, for example, and I think Kuznetsov is dissatisfied with his purchase...moreover, and I suppose I must take responsibility for this, there are difficulties, quite coincidental difficulties, arising from my arrangement with Mickey's political friend."

He explained the problems, in some detail.

"Shit. We could do without upsetting the Russians...and the other thing...not worth the risk, is it? So, you think we should wind it up?"

The tall man nodded.

"As I said, I'm sorry. But it has been very rewarding. Maybe we can try placing one more, perhaps two."

Johnson had been looking out of the window. He opened it, and scattered a few seeds from a paper bag onto the ledge. The pigeons were there in a flash. He looked at the tall man who thought he could see sadness, a sort of wistfulness, in his expression.

"It was such a neat scheme, wasn't it and so, so *tidy*. No harm to anyone, money all round, a truly victimless crime, as they say. I mean, who suffers? Who do we rob? No-one. There's a philosophical principle there, you know."

The tall man, who had collaborated with Johnson for some time now and knew exactly how philosophical and principled was his behaviour, interrupted.

"Covered moral philosophy, your course, did it? I thought it was how to change oil and mend carburettors."

This annoyed Johnson, who was not accustomed to being talked down to, except by the Chairman and, naturally, Lord Stuck-up-Bumfinger, one of the non-executive Directors brought onto the board as window-dressing. He had already planned where and when his supercilious lordship was to receive a slap.

"Don't be so fucking patronising. So you've got a degree, when did you last do any, what did you call it, literary humanities, some pretentious crap or other?"

The tall man smiled coldly, but spoke in a conciliatory tone, "You've got a point there; I'm sorry, I must be a little tired. But we should agree on the next step. I've bought a little time, that's all. I came here so that we could discuss it now and make a decision."

"Look, I'm quite happy to leave it to you. You decide, whatever, it'll be OK by me. Just don't take any unnecessary risks, will you?"

The tall man turned fractionally, with a ghost of a frown, which might have meant that he didn't really understand what the other man had just said.

"I go to enormous lengths to minimise risk, you should know that by now."

His companion's ears were not sensitive to the harmonics of this statement, otherwise he might have felt a little uneasy.

Leaving the room with the Chinese theme, the tall man walked past the oil paintings lining the Turkey carpeted corridor: East India Company nabobs with faux turbans and tiger skins, eighteenth century sugar and slave traders, nineteenth and twentieth century coal and cotton millionaires, ship owners, politicians, brewers, all with the rounded bellies and tight waistcoats of wealth and success – such a tradition of mercantile endeavour, of that individual pursuit of riches which British philosophers and economists had guaranteed would so greatly benefit the entire globe. A tradition, he thought, of hypocrisy, exploitation, racism and cruelty. And now, who guarded that tradition? The so-called private equity company, the anonymous – although not to him

– crew of gangsters whose billions had turned a moribund trading company into a giant vehicle for translating the fruits of international crime into respectable dollars and pounds.

Outside the office building he set off in the direction of Charles Street, where he turned left to cross Regent Street and return to Soho. Rather to his own surprise he retained a strong mental image of the chubby pole dancer, and he saw no reason why he should not spend the evening with her. He did not doubt that she would be happy to spend it with him.

June 23   The tall man   A drunk

    The tall man would not have been recognised by his colleagues in the trading company. No cashmere overcoat, no light-weight Oxfords; a black fake leather jacket, trainers. He wore gloves, although it was not cold, and his fair hair was tucked away under a dark green beanie. A scruffy beard softened his jaw line. Taking a tube to Bayswater, he worked his way steadily through the network of streets surrounding the Orthodox Cathedral until, on the corner of Orme Lane and Caroline Place, he saw a parked car which met his needs. This was a smallish silver hatchback of a particular but common make and model, six or seven years old, with various cosmetic enhancements such as a widened exhaust pipe and polished wood steering wheel. It might or might not have an alarm; that did not matter. He would take the chance that no immobiliser had been fitted – if it had, he would walk away and look elsewhere. He swiftly broke in and shut the door behind him. The alarm shrieked, which he ignored. A passer-by looked at him through the window on the nearside door, he smiled, shrugged, made an 'oh what a nuisance' gesture with his hands, the passer-by smiled, returned the gesture, and walked on. He had the engine started in under half a minute, and drove quickly up to the railway line near Paddington where there was some rough ground by a chain link fence, opened the car's bonnet and disabled the alarm. It took him about half an hour to crawl through the Maida Vale traffic to Kilburn, where he parked a short distance from the Loyal Victorian, a pub which sat uneasily between areas which had just about maintained a modicum of respectability, and those which had not. A CCTV camera was fastened behind the window of a late night off licence on the opposite side of the road, and he was careful to park outside the sector covered by its lens. He removed his beanie, pulled off his beard and changed his bomber jacket for an old brown Barbour. He placed the items which he had discarded in a holdall, and put it in the boot. The end of the terrace was only a few paces away, where the building on the corner, even if it had not displayed a swinging sign proclaiming allegiance to the previous century's eponymous monarch, would have been recognisable as a pub by its fancifully patterned, smooth-finished brickwork, and rope-pattern courses of dark green glossy tiles. When this had been built, by a famous London brewer in the late nineteenth century, its door had been a masterpiece of carved oak and stained glass, but a century of drunken shoves and kicks had put paid to this door long since. The tall man pushed open a mean and temporary-looking plywood affair, designed only to be cheap to replace; at night, metal bars were fastened over it, but the pub's main security sat alternately scratching its belly and licking its privates, chained to a ring at one end of the bar.

"Hello Arthur," he said, walking straight over to one of the tables. This was a very recent acquaintance who drank heavily most of the day, who could drive a car, and had been arrested at least once for assault; he may or may not have been married, but at present lived on his own. Arthur had taken off his own beanie, green and greasy as the Limpopo, but still wore his shiny black bomber jacket. He clearly hadn't shaved for some time. They had talked, or rather, the tall man had listened while Arthur talked, about football and snooker. They had played darts once, but the barman had stopped them because Arthur had become too drunk. The tall man had said next to nothing about himself, beyond hinting that he could often get hold of cheap, presumably stolen, whisky.

"What are you drinking? Two large Bell's please."

He let Arthur tell him at length about an extraordinary break played by some East End hero of the snooker circuit, but when Arthur rewound himself to start again at the beginning the tall man mentioned that he'd had a delivery from his lorry driver friend, and he didn't mind sharing a bottle with Arthur, if Arthur would fancy some? Nice drop of Scotch, might even be from Scotland. Arthur looked puzzled, but ignored this attempt at a joke, he didn't give a damn where his booze came from. He pulled his beanie back on and headed for the steps down to the subterranean lavatory.

As they walked to the car, the tall man asked Arthur to remind him what sort of car he had? Fast one, was it? Had he got his licence back? Arthur was, it seemed, between cars, but used to own a Vauxhall Senator, ex-police, went like shit off a shovel, cornered like a fucking Ferrari. Fell to bits; fucking filth had fucking 'ammered it, 'an't they?

The tall man indicated his seen-better-days boy racer, pointed at the gaping exhaust and suggested that in fact this vehicle was at least as fast, probably faster, than any sort of Vauxhall. Arthur could not agree to this.

"Go on then, take it round the block. Bring it back in one piece, eh?"

Arthur wasn't quite sure how to play this one. How could he show this twat, he didn't even know his fucking name, that his car was crap but, on the other hand, that he, Arthur, was a shit-hot driver? In the end he drove it round the back streets as fast as he could, swerving and screeching to a halt near the tall man, staggered out and swore that it was like trying to steer a fucking fork lift truck. They sat for a while with their whisky on the low wall of an overgrown garden, in a litter-filled corner shielded from houses by laurels and dusty holly trees.

Arthur wanted to drive up to Primrose Hill and continue his boozing on a bench which he knew well, he said, a fine place to have a dram or two, up on the grass there, but the tall man was surprisingly adamant that they should stay put. There was no-one around, he said, it was pleasant enough, the low wall was comfortable, wasn't it? Arthur was up-ending the bottle and drinking deeply; the tall man wondered if he might be sick, but Arthur had passed that stage in his life, and his drinking career, when too much alcohol in the stomach would make him vomit. The tall man had been careful to swallow none himself; since they had been swigging from the bottle Arthur had not noticed this. Probably, the tall man thought, they should try and return to the car before Arthur passed out; this would quite likely be soon because he had reinforced the whisky with rectified spirit.

"You got chilblains?" Arthur suddenly asked as the tall man walked him carefully back to the car, supporting him by holding Arthur's left wrist on his, the tall man's, left shoulder, with his right arm round Arthur's waist. "Never take your fucking gloves off, do you?"

"Yes, that's right," replied the tall man as they reached the car, but Arthur was asleep now, his head lolling like a two year old's, and his feet dragging sideways along the pavement. The tall man pushed him onto the back seat and covered him with a thin rug which he took from the holdall in the boot, pulling the cloth right up over his head. He changed into his black jacket, pulled on his beanie, and fixed back his beard, then started the car and drove back in the direction of Bayswater, in perfect time to encounter Winterbottom crossing the road as he walked home from the tube station to his flat on Porchester Terrace.

June 26   Sir Richard   Henry   Dame Jennifer   Carol   Jane

"So, that's curtains for the Children of Love, then?"

"Yes, Richard, closed at last after a distressingly long run. It is such a worrying phenomenon, though. These people just seem to pop up, out of nowhere."

"That's the thing about messiahs, Henry."

"Exactly. They say it's all to do with the eyes, but I'm not so sure. It's quite possible to manufacture a messiah, you know; look at North Korea."

"I think it may be fairly fruitless at the moment to discuss the qualities of charisma, Henry."

"You're quite right, DG, we should move on. To conclude, the cousins were surprisingly cooperative, he got three terms of ninety-nine years."

"Consecutive?"

"Yes. Mind you, that might be inadequate."

"Really?"

"One of his attributes was immortality, you may remember."

"Hmm. Now, Henry, the next item, where are we, number six. This is the one you put in my tray the day before yesterday, isn't it? 'Note from Winterbottom.' I don't find any papers attached, certainly no note. Is it on file?" He turned to his desktop and reached for the mouse, but paused before Henry could remind him that this was an off-the-record meeting.

"No copy, even?"

"No, Richard. Here, take a look."

He handed the Director General a thin file, opened at a single sheet of paper, a smudged carbon copy of three paragraphs of text.

"Is this *typing*, Henry? I mean, as in *typewriter*?"

"It is indeed. Very old fashioned, was Winterbottom. Our winger at the Screws acquired it."

"Good God. Well, what does it say?"

He quickly read it.

"Henry, for goodness sake, you can't take this sort of crap seriously? And, who the hell is Winterbottom?"

"You know, DG, journalist, also writes a crowd-pleaser in the Shield?"

"Oh, that Winterbottom. Writes what's it called, God's Own Country?"

"This Sceptred Isle, I think, DG."

"Quite. Too William Hickey for me. So what's she called, Nicholson isn't it, picked it up, did she?" He paused, biting his lower lip and waggling the index finger of his left hand like the arm of a metronome. Henry waited for the DG to remember that it was Winterbottom who had uncovered a rather nasty scandal involving passports, drugs, and officials of the Home Office.

"Of course, yes, couldn't fault him on that one, could we? But this is just silly, don't you think?" Before Henry could say what he thought, the DG continued, "Well, what are we supposed to do? Warn Armstrong that someone's out to get him? He gets dozens of threats, surely? All politicians get hate mail."

"I see you've worked out who the *subject* is - it took me a minute or so longer."

"Come on, Henry, enough clues, I would have thought. Liverpool – skiing – and I have occasionally encountered him at the Acol."

"Ah, bridge. I don't play."

"You should, Henry. Too taxing, after work, perhaps?"

"Spot on, DG. I quite like crib."

"You said that for humorous effect, Henry, but I do actually happen to possess a remarkably attractive cribbage board, Tunbridge ware, you know what that is? Where did Nicholson find it?"

"She saw him typing it up from some notes, or something. They usually use email of course, so this seemed very odd. I don't know how she got hold of it, but it's on the way to the editor, she thinks, probably to be discussed at their next Thursday meeting."

"Well, we'll just have a quiet word, shall we? We should let Armstrong's protection unit know, at the very least."

"I don't think it's quite as simple as that, Richard. The next item in the file you're holding," – the DG folded back the note from Winterbottom to reveal a scrap of newspaper –"is a cutting from the Screws. It was in the other papers too; perhaps your briefing team missed it?"

The Director General read the cutting.

"Hit and run, eh? We don't like coincidences, do we, Henry? But I don't think we can blame my briefing team, whom I normally refer to as Susan, for missing this. Winterbottom only helped us once or twice – he must have made lots of enemies elsewhere. She would have little reason to make a connection. The police are satisfied, I see; the car was driven into a lamp post – only ten minutes after – dead drunk driver, no, both, I see, drunk and dead?"

"Yes, DG, the next paper is a copy of the police report, and a summary of the autopsy. Blood alcohol sky high, liver completely shot. Then, as you see, they called in all the CCTV images near where they presume he stole the car – well, someone stole it because it was reported missing just before the accident."

"*Before*, Henry, are they sure?"

"Yes, and much to the annoyance of the AC, I had Taylor check their logs. They turned up three sightings, two of them on newish cameras, where you could just about make out the driver's appearance; quite consistent with the dead man. He'd got form, of course, that's how they identified him, fingerprints all over the car, door, steering wheel, and two, rather surprisingly, thumb and index finger, on the leather part of one of the rear seats."

"But you don't like it, smells wrong to you, does it, Henry? It's not much of a coincidence; and they do happen, you know. Let's have another look at that paper Nicholson picked up." He read it again carefully, then aloud.

"'Subject drives a vintage Bentley, owns a first edition of The Origin, a flat in St Malo, a number of extremely valuable paintings of the mid-twentieth century and has recently acquired a large Riley. He plays cards and takes his entire family skiing every year at Méribel. His grandfather worked on a farm near Warrington and his father was a gardener on the Earl of Derby's estate at Knowsley. Before he entered Parliament he was a student, then he took a PhD, then he taught physics in Liverpool. 'Subject'! Pompous blighter. Sorry, de mortuis, eh?"

"The point is, Richard, where did he get all the moolah? He doesn't just seem to be comfortable, like ourselves, you know, twenty years in a reasonable job, paid off the mortgage and all that. No, he seems to be rolling in it, doesn't he?"

"Well, only on the assumption the late Winterbottom's information is correct," said the Director General, "Let's see, he's been a Minister for, what, almost ten years? As you say, reasonably well paid, not excessive though. Perhaps his wife's got hold of some money? It doesn't seem as if *his* family would have any, does it? He gambles; perhaps he wins? Not likely, I admit. Vintage Bentley, eh? Does he collect old cars? I didn't know they ever made a large Riley. Nice little sporting jobs, mind you."

"I do think we should take this a little bit further, Richard. One does worry sometimes. Winterbottom was a bit of a tit, I grant you, but, you see, Green tells me that the passport affair, which you obviously remember, wasn't the only bit of useful snooping he did for us; also, it seems that he gave Ted Lancashire in GR2 one or two snippets which were quite without tarnish. Not that he was ever on the payroll, you understand; he was an old fashioned patriot, is what he said to Ted. So, however unrewarding it might prove to follow up this little billy-doo, I honestly think it would be negligent to ignore it. Certainly, I would like one of my chaps to look into the hit-and-run, and as far as Armstrong is concerned, I'm only suggesting that we make a few enquiries to, how shall I put it, update the file. That shouldn't present too many problems? Oh, and it's a *Bridget* Riley, an abstract painting. It would give you a headache, Richard, and in any case I doubt you could afford it."

"Not too many problems." The DG corrected the alignment of pen and pencil on his blotting pad and dropped his head in a little pantomime of exhaustion. "I fear you are being disingenuous, Henry. *Performing* such an enquiry would indeed be simple, I grant you. So would you care to approach the Prime Minister and ask his consent?"

The person whose name was typed at the top of Winterbottom's paper was one of the most effective and loyal members of the Cabinet, in a Government which was a coalition of more or less inconsistent ideologies and interests, and his job was to reconcile these disparate strands and to deliver a majority to the Premier on all important issues. The Minister's previous cabinet post had been Secretary of State for Export and Trade, but he now had no departmental responsibility and the honorary position of Treasurer of the Hundred Levels. He was the Premier's confidential adviser, and almost a close friend; the Minister himself had many friends in politics, but none particularly close, and many acquaintances, who trod carefully in his presence. Henry was, of course, being disingenuous, but he felt uneasy about the apparent – at the moment only alleged – inconsistencies between the Treasurer's lifestyle and his overt sources of income. With Henry, minor unease often modulated into major suspicion, and, in his line of work, Henry did not like to neglect his suspicions.

The Director General continued, "You must know that the PM hates us poking around in the private lives of his friends. Here and abroad." He placed his hands on the desk and leaned forward. "I had the temerity to warn him about his mateyness with Floorboard, wanted Jennifer to send one of her teams over to help the locals find out how long he could last, but the PM wasn't having it at all. Apparently Floorboard was going to support our bid to host the world mud-wrestling championships. Or something of that ilk. Not to speak of entertaining the finest in our land to holidays on his yacht."

Henry remembered the person codenamed Floorboard well. He also remembered the PM's motives, which were rather more political than the DG was implying. The DG was prone to make rather binary moral judgements at times; it was his upbringing, of course, the strict code of the Scottish Islands. The poor man's adolescent Sundays had been spent struggling to reconcile the internal contradictions of a peculiarly anal version of Calvinism, and he had never quite wriggled out of its gloomy straitjacket. Jennifer found the occasional insertion of moral absolutes into her activities particularly trying.

On this occasion, however, when the DG – 'C', as he was still sometimes known – began to explain in some detail the practices which were rumoured to occur on Floorboard's yacht, The DD (O) became aware that his purpose was to sidestep the issue. Not, of course, officially to refuse a formal proposal, merely to put what he judged the best distance between himself and, in this case, the notion that Armstrong was anything but straight-down-the-line kosher; a considerable distance, but not so great that he couldn't tiptoe back if some enterprising journo were to find Armstrong tucking into a bacon roll.

The Deputy Director put down the red file and they turned to staffing matters. They had recently taken to advertising for staff, partly because there seemed no reason not to, and partly to entrap, and possibly turn, unfriendly persons who might – who undoubtedly would – apply in order to infiltrate the service. They discussed the screening procedures which had been put in place. The DG was concerned; he was even concerned about the loyalty of the screening staff. Issues of loyalty inside the service were one of his major concerns; the enemy without, he thought that they could deal with more or less effectively, or at least according to sensible and consistent strategies; the enemy within was a different matter. It went without saying that neither he nor any other member of the secret intelligence services trusted the honesty or loyalty of ordinary Members of Parliament. The so-called Wilson doctrine, by which Harold Wilson had assure Members that they would not be subjected to surveillance had, luckily, never been enshrined in law. Monitoring MPs was a standard and accepted function of the Service and the surveillance procedures were routine. The classification of sins was religious in flavour. Venial sins were met with a quiet word in club or pub, and usually expiated by means of a show of penitence and a Hail Mary or two; occasionally a hint of a threat might be employed in the case of the more distasteful transgressions. Mortal sins were usually discussed at the Secret Security sub-committee of the Cabinet, and criminal proceedings, resignations or voluntary exile followed; very occasionally, carefully and deniably, mortal sins were just that.

The current Prime Minister, however, exercised a much closer control over the security services than had his predecessors, and by skilful manipulation of the appointments procedure for senior posts had made the job of those special sections which functioned independently – *took initiatives* was the term used, *acted illegally* was its meaning – much more tricky than in the past. He had also to an extent broken down the barriers between the two arms of the Security Services, and now not only was the collaboration between those entrusted with homeland security and the spies of what had been called MI6 much closer, but both functions were combined in a single Directorate. A number of sections were formed to undertake work which contained elements of spying and security – work which, previously, had required ad hoc co-operation between officers of the two separate services, and which had often been bedevilled by problems of communication and leadership.

Two infamous occasions, where knowledge had been acquired but not acted upon, and where lives had been lost, had precipitated the Prime Minister's action. He had first made a feint against the Special Branch of the Metropolitan Police, mooting the suggestion that it should be absorbed by the security services, but the Commissioner had rallied his friends in the press, and the tabloids had inveighed against such an over-arching concentration of power, using (quite inappropriately) terms such as KGB and Gestapo. Members of Parliament had agreed, and this idea had been dropped. The subsequent amalgamation of the security services then seemed a less controversial issue, and the two displaced Directors found that they could marshal little opposition to the plan. The Security Directorate had also been given a remit to monitor, and in some cases control, police action against cross-border crimes such as gun running and human trafficking. There were fewer operations in Northern Ireland since the recent agreement, but the Deputy Director (Ireland) still controlled a powerful section which, for historical reasons, worked more closely with the police and army than did other branches of the Service.

One of the PM's requirements of the re-organised Service was that none of his close cabinet colleagues, nor any of a small list of powerful others, should be investigated without his permission, which although formal was not a formality, as the deputy Directors soon discovered.

At the end of the meeting, as Henry was making his way to the door, crossing the fairly wide expanse of quite good quality and reasonably unworn Iranian rug which the procurement Directorate deemed appropriate to Sir Richard's rank, Sir Richard himself rose and beckoned him back. They met over the central lozenge, and the DG, a tall and handsome Coldstreamer, laid an arm over Henry's back and, clasping him by the shoulder, walked slowly to the door, stooping slightly to speak confidentially into his ear.

"I should get a move on with that little inquiry of yours. I expect the Screws will put private dicks onto it toot sweet. We don't want egg on our faces, do we?"

In the canteen afterwards – and they all used the canteen, the senior people no longer strolled through St James to the Reform – the DD(O) spoke to the Policy Adviser (Temporary Initiatives), who was at the same level of seniority as the Deputy Directors, but had a slightly less well defined role. Her amorphous department was commonly known as Ticklish Issues. She was known as Patty, but not to her face.

"Jennifer, can I tempt you to treacle sponge?"
"Coffee please, black"

"Two black coffees, then." Without at this stage going into details, he brought the conversation around to the PM's protective attitude towards his most senior supporters. This was not difficult because it was an issue which worried the Service, unused as it was to circumscription of its activities by politicians. Jennifer, who never spoke unguardedly, stirred her coffee for a moment and then said, "This isn't just a general chat, is it? What have you heard, Henry, and about whom?"

Henry outlined the information contained in the note from Winterbottom, without mentioning the journalist's name. Jennifer replied, "I don't get on particularly well with Armstrong, you know that. When he was at Export he could be damned obstructive. I sometimes feel that C could be a little more assertive – it should be quite a simple matter to check Armstrong's wife's money, and his gambling of course – as a matter of interest, are spouses covered by the same embargo?"

"Not explicitly – but I think the PM's attitude is fairly clear."

"Well, I suppose that does make it all rather difficult, doesn't it?"

"I don't know, Jennifer, I don't like the smell of it at all. Can't you think up a wheeze?"

Two junior officers approached the table.

Smiling, the younger one said, "You don't mind do you? It's getting very crowded. She hooked her bag over the chair back, wriggled her skirt up a bit, and sat down. Her companion hesitated a moment, smiled briefly at the table top, and sat down also.

The girl turned to Henry. My name's Carol. I work in non-comp cross referencing?"

Henry smiled. "Well, I work here too. What's non-comp cross referencing?"

The girl looked arch. Her friend continued to stare at the cutlery.

"We're not supposed to talk about our jobs, are we?"

Without looking up, but with a note of exasperation in her voice, the other girl said, "It's all right Carol, we're all friends here," and then, to herself only, "if not exactly on the same pay grade."

"OK then. It's just correlating things which haven't got a susp-act code yet."

"Ah, fascinating."

"What do you do?"

Her friend exclaimed, "Look Carol, there are Ted and Maureen – perhaps we should go and join them?"

Carol beamed at Henry. God, he thought, she's a pretty little thing.

She said to her friend, "That wouldn't be very polite, would it?"

Henry asked her how long she had been working there.

"Only four months. I saw the ad in the Custodian and thought, why not?"

"The Custodian. Yes, do you know, we had a good response from those advertisements. Good ethnic mix, too. Which University did you go to?"

"North East Kent. A poly, really." She nudged her friend. "But I got a good degree. And now I'm a clerk."

Jennifer asked, politely, "And your friend?"

The other girl looked up. "HR have just told me that I'm being attached to your section. I hope I've had enough experience to merit it. My name's Jane Ryan."

"Yes, of course." She pushed her chair back. "I look forward to meeting you again soon. I am aware of your experience. Come along, Henry."

"O K. Goodbye both." he said, smiling at the young ladies.

As he left with Jennifer she said, "Have you seen the new Dogme film at the Kennington Arts?"

"'Exclusion'? No, I haven't. Rear stalls? Tonight?"

"Yes. We can have an informal chat, don't you think?"

Jane said to Carol, "Have you the faintest idea who they were?"

"Oh yes, well, him certainly. He's the Deputy Director, Operations. I've been trying to meet him for ages. I don't want to be stuck in bloody non-comp for another four months. Do you think he fancied me?"

"Very probably. Do you know who she was?"

"That dog? Not the faintest."

"That, my dear, was the Policy Adviser, Patty, Dame Jennifer to us."

"Oh fuck! Fuck! Were my knickers showing?"

"Only slightly."

Chapter 2

August 2   Anthony   Peter   Emily

Anthony, fiftyish, was woken by the light and the silence. It was high summer, but the air was sharp and little beads of moisture dribbled down the concave plastic window. He reached up and wrote his initials in the condensation, then wiped off a square, but couldn't see much through the scratched perspex. Hooking his feet over the end of the bed he pulled himself carefully down the thin mattress, avoiding the hard, cold lump of metal which had found its way from his pillow to the middle of the bed, slid to the floor, unlocked and pulled open the door. Without putting on his shoes he stepped outside and carefully picked his way over the verge and behind the hedge to relieve himself. The dewy grass and slippery soil dampened his feet as he returned, and worm casts left sticky deposits of soil between his toes. The sun slanted through a band of brilliant yellow and blue sky to the east, where a gap had opened between the distant clouds and the sea, and, outside the van, he could hear one or two birds singing and the subdued rattle of waves upon a beach, dragging small pebbles to and fro.

He made coffee and ate the remains of Tuesday's sandwiches. He wondered whether he should clear up the interior of the vehicle, which had become surprisingly dirty and untidy in less than two days. Monday night he had spent in a cheap hotel just outside Brighton, because he had been too tired to tackle the secrets of the Dormobile. The bed, which he had hauled down with difficulty the night before, obscured the view through the rear window, and he was surprised that, although a double, it swung easily upwards and clicked back into its position under the roof. Drawing back the curtains, he wiped the rear window and peered out. The field in the foreground had been partly ploughed, but at least half had been left untouched since the previous year's crop had been taken – or perhaps longer than that. Unlifted roots poked out from the soil; creatures had been nibbling at their ochre skins.

The middle distance was more attractive; there were hedges and green fields and stands of broad leafed trees, the nearest clearly defined, those further away paler and less substantial. In the vestigial mist each copse seemed separate and without depth, like painted scenery on a stage. He couldn't see the beach which must have been close, but well below him.

To the right there lay a field with a small pony standing quietly by the gate, next to a low rectangular farmhouse, granite built and slate roofed, with a range of outbuildings across the yard. No person was to be seen, but he became aware that a tractor had started up and was working nearby.

The excitement of the last four days had drained away, leaving him flat and depressed. He had felt astonishment, fear, panic, but also exhilaration. Now, as the effects of the adrenalin faded, he would be able – forced – to make a more sensible and realistic assessment of his predicament. And predicament was putting it mildly.

After washing up his coffee jug and cup he replaced them in the neat rack above the circular steel sink and let the water run out, presuming that it emerged somewhere underneath the vehicle. Then the cut and bruises on his leg needed to be dressed, and he shaved and washed at the sink, using the rest of the water which had been boiled for coffee. In a sort of tall plastic cupboard there was a lavatory which he used, hoping that none of the taps which he turned would activate the dangling shower head. The news would be on the radio soon.

He lowered the window in the driver's side door. Patches of mist lingered, despite the early sunshine, and the birds had fallen silent. The farm tractor had also stopped and the waves could now be heard, only faint and indistinct. He reached for the radio, inconveniently located near the floor, retuned it from some popular music channel to Radio Four, and turned the sound low. He tried to think clearly once more about the extraordinary situation which had developed so suddenly, its horrific resolution and the bizarre chain of events which had followed, but he found it very difficult because not only – obviously – had nothing remotely like this ever happened to him before, but the fairly simple moral rules according to which he had been brought up, and which had by and large governed his behaviour, seemed all of a sudden irrelevant. And on top of it all he was worried about the speed with which, out of rage, and fear for himself and his family, he had discarded them. Would he know when and how to return to normal? Perhaps his idea of the normal would have changed forever?

Through the window there was visible another field of turnips, or some similar crop probably intended for animal feed. The fields here were smallish enclosures, bounded by rough and grassy walls, constructed from lumps of granite laid apparently at random, but which after a moment's inspection showed a careful gradation in size from very large at the bottom to small at the top. Gorse bushes grew from the apex of the wall, and small birds hopped in and out of the brambles at its base. In the far corner of the nearest field, where the land sloped sharply uphill, boulders, some with edges which seemed to have been worked straight and smooth, partly surrounded what appeared to be a cave entrance. He was cold now, his stomach began to feel uneasy, and he shivered a little. The cave symbolised security; he imagined it with a comforting fire at the entrance, to cook him a hot meal and protect him from wolves.

The passenger's door opened gently.

"You can have all they turnips for fifty quid. But you'll have to lift them yourself."

The tractor driver, who was the farmer, had naturally noticed Anthony's arrival the previous night. Since Anthony had admired the farmhouse earlier in the morning he should have realised how unlikely it was that he himself would have remained unobserved, and in fact both the farmer and his wife had seen and heard his vehicle when it arrived in the dark, but being used to campers and caravanners – indeed, making more money from them than by growing turnips –

and, what with one thing and another, had decided to wait until morning to ask for their payment.

Anthony emerged from his reverie, and replied.

"Good morning. Sorry I just parked here, but it was very late and I'd driven all day. I didn't know I'd actually pulled onto the field, I thought it was sort of a big lay-by, well I really didn't think about it I suppose."

"Don't give it another moment's thought, flower. Just my little joke. There's no money in turnips no more, as you can see. But, I'll tell you a thing, there was a couple of blokes the other day, perfect strangers they were, who wanted to buy some old stone" – he pointed at a small heap of squared granite near the cave – "and I thought the buggers just wouldn't go away. I'm going to use they, I told them, and that was that. They looked proper angry. Still, that's it isn't it?"

"Do you have a campsite, by any chance?"

"Yes we do, me 'ansom. We charge five pound a night – I don't know about last night. Why don't you go and see my wife up the farm, I expect there'll be a brew on. Tell her how long you want to stay, if you do, that is."

"Thanks very much, that's very kind of you. Actually, I'm looking for a farm, maybe just a farmhouse, called Boselloe. I think it should be close; you don't know it, do you?"

"I certainly should. That's ours, that is. You're on it. That's the house, and yes, we do still run the farm, not that we make any money out of it, but that's farming isn't it?"

"Oh that's wonderful. What a bit of luck. A friend told me about your campsite, said it was idyllic, I couldn't find anything nicer."

"Did he now? I wonder who that might be? Very rural it surely is, squire, very peaceful. We never take lads, without families or girl friends, that is."

"Why not?"

"Why not? Are you joking? Drunken mayhem, that's why not. No, you'll find it quite peaceful here. The wife handles all the money, you go and see her. By the way, did you know that you've got bits of black tape hanging from your number plates? And whatever you do" – he pointed at the cave entrance – "don't go near that bloody shaft. It's a death trap. Well I'll be off now, see you dreckly."

What? And damn it, he thought, after all that effort. When had the wretched tape peeled off? The tractor started up, and the engine noise receded. The weather had deteriorated and it started to drizzle.

The farmer's wife came to the door promptly, and invited him into the kitchen. She was small, neat, well dressed and Japanese, and this momentarily surprised him, although it would probably not have done in the town where he lived. She was also younger than her husband. He took off his shoes and placed them just inside the door. She told him it wasn't necessary, but thanked him all the same – "but this is a farm kitchen you know, lots of muck in here." There didn't seem to be.

The farm house was also a surprise. It would originally have been nothing but a run of small square rooms built in a straight line, the one leading to the next without any separate passageway, the end room joining the livestock barns; an arrangement which leads to appealing external proportions, but, partly upon account of the thick walls, a cramped interior. In this case, however, an extension to the rear and the removal of some internal divisions had left the house as attractive inside as out. The furniture was simple and modern, the walls a powdery white and the curtains a dull cream loose weave. And there, on the powdery white walls, at the other end of the long room, were the pictures. Five or six Festival paintings of the mid-fifties; and not just of the Festival school but almost certainly all by Hopkins himself. The wireless was tuned to a farming channel, listing the market prices for commodities, or possibly animals, unknown to him.

"Your husband – he came down on his tractor, I think – asked me to come and pay for my night's stop."

He was about to explain again, but decided not to.

"Did he now?"

She turned the radio off and gestured at a chair by the kitchen table. "Sit down, please."

She filled a kettle and switched it on, and offered him tea or coffee. When she had made the coffee she sat down opposite him and poured out two cups. "My name's Emily, Emily Williams."

"Alfred Campbell."

She seemed not to have heard. He must have told lies before, as a child, obviously, but also, surely, as an adult? Yet this straightforward, planned, deception seemed different, much more perspicuous. He half expected her to laugh and say, "No you're not, don't be daft, you're Anthony Evans!"

"Have you travelled far?"

"From London, yes."

Dear me, he thought, remembering his experience with the solicitous shopkeeper in the village with the boarded-up pub, now he might have to invent an address and a route.

"It took me much longer than I imagined it would. I haven't really got used to the motor home yet, and I didn't realise that it would be quite so slow."

"Are you on your own, then? Have you come down for the surfing?"

He smiled. "Yes, and no. I don't think surfing is quite my thing, but it's very kind of you to think I might be up to it. I've just come down for some peace and quiet, really, and to look round the little galleries. Occasionally there's something quite nice, so I'm told."

She took his cup and gathered up the remaining breakfast dishes which she carried to the sink. He moved out of her way as she brought a cloth over to wipe the table, and glanced at the pictures which were hung at the further end of the room. His glance was brief, but she had noticed.

"Do they class as quite nice, then?"

He looked at her, raised his eyebrows and turned his head towards the pictures. May I look at them, he was saying. She nodded. He stood up and walked further into the room, to where the pictures hung. He opened his eyes wider, and after hesitating for a moment stepped closer to the nearest of them. He had, of course, recognised it as a member of the Industrial series, and he could quickly see that the brushwork was either Hopkins', or so similar that only microscopic examination would reveal any difference, and even then, nothing that couldn't be argued over. Paintings of Hopkins' Industrial series were generally recognised to be among the very finest examples of the entire Festival school. She was observing him as he peered rapt at the paintings. She had an amused expression, her hands clasped in front of her and her head held at a slight angle.

"I don't know what to say. Aren't they marvellous? I thought they must be prints."

"No, no, they're originals, oils, by an artist called Hopkins. You've heard of him? He was a close friend of my husband's father. Would you like another cup of coffee?"

He demurred, then accepted. As she made the coffee his eyes were drawn back to the pictures on the wall; indeed, they spoke directly to him. Look at us, they said, while you have the opportunity; never mind if it's rude. It doesn't matter what impression you give to this lady, it doesn't matter why we're here, on these walls, just stand, stare, and enjoy us. For a moment or two at least you should forget everything else. He hadn't really believed that his flight to the rocky tip of England would end in anything but bathos – perhaps signed prints, perhaps feeble imitations. This was treasure trove. He felt as if he had stepped into a seaside hotel for tea, and found that the musical entertainment in the Palm Court was Yo-Yo Ma playing the Bach cello suites.

He was unable to keep silent, although he was unable to express his delight coherently.

"They're stunning, aren't they, quite stunning. This one, the splashes of magenta here, they seem, I don't know, almost backlit, it must be the juxtaposition with the dull green there, by her elbows, where her sleeves are rolled up. And her expression; it makes you wonder sometimes why any of the others bothered."

He stopped. He hadn't really meant to say that. After all, he had bought two Bradleys and he liked them – well, definitely one of them – very much. And in another way it was a very ill-judged comment; he should be more careful, since he was very aware how easily art collectors – or art owners – could interpret the most casual, tangential, comment as an attack on their taste, or knowledge, and this family might have other paintings of the same school. And, he had to remember that not everyone thought so highly of Hopkins; some art historians treated Michael Harris as the first, and possibly the best, Festival painter, which was of course ridiculous but had become a pose – an angle – in one or two of the art schools which had recently insinuated themselves into universities.

Anthony's job involved the careful and detailed assessment of complicated alternatives, and the need to support with reasoned demonstration each step taken towards his conclusion. Serious errors could have serious consequences, in industrial, administrative, and, very occasionally, in military settings. He enjoyed the contrast of the art milieu, where he spent much of his leisure, and where subjectivity, cult, prejudice and absurdity were accepted, indeed encouraged. He had been amused – gratified, even – to find that he had his own artistic prejudices, which he recognised as such and which might lead to arguments but seldom ridicule. And there was no doubt that some art evoked from him an immediate emotional response – but, whatever the medium employed, whether intended to express simple or complicated ideas, or to capture directly the beauty of an image, to satisfy him a work had to exhibit great care and skill. Anthony was neither a minimalist nor a conceptualist. He would admit to his friends that it was just a matter of his taste, of course, and that others were perfectly entitled to admire a row of dots or a few parallel lines. But he kept his fingers crossed behind his back when he said this.

"No, that's unfair, there were some other decent painters who followed him. Bradley, for example. But Hopkins was certainly the best, I'm sure, whatever that," he made a quick verbal substitution, "*chap* Henderson, thinks."

"You seem to know a lot about them. Yes, the Cherry Girl's probably my favourite. Hoppy gave it to Peter's father before Peter was born. And one of the others – that dull one with the jeep in it. They had been in the army, doing their National Service, and they'd had some, well, rough times together. Especially once. He might tell you about it. Actually, he's bound to. In fact, all the paintings were gifts." She handed him the coffee. "I think I've heard of Henderson, he's been on TV?"

"That's right, I suppose he's generally accepted to be an expert, the expert, on the Festival school, and he thinks that its most important member was Michael Harris, not Hopkins. He's actually an old – a bit too self-confident, shall we say, and he's eminent because he was at school with Watson, and Dowlands use him a lot to do their authentication."

"You've lost me there, I'm afraid. Who's Weston?"

"Watson. He's the chairman of Dowland and Prendergast, but I'm sorry, I was rabbiting on. Talking too much as usual. I'm very interested in twentieth century art, mainly before its definition was changed, that is. Not that the Farrier's stuff isn't occasionally interesting, but more to an ethnologist than an art lover I can't help thinking."

"You've struck lucky then. We like these paintings, and my husband is very sentimental about them. There's no other reason why we've got the alarms" – she pointed at the little plastic sensors fixed round the room – "which actually cost a fortune to keep going, but the insurance people insisted, and on the special doors and windows to the room. Peter thinks it's ridiculous, because of the dogs."

"I'm sure he's right, not that it's any of my business."

"Don't worry about that. I'm supposed, that is the insurance company said that if visitors seemed to know about the value of the art we should draw attention to the" – she drew two notional inverted commas with her index fingers – 'comprehensive nature of the alarm system'. So there you are, you're a suspected thief. Like a lot of our visitors including the minister. Rector, I mean. It's all connected by its own mobile phone to a security firm in Penzance." She smiled at him. "The sensors you can see are the ordinary infra-red type - but the entire floor and ceiling act as vibration detectors. The doors and window frames are steel. They look authentic, though, don't they?" She hesitated, embarrassed by his slightly puzzled expression. "But you don't want to know all this."

Anthony had only half heard what she was saying about the alarms, but wasn't surprised. Each painting must have been at least twice as valuable as the house. He had in fact been wondering why she had called the picture the Cherry Girl.

"Well, I suppose it's an artist's attempt at humour. Bit heavy handed. Look at what she's doing."

The painting, in various shades of brown and ochre, showed a wan girl, wearing buff overalls, with her hair tightly bound in a turban of the same material. She was leaning over a wide conveyor belt covered with little fancy cakes, and appeared to be flicking one of them into a trough in the foreground of the picture.

"He had just been shown round the latest production line in Bennett's. It was what passed for automation in the fifties. This girl's only job was to spot the cakes where the cherry had been misaligned by the machine, and to flick them into the trough. You can see that she can't quite reach the trough; I think he told Peter's dad that was to make sure no-one on the line could pocket any of the cakes."

"I hadn't realised how sly he could be – he'd been commissioned, hadn't he, to paint a series celebrating new industrial processes – taking the drudgery out of labour indeed!"

"He could be sly all right. Look at that one."

She pointed at the painting on the wall opposite. Anthony turned to look at it, and, startled, said, "But it's The Overseer!"

"One of The Overseers. He painted two, a year or so before the Cherry Girl. The one in the London shows three girls and the foreman; this one has an extra girl. And do you see? Look at the girl on the left."

"Do I see what?" He looked at the girl, who was standing upright, her hands pressing against the small of her back, while her colleagues were bent to another production line task, fixing some cloth lining panels to the inside of a car door.

"She's pregnant."

"Pregnant?"

"Yes. Can't you see? Her expression, and her complexion too. And how could she not be? Look at the foreman's eyes. Never mind, I've been able to look at them every day for nearly four years now."

Connoisseurship, he thought, was so different from insight. He could see it now, but would he have done so had this girl not pointed it out? He was damn sure that Henderson wouldn't see it. He would say he had, though.

"Four years? Is that how long you've been here?"

"That's how long we've been married. I love the paintings and when we decided to move here I made sure we decorated it right and put the right curtains up and in fact I suppose that the house is organised round the paintings rather than just fitting them in. Not that we've been here long, just a couple of years, and we were away most of last summer – had to put the pictures in store – I'm not sure how many of our friends are crazy about them; they're always very polite because they can see how much they mean to me. There's a lot of art round here, you know, but quite a lot of it is, well, rather..."

"Simple?"

"Yes, that's a good way of putting it. Simple."

They both clearly thought that simple wasn't a particularly good way of putting it.

Anthony said, after the briefest of pauses, "I had only intended to stay for a couple of nights here, but perhaps, after all, it would be a good place to spend the first week of my holiday. The..." – he paused again – "scenery, the countryside, the sea, yes, perhaps I could get in a swim or two. No surfing. But, as you said, what a bit of luck – not many campsites have a fabulous art collection on the doorstep." He went pink. "I'm really sorry, I know it's not an art gallery, how presumptuous, what..."

Emily laughed."Don't be embarrassed. I love showing the paintings to people even if they don't like them and have never heard of Hopkins. It's a treat to have a visitor who knows so much, and likes them too. The last person I showed them to who knew anything about it was quite polite, but I think he had just done some sort of art appreciation course. He was quite certain that the last two" – she indicated the hall beyond the sitting room – "showed 'Hopkins' failing powers in old age' of all ridiculous things. They are late paintings, that's true, but, really...so don't worry about offending me, far from it. You must come back up when Peter's finished work, or tomorrow perhaps. I'll show you the pictures properly, and he can tell you something about Hopkins, and what he got up to with Peter's father."

"I met your husband outside just now. As I said – which reminds me." He took five pounds from his wallet and handed it to her. She smiled, and took it. "He was driving the tractor. He tried to sell me some turnips; he was joking, of course. He's...very friendly, isn't he, considering I was trespassing on his land?" What he had stopped himself saying, was "He's much older than you, isn't he?" But he was, obviously, much older than her and he seemed such a different type from this cool, well-spoken young lady. He chided himself for his prejudice; he knew that posh girls quite often fell for farmers. She had said, had she not, that the Cherry Girl had been given to his father before her husband had been born?

"Do you have a large farm? Is it mainly cattle?" he asked.

"Well, yes, all livestock really, but we grow a lot of our own feed. It's only a very small farm. We started a kitchen garden which is meant to be organic, at least it will be organic soon. It would be now if we hadn't used some horse muck with wormer in it last year. And we hope to send a lot of the veg we grow to hotels locally. Peter expects to make more money from that and the campers than he will from the beef.

I don't really know, though. I enjoy a bit of weeding from time to time, but that's about as far as it goes

She walked towards the window, picking up the coffee pot and moving a vase of flowers more precisely to the middle of a side table. Although she continued to explain the difficulties of small scale farming on a stony, thin and acid soil, Anthony paid only enough attention to respond reasonably appropriately, he hoped, from time to time. He was in fact trying to work out the chronology implicit in what she had told him about the gift of the painting. Peter had to be considerably *younger* than himself – the Overseer or now, it seemed, Overseers, had been painted in nineteen fifty two, so the Cherry Girl had been painted in fifty three so Peter had been born in about nineteen fifty four. Which would make him forty six. Even allowing for the wear and tear of agricultural life, surely he looked older than that? There seemed to be a silence and he assumed she was expecting him to say something.

"If – if farming has changed so much, as you say, I wonder sometimes why people still seem so devoted to it. I know change is always a bit difficult, but look at coal mining for instance – it's all gone now, and most of the mining areas, not all of course, have replaced the mines with other employments, and of course most of the ex-miners would have retired in any case by now."

He was perhaps – he didn't know – talking nonsense, but he hoped at any rate that he had disguised his failure to listen closely to what she had been saying.

"Well, round here many people used to be both, you know. Miners and farmers, that is. But farming isn't in Peter's blood – and in any case, don't you think that it's a bit of a romantic myth that a job can be in your blood – in your culture maybe, which is a very different thing. Soldiers and doctors and priests may follow a family tradition, but I don't think that's genes, it's just example, surely?" She smiled and looked slightly embarrassed, as if it might have been impolite to disagree with a guest.

"I'm not sure about that," Anthony replied. "What about musicians? Writers? Painters? And, well, you mentioned soldiers – I bet bravery, or whatever, is in the genes, and then look at the mafia families – no, that's not a very good example, clearly – although I suppose you could say that some criminals are quite brave as well?"

"Perhaps. I wouldn't know. Look, it's cleared up. Would you like me to show you the facilities?" She enunciated this word very deliberately, perhaps because it was a term used by the Tourist Board, or because it was a euphemism for water closet.

"That's very kind of you. Yes, I should like to see round. Then I think perhaps I'll go for a walk round the coast if the rain holds off. Is the coast path close?"

"Yes, of course. It's bound to be really isn't it? You can hear the sea. Come and see the campsite. It's hardly what you might call full, most bookings are for the second half of August and we don't get much passing trade. I don't think we advertise it properly."

She showed him through the kitchen to the farmyard at the rear, where a few pots and tools stood by the wall against which grew a fig tree and a nondescript climbing rose. A path led past a stone barn which had been renovated, with shuttered windows and a new slate roof, to a smaller outbuilding. This was adequately, but no more than adequately, fitted out with a couple of water closets and hand basins, and a cement-rendered cubicle with a half door, behind and above which he could see a shower.

"And we have to have a room for washing clothes and drying them," she said, "but most people use the hand basins."

He could see why: the laundry was a small wooden shed with an old cracked Belfast sink and a floor whose boards were only kept intact by the lino which covered them.

The camp or caravan site itself was, in contrast, glorious. Simple terraces had been cut into a gently sloping field which was enclosed on three sides by dry stone walls and on the fourth by a low bank of gorse and bell heather, beyond which, calm, grey and lustrous in the faint mist, lay the Atlantic. Two tents only were pitched, close to the western wall, no cars but one dilapidated van. Anthony was surprised; this was the second week of school holidays.

"Come in and meet my husband properly this evening. He'll not mention turnips, on the contrary I expect he'll want to talk to you about Hopkins. The village and the pub are just over the downs" – she pointed to the east – "and you can get a pint and a pie there. I'll be going back now, so see you later. Park anywhere you want."

He chose a spot by the wall opposite the tents, and set out for the facilities. He locked the van, but had also gathered together his wallet, phone and binoculars and placed them in the shoulder bag which he took with him. The gun remained under the mattress – he had forgotten it. The sun had now dispersed the low mist, and a thousand tiny gems sparkled in the long grass. Within seconds his sandals were shining wet and his feet were soaked.

On his way to the ablutions, as he passed the Transit which was well used and shabby rather than decrepit, one of the rear doors swung open and a shortish man, stooping then straightening as he emerged, stepped into his path. His grey pony tail was secured with elastic bands.

"Give us a hand with this will you?"

He hauled a large, square, thin packing case, made from wood and secured with heavy nylon tape, from the interior of the van, and held it balanced on the mudguard. He stared expectantly at Anthony and waited for him to grasp the other edge. "You can leave your handbag in the van."

"I'm blowed if I will" thought Anthony, but then he realised that he had little alternative: he couldn't carry it with him, it would take too long to go back to his own van, and just to refuse would be churlish, despite this rough bloke's abrupt tone. "All right. Where is it going?"

"Into the bandit's hideaway. The Mexican's lair. The shed, the big shed over there by the bogs." He jerked his chin towards the stone barn which Anthony had passed earlier.

They lifted the case and carried it to the entrance. It was awkward rather than heavy. The barn shutters had been opened, padlocks swinging on the loose hasps, but the door was locked. The man with the pony tail didn't bother to knock, walked up to the nearest window and shouted, "Hank's here. Delivery. Look sharp." He turned to Anthony, "And thank you very much, I don't know what I'd have done without you." He didn't sound particularly sincere.

Anthony put down his end of the packing case and walked back past the hippy bloke's Transit. He noticed the tractor parked close, between the barn and a fairly tumbledown shed. He turned to walk across the field back to his own van, but remembered that he had left the bag – his stolen man-bag, which was obviously not a handbag – in the Transit, and also that he had not actually achieved the initial purpose of his expedition. He had pushed his bag towards the front of the Transit, the rear doors of which had been kicked shut by the Hank person, so he pulled open the passenger's door, climbed in and rummaged for it.

"What the fuck – oh it's you, you're after your bag, come on out, I'll get it."

Giving Anthony his bag back, he offered him a smoke. "It's only a roll up but it's got a little bit of oregano in it, know what I mean? Makes it smell nice, doesn't it?" He smiled. "Pardon my manners. I didn't want that parcel to get wet, and Pete won't come out to help once he's opened up his shop. He's what you might call both lazy and obsessional. It's a tiresome combination. If you don't want a smoke, how about a cheese sandwich?"

They sat on the tailboard of the Transit. Anthony would have felt bemused had he not remembered that he had in fact taken leave of reality two days ago, so sitting on the back of an old van at nine in the morning, chatting to a hippy and, out of politeness, or nostalgia, taking an occasional drag on a joint, was probably just the sort of thing to expect in this new not quite parallel world.

"Why do you call Peter Williams 'the Mexican'?"

The hippy leaned into the van and reached for his hat, which was of Australian or American design, made of leather, now greasy, with a thin band and little tassels dangling. "It's a sort of feeble running joke. It gets on his nerves, but not mine. I expect you're too young to remember Whirligig on what used to be called children's television, on a Saturday evening?"

Anthony blinked a bit and waved his hand around in disagreement. "Too young my arse," he was surprised to find himself saying, "I'm older than you; wait a minute. I expect you're called Henry..."

"Yes, you've got it. That's what I was christened."

"So you're Hank, and he's Peter, of course."

"Everybody calls him Pete except Mee – Emily"

"Sorry?"

"Emily."

"Mexican Pete the bad bandit. Right. Got it."

What a strange bloke. Never mind, it takes all sorts.

"And we fire our pistols at each other, and yell a lot, but if there's only one good man and one bad man how could you have another episode if either of them got shot?"

He replaced his tobacco tin in the pocket of a waistcoat which was knitted and patterned in horizontal hoops of reds and greens. Each side of the front dropped to a point and it had buttons of polished and folded leather, the bottom one of which he had left undone. "I buy all my clothes at the school fete. Well, not my trousers." He was silent for a moment. "Goodies and baddies – that's a laugh, isn't it?"

The walk along the coast path to the village with the pub where you get a pie and a pint was along the cliff tops and beaches of a coastline which possessed a beauty belied by the bare inland downs. To the north-west lay the calm sea, many shades now of blue and green. The path, its margins dotted with the tiny white and golden stars of stitchwort and tormentil, wound laboriously from bay to bay, sometimes along the side of a sloping meadow, through gorse and blackthorn, sometimes climbing up and down granite cliffs and heather carpeted headlands. Birds of all sorts, gulls, crows, stonechats, pipits, small brown ones of numerous species, fluttered and wheeled and hopped around. Buzzards circled high, and a kestrel hovered at the cliff edge. There was a seal watching Anthony, but he didn't notice it.

The village seemed charming; the pub, to Anthony, hot and sweaty now, even more so.

He turned round from the bar with his pint, looking for a seat. It was quite early, and there were very few customers. But in the corner, by the fireplace with its seasonal vase of hydrangeas, a drink on the table in front of him and his eyes fixed upon Anthony, sat a dead man.

Chapter 3

July 29   Anthony   A Scandinavian   Smith   Brown   Helen   Walter

Half way through a fortnight's holiday, Anthony had been looking forward to Saturday. He had been wearing his slippers and dressing gown when his sister Helen and his son Walter set off early from his house in Broadharbour for her country cottage, a terraced estate worker's house on Dartmoor, not particularly tarted up, in the village which used to belong, together with the labour and votes of its inhabitants, to a nineteenth century brewer from Exeter. He thought that before breakfast he might have another cup of tea and re-read the condition report which Dowlands had sent him on the two Festival School paintings which he intended to bid for at their sale that day.

Not only was he excited, he was quite nervous. He never felt that he was wasting money when he bought works of art, but he had never before been prepared to spend so much. His senses felt unusually acute; his ears seemed to differentiate precisely between many, even simultaneous, small noises, and to hear them as individual exceptions to an enveloping silence. His vision was also different, and he saw his immediate domestic surroundings not as a comfortable and familiar setting for eating and drinking and reading the newspaper, but as a sharp design of line and colour, clear and distinct in a formal and elaborate perspective. Both sunshine and rain were forecast today; at the moment the sky was clear, and the gothic tracery of the double pointed window was projected, pin-sharp, on the opposite wall. He placed his cup on the elongated wingtip shadow of the little Elizabeth Frink bronze eagle. The cup's shadow slipped over the edge of the table but vanished into the carpet, lost in the complicated Islamic geometry.

Since it was a Saturday, the auction started at ten, and these two paintings would come up at about half past. It was a little unusual for two such valuable works by Quentin Bradley to be offered in a provincial sale, and their provenance was slightly mysterious. He knew the series of paintings of which they were examples, a series inspired by the fragile and now largely forgotten optimism of the late nineteen forties and early fifties, the feeling of relief and the return of national confidence. The British people believed that, after the determined but grim post war years, during which people felt – perhaps wrongly – that the construction of the welfare state and the repayment of American loans had entailed poverty greater than during the war itself, the nation's reward would be a new, richer and more exciting society. Consumerism – the attitude, not the word – was a popular response to the use of advancing technologies to produce modern, desirable goods available to all, not just the rich. The first picture in this series, painted in a style still heavily influenced by Stanley Spencer's work on the Clyde, showed men in white overalls rolling a Morris Minor off the line at the Oxford factory. A couple of years later the Festival of Britain handed them a wealth of subjects, from the Skylon to stacking chairs, and it was in the early nineteen fifties that the name 'Festival school' was coined. But the painters got older and became disenchanted. Automation had not fulfilled its promise to accelerate the arrival of the new millennium, which seemed reluctant to appear. Factory work was still hard, poverty still rife, despite factory-farmed chickens and Yugoslavian wine for the middle classes. So their paintings became gloomier, like dark cartoons, or glossy and brittle with not particularly subtle irony. The market in the bright and shiny ones was now very strong, especially in America.

The two up for sale today were from the middle period of the series, expressing neither the exuberance of the Festival and the apparently magic potential of technology, nor the anguish of the Suez and Kenya paintings. He thought he knew most of the collectors who would have been likely to own them, but the references in the catalogue were very sketchy and rang no bells; perhaps the auctioneers had slight misgivings – feelings only – about them. He knew, as would the auctioneers, exactly the weight to be given to the sententious authentications offered by fat Barry – Sir Barwell Flyte-Henderson now, for goodness sake. Nevertheless, Anthony had examined them, had assessed the style, and studied the brushwork closely, had peered at the edges and the stretchers, and was convinced they were bona fide Bradley. They were from a series illustrating domestic arrangements in the early fifties; Bradley had a penchant for women ironing, and the pose of the lady wielding an electric steam iron seemed very characteristic.

The paintings were unframed. A telephone chat with a young man in Dowlands' Modern British department had confirmed his suspicion that they had come in framed, contrary to the usual instructions of the artist, and apparently in unsuitable eighteenth century gilded gesso. The frames themselves were valuable, and were being included in a different sale.

The reproduction of the pictures in Dowlands' catalogue showed the colours as more vivid than in reality, partly because this is a characteristic of small scale reproductions, and partly, he suspected, because the photographers could not resist the slight adjustments to brightness and saturation which were becoming technically so easy. Many pictures, which may in any case have faded from their original appearance, are enhanced by this process; but not the Bradleys. The restrained, pale washes, the subtle gradations of tone and depth, the infinitely careful juxtaposition of colours were, if not lost, made cruder by the devices of reproduction. They were in a sense pictures for artists; when they flourished, in the fifties and sixties, painters such as Bradley and Hopkins were revered by their contemporaries, as much for their unmercenary dedication to their ideals as for their unusual skill and vision. But this reverence did not preclude condescension; however hard they might try, the rich can seldom defer for long to the poor, and some of their contemporaries became very rich indeed by feeding a public taste for the obvious. The followers of the Festival school remained relatively poor. Forty years on, however, the solid worth, if not the genius, of its principal exponents had been realised, and following the purchase of Hopkins' *Pylons* by the Union of Communication Workers, saleroom prices were rising fast. Anthony had been buying minor paintings of this school – watercolours and gouaches – for ten years or so, and felt that the time had come to consider some of the more important oils. Soon they would be out of reach.

Anthony put the catalogue down on the kitchen table. He didn't need to look at it again. He was only interested in two paintings, he knew when they would come up, and had decided, or thought he had decided, on the limit to which he would bid. He picked up the newspaper. It led with the story of what it termed a daring raid upon a jeweller's in Bournemouth: the manager's son had been kidnapped and threatened with mutilation if the safes were not opened. Sick, thought Anthony, sick and disgusting, not daring. He thought of his own son, seven year old Walter. Anthony's sister had taken him to stay with her on Dartmoor, and she was a sensible, trustworthy woman, but she had no children; did she realise the extent of the dangers to which boys can expose themselves? And how it takes an experienced parent like himself to read the real intentions of children when they make innocent sounding requests – and they often are innocent, the children themselves not realising how far they might be tempted to stretch their licence? And how quickly a seven year old boy can run if he sees something interesting, and how easily he can get lost?

"You'll ruin your life by worrying if you're not careful, Anthony," his dependable, adorable, wife had said, and on the whole he had managed to suppress his most disabling fears. Estimating probabilities and risks was a large part of his job, and he could tell himself that most English children survived to adulthood despite the extraordinary range of theoretical reasons why they might not. "*The thing you worry about never happens,*" she used to say, and perhaps his worries were a form of protective superstition. In a way she had been right; he had seldom worried about her health. After all, she had been twelve years younger than him.

He shuffled to the toaster and started to prepare his breakfast. His dressing gown seemed scratchy on his skin and his slippers were too large – he was unused to rising so early, and they had hardly ever been worn since he had bought them, unnecessarily, for a short hospital stay to correct a minor misalignment of his ankle. Last night he had slept badly, partly because his sister and Walter were setting off early, but mainly because he was very excited by the prospect of buying the paintings, and desperately worried that he might be outbid. He took his breakfast to the little table under a window through which the sun only shone early in the morning, and opened the instruction manual of a small digital camera which he had bought the previous day. It seemed unlikely that such a small item could take photos of such quality – better, the salesman had told him, than his old film Leica – and he decided to try it out. He photographed a vase from one or two different angles, wondering whether the camera's programs could cope with the different lighting effects. The images on the screen seemed all right, but they were so small it was difficult to be sure. He fiddled with the controls to enlarge the shots, decided they were surprisingly good, and deleted them.

He had worried about the vulnerability of the unframed paintings. Some few years previously he had bought a painting which needed restoration. It had suffered from damp and from the inconsiderate use by the artist of compressed breadcrumbs as a medium for enhancing the texture of certain small areas of landscape. He had been fascinated by the atmosphere of the conservator's workshop, where a completely matter of fact, in some cases almost disrespectful, attitude towards the phenomenally valuable and famous paintings did not prevent their restoration being undertaken with at least the care, and almost the expense, of cosmetic surgery. There he had seen an oil by a well-known modern artist who also stipulated that her paintings should not be framed, and effected this by signing them on the edge. The picture had been damaged quite severely on an unprotected corner. But that had happened, so he was told by the conservator, at a party held by the rock star owner, so he tried to stop worrying, and reassured himself by considering the long experience of the auctioneer's porters and the security of their strong room – but, there again, this was a provincial branch, not the Bond Street saleroom. He couldn't shake off his anxiety.

Only five days previously the Irish government, slightly bemused by the run-away growth of its economy, had asked him to join a small group of analysts to suggest a ten year transport plan. He knew some of the other people who would be involved, and had accepted the offer of an exploratory meeting, and would be travelling to Dublin on Tuesday. If he managed to buy the paintings it would be necessary to get them safely to his conservator before he left, so he had arranged with the auctioneer that were his bids successful at the auction he would collect them immediately, paying by banker's drafts and debit card, and deliver them personally into the care of Safetrans. He had expected that making all these arrangements would have exasperated both the auction house and the bank, but the auctioneer had been most obliging, effusive even, and in the bank he had been passed smoothly from receptionist to cashier to assistant manager, all wearing the polite and distant smiles of persons thinking about their dinner. The auctioneer had certainly tried to winkle out of him an indication of his upper limit – unsuccessfully, he hoped.

By making only a small detour he could walk to the sale rooms by way of the promenade. The tide was out, and turnstones ran among the pebbles, throwing strands of seaweed about as they searched for sand-hoppers and shrimps. An egret stood at the water's edge, and he took a couple of photographs, experimenting with his new camera's zoom, which seemed to have an extraordinary range, the telephoto facility almost filling the screen with the bird. The wide angle function of the lens wasn't quite so startling, but he took some good panoramic shots of the harbour and the High Street.

The sale room was crowded and, like most rooms outside the grand salons of Bond Street, Manhattan and Paris, seemed more suited to the eclectic mix of furniture and ornaments which was its mainstay than to this sale of paintings and sculptures which were a couple of orders of magnitude more valuable. Squeezing along towards a vacant chair, past a row of potential purchasers or spectators, who all seemed to be wearing at least one unnecessary layer of clothing, he recognised the owner of a gallery which, only very occasionally, had a few decent pieces. Not that Anthony bought much from galleries; in his own field he was more of an expert than any gallery owner he knew. In fact, he also considered that he knew more than most of the precious old men who floated around in bow ties, pontificating on the telly and advising footballers to buy Hockneys. So he told himself.

But despite his familiarity with sale rooms, he was nervous, and it showed. His acquaintance leaned over, noticing the numbered paddle on Anthony's knee.

"Hello Tone, how's things? What are you after then? Not the Lamberts, surely?"

"Don't be facetious *William*. I might be interested in some of the art."

"Well you've timed it right then. Bradleys are up soon. Five before, I think. Oh, so you are then? Hope you've got a deep pocket old son, Ward's just over there, and Marryat's on the phone."

"They'll be after the Hopkins, shouldn't wonder."

"True, and there are two more phone lines; look, no-one on them yet. But the Bradleys are very attractive, especially, which one is it, yes, the first one up. Marryat wouldn't mind one of them, I'm sure. Aren't you interested in the Hopkins?"

"Come off it. I haven't won the lottery."

"It's an odd one, isn't it? Difficult to interpret?"

"Oh, I don't know. But I'll just keep my fingers crossed the Bradleys don't go wild. What are you after?"

"Usual tat, a few of the pots, perhaps. Stop twisting your paddle, it's not a bloody propeller."

"Mary's over there, I see. Never misses, does she?"

Mary had a junk shop in an old bus depot. She sat sideways in her chair, more swaddled than most, one leg propped on a large plastic holdall, nursing her paddle and a bottle of Evian water which those who knew her swore was neat vodka. She was the sort of person about whom fanciful stories developed and spread; her dim shed was a perfect incubator of rumour. She had seldom been seen to bid.

Anthony's friend Bill bid successfully for two pots, a Kawai and an early Coper, and declined to bid for the third, a Bernard Leach.

"It's a Fetherstone special" he whispered to Anthony. Nevertheless, it sold for four thousand five hundred pounds.

As the bidding for an early pen and ink drawing by Mark Gertler got under way, the man sitting two seats away from Anthony stumbled abruptly to his feet and pushed his way to the end of the row and to the door. As he passed, Anthony heard the buzzing vibrations of a mobile phone set to silent. Anthony knew him, a dealer who owned two well-known and purportedly profitable galleries. Strange that he was leaving as the Bradleys were coming up – they were among the stars of the show.

The first of the two Bradleys was held up by the porter. The auctioneer repeated almost verbatim the description in the catalogue. The man holding the phone looked up at the rostrum and nodded to the auctioneer.

"The bidding will start, ladies and gentlemen, at fifty thousand pounds. Who will offer me fifty?"

The bidding rose quickly to one hundred and fifty thousand, thirty thousand over the top of the auctioneer's estimated range. There were four people bidding, Anthony, a dealer he knew, a lady whom he did not know, and the person at the other end of the telephone. The bid was with Anthony. The auctioneer looked at the two others who had been bidding, then round the room. No-one moved. The auctioneer then looked down to the telephone man, who nodded. Anthony was now bidding only against the unknown person, perhaps Marryat, on the telephone. The bidding reached one hundred and sixty eight thousand; the bid was again with Anthony. The room was silent. All of the dealers and most of the private collectors knew that no Bradley oil of this modest size and subdued colouring had fetched more than ninety thousand pounds at auction. Their concentration, almost excitement, carefully restrained yet clearly evident, was now shared with the rest of the room. Eyes pivoted from Anthony to the telephone man, who nodded twice.

"One hundred and seventy thousand on the phone" the auctioneer said, looking, like everyone else, at Anthony.

Anthony's limit had been one hundred and sixty five thousand.

"And ten" he said.

The man on the phone made no move, then shook his head. Anticipating the auctioneer's confirmation, many of those present started to clap. The auctioneer made sure that the bidding was finished, and knocked the picture down to Anthony.

Mary, who had appeared immune to the general interest, heaved herself round in her chair and spoke over her shoulder, in Anthony's approximate direction, her chair creaking in sympathy with her neck, "That wasn't Marryat on the phone, you know, he's in New York after the Rothko, he isn't interested in the Festivals any more. Don't know who it was though. Nice painting, got style, Bradleys have, that one especially. Wish I could have afforded it."

"Come along now Mary," Bill joined in, "all you have to do is open up your handbag. It's like a piggy bank, that handbag, anything goes in but you've got to break it to get it out."

"Piggy pot yourself, that's what you are." She gave a terrible, metallic grin, revealing where at least some of her wealth had been invested. "That's a good name for you, rows of little pots on your shelves, can't bear to sell them." She leaned further forward, "Which accounts, young William, for your ridiculous prices!"

Pleased with her wit, she swivelled lumpily back, accidentally knocking over her Evian bottle. If it was vodka, she took its loss very calmly.

Anthony would normally have contributed, not particularly effectively, to the crosstalk. But he was intent upon the rostrum where the porter had taken down the first Bradley, and was now replacing it with the second, a wide East Anglian scene, with wheat field and combine harvester. The bidding started, and proceeded slowly, much more slowly than usual. The other potential purchasers in the room soon dropped out except for the dealer who had been bidding for the first painting, and Anthony was fairly sure that he wouldn't stay the course because he would usually only buy if he thought he was picking up a bargain – and today's prices were not low. At a hundred and ten thousand the bid was with Anthony, and the dealer in the room remained motionless. The auctioneer looked at the telephone man, who made no response. The auctioneer stared, openly frowning, at his assistant, willing him to speak. But he shook his head, and the auctioneer had no choice: the picture was Anthony's.

"Just time for a quick one then. On you, I think, if you've any money left." Bill had grasped Anthony by the elbow and walked him to the Schooner, just off the promenade, before the morning sale had ended, and after Anthony had thankfully handed his paintings over to the Safetrans driver. "Taking a punt on that first Bradley, weren't you?"

"Yes, it felt very strange. I'm usually more disciplined than that. But you see, Bill, I really like that painting, not just as a collector, I know it's not very, how should I put it, *striking*, but I do think it's one of his best." He nodded vigorously, perhaps to forestall disagreement."And I got the second one cheap."

"You were lucky there. If you rate it, that is. I wonder what happened to the bloke on the phone?"

Anthony's walk home took him back past the auctioneer's. The Hopkins, a painting entitled and featuring a Morris Minor, (although 'featuring', in the works of this artist, did not mean that the car was painted large, or centre stage) had been sold to one of the three telephone bidders for eight hundred and fifty thousand pounds; high, but not extraordinarily so. No-one in the room had bothered to bid. Two or three Victorian genre paintings and a couple of eighteenth century conversation pieces followed, then interest faded as the quality of the lots diminished, the auctioneer efficiently knocking down a miscellany of low value items while subdued and sporadic conversation replaced the previous tense silences. A small group of smokers stood by the double doors of the sale room, among them one of the assistants who had handled the telephone bidding. She threw her cigarette down, and hurried to join him.

"There you are! What a relief; I didn't know where you were, you just vanished!"

"Only to the pub with Bill Sanders, you should have guessed, free pint he was after, always is, isn't he? Why, did I leave something?"

"No, no, I've got a message for you, it's important. The man on the phone, he's sent someone to see you, he's waiting in the Angel now."

"Now? How could he do that, it's only just twelve? Where was he ringing from? In any case who is he?"

"I can't tell you that, but his, representative he said, is in the Angel bar, and asked you to please go and meet him. You know what it'll be, he'll want to make you an offer for those paintings. Something went wrong with his bidding, I'm sure. At any rate, that's the message, and please go or he'll think I didn't give it to you."

"Well, what's so dreadful about that?"

But the woman had retreated into the sale room, turning and waving slightly before she vanished.

Should he go? The Angel was only a stone's throw away, overlooking the beach. It seemed to have little custom except for busloads of the elderly, and a few commercial travellers. Obviously whoever it was who failed to secure the paintings was going to make him an offer; he would refuse, of course, unless it were quite exceptional and – no, he would definitely refuse – or at least he certainly wouldn't part with the first one. Well, no harm in seeing who it was.

He had never been into the Angel. The bar was as depressing as he expected, as depressing as any large room in a hotel built for Victorian holiday makers and for the owners and managers of industries long defunct. Nothing was particularly dirty, there was no smell of boiled food, the chairs were quite comfortable, the waiters were youngish and walking around with peanuts, but somehow it was impossible to believe that it could actually be profitable. Two or three groups of old ladies, one table of middle aged men, one well-dressed man on his own, his smart camel coat thrown luvvy style over his shoulders, sitting at one end of the bar, a couple of bar flies at the other – how could that pay for the kitchen staff, the waiters, the management, the heating, the repairs – he couldn't account for it. At least it was obvious whom he was meeting.

"I imagine you're waiting for me? I just bought the two Bradleys at Dowland's. Mrs Poynter said you would like a word?"

"Thank you for coming. It is very kind of you to take the time. Drink? Another glass please. Have some, it's not as bad as you might expect."

What would you call his accent? Not regional. Educated middle class? North European, that was it; Dutch, perhaps. Dutchmen often spoke perfect English. Perhaps a little pedantic. Anthony accepted a glass of wine. The man continued.

"I am sure that you know what I'm going to ask you. My client in this matter is a gentleman with many business interests, and that is why he – or, to be exact, his London attorney – has been able to command my services at such short notice. Here is my card."

He handed Anthony an engraved card. Ah, a quick glance, Scandinavian name, some sort of accountant.

"My client is a connoisseur of fine art, and has decided to add representatives of the Festival school to his collection, and he gave certain instructions to his agent with the aim of securing the two Bradleys today. Unfortunately there was a – ah – balls up, and his instructions were misinterpreted. And the rest you know."

"So he would like to buy them from me. I thought that might be why you wanted to meet. No, no more wine thanks."

Mr Something-sson nodded, and refilled his own glass. He had been looking through the bar window towards the harbour; now he turned and looked directly at Anthony. "Not both of them. He feels that what you paid for the first one was a sum which he would not wish to exceed. Frankly, he prefers the second, which is more to his own taste."

"Hmm, yes. It's brighter, isn't it?"

"More vibrant, is how he put it. Myself, I have no feeling for these things. I have not seen either of them. But to, ah, dock a long tail, he would offer you one hundred and fifty thousand pounds; a reasonable profit, I think."

Nearly twenty-five thousand pounds profit, that would be, after the buyer's premium to the sale room. Anthony replied.

"I only came here to see you because I wasn't sure of my own mind. I'm not even completely certain now – your offer is very generous, but – would you hold it open for a couple of days?"

"Yes, I think my principal would agree to that. But he will not raise his offer."

"No, of course not, I'm not...wouldn't dream ..."

The bartender, at a glance from the Scandinavian man, had immediately detached himself from an argument about snooker at the far end of the bar and topped up their glasses. He opened a packet of cashews, poured them into a saucer and pushed them across the bar.

"With the compliments of the hotel, sir," he said, stood uneasily behind the bar near to them for a moment, then edged back towards his friends.

"Jolly nice wine, this, thank you," said Anthony. "Is your, er, client, interested in other artists of the Festival group? Hopkins, for example? Many critics think he was probably the most important of the Festival painters – but perhaps you know that – many apologies!"

"No, I am by no means an expert!" he replied, "My client is – well, he takes a great deal of trouble over his art collection, whether you would say he was an *expert* or not – actually, it is interesting that you mention Hopkins, he bought a painting by Hopkins a little while ago, but he told me that he doesn't actually like it much now! I said to him, Mickey, I said, you mean you expect to *like* the art you buy – what has liking got to do with it? The little name in the bottom right hand corner, that's all you want, surely? I was joking, of course, but my joke ballooned rather, no, sank like a balloon, no, that can't be right, *helvete*, what do you say?"

"Sank like a lead balloon."

"Of course. What a vivid metaphor, thank you. Yes, I thought he might strike me. He did not wish to be confused with the others, the other Russians, and the Arabs, who buy in ignorance and lock the articles up in their banks. So, he has loaned this picture to a friend to put it on his wall, but I expect he will sell it quite soon."

"Really? What's the subject, do you know?"

"I haven't seen it but Mickey said it was one of the Cowley series. Production of cars, I imagine."

"Oh yes, yes indeed. And Mr um, Mickey, doesn't like it? I wonder why not?"

"I couldn't say. Perhaps it is just not to his taste. One does not have to like all the work of a great artist, presumably?"

"No, of course not. Well, I'll keep an eye open for it, the Morris paintings don't come up often. Sotheby's?"

"No, he intends to sell it privately, I believe."

"Right." Anthony drank the remainder of his second glass of wine. It occurred to him, with the optimism engendered by beer and wine on a fairly empty stomach, that he might know Mickey's friend, if he was a devotee, or collector, of the Festival school, and that it would be nice to see the painting, not with a view to buying it, of course – but before he could mention this the Scandinavian man raised the topic himself.

"You would be surprised to learn upon whose wall it hangs at present."

Anthony took this as an invitation to guess, so he mentioned one or two names, but Mr Something-sson shook his head.

"I will tell you. I do not suppose Mickey would mind, but perhaps you should keep this to yourself. It hangs in the drawing room of Mr Armstrong, the Lord Treasurer or whatever you call him."

"Good Lord! D'you know, I think I've been told that he's got a bit of a collection. But Hopkins, well, out of his league, I would have thought. He's not a particularly rich man, is he?"

"No, I believe not, but Mickey tells me that his enjoyment of art is genuine, as is that of his wife. In any case, he is not in any sense a prospective purchaser."

They stood silent for a moment, sipping wine from glasses which had been refilled by the attentive barman. The bar was almost deserted now, as lunch service was well under way. The barman was filling up a tray of drinks for one of the waitresses. The argument about snooker had been resolved, or suspended, and the bar flies had departed. The coach party ladies were now in the dining room, drinking oxtail soup or grapefruit juice. But Anthony's wine, probably from a second bottle by now, immersed in an ice-filled bucket, was excellent.

"I know!" said the Swedish man suddenly, "Let me arrange an introduction for you with Mr Armstrong! I'm sure he won't mind, if I mention Mickey, he'll enjoy showing you his paintings, especially since you're a bit of a Festival school expert, eh? And you can get a good look at the Hopkins. And, of course, if you have interest, perhaps you might consider a part exchange?"

"What?" Anthony's head, if not exactly spinning, seemed rather more prone to wobble than usual. "Oh, I see what you mean! A Hopkins, eh? But won't Armstrong be far too busy? He's got his fingers in everything, that man, never stops, runs the country really, don't you know about him?"

"Well, maybe. But his wife certainly isn't. No, I'm sure I can manage it. Look, I will phone you. Have you got a card?"

Anthony found one of his business cards and handed it to the Swede, who looked at it quite closely, maybe not focussing quickly on the small engraving-style print.

"Your own business? Is it like management consultants?"

"Perhaps a little; I think we use mathematical modelling more. And yes, it is my business."

"It must be difficult at parties and such-like. Much easier to be a postman or a doctor. Everyone knows what they do!"

"You're absolutely right," said Anthony enthusiastically, "it takes ages, and they always get bored half way through, so they assume you're boring. But then," he added, "I suppose that might be true."

"Not at all, I'm sure. In any case better boring and successful than fascinating and a failure! You do quite well, I imagine?"

"Well, I must say, fortune seems to be smiling at the moment!"

What? He must rein in his tongue. *Rein in his tongue*? Shit and derision, it must be the wine. But, hell, boasting aside, he *was* doing well. He could buy a Hopkins if he really wanted, part exchange or no part exchange. Good investment, too.

"Well, as I say, I'll ring you. It might be fun, you might meet Armstrong himself."

"Yes, well, thanks, can't do any harm, can it? Sorry, I mean, thank you very much, most kind of you."

The Scandinavian man slid from his bar stool. He was a certainly a Viking; tall, fair, green eyes, sandy hair.

"I have just to make a short phone call, please excuse me." He left the bar through the door which led into the hall, and Anthony could see him through the bay window, standing on the promenade and silhouetted against the sea and sky, making what seemed to be a number of calls on his mobile. Anthony glanced again at his card – his name was Axel something. He put the card down on the bar. Axel returned, and was now smiling broadly, almost grinning, an expression which Anthony had not seen previously.

"I have for you an invitation, Anthony, to tea – well, at what is tea time so I can't imagine you will not be offered tea," his mood was now definitely jovial, "with Mrs Armstrong, at their house in Victoria Park, a week next Tuesday! I think there will be one or two other guests, gallery people I imagine, and she is showing off her pictures. The Hopkins will be there also." He coughed, and looked slightly embarrassed, and continued, "I described you as a well-known expert and collector of Festival paintings, that is true, I am sure. I hope you don't mind?"

Anthony, although very surprised, found that he could, at the moment, take this turn of events in his stride remarkably easily. He knew quite as much about the Festival school as any of the pretentious crew of critics and art historians who had written books or articles about it, and tea with the Armstrongs sounded great fun. But a quick flash of insight told him that it would be sensible to confirm the invitation in a couple of days.

The Swede put his coat on properly and buttoned it up against the weather, which had taken a turn for the worse. He suggested that that cold spells in the summer were becoming more common, and Anthony agreed with him, probably something to do with the Gulf Stream? He was taking part soon in some sailing event in the Baltic, and his interest in art was fairly superficial, except where the collection of his principal was concerned. The wine had made his manner less formal now, Anthony thought, and his English a little more idiomatic. They shook hands, Anthony wished him good luck in the yacht race, and he left.

Anthony thought he might as well have another glass of wine, since the bottle was not yet empty. *Very* nice spot of white, it was, and now he was in no danger of its clouding his judgment. He looked at the label. Heavens above, Montrachet. In the Angel? Well well.

*****

The log effect gas fire glowed and flickered as it was supposed to and Anthony sat comfortably in his own armchair, the morning's sale catalogue on his knee. He had intended to make some beef sandwiches for lunch; the beer and burgundy had overcome him, and he slept. He was woken in half an hour or so from the strange dreams of diurnal sleep by the creaks of the bedroom floorboards and the unmistakeable scrape of the wardrobe door, as his cleaning lady put away the two hundred and ninety clean purple towels which she had just brought to the house on a milk float. The noise continued, and, fully awake now, he became alarmed. The house was empty save for himself; it should be silent, it was not the sort of house which responded noisily to vagaries of plumbing, or changes in wind direction. Perhaps the occasional patter of a mouse between upstairs floor and downstairs ceiling – a different noise altogether.

In the hall the front door was closed, but the thick chenille curtain which hung on oversize rings from an unnecessarily thick mahogany pole, and was intended to stop draughts, was drawn back. He might easily have left it like that, however, when he had returned, elated and, admit it, slightly drunk, from his sale room coup. Without forming any particular plan about how he might cope with the situation if there really were an intruder – and what other explanation could there be for the noises? – he crept upstairs.

There was indeed an intruder. The door to the main bedroom was open, and he could see that the wardrobe doors were open, and the drawers in the chests pulled out. Stooping down in front of the cheval glass there was a man dressed in dark clothes. He appeared to be looking under the bed. Anthony, shocked and dismayed, realised at once that he hadn't the faintest idea what to do next. The man straightened up and looked at him. He didn't seem startled; maybe, from the slight downward twitch of his mouth and creasing of his forehead, a trifle put out – no more.

Anthony found his voice.

"What the hell do you think you're doing?" was all he could think of saying. It was really quite obvious what the man was doing.

At this point, the calm and almost motionless eyes of the man in the black jacket flickered for an infinitesimal moment towards the door to the landing, behind and slightly to the left of Anthony. Maybe there was also some very slight noise, registered only at a subconscious level, or some equally indefinable change in the atmosphere; but when Anthony turned towards the door, he had no doubt at all that he would see another person there. The man who was standing on the landing, quiet and still as if he had been present for a while, although Anthony was convinced he had not, was, at least on one level, somewhat of a disappointment. He was middle aged, grey haired, and wore an overcoat in a knobbly brownish material, tailored in a style called Raglan, unfashionable for decades. He spoke in a voice devoid of accent or colour.

"Mr Smith has clearly failed to find what we are looking for. I am sorry that we disturbed you, but in these circumstances " – he frowned slightly at the man whom he called Smith, whose expression in turn exhibited, but only very slightly, a modicum of contrition, – "we would in any case have been obliged to awake you and ask for your cooperation. I gather from your neighbours that your sister and son," – he paused, and repeated, "your young son Walter – are spending the weekend at your cottage in" – he looked at a page in a little notebook – "Pond Street, Anford. Nice little hideaway I expect? Not too far away, though? And you intend to join them tomorrow?"

He paused. Anthony looked from one man to the other. He wondered how quickly he could get downstairs to the phone, which was in the sitting room, and whether he could dial while leaning against the door to keep it shut. His mobile was where he had emptied his pockets before he went to sleep. He couldn't remember where that was.

The grey haired man continued, "It is in your own interests to help us." He looked round him as if he were appraising the contents of the house for a valuation, "I don't imagine that you're in any immediate need of cash, but my proposal might perhaps add a case or two of decent claret to your cellar. But first, I must ask you an important question. Have you looked at all closely at the pictures which..."

Anthony found that although he seemed not to have lost completely the power of thought, he had certainly lost the power of intelligible speech. The neural connection between the speech centre of his brain and the physical arrangements which constituted his voice seemed totally severed. His heart bounced against his diaphragm like a fly in a paper lantern, the rhythm of his breathing was that of a child beating a saucepan with a spoon. Bees buzzed close to his ears. With difficulty he found one or two words which he could express between gasps. They were not polite words, and the man with grey hair possibly took exception to them. At any rate, he moved towards the head of the stairs.

"I shall leave you with Mr Smith now. Are you happy with that, Mr Smith?" He looked at his watch.

"Quite happy, thank you, Mr Brown".

As soon as Brown had left, quietly by the front door, Smith turned to Anthony.

"Don't try and talk now. Come downstairs with me, sit down and get your breath back. Then I'll explain."

He propelled Anthony to the stairs and grasping him by the upper arm walked down with him, taking care not to let Anthony push ahead. Near the foot of the staircase it turned through ninety degrees, and on the little landing Smith loosened his grasp, causing Anthony to miss his footing and fall heavily against him. Anthony noticed two things; first that falling against Smith, who was if anything lighter than Anthony, provided a demonstration of the inadequacy of the laws of physics to explain human encounters, Anthony in this case supplying the action, but Smith no palpable reaction – and secondly that Smith was carrying a gun, a very conventional looking small revolverish affair in a polished brown leather holster attached to his waist band.

In the kitchen, Smith sat Anthony down by the door in the Ercol bentwood easy chair, a sort of low-slung fifties take on a Windsor chair, and under the cushion of which Anthony kept old copies of the Antiques Gazette. Confident, presumably, that Anthony was of negligible consideration as a physical opponent – and in general this was no doubt correct – Smith picked up the kettle, filled it at the tap and put it on the gas stove. For a moment Anthony thought, absurdly, that he was about to make tea; but then he realized, with a fresh onset of panic together with its disabling physical concomitants, that Smith was preparing for some dreadful interrogation. But even as he shrank back in fear into his chair, Anthony suddenly realised how ridiculous this situation was. He had been furious when the man called Brown had offered him, what was it, the cost of a couple of dozen bottles of wine for two pictures which, although not perhaps absolutely top rank, were certainly worth the two hundred and ninety thousand he had paid for them. But, for God's sake, his insurance, or the conservator's insurance, would pay out, of course it would! He would just tell this Smith where they were.

As he was about to do this, his right hand, which was brushing against the floor at the side of the chair, touched something cold and hard. This was his doorstop, a grotesque iron money box cast in the form of a nineteenth century African minstrel's bust, complete with parody mouth and rolling eyes. If a coin were placed in its left hand, and its right arm pushed down, the red lips would part, the left arm and the eyeballs swivel up, and the coin would vanish between glistening rows of white enamel teeth. Both Anthony and his wife had thought that it was tasteless, offensive and altogether horrible; but it had belonged to his wife's aunt who had been a sort of surrogate mother to her, and they had never quite got round to throwing it away. Anthony hid it when his black friends visited.

Anthony's rational thoughts concerning the insurance companies and the prudent way to behave vanished in an instant. He grasped his missile firmly and hurled it at Smith's head. Of course, he missed. The money box struck Smith a glancing blow on the left elbow, hit the wall and fell to the floor, where it lay rocking on its back, eyes blinking and right arm waving at the ceiling. Water spouted from the kettle onto the gas ring, hissed and spluttered and extinguished the flame. Smith ignored this, and turned quickly to face Anthony, who had jumped from his chair with some idea of following up the advantage which he would have derived from the violent blow to the head which Smith should have received from the iron box. The speed with which these events had occurred, the smell and hiss of the gas, the failure of his attack, robbed Anthony of any residual good sense. It should have been clear to him that his adversary was better at this sort of thing than he was; that Smith almost certainly did it for a living, that he was very strong and very fit, and above all else – way, way above all else – was armed with a revolver.

But the new bit of Anthony's brain, the thoughtful bit, which had been developing in his species for less than a couple of minutes in the six days of creation, had by now been engulfed by a wave of primitive emotions left over from pre-sapient times. In Freud's convenient shorthand, his ego had surrendered to his id. (His super-ego was not involved). Too much adrenalin had flooded his bloodstream and he responded again to the territorial challenge. As Smith leaned over to the cooker and turned off the gas, Anthony pulled open one of the kitchen drawers, seized the first knife he saw and threw himself at Smith.

Surprised by the fury of this attack, and irritated by the turn of events, Smith prepared to disarm Anthony and to sit him down again in the Windsor chair. He discovered, however, that the blow from the money box had temporarily numbed his left arm, so he was forced to parry the knife attack more clumsily, and with more force, than he would have preferred. Anthony fell heavily against the wall but, ignoring in his rage the pain of the impact, and the jagged cut where his leg had scraped on the sharp edge of the cooker, he pushed himself up and stumbled again towards Smith, screaming oaths which he was hardly aware that he knew. Smith turned, in order to achieve better balance for his retaliation, but in so doing slipped on the pool of water which had splashed from the kettle, and as he fell, in an immediate reflex action, drew the revolver from its holster. But he fell awkwardly against the corner of the washing machine, the gun evaded his grasp and skidded across the floor to Anthony who picked it up, pointed it, and pulled the trigger. He had never held a hand gun in his life before. Nothing happened, and for a split second both men stared at the weapon. Anthony put the index finger of his left hand over that of his right, and pulled, much harder. The noise was staggering in the enclosed, uncarpeted room, nor was his wrist prepared for the recoil. But Smith was lying quite still on the floor. Anthony stood, like an action man new from its box, waiting for its arms and legs to be arranged in a lifelike position; the first finger of his right hand remained motionless on the gun's trigger, his left arm was frozen horizontal. After an hour, during which time the second hand of the kitchen clock moved through forty-five degrees or so, Anthony saw the blood, staining Smith's dark blue shirt purple, seeping out onto the tiles, running in little rivers along the grouting until the floor around him was a matrix of white squares outlined in red. Smith's eyes were open, staring at the ceiling; his body had not moved.

Anthony leaned against the wall, and slid to the floor. He still gripped the gun. He still pointed it at Smith. After a little while he found that his breathing was no longer a series of trembling gasps, and he thought that his knees might once again support his weight; but an attempt to stand proved him wrong, and he was forced to crawl towards the door. He reached the sitting room and levered himself into the chair by the phone. But before he had dialled the third nine he remembered the grey haired man, and the words he had spoken, the information he had received from the neighbours, the implicit threat to his family, no less compelling, no less terrifying for its banality. Who were these people? Would the police know and would they be able to protect his family – and himself? It was well known that art theft gangs were international – hadn't there been something foreign in the plain and careful diction of the man in the overcoat?

And, in any case, he had shot the man called Smith – had killed a man with the very first shot from a gun that he had ever fired. His mind was in a whirl, and he tried to concentrate instead on what must be done next; and this at least seemed blindingly obvious. He must put distance between himself and the crime scene – but whose crime? Over and over again he had read of householders charged with crimes of violence, even murder, when confronting burglars. How would the police know whose gun it was? They might claim that he had clipped his holster to Smith's belt. As he said this to himself he realised that it was the futile, undisciplined train of thought of a man who was near to panic – he was no detective, he hadn't the faintest idea what the police would or would not believe. His next priority was to get his sister and son away from the cottage on the moor, and find them somewhere to stay where they could hide away anonymously for a little while – then maybe he would ring the police – it shouldn't be more than twenty four hours or so – at any rate, his family would be safe. No, he didn't know what he would do after that.

He should prepare his sister for his arrival, of course, he should phone. From the car, he would phone from the car. Where was his mobile? He had taken off his jacket and put the contents of its pockets down somewhere, but where? He had hung his jacket and waterproof up in the hall and they were still hanging there – wait, he remembered carrying his wallet through to the sitting room. Yes, thank goodness, there was all his stuff, dropped between the cushion and the chair-back. He grabbed it and fled the house, automatically setting the burglar alarm, but then de-activating it again. His alarm sent an instant mobile phone message to a private security firm, actually, two men and their dogs, who would respond immediately. He had imagined the carnage which might ensue if Brown were to return with, God knows, Jones or Robinson. He drove to the ring-road and parked in a lay-by to phone his sister. But what on earth could he say?

"Hi Helen, it's me, drop everything and pack a bag for yourself and Walter for a few days in a hotel somewhere. I've just shot a burglar dead and his accomplice is coming to abduct Walter and hold him as a hostage until I hand over some paintings."

What would be her response?

"Yes dear, of course, Walter's got a bit of a snuffle so could you pick up some Calpol on the way?"

Nor could he just say, like men in films, "Trust me, Helen!" because that wouldn't work either. He was sure that there was as much trust between himself and Helen as was possible between siblings. Yet this was within the context of a relationship between people who understood each other, who broadly knew what each other was like, who, after fifty years or so, could set limits to each other's unpredictability. What had happened this afternoon was way outside this boundary, and, quite simply, she would need proof that he had not lost his senses. In any case, perhaps the grey man – and he talked of 'we' so perhaps he would not be alone; he talked as if he were part of an organisation – already had people watching the cottage. She would have to leave immediately, before Smith found out what had happened in Broadharbour. No doubt she would be followed. So he sent her a text, "Both meet me in Marples at six pm v important got lovely surprise tell Walt."

Marples was a popular delicatessen and restaurant, in an Exeter mall where the throng of shoppers would, he hoped, deter any kidnap attempt. She would be early, he would only be slightly late.

Anthony was correct in his expectation that he would arrive at the shopping centre later than his sister and son.

The A30 had been glassy with rain and the left hand lanes almost solid with traffic, the lorries, taking to the road again after their brief dinner breaks, throwing up clouds of spray which would suddenly reduce visibility to something approaching zero. Cars sped by, flashing their lights and disappearing almost immediately into the murk. Anthony, not normally a particularly timid driver, did not on this occasion dare to follow. His mobile rang twice, but he didn't answer.

Arriving in Exeter in mid-afternoon, he impatiently followed a police car driving for nearly two miles at twenty eight miles per hour, fought his way to the city centre then turned into a narrow lane which he did not notice was one way – luckily no cars were coming in the other direction – and left his car near the cathedral on a double yellow line. Normally he was a legal parker, but in the present circumstances he decided, quite quickly, that the risk of a parking ticket was somewhat less grave than the risks attendant upon delay. He hurried to the shopping centre. A sizeable crowd of people had found shelter from the rain there, and Anthony had to barge through a throng of startled, annoyed and in some cases vocal shoppers to reach the entrance to Marples. Almost immediately he saw Walt and his sister queuing at the patisserie counter. As he manoeuvred his way towards them past umbrellas, pushchairs and chattering shoppers he saw, standing quietly by a rail of partly eviscerated rabbits, the man watching them. He was ordinary, so one might think, but he had that quiet, alert, composed manner which had been so noticeable in Smith and Brown, and he was wearing a blue-tooth earpiece with a small microphone.

"Anthony! What on earth's this all about?"

"Daddy! What's the lovely surprise?"

"No time for cakes, you two, we haven't got a moment to lose, I'll tell you in a second, come along COME ALONG sorry madam, sorry, my sister's..."

Grasping Walter's hand he pulled them towards the exit.

"We must hurry to the car, I left it on a double yellow, I'll tell you as soon as we start off"

"But daddy, Auntie Helen said I could have a bun, daddy why can't I, daddy I don't like lovely..."

"Walter, shut up..."

"Anthony!"

"Sorry, sorry..."

Anthony looked back and saw the watcher turn round slowly, looking towards them, and start to follow. He was speaking into the microphone.

Helen, of course, wanted to stand there, in the rain, and sort out what on earth was going on. Anthony's behaviour, this obviously contrived urgency, was so completely uncharacteristic that it couldn't possibly be explained by the opportunity of some unexpected treat. But she realised that there would be no explanation, credible or otherwise, until they reached the car. Anthony was hurrying them along, breathlessly making Walter all sorts of improbable promises – to little effect, because Walter, deprived of buns, had taken against all other treats.

They soon reached the car. A parking ticket was, not unexpectedly, taped to the windscreen. But Anthony had forgotten about wheel clampers – and there, with his little yellow van parked down the road, was a burly, head shaved, ear-studded young man, bending down to screw a clamp onto his front wheel. He looked over his shoulder at Anthony,

"Sorry mate, you're just too late. Got to do it up now."

"For God's sake, how much? I'll pay now, straightaway, please. We're in a desperate hurry." He opened his wallet.

"No chance. I can't take money, you'll have to wait till the guvnor comes. And then it'll be forty quid." He continued to fiddle with the clamp, awkwardly reaching under the wheel arch.

Anthony looked back up the road. No-one there yet. "Get into the car with Walter, now," he said to his sister.

"What? It might be ages before his boss comes. What's up with you? What's..."

Anthony cut her short. "I'll explain, honestly. But please, please get into the car. I'll settle up with this guy."

He turned to the clamper. "How much, now, in cash, to take it off?"

The clamper straightened up. "You trying to bribe me?"

"Yes, obviously."

"Fifty?"

Anthony counted out five tens. The man bent down and pulled the clamp clear; it wasn't locked. Anthony drove off, quickly looking back over his shoulder to check that the man tailing them had not turned the corner.

Outside the shopping centre the man with the telephone earpiece was joined by his wife who had been looking for a Jaeger skirt in the department store over the road.

"Nothing that fitted, darling, I'm afraid."

"No sweetbreads here either. Hardly any offal at all. What a waste of time." They hurried through the rain to the taxi he had just called to take them home.

By the time Anthony had driven to the outskirts of the city, and the traffic had cleared a little, Helen could contain herself no longer.

"Anthony, please tell me the point of all this? What's the tearing hurry? And what about my car? It's parked in the Cripplegate multi-storey, and that closes at eight thirty. You must tell me what's going on. Do you realise how mad you're behaving? Stop the car, stop it now."

"I will explain, I promise. You'll understand. Let's get to a café or a service area. I'll tell you then"

Walter was still cross. "Yes, dad. Why didn't you just kick him up the bottom? You wouldn't have had to give him any money then. You're weedy."

"Don't speak to your father like that. But, Anthony, honestly, what has got into you, you haven't answered my questions at all, what about my car, you can't just drive away from Exeter ..."

"For God's sake don't fuss about your car, it'll be safe, we'll just have to pay to get it out, it hasn't got a hi-fi or anything to steal in it."

The policeman, whose panda car had been parked in the back entrance to the shopping centre, strolled up to the clamper, who was just returning his mobile to its pocket.

"You got here quick. Nice little earner, eh?"

The clamper stared at him. He spoke deliberately. "Well you can just bugger off, can't you?"

Anthony drove as fast as he dared onto the motorway. He was fairly sure that no-one could be following them, but in any case he hadn't watched enough television to know how to shake off pursuers. As a sort of gesture to evasion he came off the motorway at junction twenty nine, drove around the lanes for ten minutes, then returned to the motorway and turned south. Helen had reached over into the back seat, grasped Walter's hand tightly, and closed her eyes.

Walter's curiosity had overcome his anger.

"Are we doing a runner from the filth, dad? So why are you driving like Granny?"

Anthony tried, but failed, to keep his self-control.

"I told you, Walter, I'm taking you and Auntie Helen on a very special holiday. We are not running from the police. And I am driving within the speed limit, so that we are not *stopped* by the fucking police, OK?"

"Daddy you said the eff word Auntie Helen Daddy said the eff word put him on the naughty stool put him on the naughty stool put him ..."

Aghast at the sudden concerted response to this Walter fell silent. When tears elicited no sympathy he realised that something very unusual indeed was happening. He sucked his thumb, and fell asleep as Anthony pulled into the service area.

Quietly, in order not to wake the child, Anthony explained what had happened. His sister remained silent; Anthony could not tell whether, or how much, she believed him. Reaching onto the back seat for his overnight bag he started to unzip it.

"What are you doing?"

"I'm going to show you the gun."

Helen caught her scream before it left her lips. "Don't you dare! I don't want to see it, what are you thinking of? Shut your bag up!"

"You don't have to touch it. You could – you could smell it and see that it's been fired?"

"Don't be ridiculous! Oh Anthony, Anthony, what is all this?"

She was crying now, and could only speak between sobs. She had indeed caught a glimpse of the obscene black metal thing in his bag.

"Anthony, dear Anthony, you've never fired a gun in your life...my God, what are we going to do? But why didn't you call the police?"

"I've told you why."

"Yes but that's daft, you should have rung the police, they'd know you weren't a criminal."

"Maybe I am. I killed him. Do you realise I killed him? I could have – I don't know, just pointed it at him and rung the police. But who was he? What sort of art thieves go round like," he paused, "mafia mobsters? No, not mafia, are there English gangs – organised gangs with, well, sort of cold and efficient types, not rough yobs?"

"Yes, there are bound to be. Did you see, that horrid picture of Cardinal what's-his-name went for thirty five million – *thirty five million*? And he wasn't even a pope."

"Come on, Helen, don't be such a philistine. It was a brilliant painting, it wasn't meant to be flattering! Of course, it wasn't a commissioned portrait, I'll tell you about Ottaviani, he wrote a..."

"For goodness' sake Anthony, I don't care about bloody Mantovani, stick to the point, can't you?"

"Yes, I know. Sorry. But you don't often hear about art thefts – I mean, compared with banks, or post offices, or jewellery."

"They must happen though, all the time. We just don't hear about it. It's all kept quiet and settled by insurance companies. It's only the...the...glamorous thefts that the papers get hold of – like that one where they abseiled down the tower at Windsor. So you've got to go to the police. They're certain to know who this lot are – and what sort of people – they'll know your life was being threatened. You've got to go back, now, and call them. We'll all go. I'll take Walter to see Stan and Miriam up the road. This kidnapping stuff is just rubbish, you know it is."

But Anthony did not think it was rubbish. He looked out of the car window. The rain had eased, and the semi-tame rooks in the car park, bright eyed and glossy, were restarting their day-long meal. He hadn't previously noticed how sharp their beaks were, like the little black daggers of Medici assassins. One seemed to be staggering around from car to car, only with great difficulty retaining its balance – but the more it limped the more crumbs, crisps and crusts were thrown its way and it was, if anything, sleeker than its sure footed companions. Survival of the lamest, Anthony thought; then, mutilated beggars, limbless children he had seen in prams outside cathedral doors – he wrenched his vagrant thoughts back to the present.

"All right, Helly, I'll go back, I promise. But I just don't want you and Walter anywhere near until I've sorted things out. And I don't want you to go back to the cottage. I know you think I'm daft, but please humour me. Take Walter somewhere nice, what about Brighton, give him a good time, there's lots to do, fairs and the pier and things."

Eventually he persuaded her. She thought, initially, that she would agree in order to placate him, and then leave Walter, with their cousin in Ide perhaps, and follow Anthony to his house. By now, however, what she thought of as Anthony's paranoia had started to affect her, distorting her reason and preventing her, she knew, from judging things with her usual common sense. And there was no getting round the gun, hard, solid evidence impossible to ignore.

Anthony left Walter and Helen at the Earl of Strafford hotel. First thing the following morning they were to travel by taxi to the station, and then by train to Brighton, where they were to take a room in one of the many boutique hotels near Regency Square. Anthony would phone them with news when he could, and in the meantime Helen would pretend that he would join them soon for a holiday together.

Chapter 4

July 29   Anthony   Paul and Anne Baxter

After seeing his son and sister safely checked into the Strafford, Anthony had driven home, arriving late in the afternoon. He had attempted to make some sort of plan; had been going over the various possibilities in his mind, appraising the options, in the jargon of his trade. He had never in the past had much sympathy with interviewees on television who would duck an issue by refusing to answer a 'hypothetical' question. Any planning which does not involve the answers to hypothetical questions must be very simple, he had thought, not really planning at all. Like going out shopping with a list and coming home without any vegetables because the sprouts were sold out. But now he could, if not sympathise, at least see clearly what the word 'hypothetical' encoded – something not in itself impossible, but either so awful as to be impossible to contemplate, or so difficult, painful or embarrassing to solve that the interviewee would much rather not talk about it. And the problem was, and a very big problem it was, that all the 'thens' which would follow the present situation's 'ifs' were dire in the extreme.

He had more or less decided that he would, after all, call the police, or, if they were already at the house he would tell them his story. Mental – and possibly physical, although he did not recognise this – exhaustion had catalysed his decision, and it had seemed to him, as he kissed Walter and his sister goodbye that his aspirations to emotional self-sufficiency were unrealistic. The picture of himself, half formed in the past eight hours, as a sort of *Rogue Male* figure, was fading fast as chemicals drained. All that he was left with was the anachronistic notion that the police would believe him because of his nice suit and Oxbridge accent.

There seemed to be no-one about the house. His neighbours' lights were dim in their front room, and the changing colours flickering over the wallpaper showed that they were watching television. He walked up to his porch, let himself in, turned off the alarm, shut the door behind him and stood for a moment in the hall facing the kitchen door. There was a certain odour overlaying the scent of the entirely appropriate white lilies in their vase on the hall table – he had been vaguely expecting something like the smell of a butcher's shop, from the kitchen floor pooled with Smith's blood – but this seemed to be more like bleach, similar to his lavatory cleaner. Next to the vase was a folded sheet of writing paper, which he didn't remember seeing in the morning. He picked it up and saw that it was a note in the handwriting of their Polish cleaning lady. He had, of course, forgotten that she came on a Saturday afternoon. It apologised for her lateness and complimented him, in a characteristically arch manner, upon the general cleanliness and good order of his kitchen, but mentioned that he must have dropped a steak or a lamb chop on the floor just behind the waste bin, but never mind she had scrubbed it clean with a bit of Vim. And, he had forgotten to turn the alarm on.

The kitchen was spotless and uncorpsed. He sat down in the Windsor chair, throwing the Antiques Gazettes onto the shining tiles. Had he been drunk and dreaming? No, he hadn't. It was all too consistent for a dream – up to now? But obviously there had been blood on the floor, not from a lamb chop, and...and, neatly placed by the door was the minstrel money box, madly grinning. But its left arm ended in no hand cupped ready for a coin, only a broken stump. He could see, just under the washing machine, a black cast iron disk, a severed wrist, four forlorn fingers and a thumb, curled in the now hopeless expectation of alms. No, he had not been dreaming.

First he must phone his sister. He dialled her mobile, there was a brief pause and he was asked to leave a message. Momentary irritation overlaid his anxiety – surely she hadn't let her battery run down? No, there could be any number of reasons – he would try later. He said that he was all right and would ring again.

Secondly, he ought to check that the robbers hadn't traced the paintings to Safetrans, and stolen them from the van, or the depot. He presumed that the employees of this very well-known firm were trained in all sorts of security procedures – but, somehow, Smith and Brown had made such a frightening impact upon him that he could not believe that their organisation would have any difficulty lifting the paintings wherever they found them. Smith, it was true, was dead, but only by an extraordinary fluke, and Anthony was still, amazingly, carrying the gun which had shot him, in his coat pocket, like a camera, or a pair of miniature binoculars, or a heavyish book. No, only like a gun.

He would phone Safetrans. They would surely have a twenty four hour service. They did. Would he give them his security password? He did. The paintings were located in the Reading number three depot, bay 41. There had been no other enquiries.

He sat down again in the Windsor chair. He should make himself some tea. Why tea? Instant coffee was simpler and quicker and had more caffeine. So he made a cup, poured it down the sink and made a pot of tea. He should eat. He buttered a stale bath bun and managed to eat half of it.

It was clear that he couldn't ring the police. What could he show them? The gun? Absurd. And what if Brown returned? He was suddenly afraid, and realised that he would not sleep, and could achieve nothing by staying in the house. But where to go? Maurice was his oldest friend, they had lived on the same staircase at Brasenose, and it was Maurice whose delight in art, especially British painters of the twentieth century, had communicated itself so strongly to Anthony that it soon became his passion also. Maurice now lived on the edge of Exmoor – not too far to drive – and would be more likely than anyone to believe his story. But wasn't Maurice in Italy, researching a book on Harris? Perhaps he could ring Paul and Anne Baxter, good friends whom he trusted, and Paul who had some government job in Exeter would at least be able to talk it through with him, and give some advice. He needed, desperately, to talk. So he telephoned Paul, told him he had a serious problem and asked for his help.

Paul and Anne lived about an hour's drive away, in one of the wooded valleys of South Devon. The drive took him through the arts and crafts settlements of Dartington and Totnes, and through beautiful countryside dotted with the immaculate houses of rich and concerned people who would turn their AGAs off in August to prevent global warming. Paul and Anne, who had two children, were not rich, and spent what money they had left over on a boat which they kept at Dartmouth. The light was beginning to fail as Anthony arrived, and Anne was reading their younger child a bedtime story, so Paul took him into the living room, offered him a drink and asked what was wrong.

"I think I should stick to coffee, please."

For over six years now, since the death of Anthony's wife from ovarian cancer when Walter was not yet one year old, hardly weaned, still in nappies, Anthony's friends had been anxious – initially deeply worried – that looking after Walter largely on his own, with sporadic support from his sister and cousin, would prove too great a burden. Anthony had not shared their doubts. He saw the physical care as a fairly simple problem of logistics, and he was quite prepared to sacrifice whatever was necessary to ensure that the love and emotional support which his son received was little less than it would have been were his wife still alive. In fact it was only his friends – mostly male – who used words like 'sacrifice', or who wondered how he could bear to stay at home every evening, cooking fish fingers, running baths, reading gross stories about sweet factories, and ending up (they imagined) with whisky in front of the television. Or organising children's parties, buying children's clothes, – and not being able to go to the pub. Anthony had managed perfectly well, first by organising friends and neighbours, then, as his income increased, buying good nursery care. As he became richer, the mechanics of care became easy. He still stayed in most evenings, but it was easy to find baby sitters – perhaps too easy. Anthony had married late. Since Amy's death he had had no relationships of any significance; he thought her irreplaceable.

His friends more or less accepted that Anthony was living a happy life as a single father and that Walter was also happy, normal, well adjusted – or, at least, about as much so as their own children. But it's always difficult to tell, they would say, and naturally Walter is bound to *seem* very bright because Tony taught him to read so early and then playing chess with him of course, and he is a bit *rough* in touch-rugby; but most of Anthony's friends, and their children, liked Walter, and invited him to tea, or to parties, and their gossip about him was more a matter of form, when they had exhausted the more interesting topics of their own children.

Nevertheless, Paul first asked if Anthony's problems concerned Walter, and when this was immediately denied, looked initially relieved, then apprehensive.

"Are you ill?"

"No. Please listen, and please try to believe me. I honestly think you and Maurice are the only people who might."

Anne came in at this point, closing the door quietly behind her. She glanced at Paul who frowned very slightly, and shook his head. She greeted Anthony with a kiss, sat down, and listened to his story. She was younger than her husband, had not known Anthony quite so long, and found it difficult to believe him. Paul was making a greater effort, but it was obvious that he too was considering the possibility that Anthony had been overcome by a paranoid illness.

"You say that there were no traces when you returned?"

"None at all. Except Ira had left a note saying there was blood on the floor."

"Yes, but it could have been anything? A bit of ketchup?" Paul immediately regretted his tone. He didn't mean to imply disbelief. If Anthony had really succumbed to delusion, reasoning wasn't going to help, and if he hadn't then the cleanliness of the kitchen was a minor detail. Anne left the sitting room, looking dazed, saying that she was going to check the children were asleep.

Anthony and Paul sat in silence for a minute or two. Anthony felt relieved, as the need to share his problem had become so pressing, but he knew that this was an illusory feeling, since what he needed was advice – instructions – not comfort. Anne returned.

"Anthony, I hope you don't mind, I've got your sister's mobile number from when you came to our party, remember, and I've just rung her..."

Anthony sat forward on his chair. "I tried, there was no reply, is she all right?"

"Yes, fine, they both are. She was having supper, Walter was with her. Anthony, she says that you showed her a..."

"Yes, yes, of course, how stupid of me, just a minute."

He ran into the hall, pulled the gun from his coat pocket and returned quickly. Paul and Anne were standing together, Paul in front of Anne, the other side of the room.

"Here it is, oh I'm sorry, look I'll ..."

He threw the gun onto the settee near to Paul.

"I've never touched one in my life before. Have you?"

"Yes, I have actually."

Paul bent down to pick up the gun, intending to unload it and check whether any rounds had been fired, but Anne pushed him violently away, shouting at him not to touch it.

After a moment they sat down, no-one choosing the settee.

Anne said, "Anthony, you know you must ring the police. You've got a solicitor, surely? Why don't you ring him?"

"No, Anne, I haven't *got* a solicitor. Why should I have? I *know* a few solicitors I suppose, but I don't see them helping. A madman with a gun?"

Paul said, "Yes, Anthony, Anne's right, of course you should ring the police. And you've got to calm down. But what do you want us to do? I don't see how we can help."

The telephone in the hall rang. Paul came back after a few minutes. "Only Mary."

Anne looked at him in surprise. "Mary?"

"Yes, you know, Mary from work...she wanted to know if I was coming to the planning meeting tomorrow."

"Well, you took your time, didn't you?"

"Well, she does...you know ..."

Anthony put his hand to his face, and pressed his fingertips against his forehead as if trying to avert a headache. He looked, and was, exhausted.

"I'm so sorry. If I could just have a bed for the night, the sofa's fine, I'll be gone first thing."

Paul hesitated, and then said, "Well, at least you ought to have something to eat" – he looked at Anne, who stared back at him and said nothing, "so I'll go and get you a bite to eat, a sandwich or something, shall I?"

Anne stood up, glared at her husband, and said, "No. He can't stay. Not as he is, not with a gun and, well, for God's sake Paul, think of the children. You don't believe a word of it, do you? So what does he want with the gun?" She turned to Anthony. "Please understand why you can't stay, not a moment longer. Please go away now."

Anthony looked up at Paul, who was hesitating and gesturing towards the kitchen, and who then said to Anne, "But surely there's time to make him a sandwich and a cup of coffee? That wouldn't do any harm would it? I think he should stay for that?"

"Why are they having this argument?" thought Anthony, "I just ought to go."

"No he shouldn't stay for a sandwich" said Anne. She appealed to Anthony, "It's the children, you can see I'm thinking of the children, can't you? How can we take this sort of risk now?"

Anthony understood; he thought momentarily of Walter; of course he understood. There had been a time when they were younger, when they took all sorts of risks. They had all sailed across to Brittany and then to Santander once, in a thirty two foot sailing boat without a life-raft, RDF, radar, anything. Anthony was the oldest, but had done more sailing; Anne had only just left school.

Anne continued "Why didn't you ring Maurice? He wouldn't mind what you'd done – I mean, he would help whatever had happened?"

"Because Maurice is in Italy. He's gone to Padua to find Harris's daughter."

"No he hasn't. It was called off. She's ill or something."

"Oh. So he's in Tynsleigh now?"

"Yes. Look, ring him from here."

It was obvious now that he should ring Maurice as soon as possible. He would have phoned him in the first instance had he not thought Maurice to be in Italy. It was true, as Anne had implied, that Maurice was the least judgmental of his friends, in that he would certainly understand quickly how pressures and events can combine to produce a situation where behaviour normally thought culpable becomes almost inevitable. He would not have made a good policeman, or an efficient magistrate, because the thought of exemplary punishment repelled him. But being by nature absolutely honest himself, he could be unexpectedly and pointedly critical of his friends when he thought that their behaviour fell short of his own, occasionally idiosyncratic, standards of rectitude, so he could at times be an awkward companion. He was a fairly successful art dealer, but would have made more money if he had been prepared to deal in paintings and sculpture which were fashionable but in his view meretricious, and if he had been less scrupulous in his dealings with his artists and the Inland Revenue. In any case, he would always claim that he only bought and sold in order to finance his main interest, a study of the ways in which social developments beget and interact with artistic movements. He was trying to find out whether art actually serves to reinforce, or undermine, the social order. Reinforce, obviously, in authoritarian regimes; he was wondering if that was also true in democracies. It was an intractable subject, and on occasion he despaired of reaching any conclusions. Then he would, at considerable length, share his gloominess with his friends, who at times found their capacity to sympathise somewhat overstretched. But this would not be such an occasion.

Anthony wanted to telephone him, but felt inhibited from doing so in the presence of Paul and Anne. He decided to leave immediately, and phone from his car. There was no point in staying – he should never have come. Paul tried once more to persuade him to eat something before he left, despite his wife's incredulity and obvious anger. Apologising again Anthony picked up his coat, then stepped over to the side table. Paul also moved quickly to the table, and they spoke simultaneously.

"I think I should take this with me. It doesn't belong here, does it?"

"I should leave this here if I were you, I'll say I found it ..."

Anthony was quicker. He picked up the gun, put it in his pocket and left the house.

The darkness outside was the deep black of a starless night in woodland far from a town. In about a quarter of a mile he turned down a side road and pulled up in a gateway, turned his car lights off and opened its door. He saw the headlamps of two cars driving fast along the road he had just left, then nothing. Leaning against a tree, he made an effort to breathe calmly and deeply, willing his heart rate to slow, clearing his mind and trying to absorb the peace of the dark and quiet wood. After a little while he returned to the car, and dialled Maurice's number.

The police, six of them, all bulky with body armour and carrying an assortment of weapons, had surrounded the house soon after Anthony had left. They had asked Paul, when he rang them immediately after the phone call from Mary, to distract and delay him if possible. When they had been told where he had said he was going, two stayed in the house, still with their weapons ready, and the remaining four drove away in pursuit. Paul and Anne were told to stay in the sitting room. Anne wept when she heard one of the officers radioing for a police woman and, if possible, whoever was on call from Social Services. He tried to reassure her, but explained that there were very explicit rules which had to be followed at a suspected gun crime scene.

"But there hasn't been a gun crime, and in any case he took it away with him!"

"I'm afraid that's yet to be ascertained, madam."

The children were quiet; she didn't know what would happen if one or both of them woke and came downstairs, and she suspected the police didn't either.

July 29   Anthony   Maurice

"I doubt they're still serving. I'll try and charm a couple of sandwiches out of them. Cheese OK?"

Maurice took their order to the bar, and came back with two pints.

"You look completely done in. Shagged out. What's all this about then?"

So once again, Anthony told his story. He embellished nothing, and kept nothing back. Maurice had chosen a sensible rendezvous, a large and noisy road-house where food, of a sort, was served until late.

"Drink up," Maurice said. "I've booked us a room. You don't look fit to drive in any case."

Anthony didn't respond, but sat silent, staring at the fireplace. He had started to tremble.

Maurice was also quiet for a moment.

Then he continued, "Mind you, we never used to bother much about that, did we? Goodness me, those old bangers we had. You had a Morris Eight and I had a Beetle with a dickey steering worm? Well, that's what old Tommy Allsop said, I distinctly remember the phrase, it sounded most unlikely. I had it repaired by that German chap in Headington, and nearly drove it into the ditch when the car actually changed direction the minute I turned the steering wheel. First time it had done that. Very disconcerting."

He chattered on, pausing occasionally to smile at Anthony. He was unsure whether conversation or silence was more appropriate; there was, however, one issue which he wished to raise. He worried that he would give offence.

"We had a few jolly evenings at the Chub, didn't we? No breathalysers then; someone had chalked a line on the river terrace. As long as you could walk along that without actually falling down you were OK to drive home. Do you remember the little green lights we had to have on the bumper, and the proctors stopped people, ordinary citizens, not necessarily students, can you imagine it, to ask them if they were undergraduates? It's almost like a false memory, isn't it? Something you've seen on the box? Well at any rate..."

"Look, I know what you're getting round to. I could put it away all right – just like you, I may say – and I do remember the occasion when I saw the Principal dancing a waltz with the Senior Tutor in the buttery and very few of my friends, you included, could bring themselves to believe me. Yes, of course I remember. I have never hallucinated since then, I do not booze like we used to at Oxford, does anyone, and I have here in my pocket what is I believe known as a Smith and Wesson Airlite. At least that's what's printed on the handle. Stock. Grip. The bit you hold. It's a revolver, Maurice, like, you know, a cap gun but bigger. *A revolver.*"

His voice was becoming louder, dangerously close to the volume of the other drinkers.

"Revolver eh?" Maurice raised his voice in reply. "Wonderful disk! You can keep your Stones and your Led Zeppelin, Eleanor Rigby, now there's a fine song. Written in the Dorian mode you know," his voice dropped, "please keep that thing in your pocket. Whatever make it is. I am truly sorry if you thought I doubted your word."

But no-one had heard. Maurice returned to the bar and bought whiskies.

They took coffee in their bedroom. That is, they carried it upstairs themselves, spilling onto a British Railways tray, with little brown plastic pots of bleached turnip extract, and paper packets of salt which didn't matter because neither of them took sugar.

Maurice sniffed the barrel of the gun. Anthony laughed.

"You've been watching too much Poirot. Zis gun as not been fie-herd, Aysteengs. Well it bloody has. And by bloody me."

"As a matter of interest, Anthony, setting aside whether or not your story is actually true – no, don't be upset, I'm sure you can see what I'm getting at, – do you really expect me to believe it?"

"I just don't know," Anthony said miserably, "But I thought that you might. It's true that I couldn't think of anybody else who would."

"But you went to Paul's? Did they believe you?"

"I don't think so. Anne panicked. Once I'd shown them the gun I could see that no explanation of mine would help. Perhaps it was the children – being in their house, with their children – maybe it's different here, you didn't panic. I think seeing this wretched gun drove what I'd actually said out of their heads. I only told them once, I shouldn't think they would remember any of the details. People don't, do they?"

When Maurice merely frowned, Anthony continued, "Come on, surely you remember the vacation job we did one summer for that Austrian psychiatrist at the Maudsley? Well, he wasn't Austrian, was he, he was just pretending, now he was *really* doolally. The job where you and I were interviewing old biddies to see how potty they were?"

He recited:

" 'I'm going to tell you a little story, Mrs Smith, and then let's see how much you remember in ten minutes. In the meantime please count backwards from ninety three in sevens, and who is the prime minister's uncle?' "

"Only in this case, 'just have a butcher's at this weapon of death and destruction will you?' is that what you mean?" said Maurice.

"Yes, that's what I mean."

"Yes, you're right Anthony, but I *can* remember your story. Of course I'm not panicking. Maybe I would be if you hadn't put that thing back in your pocket. But surprised. I think I can fairly say that I'm surprised. Look, I know you're exhausted, but can you possibly stop jigging around for a minute or two, and I'll tell you about something that's happened to me?"

"If you must. I can't promise to concentrate."

"You could try. It might be relevant. A couple of months ago I had a phone call from some far-back type, you, know, he wundahed if I could ahh – who said his boss, called him his principal, would like some advice on a couple of

Festival paintings which he'd just bought. I asked what advice he meant, if it was about conservation then I wasn't his man, he should go to Patrick Olds in Dulwich. No, he said, and I could tell he wanted me to authenticate them. Or not, of course. I asked this secretary chap when and where his boss had bought them, but he clammed up. Then when he told me the fee, I just asked him the time of the next train.

"Well, I dare say Peter the Great had a bigger house, and more golden cherubs, but this chap would have run him a close second. You read about these sorts of lifestyles in Hello – in the barber's, of course, where else? And I suppose we tell ourselves that it wouldn't suit us, that we wouldn't take to it at all. Not true, I'm afraid, for me at any rate. After twenty minutes, a couple of glasses of the Widow with a very nice young man – personal assistant, he called himself – and a spoonful or two of fish eggs, I was feeling quite relaxed enough to submit without turning a hair – or, indeed, showing any other reaction – to a really quite intimate body search from a very large gentleman. When I finally attained the presence, the man himself didn't mess around. Two pictures were propped up against a sofa, and he asked me who had painted them. I didn't think it was meant as a test – they were obviously Hopkinses, or meant to be Hopkinses, from the people's cars series, really big oils, you know, a bit showy – not like the Bradleys you prefer – but a damn sight more valuable. Just the sort of things to appeal to a Ruski. About three parts of a million each, I should imagine. Possibly more. I don't know where he got them from, certainly not an auction.

"What was he like? You know, looked about twenty with a silk shirt and stubble. No tie, dangerous eyes. No, I was never told his name. To continue, I did my well known Brian Sewell imitation – but I didn't have to spin it out. One of the paintings seemed OK – it was an Auto Union, one of the small ones, – but the other wasn't. And here's the really interesting bit. I couldn't tell the difference from the techniques. The forgery was about the best I've ever seen. Colour, brushwork, balance, signature – damn near perfect.

But the date was wrong. Ivan didn't need an art expert, he needed someone like that Clarkson chap."

"What? What are you talking about, Maurice?"

"You know, tall bloke on telly who knows all about cars?"

"Yes, I know who Clarkson is. Can't you get to the point?"

"Well, the point is, the picture was a very early one, signed and dated April 1950, and it was a Beetle, like mine, but with a single oval rear window. Now, I know nothing about any modern cars, but I do know a thing or two about old Beetles. As I have just reminded you, I used to drive one when we were up at Oxford. You will no doubt remember how absurdly devoted to their cars VW drivers were in those days, we used to give each other funny little waves when we passed on the road; there was a sort of secret expression we had, like two gays at Twickenham. Well you wouldn't, would you? Oh yes. More than once, actually. But I digress. At any rate, the one-piece rear window was introduced in 1952.

"No, I didn't actually *know* that to start with, but it just didn't seem quite right, and it took me a couple of phone calls. So there you have it. Ivan had been scammed, and so might we all be if matey's a bit more careful next time – or the previous time, God knows when he started. But I tell you, it must have taken some nerve to put one over this Russian. Not the forgiving type, I imagine. He didn't react a lot, mind you. Looked a bit more dangerous, not that there was much scope for that. Said that he would do a bit of checking up, and would be obliged if I would let him know if I came across any more ripples in this particular pond. Told his secretary to give me a phone number – one of his people could always pop and see me at a moment's notice. At this stage I rather regretted taking his shilling. But he added what he called a modest retainer to my fee. Modest enough to keep me in Lafite for a year or two."

Anthony had stopped fidgeting now, and was waiting impatiently for Maurice to draw breath. When he did pause for a moment, temporarily distracted by the thoughts of self-indulgence raised by his last conceit, Anthony asked a question which he had wanted to ask half way through Maurice's last speech.

"Are you sure that the other painting wasn't a Morris Minor?"

"What?"

"They look quite similar, and there's quite an impressionist feel to his middle period?"

"Well yes, that's true, but as it happens I'm quite certain. I remember the Auto Union well because there was one at a steam fair I went to in the Beetle, it was in Kent at Knole – hang on, you came as well, there was a Gavioli organ playing *Is this the way to Amarillo*?"

"Yes, you're right. Friggers was there too, wasn't he? He was beside himself. He's got perfect pitch, did you know?"

"I think we all knew that, dear."

"But I don't remember the cars; the reason I ask is because the Hopkins in the Dowland's sale was a Morris Minor. At least, that's what it said in the catalogue."

"Well, I do remember the cars. I was much more interested in the cars than you were. It was an Auto Union. Definitely."

"You're sure?"

"Oh, for Christ's sake, yes, I'm sure. Look, I know it's sad, but I just am. You just have to look at the radiator, in any case."

"Actually, I don't think I've ever heard of an Auto Union?"

"They changed their name to Audi."

"Oh. Well, there you are then."

Although he couldn't really put his finger on the reason why, Anthony was beginning to feel more relaxed, only slightly, but enough to give him some hope that his mental state might have reached its nadir, with the possibility of an improvement to come soon. To find confirmation, not of his story, because of course he was sure that his story was true, but rather that what had happened to him might actually be part of an explicable series of events, rather than a sort of random visitation of horror, was in one sense a relief. His story had become credible; it could easily be an element, perhaps a small element, of a larger and at present obscure pattern, and perhaps Maurice was wondering about this too. But at the same time he had been subconsciously and unrealistically hoping for an explanation along the lines of a doctor comforting a worried patient with the reassurance that all his painful and disabling symptoms were due only to a passing virus. And this was not the case. The condition was not benign.

Maurice continued, "You're sure the Scandinavian accountant with a penchant for expensive Chardonnay didn't mention who his boss was? No clue at all?"

"No. But the paintings I bought aren't forgeries, or if they are, why should anyone want to buy one so much that they'd pay me an extra forty k? Or organise an armed robbery in, what, about three hours? And they're nothing like as valuable as Hopkinses. I mean, this gang would have had to be there already, surely?"

"Well," said Maurice, who was busy thinking up all sorts of arcane connections and plots, "rich Russians do travel around in some state, you know, especially if they've offended the czar."

"Has he? So do you know who your bloke is? Where did you meet him? They live in Kensington or Regent's Park don't they?"

"No, I don't know who he is. His secretary said that he has a house in London and I got the impression that he also had one in the country, but apparently neither was convenient. I'm afraid I was being slightly misleading when I mentioned the train times. Plane times would have been more accurate."

"Good God, I should have guessed. Lenin...St Petersburg."

"Yes, St Petersburg, for nearly ten years now. Ten years, Anthony."

"Of course. Some habits are hard to break. You're an old lefty too, Maurice, or is that all in the past?"

"Old, yes, I fear. Lefty too, I suppose. Am I still? I really don't know. What a shambles now, eh? Are you still a party member?"

"Come on, Maurice, you know I'm not, Czechoslovakia finished me off. We were still at Oxford, you must remember."

"Not the CP you prat, the Labour Party."

"Oh that. Of course not. Nothing now, I'm afraid. Might try the Greens. That was a joke. Could we talk a bit about my, what shall we say, quandary, please?"

"I'm not sure that I can say much more to the point. I still think you should go to the police. What can you do on your own?"

Anthony walked slowly around the room with his hands in his pockets, looking at the carpet. For a few minutes neither of them said a word. Maurice broke the silence.

"I did hear that some surprise Hopkinses have suddenly popped up in Cornwall. Place called Boselloe, near St Just. Perhaps they're a bit iffy? Or something; I don't know."

"Where?"

"Boselloe. Don't know how it's spelt."

"St Just's near Falmouth isn't it, across the river?"

"The other one, I think, near Land's End."

Anthony waited for him to continue, but he remained silent. Anthony gave him a moment or two, then spoke.

"Maurice, you're being cagey, that's not like you. Come on, what's the story?"

"Well, I heard a bit of a rumour, so I – do you remember Ratty?"

"Chap who got a first in history and never changed his jeans? Yes I remember him. Prodigious memory, could be a bit boring about the Hohenzollerns couldn't he?"

"He could. And the Habsburgs. Attractive little sod, but, as you remember, a bit on the smelly side. In any case, he was straight, you know."

"I do. I believe a few of us were."

"At any rate, he was at the last gaudy, which you missed."

"You know I never go to gaudies. They're all Lords Justices of Appeal now, or Permanent Secretaries, or billionaires."

"Or art dealers or, in the main, greying school teachers. As is Ratty. Nice chap now, married, kids, even wears clean clothes. He's apparently head of Liberal Studies at Tregethnan College, and, like so many down there he's a sort of art buff. He buys the occasional painting, he says. His favourites are the naives. Can't afford Alfred Wallis, of course, but there are one or two others – he doesn't even mind some of the pretend naives. However, he likes nosing out Wallises: they turn up in all sorts of odd places and he heard that some farmer out in the wilds had no less than five, biggish pretty ones, all with lots of boats on."

"The number of boats matters?"

"Certainly it does. There's a way to work out how much Wallises will fetch, you know. It's an equation, apparently the value's a function of size, number of different colours, number of boats – masts, actually, to be precise. And the ones painted on bathmats are more valuable than the ones painted on biscuit tins?"

"Dummy variables, that's how you – oh, for goodness sake, Maurice, tell the truth occasionally, there's a good chap."

"Sorry. Well, he found this farm, near St Just as I said, and asked very prettily if he could see the Wallises. Bit of a cheek, but they could only say no, probably not set the dogs on him. The farmer said that his wife was the art collector, and she was out shopping, but he let him have a quick look. Ratty was slavering over them when the farmer's radio thing buzzed, and he said that there was a problem with calving or something, and they would have to leave. He escorted Ratty out, shut the door and locked it with about five separate keys. It was Easter holidays then, and Mr and Mrs Ratty and the little Ratlings went off to Florence for a bit of foreign culture before the b & b prices went up. They came back in a fortnight and Ratty thought he could pop up and see Mrs farmer and gawp at her pictures again. He did just that – but, in the fortnight he was away, the pictures had gone; sold, she said, to an American dealer, all five of them. She was very short with him; brusque, he said, he was left standing on the doorstep."

"Maurice, I was buying a Bradley, a Festival painting, not a naive. They're about the least naive paintings since ..."

"Hang on, hang on. The story continues. I correspond sometimes with a dealer in Penzance. Strange bloke, sartorially challenged, odd sense of humour, – but that's neither here nor there. He rang me only a couple of weeks ago because he knows I sometimes do the Festival school, and he said that a private owner had recently shown some extraordinary Hopkinses to a friend of his. Told him they'd kept them in the family home in the Midlands, but now had them down here. And yes, same address. The Wallises had been replaced by Hopkinses. The walls were no longer bare. And I am told that Alf's been to see them – you know him, surely, writes the odd article for the coffee table trade."

The hotel was silent when they eventually turned in. Maurice had decided he shouldn't drive home, and there were twin beds. No resolution of Anthony's problem had been reached. Maurice, his normal bed-time reading not being to hand, mulled it over once more. He could not really believe that Helen and Walter were in any danger, because this gang, if such it was, could easily find the pictures at the conservator's so what else could they want Anthony for? Anthony may have thought that he had examined the paintings carefully, but hardly any non-scientific examination would be sufficient to rule out a counterfeit, especially if the quality of the forgery were as good as that of the beetle picture. And in any case, Anthony was expert for an amateur, true, but not as expert as he thought he was. Maybe there was some anachronism, as in the beetle painting, which Anthony just hadn't spotted? But, then, did the bad men know that he hadn't? Had he managed to answer the grey man's question? Grey man, wasn't he called Brown? Confusing. Wasn't it about then that Anthony said he had flipped? And goodness, if this was to do with forgery, the conservator would be the one in danger now.

This phrase, 'in danger', was one which Maurice realised he had read, in books or papers, a thousand times, but had never applied to anything in his own world. What sheltered lives English baby boomers had lived! Driving without a seat belt was probably the most dangerous thing he'd ever done. No, perhaps occasionally...he fell asleep.

Anthony's thoughts had been along much the same lines. He decided he would telephone the conservator's again in the morning.

They were both, of course, very tired, more than a bit drunk, and had consigned the shooting to a sort of limbo of the imagination.

Chapter 5

Previously   Maurice   Patricia and Christopher

After his encounter with the oligarch Maurice had looked up all recent sales where Hopkinses had appeared, and nothing odd seemed to be happening; prices were rising, which was only to be expected, as the Festival school was in favour at the moment. He had put himself about in the galleries, including the great nationals, but the buzz had not included rumours about counterfeit Festival paintings, nor did he notice any raised eyebrows, no marginally altered expression which might have indicated the germination of even a tiny doubt when he mentioned names such as Harris, or Hopkins.

But this was London, New York, Paris – and pedlars of fake art often find the provinces an easier theatre to work their stage magicians' tricks in. The audience is less sceptical, the desire to believe stronger. Only quite recently the art gallery of a largish town in East Anglia had bought a painting, discovered in the back parlour of a decaying tavern, which was confidently attributed by the local auctioneers to, of course, John Constable. Appeals had been set up, parents had spent hours glueing and painting cardboard hay wains for school prizes, finance officers had sat head in hands over their computer screens, inwardly ululating, desperately searching for a budget to rob; the pressure on the London expert to authenticate the painting was enormous; she did her best, no-one took any notice of her mild caveats and house-surveyor style disclaimers. The corporation bought the painting before auction, for a bargain price which reflected the wish of the owner, the licensee of the inn, to 'do a bit for the town whose citizens had put a few coppers in his purse'. A bargain price for a Constable would nevertheless have built a good few bus shelters, even a bus terminal. The painting was, naturally, a forgery. The public-spirited licensee and all the pub staff vanished, and it turned out that his lease was only months old. Lawyers were still arguing over who should bear the cost.

But this story was well known now; the forgery, however, was said to be more than usually competent, and Maurice felt obliged to examine it to find out if the work was in any way similar to that of the one he had seen in St Petersburg. It seemed very unlikely, and in any case he wasn't at all sure that he would be able to spot any identifying characteristic of an artist who could work in the styles of both Constable and Hopkins and produce paintings in each good enough to fool experts. He almost certainly wouldn't have identified the Hopkins as counterfeit had it not been for the mistaken date.

Nevertheless, he thought that he owed it to the Russian – well, considering the size of his fee he certainly did – to follow up any lead. He rather fancied himself, in fact, as a detective; weeks later, Anthony's little dig when he sniffed the gun barrel, far from embarrassing him, struck him as surprisingly apposite, conjuring up the make-believe world of the educated, sensitive detective of English female crime novelists.

He had telephoned the Met art squad, who used to visit him occasionally to find out if he had been offered any pictures which were on their stolen list. He had only encountered fairly junior policemen except on the famous and recent occasion when the Duke of Redgrave's Vermeer had gone missing, along with four or five modern British paintings, including a Bacon and two Hopkinses. Then he had been visited in his little Exeter gallery by the nearest approximation to a fictional detective that he could imagine, a well-spoken young man with longish hair and designer jeans, an engraved card and two degrees, called Chief Inspector Green.

The chief inspector had initially spent some time looking around the exhibition, which was a retrospective of an elderly painter whom Maurice rated highly but who had never had much commercial success, and at one stage he looked so intently at a painting of the famous tombs at

Fontevraud that Maurice thought for a moment that he might actually buy it. Alas, he then introduced himself, and explained that although he doubted – and Mr Symes-Franton must not, please, be in the slightest degree offended – that this gallery would be the very first port of call for a thief wishing to dispose of a Vermeer (or a Bacon, Maurice said to himself), nevertheless it was well known that Mr Symes-Franton was very much in tune with the market for Modern British. So had he been approached, or had he heard any rumours, about the stolen Redgrave paintings? Maurice's demurral, and the subsequent enjoyable chat over Earl Grey and madeleines about the opportunities for dishonesty offered by his trade, saw them through a rainy afternoon, uninterrupted, as was not unusual, by customers. Looking back on this meeting Maurice realised that Green had probably been on what he believed the police called a fishing expedition. But perhaps not; perhaps he was actually being friendly, and had stayed because he had a late train to catch.

On the basis of this earlier encounter, Maurice rang the Metropolitan Police, and, when he eventually got past the gatekeepers, asked the Art Squad detective constable if he could speak to Green. Apparently he could not. Chief Inspector Green had been on temporary secondment from another branch of the service, and had moved on. Maurice was surprised; he had seemed very knowledgeable for a temporary officer; what branch had he gone back to? The constable either didn't know or wasn't telling. But he could tell Maurice that as far as he was aware there was nothing special going on concerning the Festival school. No more than usual, that was. Which was all he was saying. So Maurice had found no titbit under this stone, but he had at least turned it over, which was what he had felt obliged to do.

After his unproductive telephone conversation with the police, Maurice rang the Director of the municipal gallery in the East Anglian town, in order to arrange a visit when he might have a look at the fake Constable. Maurice was friendly, or acquainted, with most gallery Directors or senior staff, or had at one time or another bumped into them at an exhibition or an opening. He had met Ruth ages ago, at an exhibition of British Surrealist art, which she had curated. She had been very young then, and had written a catalogue which sounded as if she really believed what she had written about the painters and their work. Coming across her at the bar, and after his second gin, he had alluded to this in humorous yet affectionate tones. After the ensuing short discussion he decided that she must be a little on edge, what with this being her first exhibition, and the Director of the London and other such luminaries invited. Spiky, he had thought her then; her dark gelled hair, pointed shoes, long black fingernails and jagged black skirt. And, especially, her conversational style. He wondered whether she had changed much.

She may have done; he had at first little opportunity to find out. She didn't remember their meeting, nor, partly because she had moved on – or back – from the British Surrealists to the Spanish Enlightenment and their main artistic interests were therefore separated by one hundred and fifty years or so, did she recognize his name. Although understandably reluctant to talk at any length about the fraud, she told Maurice what he ought to have realised, that the fake Constable was no longer her concern, being held by the police as evidence in case they either traced the publican or found the forger. She expected that it would be possible for him to see it, if, that is, he could persuade the Cabinet Member for Leisure to make arrangements with the Chairman of the Police Authority. Perhaps he could persuade these officials that his line of enquiry, involving as it did an unnamed foreign magnate and a painting by an artist almost certainly unknown to either of them, might help the local investigation. No, he thought, she hasn't changed much. He thanked her, congratulated her on the vertiginous trajectory of her career, and rang off.

The lady on the Eastwich council switchboard put him straight through to the office of the Cabinet Member for Leisure.

"Chairman's office how can I help you?"

"I was rather hoping to be able to speak to the Cabinet Member for Leisure please."

"One and the same dear I expect I'll get used to it he's in a meeting can I help?"

"Could I make an appointment to see him?"

"With reference to or concerning what?"

He explained as simply as he could – which was not very simply, not only because he felt that he should conceal at this stage the involvement of the unnamed oligarch, but also because he was not very good at simplification, being of a periphrastic bent. He managed to extract a provisional appointment for ten days' time, but was warned that it might be cancelled.

He then phoned the number given to him by the Russian. It was a freephone number, and as far as Maurice could tell the person who answered could have been in Timbuktu. He gained the impression that he was doing what was expected. But he also inferred that sorting out a small art fraud was not one of Ivan's highest priorities. Maurice wondered what fees were paid to persons working on these.

He contacted two or three well known collectors. One was rather grand, and he referred Maurice to his adviser, a pundit who floated from the position of respected consultant to that of commissioned salesman, and back again, with insouciant ease. Maurice, who knew this louche character well, learned that he had indeed been offered a rather tempting little Bradley for his patron's collection, but had not followed up the offer because at the time he had been busy chasing a delectable Sargent. Who had made the offer? Perfectly respectable, Deborah at Todd's. Deborah had been cagey, of course, and Maurice was not convinced that she knew much about the painting, which had been returned to its owner; and no, of course she couldn't tell him who that was. Nor would she like dinner at the Ivy, nor – especially nor – to accompany Maurice to Swan Lake at the Garden. He sat around in the ante-rooms of various other magnates, feeling annoyed when he was kept waiting, but only because he was not on this occasion trying to sell a painting. When he was peddling his wares he was quite prepared to wait at the tradesman's entrance.

His last visit was to Battersea, to Ellen Terry Mansions, an enormous red brick block of flats built in the late nineteenth century, one of a number of matching blocks overlooking Battersea Park. Evening was the best time to visit, because the couple living here, as well as being collectors, were old friends whom he knew both worked during the day. The building, solidly constructed and carefully finished, had been designed with a kind of mechanical logic, eschewing, it seemed, any attempt to convey atmosphere or personality. There was nothing about it which would lead an occupier to any warm 'home at last' feelings after a day at work in the city or Westminster. The decorative features, the inset limestone lintels, and the specially shaped bricks around the windows, were all external; inside, the halls and staircases were plain, functional and ill proportioned, the lifts utilitarian and ugly. The flats were very large but to modern eyes dark and ugly – gloomy corridors with seven or eight rooms, all too long, narrow and high, the middle rooms only gaining natural light from narrow wells piercing the centre of the block. But sunlight was the last thing in the mind of the architect, whose plans had been illuminated only by the newly invented electric light bulb.

To Chris and Patricia, however, their flat was perfect. The natural world was only of interest to them in reproduction. The occasional vignettes of the countryside which they glimpsed from train or aeroplane window served only to convince them of its inferiority to the idealised landscape compositions of the seventeenth and eighteenth centuries. At parties, which they enjoyed as much as anyone, they would sometimes follow guests from room to room, nudging each other and whispering the names of the portraits or pictures of which they were reminded. Chris's evening was once ruined, his Sancerre soured and his hollandaise separated, by the Duchess of Portsmouth's thick ankles.

They had set about creating a private gallery, blocking out the daylight, installing suspended ceilings, illumination, air conditioning and security systems such as were used by museums. Their taste was eclectic, but best of all they liked twentieth century British painting, especially the Festival school. The proportion of their flat devoted to ordinary life, to eating, sleeping, bathing and listening to Mozart (they had no television) shrank each year, until now it was not much bigger than a student's bedsit.

As with many amateurs, their appreciation of art was more rounded than that of most critics, partly because they took a genuine delight in it, partly because they had acquired no prejudices during their education, and partly because they were not obliged to take revisionist views of great artists in order to attract the attention of television producers. And they knew far more about it than most practising artists, although they were friendly with a number of these, and would often drop by their studios, sometimes with a cheque book, and always with a bottle or two of malt. Maurice didn't know where their money came from. No doubt they bought and sold at a profit; no doubt their day jobs were well paid; but sometimes they would spend a prodigious amount at a single sale.

They were delighted to see Maurice, handing him a bottle of beer and pointing him to the settee while they finished their supper. Their meal grew cold, or perhaps it was already cold – Maurice had once shared with them a meal of beans and sweet corn straight out of the tins – as they exchanged stories about their recent acquisitions and sales. As Chris cleared the plates and started the washing up – this meant that Patricia had prepared the meal, it was a strict rule with them, and it was usually to the advantage of the cook – Patricia poured whiskies and sank back into the sofa by Maurice. Her hair had been long, golden and curly. Greying now, it was tied back tightly into a fairly unbecoming pony tail. She was tall and remained slim, but her figure was concealed by indeterminate layers of wispy cotton. Nevertheless, Maurice could see that she would still be counted beautiful – which was more than could be said for

Chris, who had thrown his tea towel onto the draining board and pulled up an easy chair to join them.

"Tell me, Chris," said Maurice, "the name of a Russian collector, new to the game I think, who lives – or has a house – about thirty kilometres from St Petersburg, young, piercing stare, green eyes – and not...", here he listed some names of Russian millionaires well known in the sale rooms.

"Yes, I heard you'd been to see Kuznetsov. Taxis, fruit, cheap menswear and ice cream. Self-made, above board – well, what counts for above board in Russia. He hasn't bought much yet, but he's got a few scouts out. Same Scandewegian bloke runs around for him that other Russian, whatsisname, uses. Picked up a nice Poussin a month ago – you remember, Fischer bought it at Bonhams in the New York OMs? Well, that was for Kuznetsov."

"Good God, Chris, how on earth did you know all that? I tell you, I didn't even know who he was. I just ring up a mobile phone number, could be anywhere, and it's not him answering."

"Garry, in this case."

"Of course." Maurice tut-tutted and leaned back in the sofa. "Your usual technique, presumably?"

"Not too difficult with Garry. Couple of glasses and he's away."

"Did he know what this – Kuznetsov? – wanted from me?"

"Not a bit. In fact, he asked me if I knew. So, what *did* he want?"

Maurice was prepared for this question, because he had expected the conversation to come round to his meeting with the Russian, although not so soon, nor so abruptly.

"He's interested in the Festival school now, and I think, I mean, I hope, he might ask me to look out for one or two. He'd apparently heard, I don't know who from, that there were some iffy Hopkinses about, very good technique it seems, and he wanted to pick my brains about them. Well, it was news to me, and I told him so."

"Festival stuff's a bit low key for him, isn't it? Idiosyncratic for a Ruski? And so English. But if it were Turner, or Constable – actually, there is a fairly competent Constable copier at large, isn't there? The Eastwich chap?"

"Have you seen that?"

"No, just heard about it from Rosie. She thought it was right, you know, without putting it in the body scanner and all that"

"So I gather. But did you see what that Hopkins fetched?"

"Nine hundred and fifty? But remember, the last Poussin went for four million. And that was the most ever paid for a Hopkins – and the Bradleys and Foresters go for much less. But I suppose on the whole it's safer to forge something less than six figures. A good provenance, that's the thing, people are so anxious to prove themselves right that they avoid the tests which might show they're not. It's like going to the doctor's with a pain in your side. Avoid the young whizz kid who might send you for a neutron scan or whatever, and see the nice comforting old bloke who says it's bound to be indigestion. So spin them a good yarn. You remember the Discobolus miniatures?"

Maurice did, vaguely, but had begun to feel very warm and comfortable. Catching Patricia's eye he gave her the merest semblance of a wink and she smiled, pointed to the whisky bottle, he nodded and she filled his glass. "Tell me about them," he said.

"Roger Mallbury. World famous sculptor. Died in seventy three. Durham and Monmouth Yarns commissioned a vast bronze from him to stick in front of their factory, back in, oh, the sixties? And he based it on the Myron Discobolus – he liked bronze discs. Don't like it myself, the Mallbury, that is. But there it stands, what would you say, fifteen feet high? God knows what it's got to do with fibres, cardigans and suchlike. Well, in nineteen eighty five, Christmas time or thereabouts, I was walking around near the BM looking in the windows for something nice for Pat – there were some very pretty little

Roman bottles around then, you know, before we had much cash..."

Pat leaned further over to Maurice and whispered loudly, "Some scent would have been nice."

Maurice sensed that Pat had taken her cue, that this was a story Chris had told before. Chris continued,

"....and there in one of the windows was a stamping great photograph of the Mallbury Discobolus. But it wasn't. It was a photo of a different sculpture, much simpler and tiny. About thirty five centimetres high, no more. But clearly based on the Mallbury. I went in and spoke to the girl behind the desk – it's not there anymore, it was only a small saleroom – and she found the catalogue entry for me. Apparently the Chairman of Durham and Monmouth had thought it would be a good wheeze to get the old boy to run up an edition of miniatures for him, so that he could distribute them to the great and good, or his mistresses or mates, whoever. And he'd given this one to his fishing buddy, who had handed it over to his daughter. There was a letter, much folded and scuffed, on Durham and Monmouth Yarns writing paper, from the Chairman to his friend and a note from the friend to the daughter. And a receipt, signed by the daughter, for the six thousand pounds she had been paid by the chap who was now selling it. How interesting, I said. It was an edition of seven, and this was number three. I liked it; much nicer than the big one. In fact, I bid for it at the sale. Nicer than a Roman bottle for Pat."

"This was before you had much cash?"

"Yes. What do you mean, much cash? Anyway, I didn't get it. It went for sixteen grand, and that was nineteen eighty five, remember. Then another one came up, and this had come down by descent from the Chairman's secretary. Same story, slightly different paperwork, this time a gift card inscribed to the secretary from her boss. Scruffy again. I missed that sale, but it went for twenty three. The third was sent to Paston's, and their sculpture man sniffed it, and didn't like it. I should say he *liked* it, but thought it might not be right. He thought the casting was a bit, well, amateurish, he said. So he nosed around, but this time the model was number one in the edition, and there was actually a note from Mallbury with words to the effect of I hope you like it, is it what you had in mind? RM's writing, no doubt. And a barrage of other notes and scraps. That one sold for forty. Well, to cut a long story short..."

"No need for that, Chris." Maurice was now lying with his head in Patricia's lap, and she was twisting his hair into little spirals.

"... five came onto the market and were sold, the last one in ninety-eight. They all had a nice interesting provenance, sexed up with letters and receipts. But then Paston's got a letter, from the Chairman's son, who lived in New Zealand. He had just seen a report of the last sale, and could be completely sure that his father – who had died, of course, in nineteen eighty five – had never ordered these models. His father had never liked the finished sculpture, had been criticised by the Board for embarking on such a pointless project, had almost felt obliged to pay for the damn thing himself, and wouldn't have dreamed of commissioning any miniatures. So Paston's called in the boffins, and one of the chaps had the bright idea of investigating the dirt on the different, distressed, documents – the letter, the gift card etcetera. It was all the same. All the documents, apart from the note from Roger, had been created in the same place, in much the same way. All the vendors had vanished – they were probably all the same man. So then they traced some of the little bronzes which had been sold privately – not through an auction house. And they weren't. Bronzes, that is. They were a mixture of metal dusts – copper and tin, of course, God knows what else, and resin, you know, like Araldite. With a lump of iron in the middle to make them heavy. So if just one of them had been tested, the whole scheme would have collapsed. But none of them was, because the provenances were so convincing. And that wasn't the end of it. When the story hit the papers, five more angry people appeared; they'd all bought privately, and three of these had bought 'number one'! They all had the note from Roger Mallbury – just tracings! The crux was the original note from Mallbury. Someone found that – it could have been written to any of his clients, I suppose – and designed the entire fraud round it. Brilliant. Despicable, of course but brilliant. They've never caught him."

"Yes I've heard that tale. Surely you don't think my Russian would be caught as simply as that?" Well, he might have been: Maurice hadn't been told anything about how Kuznetsov had acquired the Beetle painting. "It's not about skill, is it; there must be dozens of competent craftsmen who could turn out a superficially credible, – let's say, how about, Alfred Wallis? – it's about belief, not just the buyer's belief about the painting, but his belief about what others will believe and so on. That's how *money* works, after all."

"Depressing, isn't it?"

"Certainly is. Marketing's the key now. I sometimes think that these dealers get together and decide who's going to be the next must-have. Then they promote him, or her, and make a f, f, sorry Tricia, fat fortune from him. And for him, of course. Or her. In fact, I sometimes think they're playing a secret game, finding out the degree of crappiness they can get the public to accept as art. I tell you, it worries me, it worries me silly, people ask me, can I get hold of a something or other, some real dross, fashionable dross, and one day I'm going to give in."

Maurice was becoming quite heated. He squirmed and got his arm tangled in a drift of Patricia's tulle. She removed it gently and re-arranged her frock.

"I know what they'll do next. They'll turn everything upside down. Not kitsch, Koons is doing kitsch. No, they'll go for chocolate box, that's it, of course, you wait, the next thing'll be chocolate box, rubbish watercolours by the Much Scratching ladies' painting circle. They'll make a fortune for some besotted spinster – "

He let out a yelp of pain. Patricia had pinched his ear. She was very fond of Maurice, because he was kind, quite good looking and of course sexually unthreatening. But there was a streak of the misogynist old queen about him, not much, but enough to be annoying at times – or was it just that all men over fifty were fundamentally unreconstructed, however hard they tried; or, actually, all men? The obverse of his lack of sexual threat was of course his lack of sexual interest, and did that irritate her? Maybe.

She pushed him upright. Chris stood up and went over to the stove to make some coffee.

Patricia said, "Chris, you haven't told Maurice about the new Hopkins people."

"You tell him, dear, I've got a sore throat"

"O K. They're not really new; apparently a family somewhere down in the South West have got at least five excellent early Hopkinses hanging up in their sitting room. There's a family connection – don't know what. Alf told us – one of his agricultural colleagues found out about them in the pub when he went down to do a story about gassing badgers. You know Alf? Coffee table journo? So Alf flew down to Newquay, found the house – more like a farm – and got to see the pictures. He was made welcome, so he says, and was very taken by the whole set-up. Impressive paintings."

Chris snorted, "Alf works for shiny magazines. He'd be impressed by a photo of St Michael's Mount in a Woolworths frame. And I gather that he was rather more taken by the very nice lady who showed him round. Be that as it may..."

"Throat better dear?"

"What? At any rate, I'd never heard of this collection. Have you?"

"No, I haven't. But it sounds interesting doesn't it?" Maurice replied.

"Come and see our new Thompson before you go," Patricia took Maurice by the arm and led him into one of the gallery rooms. Chris collected up the coffee cups and glasses.

As he was leaving, Maurice turned to Patricia. "You haven't told me where these Hopkinses are? In Cornwall, obviously?"

"Yes, at a place called Boselloe, near St Just; have your map handy, Alf said."

When they had shut the door and set its alarm, Chris turned to Patricia.

"He's a nice chap, but he does go on bit, doesn't he?"

"Look who's talking. In any case, I expect he's lonely. He's a very good friend."

"Yes, of course he is. Do you fancy something obnoxious?"

"Yes please. Lemon verbena."

"And that would be ..."

"On the shelf by the kettle, in the glass jar, labelled..."

"Lemon verbena!"

"Exactly. You have some coffee. And then, do you fancy the Titian Danaë?"

"It's not an easy part for me."

"You'll manage, I'm sure."

Chapter 6

July 30   Maurice   Anthony   Henry   An Aide   Senior Policemen

Maurice sat in a warm alcove of the dining room, drinking his third cup of coffee to 'My Way' on loop with vacuum cleaner continuo. It was a bright morning, and he had chosen to breakfast, at a time when he was usually thinking about breaking off for his elevenses, in a recess where there seemed no danger of direct sunlight. His headache had kicked in at about four in the morning, gathering strength behind his left eye, drilling a hole in the special little chamber of tears reserved for such occasions, and releasing them in a flood over his left cheek. He had some pills with him which were prescribed, at a cost to the Health Service of nearly five pounds each, to cure migraines, but he felt guilty at taking them to treat a self-inflicted wound. In this case, however, not too guilty. The subsequent slow retreat of his headache left the high ground of his hangover occupied by the various debilitating substances which his liver and kidneys had either failed to remove, or had themselves produced in their fight against the poisons which he had absorbed. As he was wondering whether he should try and eat a little toast and marmalade, Anthony came in from the street, carrying a couple of newspapers which he threw on the table in front of Maurice.

"The Westerner comes out this morning – there's nothing about the police being called to an address in Broadharbour to investigate reports et cetera et cetera. Can I have some coffee please – I'd better ask for some more; you feeling all right?"

"Thank you, yes. I can actually hear you quite well; indeed, you could lower your voice if you like. You seem very breezy this morning?"

"Yes, God knows why. I felt very strange when I woke up; but I've been for a walk, cleared my head a bit. I've decided what to do. It seems obvious, really..."

"Really?"

"Yes, really."

Anthony pursed his lips and nodded two or three times, looking closely at Maurice and frowning and blinking a little, as if trying hard to focus.

"And you were right – well, to a certain extent. I shall definitely go to the police, but not until I can give them enough information to persuade them I'm not..."

"A deranged gunman?"

"Well yes, I suppose so. How much of the stuff you told me last night can I tell them?"

"Yes, I was wondering about that too. Just keep Kuznetsov's name out of it for the time being. But I imagine it's pretty common knowledge by now. Too good a story for Garry to keep under his hat."

"So, I'll give myself three days. Only three days. I shall start by finding this little collection in Cornwall. I'm surprised I didn't know about it. In fact, if it were all legitimate I'm sure I would have known about it. Where did you say it was?"

"In a village, or farm or something, called Boselloe, near St Just."

"That's quite a pretty area, isn't it? Messing around in boats sort of place?"

"Search me. It's foreign, over the Tamar. Look, Anthony, are you sure you're all right? Why three days? Why don't you just go and meet Helen and Walter, wherever they are? They must be going spare by now."

"Yes, of course I will. I'm going to see them first. They're expecting me. But then surely to God they can put up with another day or two in Brighton?"

He stirred milk vigorously into his coffee, and plunged a croissant into the cup. It broke off and the pastry sank to the bottom of the cup, leaving a sickly mixture of butter and jam floating on the surface. He fished the croissant out with a teaspoon and ate it, then, with a look of surprise, pushed the cup away.

"Maurice, it didn't happen to you, I know you can't really believe that what I told you happened, or at least not in the way I said. But it did, and now I've got to find some way of coping with it. It's not that I'm after an actual solution; I've still no idea what that might be. I just said, didn't I, that when I had some more information, and it must be something to do with fraud, mustn't it, I'd go to the police..."

His voice tailed off, and, suddenly immobile, he stared in the direction of the cleaner, who was polishing a sideboard.

"But when I woke up this morning I had a sort of feeling that I should do something physical; perhaps go for a brisk walk, sorry, I hate that phrase, just go out for a walk. Anywhere outside. So I got dressed quickly..."

"I can see that. You look like a tramp."

"Well, maybe I do. At any rate, I found myself walking much faster than usual. I broke a stick from the hedge, and started to swipe at all the nettles growing along the lane. I was actually running from patch to patch, leaving a mess of nettles scattered over the road. It seemed to be important not to leave a single stalk standing. My heart was banging away, just like yesterday, and I was, not really gasping for breath because I was running about a lot, but it was as if my lungs would only open up a little bit so that I had to breathe much faster. I think it was the breathing which made me realise that it was a pretty standard panic attack. Not having a paper bag handy..."

"What? *What?*"

"You breathe into a paper bag to stop a panic attack, didn't you know?"

"No I didn't. Leave that for the moment. Go on."

"...I made myself sit down, by the roadside, in the ditch, and told myself it would go away. Well it took its time, but it did go away. I sat there and when I was calm enough I decided that the only way to get through the next few days was to plan them very carefully, in as much detail as possible, and to stick to the plan. It wasn't as if the panic had come on because I'd been particularly thinking about – dwelling on – how awful the situation is; it was just that there was a gap when I suppose I wasn't thinking about, or doing, anything purposeful, and all the worries I'd suppressed filled it up straight away and set off the attack."

"So have you made a plan? You told me you thought it was intractable."

"That's not the point. My plan, the plan I'm telling you about now, isn't how to resolve the real, actual problem, the shooting kidnapping thing, the picture thieves, the vanishing corpse, it's how to stop going mad with worry. I must keep reassuring myself that what I'm doing will get me nearer to a solution, although obviously part of my brain will be sending me subversive messages all the time. The trick will be to suppress these messages. So I'm telling myself that if I keep to this three day plan of mine, I shall be able to go to the police and fetch Walter and my sister, go home and we'll all be able to carry on with our life, just like before. I'm just *telling* myself. Do you see?"

Anthony had spoken more and more quickly, and had become quite breathless before he had finished. Maurice knew little of psychology, but he could see that his friend was quite ill, and he was afraid that he might become worse. Perhaps what Anthony had said made some sort of sense, but the manner in which he had said it compelled Maurice to believe that Anthony would be unable to ignore the rational doubts, the 'subversive messages', to which he would be prey. And what was that nonsense about a paper bag?

A quarter of an hour or so later Maurice had paid his bill and was waiting in the bar, ill at ease in the previous day's underwear, and unshaven. His headache had lifted, and he regretted his earlier bad tempered criticism of Anthony's dishevelled appearance. A trim figure at the bar, who was talking to the manager and whom Maurice had vaguely thought was rather casually dressed for a salesman, turned to yield a view of his face. Maurice, without hesitation, lifted his Custodian to conceal his own; he knew this man, surely? Or had seen him, maybe in the papers or on TV. Damn, who was he? It would come to him in a second, he was sure. But the vacuum cleaner had started up again, and its noise distracted him, and prevented him from overhearing any conversation; and why, he wondered, had the middle aged female cleaner, who had previously shown his delicate state such little consideration, been replaced by a much younger man wearing a bulky black vest under his denim jacket?

The hotel door opened, and a momentary shaft of sunlight illuminated the myriad particles of dust thrown up by the brushes of the clumsily wielded vacuum cleaner. Two women entered and immediately separated, one walking to the foot of the stairs and the other approaching Maurice.

"I'm ever so sorry, I think I might have bumped your car just outside. Could you possibly come and have a look?"

Unusual, Maurice thought, how honest. The woman glanced at the man with the familiar appearance, and out of the corner of his eye Maurice thought he saw him give her a slight nod. The man turned back and spoke to the manager, who immediately retired into his little office and shut the door.

Maurice stood up. The woman followed him outside, Maurice walking slowly in order to gather his thoughts. His car was at the far end of the car park, not at all just outside, where there was, instead, a silver BMW with, as far as Maurice could see, no trace of collision marks.

He turned to the woman, who was standing closer to him than he thought polite; close enough for him to see that she too was wearing a thick black gilet.

"That's my car over there, is that the one you bumped? I'll go and check, if you like."

He hesitated for a second, then started to walk towards his car.

Anthony, in his room, had just bent to close his suitcase and straightening up he glanced out of the window, which overlooked the car park. A woman was following Maurice out of the hotel and after a moment's pause, in which they appeared to be speaking to each other, he saw her take him by the arm, not like an old friend. Maurice appeared to stumble, and would have fallen had a man not stepped out from the shadows of the porch and seized him. Maurice was forced into the back seat of a silver BMW, the man followed, and the woman drove them away.

Anthony would normally have liked to take a moment or two to consider carefully how to respond to an unusual event such as the abduction of a close friend. But even he realised, and realised immediately, that in this new, strange world only two courses of action were available. He could return to bed, pull the blankets over his head, and go back to sleep, accepting the risk that he might wake up transformed into an insect. Or he could get into his car as quickly as possible and follow the BMW.

He was more than a little pleased with himself as he accelerated away in the direction taken by the BMW. Correcting the car's immediate inclination to slide into the ditch by a series of random but luckily successful jerks of the steering wheel, he settled down in pursuit, driving much faster than usual and certainly unsafely.

Only a moment or two previously, clutching his suitcase, he had taken the stairs two at a time to the bar, and without losing momentum had rushed directly to the door. At the foot of the stairs his suitcase had swung backwards and forwards, banging his leg where it had been cut on the cooker and causing severe pain which he was surprised to find that he could easily ignore. The suitcase then cannoned into a girl wearing jeans and a silly black combat jacket top, knocking her flying. He shouted an apology. On his left, a cleaner had dropped his vacuum and was fumbling with the lead which seemed to be wound round his leg. Immediately in front of him another young lady stepped forward but Anthony was unable to stop the suitcase, now a great mobile pendulum, from swinging round and hitting her squarely in the stomach.

"Sorry, sorry, I'm in a terrible hurry!" he shouted as he pushed through the door. Seconds later he was away.

Driving fast was exciting, and for a short while the exhilaration masked his incompetence. He soon realised, however, that the silver BMW might as well have been driven by Ayrton Senna for all the chance he had of catching it, and he slowed down to a pace only slightly faster than normal. Two T-junctions and several roundabouts later the odds against his being on the right road were hopelessly small. A road sign indicated the way to the M5 motorway, so he turned in that direction, intending to take the M5 north to Bristol, and then the M4 east, to London and Brighton. The green Volvo estate which was following him, unobserved because he had not once looked in his mirror, turned also.

*****

A jurisdictional argument was under way in the pilots' lounge at Bristol airport. The pilots were not involved because they had been bundled out by the airport manager. The airport manager was not involved because, among other reasons, he had had to make arrangements for the unexpected arrival of two helicopters and a light aeroplane with military markings.

"I cannot allow an armed man to drive willy-nilly across my county. For God's sake, man, if he were to use his sodding gun and someone got killed, or injured even, there'd be the devil to pay. I'd lose my job for a start, probably my pension, and I could even go to gaol, and so could Gilbert here. Never mind the poor bugger he might have shot."

The speaker took a cigarette from a pack in his pocket, but threw it angrily to the floor when he saw the expression on the third man's face.

This man said, "I can assure you that the superintendent, yourself and indeed your entire force will be treated as *Nec officio nec auctoritate* which will, of course, absolve you from any responsibility. Technically you are quite correct; until the order is laid I can't claim any direct authority." The first speaker looked towards Gilbert with an expression halfway between amazement and fury; Gilbert tried to look knowingly impassive but didn't succeed. "However, I'm expecting the order to come through any moment. So it would really be helpful if we could anticipate the formality and you would allow the man – um – "

"Evans, Director" said the only other person present, a young woman with a military bearing.

"Thank you Major, – Evans, to drive without interruption to his destination. Which may be outwith your county, of course. I do admit that this has all been arranged hastily, but Evans's behaviour has taken us by surprise."

He looked at the major, who looked at the ceiling. The first speaker frowned. The Director continued, "Yes, yes I know we are supposed to be ready for surprises, but more, how shall I say, *predictable* surprises. And, I repeat, I take full responsibility..."

"We all know what that means. Bugger all." said the first speaker. "You know there'd be an inquiry. I couldn't hide behind some bit of civil service bumf, or pseudonyms like your blokes. Sorry, *chaps,* I should say. Will any of your ministers take responsibility? Like hell they will. And your departments leak like a, like a..."

"Colander, sir?" said the superintendent.

"Is that the best you can do?"

"Tinker's pisspot?"

"Yes. And all the House committee's members' secretaries' poxy window cleaners would soon know every frigging detail, in any case it would be all over the front page of the Shield."

"Actually, our department does not leak. Well, not inadvertently. Our Spectrum teams are as tight as a nun's..."

"Don't be patronising. It's us coppers who talk crude, right?"

The major looked down at a small phone-like instrument, which was displaying a map with a red dot moving over it.

"He'll be on the motorway in a minute or two. It's quite an operation, stopping an armed man on a motorway, isn't it? Why not just leave him to us? He's not going to fire his thirty eight out of the window, is he?"

The Chief Constable looked at her in surprise.

"How do you know where he is?" He turned to Bill, "have you got a track-screen on you? That'll show us the pursuit car, won't it?"

"Not here, sir. I could get a fix sent from HQ"

"Hmm. Well," he turned again to the first speaker, "how do you know then? He hasn't got his phone switched on, we know that."

"No, we've got a beacon on his car, I imagine, haven't we, Major?"

"How on earth ...?"

"Well, it's our job, Chief Constable, isn't it?"

The major spoke, "The order's come through sir. Well well. DOR 34 stroke 5."

The Chief Constable, his surprise changing to amazement, threw up his hands and said to the superintendent, "That's it then. Pack up and go home. It's their pigeon now."

He spoke to the major, "We really need a hard copy. Is that possible?"

She pressed a button on her little machine, it whirred and ejected a slip of paper like a receipt in a restaurant, which she tore off and handed to the Chief Constable, who passed it to her superior.

"Could you sign it, or initial it, please?"

"Certainly. I'm sure I need not remind you that..."

"I know, I know," said the Chief Constable, "total secrecy is enjoined by article 34 section et cetera et cetera. Forget we've seen you, blah blah."

"Quite."

The senior man and the major shook hands with the policemen and left.

"I don't know who the fuck he was," said the Chief Constable.

The superintendent squinted at the little slip of paper.

"Madder, I think it says. Good name for a ..."

"Get in your chopper and go and catch a bank robber, for God's sake."

"Yes sir."

*****

The police constable driving the green Volvo which was following Anthony had been left without instructions for over ten minutes. He had initially been told to keep at a safe distance and wait for an armed response unit to join him. He, too, was wondering with what speed, or indeed competence, his fairly rural police force would organise an efficient road block on the busy dual carriageway, towards which his quarry was heading and which was now only a mile or so away.

He had not been told what to do if the car which he was pursuing were to brake violently in order to avoid a tractor, skid across to the opposite verge, strike a tree and bounce back onto the near side of the road, while the tractor came to halt in the middle, the driver leaning out of his cab and looking aghast at the chaos behind him.

There was, in fact, nothing the policeman could do. The car which Anthony was driving, its offside bodywork ripped open from bumper to bumper, drew to a halt some hundred yards down the road, then started up again and drove away; but the road was entirely blocked by the tractor and its trailer, hanging lopsided over the ditch. Potatoes were everywhere. The policeman turned on his blue flashing lights, previously concealed behind windscreen and radiator, and made an impatient gesture to the tractor driver who shrugged his shoulders and pointed at the listing trailer.

*****

As the major and the man whom she had called Director were walking across the tarmac to their aeroplane, she glanced at the screen on her miniature computer. The red triangle which denoted the position of Anthony's car had ceased pulsing.

"He's stopped, Henry."

"Well let's hope they've told that damn copper to go home."

"DOR 34/5 is a bit over the top, isn't it? Didn't the boss quibble?"
"I suppose he might have done, yes."
"Bloody hell, Henry."

*****

The Chief Constable's instruction was at that moment being transmitted. The policeman turned his Volvo round and headed for his station. The radio beacon which had been attached to Anthony's car by the clamper in Exeter lay in the ditch where it had fallen, bleeping in the mud under half a ton of Maris Peer.

Anthony had not seen the blue lights, but he had at last noticed the Volvo. He attached no significance to it.

His own car still responded to steering wheel and accelerator, but he found after a while that application of the brakes led the car to swerve unpredictably and violently. Moreover, a rhythmic drumming from some part of the transmission, gaining perceptibly in volume and vibration, led him to believe that some crucial bearing or joint or shaft would soon fail, probably suddenly. He slowed down and drove carefully through a village, deserted save for smokers in doorways who stared as he passed. He would leave his car at a garage and hire another. His map showed a service station on the road which led to a market town, some seven or eight miles to the east.

The mechanic at the garage was surprised by Anthony's insistence that he would deal with the insurance company himself, and suggested also that the damage to the car was so great that it might be classed as a write-off. Yes, they could hire him a car, but they would have to take a large deposit – this was partly so that Anthony would be obliged to identify himself over the phone to the credit card company. When Anthony handed the phone back to the mechanic, instead of merely confirming the transaction, the credit card voice was speaking at some length. The mechanic started to explain the circumstances of Anthony's arrival, glancing at him as he did so. Anthony's nerves were already in a dreadful state, and he panicked. He assumed that they – who? – were trying to trace him; he grabbed the card, ran back to his car and drove away towards the town, quickly and noisily.

After half a mile he slowed down and began to drive more cautiously, noticing now the acrid fumes of car parts heating beyond their design. But he soon became habituated to the smell, and did not sense its gradual, dangerous, increase in intensity. Close to his destination he took a wrong turn, mistaking the private drive of a mansion for a public road. Necessarily reversing, he was surprised to find that he was backing through smoke, possibly from a park-keeper's bonfire, which he had not noticed on his approach. The smoke became denser, and, luckily, he realised its actual cause before the entire car ignited, fifteen seconds or so after he scrambled from the car, pulling his case with him. The catalogue of the Dowland's sale had fallen from the driver's door pocket, and without thinking he had picked it up and, as he ran for the shelter of the trees, the car commenced its immolation.

Exhausted, he reached the village an hour later, by then stopping to sit on his suitcase every few minutes. The Goat and Compasses had gone the way of many country pubs, closed, boarded up and displaying a tattered planning application pinned to its door. But there was a small shop which seemed to be open.

He had drunk the can of lemonade before the shopkeeper had counted out his change.

"You look as if you needed that, my dear, parched were you? Been walking then?"

She eyed his jacket and trousers, and his tie, which he was still wearing although it was now pulled to one side, his top shirt buttons open. His case was standing in the middle of the shop. He was wearing light Italian loafers.

"No, I dare say you've broken down in your motor, have you? There's no garage, dear, you'd best get the AA out, I think. Aren't you? My Dora said she wasn't going to join either. Ran out of petrol on the M5 then didn't she? No end of trouble until the coppers came, and then, well, you don't want to know about it my dear."

"Actually, I was meeting, I mean I came with a friend, we thought we could lunch at the pub, but it seems to be, er..."

"Closed, that it is dear. Been closed near a year now. I've got a couple of sausage rolls here somewhere, I think, if that's any good to you, and there's a loaf which Mrs B didn't pick up yesterday. Have some Shippams on it, I'll lend you a knife and here's some greaseproof for a plate. Your friend gone has he?"

"Yes, that's it, I don't really want any food thank you, just another can of lemonade please. Can I get a bus to Frimmingham from here?"

"You're joking, dear. Not on a Sunday! You should have come with your friend on a Monday or a Friday, not that the pub would have been open of course, but if it had you wouldn't have needed a bus, would you? Why didn't your friend take you back with him then?"

He had no answer. Luckily the forensic shopkeeper had turned away, her attention caught by something she had seen through the window.

"Just look at that then! That's that pop singer over Longley way. He's got no idea, has he? What a place to have a bonfire!"

She pointed at a plume of dense smoke rising from a wood some three miles away in the direction from which he had come.

"Neston Wood, over there. It's famous, don't you know, that Bottomley off the telly did a programme there, ancient he said, beeches oaks and all. Barry Wotsisname won't half catch it from the Council." She paused for a second. "No, he'll be all right. Them blokes don't work weekends."

How could he get to Frimmingham? What would he do there? Get a train to Brighton? Was he still aiming to find this collection of paintings in a farmhouse? He wasn't just going to write off his car, was he? And this blasted ancient woodland, he supposed he should report the fire – surely someone else would have done so already? Possibly not;

Barry Wotsisname was probably in Beverley Hills, or Dubai. The call about the fire would have to be anonymous, so should be made from a public box. In any case, his mobile's battery was flat, and its charger consumed by the flames.

He stared at the shelves behind the counter. On the top shelf there were tins of beans, tins of tomatoes, and three large packets of caster sugar. On the longer shelf below there were packets of peanuts, jars of marmalade and six bottles of brown sauce. No, eight bottles of brown sauce. He shut his eyes and turned away. He found it impossible to put his problems in any sensible order. The loss of his car, the abduction of his friend, the potential danger to his child and sister, arson in an ancient woodland, the attempted theft of his paintings, the killing of the gunman, even the bribery of the clamper, were all jumbled together, surfacing at random from the maelstrom of his brain. He was suffering from what psychologists call experiential overload; he could no longer assess the meaning of individual events, let alone see any picture in the jigsaw which they might form.

"But you could get the shoppers' bus from Paxley, I suppose, it'll drop you at Tesco and it's a fair walk to the station but it's better than nothing isn't it?"

"How far's Paxley, then?"

"Only a mile dear, down the Milburton road. Bus leaves at half two from the duck pond. You can't miss it." She smiled. "The pond, I mean, not the bus. You'll miss that if you don't get a move on. There's only one bus Sundays. It's past two now."

He just caught the bus. His arms and shoulders ached from the weight of the suitcase, and his feet were sore in their thin soled shoes. His suitcase obstructed part of the space proper to his neighbour's feet, and he was obliged to hold it, vertically and awkwardly, on his knees.

"Why not put it in the luggage space?" she asked.

"Well, you see, I need to keep it by me because it contains a loaded gun," was the true answer, but he muttered "Oh it'll be OK, thanks." instead.

Tesco, on a green field site outside the town, was indeed a fair walk from the station. The man collecting trolleys in the car park pointed out the quickest route, which took him through suburban streets of semi-detached houses, with leafy front gardens and parked cars on drives. After only about ten minutes he was exhausted. There were low garden walls to sit on, but to do so seemed impolite. Just about managing a grin at the absurdity of this scruple, he upended his case and sat down on it. He wondered what he was going to do at the station. How could he buy a ticket if he was scared to use his credit card? It wasn't really sensible, was it, to imagine that he would be traced? He had panicked in the garage – hadn't behaved rationally, surely? He decided to draw cash from a machine up to his limit, and pay for things with that in the next three days.

In a couple of hundred yards there was a parade of shops, including a post office with a cash machine outside. A young couple were standing in front of the machine, apparently discussing which card to use and how much they could afford to withdraw. Anthony stood behind them. After a little while he cleared his throat and sat down once again on his suitcase, trying unsuccessfully to make his movement convey his impatience. Across the road a man was cleaning out a Dormobile. He was also showing off its features to his neighbour, who appeared politely impressed. When, at last, it was Anthony's turn to use the machine it responded to his request for cash with a message to the effect that he couldn't have any money, his card was being retained, and he should go into his own bank and speak to the manager. Desolate, he turned away.

Over the road the Dormobile owner had started up the motor, and, shouting over the noise of the engine, he told his friend that he would leave it running for five minutes in order to do something inaudible with the something filter, and should they go into his house for a quick coffee? They both went through the garden gate at the side of the house.

Anthony looked right and left, and saw nobody. He crossed the road, heaved his case into the van and climbed into the driver's seat. The controls were just the same as a car's. He drove away, back towards Tesco and then the main road.

It wasn't stealing. There was no intent permanently to deprive. To permanently deprive. To deprive permanently. But it had to be some offence or other; driving without permission? Taking and driving away? He would leave it undamaged. He would send the owner money. He would – damn it, he would do something, but not until he'd seen Walter and Helen, and then found these paintings in Cornwall. And it now occurred to him that he should report his own car as stolen.

He passed a police car in a lay-by; the copper was setting up an elaborate bit of kit on a tripod. He remembered that number plates could be read automatically and as soon as this van was reported stolen he was liable to be caught, especially on a main road or motorway. Could he just buy some new number plates? But what number to choose – it would have to be a real number, clearly, but did it have to be one used by a similar vehicle? How did these vehicle recognition systems work? He decided that his schemes were becoming too farfetched. He would just have to drive on and hope that he wasn't stopped.

Driving the van was enjoyable. The seat gave good support to his back, and he found the elevated position suited him. He ran his eye over the dashboard. All seemed well, but there wasn't much fuel. He had drawn into a filling station and unhooked the pump before he remembered that he had only the five or six pounds left in his pocket, but as he climbed back into the van he noticed, for the first time, the leather bag in the passenger's leg well. He initially thought that it was a handbag. In fact, it was a man-bag, with masculine trimmings of canvas on the leather, and a wide, sturdy strap. It contained, among various papers and notebooks, pens and pencils, a wallet with several cards and about two hundred pounds. Well, might as well be hung for a sheep, he thought.

There was a car show room and workshop attached to the filling station. The show room was closed, but in the workshop there was a mechanic who was fitting a new headlamp glass to a Ford Sierra. After Anthony had filled the tank, bought some sandwiches, and paid to the attendant's surprise with cash, he walked on the spur of the moment into the workshop and asked the mechanic if he could quickly make two number plates. The only numbers he could think of were his own and his sister's. So he swapped the figures round and hoped that the fictitious number sounded realistic. But when he was asked for his registration document he realised that it wasn't possible legally to buy number plates without proving ownership, identity, goodness knows what else. In any case, a non-existent number would trigger just as much interest as that of a vehicle reported stolen. Instead, he bought a roll each of black and white electrical tape, feeling obliged to explain at some length that the lights on his trailer (the putative destination for the now abandoned number plates) were shorting out. He need not have bothered. The attendant was thinking about his girlfriend, and wondering how quickly the double time he was earning would buy him a new Yamaha.

Anthony drove past a number of lay-bys until he found one which was separated from the road by a screen of trees. He wanted to be private. Much better to break the law in private. In fact, of course, no privacy was necessary; Anthony was suffering from the acute self-consciousness which affects newcomers to the underworld. Experienced criminals know that the majority of people are self-absorbed, and most of the rest unobservant, unlikely to notice any crime short of armed robbery, and certainly wouldn't interfere if they did. A man fiddling with his number plates – in fact, changing a five to a six front and back – would attract no attention. Anthony hoped that the next registration number after that on the van would have been put on a similar vehicle. At any rate, it seemed worth a shot.

He drove on through the twilight, following the motorways east towards Brighton. Near Fareham it suddenly occurred to him that breakfast, about twelve hours ago, had been his last meal, and as soon as possible he pulled into a service area. He placed the case with its lethal, illegal contents under the café table, trapping it awkwardly between his feet. Exhaustion overcame him; the meal, and the surprising availability of bottled beer, restored his spirits somewhat, but it was clear that he was in no shape to drive on. There was a cheap travellers' hotel on the site, and he took a room for the night, where he dropped his case on the bed, sat down beside it to take off his shoes, and woke up at two in the morning, joints set painfully in unusual positions, and a shoe remaining on his left foot. In his sleep he had embraced the suitcase.

There were numerous packets of dehydrated drinks, a kettle and a twin pack of custard creams. He made some tea and prepared himself properly for bed. The room was too hot with the window closed, and too noisy with it open, but he found the heating control, turned it off, and opened the window with the intention of closing it when the room had reached a tolerable temperature. Some magazines propped up by the diminutive television caught his eye, but their subject matter, video cameras, motorcycles and erotic clothing, didn't interest him. Presumably they had been left by the previous occupant, rather than placed there by the management. Nor did he bother to read the detailed instructions about how to cope with various emergencies, which did not include the surrounding of the building by armed police.

The auction catalogue, he remembered, was in the outside document compartment of the case, where he had slipped it after it had fallen from the burning car. How long ago was that? A month?

He retrieved it, and leafed through the pages while drinking his tea. The illustrations of the two Bradleys – his Bradleys now – faced each other, and he wondered why the Swedish man's employer so definitely preferred the second. It was much cruder than the first; the expressions of the subjects were so blank, so lifeless in comparison. The colours were more vivid, that had to be the reason. But now, he wondered why he had bought it himself; because it was cheap, he supposed. He would definitely sell it; perhaps he could do a little haggling, get an even higher price?

But then, he thought, perhaps he no longer owned it; at least, no longer possessed it. In any case, he was an outlaw now. Drowsy at last, he closed the window. The auction catalogue had fallen open at the centre pages, which were entirely devoted to the Hopkins painting of the Morris Minor; the well-known small family car driven by elderly ladies and vicars in the countryside and nineteen fifties B feature movies. But, was it? He had only glanced at it previously; now he looked closely. The car was parked on the edge of a meadow, a copse and stream nearby. The boot was open, and a man was lifting out a picnic basket. A rug, or carpet, was spread out by the front of the car and another man and a girl were sitting on it, leaning back upon the door and front bumper. It was midday; the sun was bright but there were no shadows. The men were wearing tweed sports jackets, shirts and ties, sharply creased trousers and highly polished shoes. One man was wearing a tam o'shanter. There was another girl who was standing by the car bonnet, pointing at the stream with her right hand. Both girls were wearing light summer frocks; one assumed they were feeling the heat, unlike their companions, because the seated girl, dressed in blue, with a blue floppy sun-hat, appeared to be pulling down the shoulder strap of her dress as if attempting to loosen it, and the other was, possibly, starting to undo her own top button with her left hand. This odd tableau, as well as grasping the immediate attention of the viewer, served to conceal many of the details of the car. It was, perhaps, a strange name for the picture, but, Anthony thought, many pictures had allusive, tangential names. Given the name, however, who would have queried the make of the car; who would have guessed that the artist had used a different car for his model? The caption was clear, 'The Morris Minor'. And, in any case – his last waking thought – so what?

Chapter 7

July 31   Anthony   Helen   Walter

"And the doctor agreed?"

"Oh yes. He asked me exactly how much I'd had to drink, and seemed to think that was quite enough to cause hallucinations – on top of the pain killers, that is."

"What pain killers?"

"I didn't tell you – I'd forgotten – I had had two distalgesic tablets for the pain in my ankle, just before I went out."

"How much did you drink, then?"

"The Swede had a couple of glasses – I suppose I finished the bottle."

"Oh Anthony, you are an idiot"

"I know. I can't tell you how sorry I am. So then, I couldn't bear not to see you, make sure Walter was all right...and you, Helen, of course."

"Thank you dear."

"Come on, Helly, you know what I mean."

"Of course I do. So you really think you dreamt it all? There was nothing there at all, no body, no blood?"

"That's right. Nothing at all."

"But the gun!"

"Yes, the gun. That's all part of it. I'll show you in the hotel."

"What? – no, hang on for a minute, the ride's just finishing."

Walter ran straight over to them from the waltzers. Neither Anthony nor Helen could quite understand how he kept his balance.

"Can I have another go please Dad?" dancing up and down, "Please, please."

"Yes, but we'll have to find someone to go on with you, you can't go on your own, it says so on that notice."

"You come on with me Dad, don't be chicken."

"I'm not chicken, you toe rag. I need to talk with Auntie Helen." He paused for a second. "I'll come on with you after we've finished. Let's find someone else to take you now."

The lady who had agreed to take Walter on the waltzers as well as her own son had moved on with her boy to the ghost train. One of the tattooed men operating the machinery called over.

"I'll go on with him, it's OK"

"Thanks very much." He added, embarrassed, "You won't leave him on his own?"

"No mate, don't worry, that'll be one pound fifty."

"So," said Helen, "we can all come home. Anthony, when are you seeing the specialist? You're not hiding anything from us, are you? Does the GP think it might be something else – more serious, you know what I mean? It could be anything, couldn't it?"

"Not quite anything, not, for example chicken pox or athlete's foot."

"Anthony, for God's sake."

Anthony found it too difficult to promise that he was hiding nothing from them.

"Amy often used to think I was irritating too. I only do it with family, honest. It's a cover, when I'm worried. But no, I'm fairly sure that I was just drunk and exhausted – by the strain of that auction. Have I told you how much I spent?"

"No."

"Two hundred and ninety."

Helen was amazed, and showed it.

"Good God, Anthony. Have you got it?"

"Well yes, I have. Business is quite good, and I don't play golf or go on cruises."

"But all the same. Well, I can understand, a bit, I think. I'll stay with you for a while and help with Walter if you want."

"Actually, I have already made an arrangement with the doctor. He wants me to have a scan straight away. Not an ordinary one, something called a petsy tea."

Anthony had heard a brief snatch of a programme about this new investigation on the radio. He didn't know what it was, and hoped that his sister didn't either, or, possible but unlikely, that it really was something to do with the brain. He continued.

"And it's only available in a few places. I'm going to have it done privately. No, don't look so worried, it's only a precaution, but Stevens said I might as well. I'm going into the Montgomery for a couple of days."

"Oh Anthony love, I'm so sorry." She took his hand, and he made a shot at a pathetic face. "Oh, it takes me straight back fifty years, you were only four. I don't expect you can remember, Daddy was at work and you had a terrible headache, Mummy went next door because our phone was on the blink and I just sat with you holding a cold flannel on your forehead. She was ages because the doctor was out or something, and you were crying like mad. He came at last, and you got better. I don't think he ever told us what it was, nothing much probably. Not meningitis, at any rate. And you haven't had much wrong with you since, have you?"

"I'm sure it's nothing, Sis, you mustn't worry, promise me."

"How can I help worrying, of course I'm worrying, how would you feel?"

And how did Anthony feel? He felt, as he should have done, that he was a very deceitful person. He thought his story was about as thin as you could stretch it, and he attributed what he saw as Helen's credulity to her pressing need to believe that they had not all suddenly landed on the square with the snake's head.

Walter didn't want another ride on the waltzers. He waved to the tattooed lad, ran up to his dad and asked if he could have a go on the ghost train.

"Roy says it's really cool. It's not just boring old skeletons and spiders, it was a telly program called Dr Who. It's not on now, is it?"

"No, it's not, it was before you were born. Dr Who was a magician, well, a time traveller, and his enemies are called

Daleks. I used to love it, it was very scary, I think I was older than you."

Walter's desire to have a go on the Ghost Train was not reinforced by the information that his father had enjoyed this Dr Who thing a generation ago, when the world was black and white and there was no MacDonald's. But Roy was still waving him over, so he stared intently at Anthony, willing him to agree. After a second or two he added, "You don't have to come with me if you don't want to."

Before Anthony could reply Roy called over to them, "It'll be OK. They're all my dad's rides, he owns most of the fair, Wally can go on his own – well, OK, I'll go with him."

Walter took this as permission, shouted "Give the man a quid, Dad" and jumped into one of the electric cars which had banged through the black exit doors and jolted to a halt. Roy half looked over his shoulder, waved to someone by the waltzers, ran over to the ghost train and vaulted into the seat by Walter. Immediately the car jerked forward and disappeared through the entrance doors, which swung shut. They were painted blue to resemble a nineteen-fifties police box, but after fifteen years or so the paint was peeling, and the previous red and orange pattern, the mouth of hell, was visible in places.

Helen said, "Anthony, what's up? You look as if you've seen...what on earth's wrong?"

Anthony couldn't contain his anxiety – his sudden panic. "Who's this Roy, he's got Walter on his own in there – how do you get in, how big is it? Has it got another exit? Helen, quick, run round the back and see. Wait if there is, see if they've got Walter, see if they're making off with him!"

Before Helen could move, before she could say a word, Anthony had jumped onto the ghost train track and elbowed his way into the maze behind the blue gates. It was pitch black and he could hear the rumble and rattle of the little vehicles on the rails. He realised that within seconds he would be knocked over, and probably electrocuted. He could see neither entrance nor exit. There was a brilliant flash which illuminated the Dalek, the lights went out, he tripped and fell over, clutching the rail which seconds before had been carrying the electricity supply.

"What the fuck do you think you're playing at you silly tosser?" shouted the proprietor, who had switched the power off, the emergency lighting on, and had followed Anthony into the maze.

"Oh God it's my dad, oh no, how could you Dad?" screamed Walter.

"Well, you were bloody right about your dad." said Roy.

As they walked back to the hotel, Anthony fifty pounds the poorer, Helen took Anthony's arm and asked him if he really thought he was well enough to drive himself to the clinic. Shouldn't she take him, and drive back to his house, or her own flat, with Walter and wait for him? Or come and collect him after the tests?

Hesitatingly, she suggested that he should also take the opportunity of seeing, perhaps, another type of doctor while he was there?

With difficulty, but eventual success, he persuaded her that it would be best for her and Walter, especially Walter, if they stayed for another two or three days in Brighton. Walter was anxious to stay and go to Water World again, and to go round the Royal Naval frigate which had moored near the marina. He was now quite happy for his Dad to go off somewhere else and leave him with Auntie Helen. More than happy, because he still ached with embarrassment.

In the foyer of the hotel, Helen noticed that Anthony was making funny little noises. He saw Helen looking at him, and said, "What a place to meet my end. Think of the obituary."

Helen knew that what seems inappropriate giggling can be no more than a nervous reaction to shocking events. When Anthony was a little boy the giggles would be followed almost immediately by tears. During one of the predictably boring family trips which counted as holidays in the nineteen sixties, when she was twelve, still mischievous and cunning, hardly protective, she had inveigled Anthony into putting a penny into a slot machine called 'The French Revolution' on the pier at Worthing. Inside the glass case little automata, tricked out like characters from 'A Tale of Two Cities', enacted a short but gruesome performance of the execution by guillotine of Louis the Sixteenth. It was extraordinarily clever; the head, struck by the blade, fell into the basket – or appeared to – and the blade of the guillotine turned red, Madame Defarge knitted, the onlookers clapped. A hidden music box tinkled out the Marseillaise. But Anthony, who was supposed to have screamed or wailed or run away, stood there giggling. What a ghoulish little beast, she thought for a second, until his giggles became sobs and he looked at her with such a woeful expression that she clasped him in her arms. His tears had been difficult to explain to her parents, and she had worried that Anthony would tell tales on her – but he hadn't.

She was not surprised when he pulled himself together quite quickly and sat them all down in the bay window of the hotel, which gave a view of the Prince Regent's peeling phantasmagoria. He ordered a pot of tea and a coke for Walter, ignoring Helen's censorious glance.

"I'll just nip up to the room for a second, I need to fetch something," he said.

When he returned he brought two carrier bags with him. From the first he produced a box of handmade chocolates and a bottle of Rive Gauche, which he gave to Helen. He gave the second to Walter without opening it.

Walter looked inside the bag, his eyes widened and he turned to Anthony.

"Gosh, thanks Dad."

He said this as if he wasn't quite sure that the contents could really be for him. From the bag he drew out a toy gun – not some shiny plastic rubbishy Cowboys-and-Indians affair, but a dull, solid metal revolver, beautifully made and perhaps designed more as an ornament for a boy's bedroom than something to play with.

"Does it bang?"

"Yes it does, there are some caps in the bag, but they're not very loud, I'm afraid."

The man in the toy shop, which also sold all sorts of models, had apologised for the feeble pop, which he had demonstrated to Anthony who could remember the explosions which cap guns used to make when he was Walter's age. All to do with health and safety, of course, the salesman said. Anthony on the whole approved of health and safety legislation, and in any case would not have dreamed of buying Walter a toy gun in other circumstances. He was fairly sure what Helen's reaction would be. He was correct. Surprised to receive chocolates and scent herself, she was astounded to see Walter's present.

While Walter was pinging around the lounge shooting the Spode, Anthony explained to Helen that he had bought this present for Walter the afternoon before the sale, and had kept it in his bedroom, intending to give it to him on his return with Helen from the cottage. It was clear to him that his disturbed mind had incorporated the gun into his breakdown – had indeed given it a pivotal role. This, of course, was the gun which Helen had glimpsed in the car – if she had held it then, and realised what it was, maybe this whole situation would have been resolved sooner?

Anthony immediately regretted this suggestion, which naturally infuriated his sister.

"Oh I see. It was really all my fault. Of course it was, how stupid of me not to realise. I should have looked at the gun more carefully. Then I could have said, 'It's only a toy, Anthony, you can stop worrying now'. You are a real pain sometimes, Ant, in fact you've never not been a real pain quite often. You've dragged us into this with your daft ideas, OK, maybe you have had some sort of turn or other, but you seem quite well to me now, apart from being barmy, of course. And buying him a toy gun in any case, after everything you've always said about, gender reinforcement. I've always said little boys like guns and it's natural, but you'd never have it, oh no. And now, you go and buy him this, this...and I don't expect it's even legal."

She exaggerated her anger to disguise her tears, but was not wholly successful.

"No, no I didn't mean that," Anthony said, "I'm sorry, of course I don't think it was your fault. Yes, maybe it is a bit over the top, it is legal, honestly. I just thought, well, you're right, he's always moaned about not having his own gun for that car theft game..."

"That what?" Helen almost shrieked.

"Oh it's based on a computer game, they don't really steal cars, well, Walt doesn't, obviously; I'm not sure about that Sebastian, though, he's eleven you know."

"Ant, if you're flippant just one more time I'm going to take Walter home with me and you'll have to get a fucking court order to, to even see him."

This was possibly the first time Anthony had heard his big sister use that word. He wasn't doing well. Why was he compulsively facetious? He hated the lying. And what a tale he was telling. When he had originally conceived it he had thought it would be reassuring, especially if he tried to seem as normal as possible, as if his turn – attack – episode – had been purely temporary. Stress and booze can certainly precipitate hallucinatory attacks, had said his fictitious GP, and this would be confirmed by the equally fictitious neurologist. Better a transient short circuit in his brain than a permanent threat from murderous gangsters. And he honestly believed that it would have been better, if only it had been true.

Chapter 8

August 2   Anthony   David   Frieda   Hank Edwards   Emily and Peter Williams   Andrew Bond

The corpse rose from its seat and approached Anthony, holding out its left hand in greeting.

"Good morning, Mr Evans. You might like to call me Lazarus."

"Smith."

"I rather hoped you might call me Lazarus now. I've never liked Smith. But I suppose I shall have to stick with it. My Christian name is David. Please don't look alarmed, I do assure you that I seek no revenge. HMG seldom goes in for revenge."

Smith was not a ghost. Anthony was severely shocked and needed to sit down straightaway. HMG – what? He recognised the phrase, but couldn't place it. Revenge?

"HMG?"

"You know, the government. The state. Us."

"Good God. The blood. What about the blood?"

"That was real, all right. Perhaps we should speak quietly? You winged me, as we say, some blood but no immediate danger."

"But you lay so still!"

"Training. You were out of control and had the gun. And I was a bit dizzy, must have banged my head on your cooker. It would have been different if you had been one of my sort, you know, professional, because you would have shot me a second time, in the head, whether I seemed dead or not. As it was it never occurred to you to fire again, did it?"

"No, of course not. I was terrified."

"The wound was clean, it was easy to patch up. Bit sore, mind you, and the arm won't be a hundred per cent for a while. They wanted me off the job, but no chance, I told them, it's the excitement I joined up for. So here I am. You were difficult to follow, we were quite impressed. Where did you go on Monday? We lost you for a while, after the potato scattering incident. What did you do with your family?"

"You must be mad if you think I'm going to tell you that. But I can assure you they're quite safe now."

"I know they're safe, of course they're safe. I told you, we're the good guys."

A group of walkers had entered the bar, trying to outdo each other in their local knowledge and familiarity with the barmaid. One man came and sat down close to Anthony and Smith, bending to retie his bootlaces.

"Yes, good for the training manual," Smith said reflectively. "I've never been in that position before, you know. Where is the..." he mouthed the word "...firearm?"

"I'll tell you as soon as I know who, or what, you really are. And I'm not moving until I'm satisfied."

"Well, I suppose that's reasonable. You're apparently known to us, well, not us exactly, but one of the FO divisions. And the MoD. And the Department of Transport, for God's sake. I'm sort of with Special Branch at the moment. Here's my identification."

He showed Anthony a small wallet with a laminated card inside, asserting, amid holographic devices, that the person whose photograph was attached was called David Smith and was a detective chief inspector in SB6 and would the person to whom it was shown be sure to assist the above officer in any way possible. He continued, "Phone if you like. Usual Met number, ask for SB6."

Anthony did just that. There was a payphone. Directory enquiries gave him the number of New Scotland Yard – Whitehall One Two One Two, that was the number Dick Barton used to ring – SB6 existed, and a voice described Smith. The call had been expected. The voice was a very careful voice, very controlled.

"Any, erm, sarcastic comments?" asked Smith, after Anthony put the phone down.

Anthony looked puzzled. Smith explained that he had had to put up with a certain amount of ribaldry concerning his less than totally effective encounter with Anthony. Then he asked, again, what Anthony had done with the revolver.

"The gun's wedged under the mattress in the van."

"Yes, the van. Why Cornwall?"

"Trying to hide and gather my thoughts of course. I thought you were criminals, killers, and I thought, a small campsite, or a farm, miles away – do you have the faintest idea what it feels like, to think you've killed someone?"

"Well, I suppose I do, yes," said Smith, letting his gaze escape from the ill-lit, shadowy, bar, through the low window, over the sloping meadow to the sea, and for a moment he seemed as distant as the horizon. Then he continued, "If we'd had time to check up on you after we'd found out who you were, then we could have avoided this whole mess. Still, you seem to have coped. Quite well, considering."

"I don't know what you mean by that. I feel shattered. What on earth do you want my pictures for?"

"We'll come to that. But, do you mind telling me what you've been doing for the FO – and why don't you tell me a bit about the Ministry of Transport connection?"

The situation seemed to Anthony weird beyond belief. Nevertheless there seemed to be no harm, at the moment, in telling Smith what work he had done for the government. It would have been incorrect to describe his judgment as suspended; it was completely untethered, like a hot air balloon, floating this way or that according to the whim of the breeze. He was also of course shaken and nervous, and spoke quickly, at some length, not always to the point.

"I've occasionally come into contact with, well, I suppose they're in some branch of intelligence, security people. I'm a logistics consultant – that's my job, I have a small firm, just me and a few young people who are good at sums, and occasionally I've tackled problems in areas of, I don't know, how shall I put it, military relevance? That was all very hush hush, of course. I don't do much of that now, don't trust the Americans. I've become a bit of a pacifist. No, that's not exactly true, perhaps I would still work on defence issues, if that's all they were. You can't distinguish them now, can you? But then, look at the Balkans...somebody had to...at any rate, I occasionally get a bit of advice from some bloke in the FO – if, for example, they know that someone – government, or oil company, perhaps – who I've got a contract with, has an ulterior motive, secret agenda is the phrase, isn't it? Especially round the Caspian. Occasionally, when we're out there, someone comes out from the Embassy to keep an eye on us. When I get back I usually have dinner with the Foreign Office chap and do my best to answer a few questions. I've never been asked to be a spy, mind you, neither by them or us. *You*, I should say. I expect that's because I didn't go to Cambridge."

Smith remained silent, and Anthony continued.

"Once, when I was doing my first job, as a temporary civil servant in the Ministry of Transport, I was involved in what they used to call 'positive vetting'..."

"They still do. And you shouldn't make jokes about Cambridge; they were just the ones whose names escaped."

"hmm...and I was called into the Under Secretary's office to answer questions about an old University friend – and flatmate – who was going into the Minister's private office. I remember the chap who was doing the interviewing was standing at the other end of the room wearing a grey suit, a white shirt and a grey tie – and I've a mental picture of a grey mac, but I've probably invented that, it was a hell of a long time ago. He wore Hush Puppies, that I can say. Do you remember them? Very comfortable. That fat Tory – you know, he was Home Secretary – used to wear them. At any rate, the security bloke was incredibly colourless and undistinguished. This was the seventies, you know, most people wore bright clothes. Maroon velvet flares, difficult to imagine now. Or was it smelly Afghan coats? No, that was the sixties.

"He asked a load of ordinary questions, checking up, I suppose, what Tom had told him, and then started on some really nasty, prurient stuff. I mean, obviously they had to check on Tom's sex life, but it was the way he worded it. And he reacted to my answers with a kind of quizzical, sceptical expression – and his replies were in a sardonic tone of voice, as if he didn't believe a word I said. I thought he was really hoping to uncover some dirty little secrets which Tom could have been blackmailed about. As I said, Tom was my flatmate, neither of us had girlfriends at the time, and I wondered whether he thought we were a couple of gays. Queers was the word then. I got annoyed and – remember, I was young – went all supercilious, and suggested he should have kept up with legislative developments subsequent to the Wolfenden report, and was he aware that homosexuality was no longer a criminal offence? I was probably quite rude, but I thought he'd asked for it. Why are you smirking?"

"Sorry, sorry, I can just picture you, all offended. Carry on, do, I'm fascinated."

"There's not much more to tell, except there was a funny incident about a fortnight later. I got a document marked Secret – red stripe, one envelope inside another, you know the sort of thing, well I suppose you do, I don't imagine secret stuff gets emailed? It was part of a spec for a new tank engine. The unit I was working in got it because of course there were implications for speed and range."

"Ministry of Transport? Surely, that would be Defence Procurement?"

"I expect so, now. But in those days we had one of the first operations research units, and we did work for all sorts of departments. So did the National Coal Board; I bet you didn't know that. The circulation list on the covering memo was the usual committee, all civil servants. Not the external advisers at this stage. This was towards the end of the morning. After lunch the Under Secretary's PA put her head round my door and said there was a call on the red phone for me. She looked surprised, as was I. It was someone from the Chief Scientist's Office who said that CS wanted the document sent to one of the externals, an engineer working for a private firm. He, the man on the phone, had not kept a copy, CS himself was out of the office, so could I do him a favour, copy it and send it on?"

"I knew the external adviser. But as I was photocopying the document – and I had to do it myself, of course – I thought it all seemed a bit strange. I phoned CSO on the ordinary line, and they knew nothing about it, nor did they know who had rung me. They phoned me back almost immediately. CS had thrown a wobbly. Under no circumstances was I to copy the document or send it anywhere. It was all a mistake. Did I understand? I had actually already copied some of the document, and I shredded it straight away. And that's all. I told my boss, of course, but that was the end of it. You're grinning again."

"So I am."

Smith leaned down and retrieved the briefcase which he had placed under the table, and took out a buff file with two red diagonal stripes on the cover.

"You've been elevated to Top Secret, you see. But there's not really much in the file yet, so I took the liberty of bringing it with me. I must be careful not to leave it on a bus. Brown would throw a freddy not just a wobbly if he knew."

"Are all you lot such sarcastic buggers?"

"Oh yes, we all watch telly, know how to behave. But if you like I can finish off the story which you've just started."

"What? It was a quarter of a century ago!"

"Security records are kept forever, surely you know that?"

He paused for a moment.

"Unless, that is, we need to lose them. If we've bumped the wrong chap off, for example."

He smiled at Anthony, who had no idea how seriously to take this last remark. Smith continued.

"Think of the spycatcher stuff. There are still plenty of Harold Wilson – what was his code name? Whitbread? no, that's not quite right, – at any rate, documents on his file which have never seen the light of day."

He paused for a moment, as if he had just thought of something.

"You're surely not telling me that Harold was..."

"No, absolutely not. But his story is relevant, in a way. Harold had every reason to feel paranoid. No minister can be completely certain that he knows the full extent of the Secret Service and its activities. Most Permanent Secretaries don't. And this is important. Harold knew that some junior, and senior, officers in the Secret Service were sure that he was a Soviet agent, and were plotting, forming some sort of cabal, with the aim of displacing him, possibly through blackmail, and possibly – well, who knows? But Harold didn't know who they were. And he didn't know whether any, or all, of the Directors who reported to him were among them. Stalin had the only really effective answer to this, but his solution wasn't open to Wilson."

"And that was?"

"Kill them all, of course."

"All except Beria. Stalin trusted him."

David swirled the last few mouthfuls of beer around in his glass, and swallowed them. The landlord looked over his shoulder and made as if to shift his bottom from the bar-stool and collect the empty glass, but changed his mind and went back to the Telegraph crossword.

"Well, there you have it. It's a matter of trust. Harold, perhaps because of his own devious nature, couldn't bring himself to trust anyone. He didn't have the gift, he couldn't tell when people were lying. Lots can, you know; there are some coppers, not particularly clever chaps, who get it right every time. But not Harold."

"Is that so? What are you going on about all this for? I mean, I don't want to seem unfriendly, but you did break into my house, and I've still no idea what you were really after."

"Come to that, you did try to kill me. But my point is, that after I have explained things a little – I hope you won't, as it were, interrogate me too closely – we shall need to make a, how shall I put it, mutual commitment of trust. I shall need to feel that I can trust you; you will need to feel that you can trust me."

"Oh. Well, we shall have to see, won't we?"

"Now I'll round off the story you told me. Incidentally, you've got a good memory, this file tells me exactly what you told the IGSS officer."

"The who? I only spoke to my manager, no-one else, I told you."

"No, an officer from IGSS was present."

"There was no-one except Dr Wilkins and his PA, I imagine, for some of the time."

"His normal PA?"

"I expect so. Wait a minute, no, I seem to remember that it wasn't Sheila, she was off, that was unusual, there was probably someone from the pool. Yes, there was, a young CO, my sort of age. I think... I think Dr Wilkins called her Jennifer. You're not telling me..."

"Yes, I am, she was no clerical officer, she was an Assistant Security Officer from IGSS. Internal Governmental Security Service."

"Never heard of it."

"Well, you were never naughty, were you? Or, alternatively, perhaps I've invented it."

"Oh God, give it a rest. Wait a minute, Jennifer...?"

"Yes indeed, Dame Jennifer now, Deputy Chair of VIPER."

"Upon my soul. Look, are you going to tell me what happened or not?"

"Nothing very dramatic, as a matter of fact. It was the man who had interviewed you about Tom Campbell who was under observation himself. His marriage had broken up, he was paying huge maintenance and he wasn't allowed much access to his children. He was in debt, his parents were both senile and should have been in a home, but neither he nor they could afford it. So he was vulnerable, extremely vulnerable. He was only given run of the mill jobs, like vetting fairly obviously zero risk employees like your friend Tom. But he wasn't turned, or anything like that. The poor sod just suddenly went potty, and it was you he picked on. He thought you were a condescending little prick and quite simply decided to drop you in the brown and smelly. If you had sent that plan to the external consultant you would have been well and truly for the chop. So, lucky for you that you smelt a rat."

"What happened to him?"

"Not much. Six weeks in a comfy bin, still got his pension, well, most of it, room found for his mum and dad in a grace and favour place. He had done some very good work, you know. That's one reason why he took against you, let's have a look, – 'arrogant little...' dear me, in a memo! He really was losing it...'privileged etc etc. ' – oh, lord, you know the sort of stuff. Well, I suppose you do. You came out of it quite well, actually, noted by the second investigating officer as 'sharp' ".

"Well, that's condescending if you like. Actually, I probably was an arrogant little shit."

"Oh, I don't know. Now, down to business. Can I repeat the question Grey asked you, and I was going to ask you before you tried to kill me? Have you looked at the pictures you took?"

"Don't you mean Brown?"

"Oh damn, yes, Brown, of course."

"I only took them to the auctioneer's office, then I handed them straight over to Safetrans and they've gone to the conservator, Prowley's, in Guildford."

"What? What are you talking about?"

"I always have Prowley's look over pictures I buy. It's quite normal to make sure that the auctioneer's condition report isn't too wide of the mark. I don't presume to know what your interest in them is, but I thought you'd know that."

Smith leaned back in his chair. He sat very still, holding his breath for a moment. He shut his eyes, then opened them again.

"No, not paintings. The photographs."

"What? *What?* What photographs?"

"The photographs you took before you went into that saleroom. The man I had in Coulton Street lost you there. He waited for you to come out, you didn't, and we had to find out who you were by showing *your* photo around."

"My photo? A photo of me?"

"Yes, of course, we had about a dozen by then. We had to show people the little screen on the back of the camera. We also had to make up a story on the spur of the moment. We told them you had dropped your Rolex on the prom. It was my Rolex actually, cost fifteen dollars in Jakarta. You thought we were after your paintings? You bought them in the sale? Oh dear."

He paused for a moment.

"How much?"

Anthony told him, and they sat in silence for a moment.

"Yes, well, that explains it, I suppose. You've got a fairly tight spring, though, haven't you?"

"I didn't know that I had. But I suppose I was quite wound up, yes – I've never spent so much at an auction before. And, another thing..."

Before Anthony could continue, the barman approached holding the handset of a cordless telephone. He squinted at David Smith's left arm, which was thrust awkwardly into the top of his jacket.

"Mr Smith? A call for you."

David listened to the phone, said "Hello Jane."

He listened for a minute or so longer, then spoke.

"I know, I know. Quite a surprise. No harm done, just tell Jennifer, please, that *all is well* – no, let me rephrase that, *so far so good*. I met him in the pub, and am about to buy him a pint."

Picking up his thread after Smith had taken the phone back to the bar, Anthony told him about his meeting with the Scandinavian in the Angel, not minimising his uneasy feeling about the nature of this man's role in the organisation of his anonymous principal. He didn't mention the proposed visit to Victoria Park to see the Hopkins and take tea with the Armstrongs.

"Yes, very stressful. But, as far as I'm concerned, not strictly relevant. Hang on a minute though. What sort of pictures were they?"

"What do you mean, what sort? Portraits, landscapes, oils, water colours; what do you mean?"

"Sorry; who was the painter? What were the, what do you say, subjects? Titles? I don't know much about art, I'm afraid"

"They were oils by a painter of the Festival school, called Bradley. One was a cannery, and the other was men unloading fish from a factory ship. Messy work. Good painting."

"Really? Men at work? The Festival school, you say?"

"Yes, British, named after the Festival of Britain. Hopkins, Michael Harris, Bradley. Why do you ask?"

"Nothing, just a thought. Now, I'll tell you how we're going to deal with this. We will clear up the mess you've made in the last two days. You haven't run over a lollipop lady, or robbed a bank while we weren't looking, have you? Good. The rest I think we can deal with, including your insurance company. And you can ring your sister, wherever she is, – she has kept her phone switched off – and tell her that all will be well. So, have you looked at them since you took them? The photographs? "

David was fairly sure that Anthony hadn't looked at the photographs, and that he had neither noticed nor recognised Armstrong and his surrounding entourage, both official and very, very covert.

"No, not yet."

"Do you think I could have a dekko? Have you got the camera on you?"

Anthony only paused for a split second; his mind was working very quickly now.

"No, it's in the van. We'll walk up, shall we? But I definitely need a little something before we go. Not a pint. A large scotch. Your shout, I think. I'm off for a quick pee."

"Fine. Malt?"

"Not on your life. Teachers with a little soda, please."

"Don't bugger off, will you? Fred and Bert are around somewhere."

"No reason to. See you in a second."

The Gents was a lean-to round the back, with a tar-washed wall to pee against, a corner-fitted basin which you wouldn't want to wash your hands in, a towel you wouldn't want to dry them on, and a windowless cubicle with a broken lock. Anthony took his camera from the inside pocket of his coat and flicked through the seven photographs he had taken. At first he had no idea what he was looking for, but as it became clear that all the backgrounds were innocuous shots of local streets and scenery – not a mobile missile launcher in sight – he realised that he should concentrate on the figures, so he used the preview zoom facility to examine the faces of the people in shot. He had, of course, not intended to photograph any particular persons, but he assumed that he had inadvertently captured – or, as far as Smith knew, failed to capture – a photo of something or someone whose presence there, at that time, should for one reason or another remain secret. Well, there was no doubt that his seventh, and last, photograph was what they were looking for. In the corner of a wide angle shot of shop windows and terraced houses a heavy featured, portly man was heaving himself from the passenger seat of a large black car. Standing in a doorway, only partly concealed by the tall figure of a man wearing flannels and a corduroy jacket, whose back was to the camera, was the Secretary of State without Portfolio. The Treasurer of the Hundred Levels. A man as powerful as the Premier himself. Nor was the rear seat of the car empty. It was occupied by a person not immediately recognisable as a public figure, but who was nevertheless familiar to Anthony. And there was Smith, quite clear in Anthony's wide-angle shot – but not with Armstrong and his companions. He seemed, in fact, to be taking a photograph of the group from a stooping position behind a parked car where, surely, he would be almost certainly concealed from them? What on earth was going on? What was so important about the photographs?

Anthony had almost completely believed Smith when he had told him that his Department, whatever it was, would do what they called 'clean up' after him; compensate the owner of the van, pacify the local police forces, square the insurance company, and whatever else he had temporarily forgotten. He had almost acceded to his sudden request for the camera without asking the obvious question – Why? Now, no longer in Smith's presence, no longer sipping a companionable half, nor exposed to Smith's calm, reassuring voice and his frank smile, his confiding patter about the need for trust at the heart of the security empire, Anthony's confidence started to dissipate. Who were the other people in the photograph? What were they doing? Why was Armstrong there? Something to do with the sale? Was the Scandinavian's shadowy principal really Armstrong himself? It was possible; Armstrong's interest in art was well known. Anthony's inflamed imagination quickly supplied several paranoid scenarios, involving foreign agents, state secrets and the roaming free-lance psychopaths employed by governments to silence their enemies. He quickly convinced himself that Smith and his crew would never be really satisfied with the flashcard; whatever assurances Anthony were to give to Smith there would always remain in his mind a suspicion that Anthony had looked at the photos, or indeed known what he was photographing in the first place. How could they absolutely, completely, ensure his silence? They could abandon him to a grim future in a secure psychiatric unit. Though why should they do that? A simple bash over the head would be safer and cheaper. Or chuck him over the cliff – there were plenty around here. Tragic accident of wealthy art collector. He realised that the flash card itself, or rather the information on it, might give him some small degree of security; he must not lose control of the data, he said to himself; it was actually ingrained in his behaviour by the nature of his job – *always keep a copy of the data somewhere else, somewhere safe.* It would be easy to copy, on his little notebook, if he could have a few moments on his own when they returned to the van. He had only just slipped the card into his wallet and the camera back into his pocket when the lavatory door swung open and Smith entered.

"Your drink's set up; I'll see you back in the bar."

Anthony returned to the bench by the fireplace, and sipped his whisky. A woman, early middle aged and attractive in a loose limbed, scruffy, freckled sort of way joined him. A bit Olive Oylish, he thought. She was wearing a gilet, green, not black.

"Do you mind if I sit here? The other seats are a bit draughty."

She could hardly say that all the other seats were taken, thought Anthony, since there was now only one other person in the bar. Bert, perhaps.

"My name's Frieda. Lovely place for a holiday, isn't it? Staying on the campsite, are you?"

"Yes; and you?"

"No, I'm staying in the pub here. The food seems very good. Surprising really – the bar's a bit basic, isn't it? There's always fresh fish, they know most of the local fishermen, quite a lot of it's caught by rod and line, you know, sea-bass and pollock. Actually, having said that, I don't care for pollock at all, cotton woolly and tasteless, do you know what I mean? The bass is excellent. And they do spider crab claws for a starter, with mayonnaise, home-made I think."

"Legs."

"Pardon?"

"Legs, not claws. You eat the legs, not the claws. The claws are very small."

"Oh."

"But you didn't do badly at all. Menu's on the bar, isn't it? Are you Fred? Not Bert, obviously?"

"I'm sorry. I don't know what you're talking about. I told you, my name's Frieda."

She sounded quite indignant. As she would have to, of course, thought Anthony. He smiled at her, while wondering.

"Sorry, ignore that. I must have sounded rude, but there's an old schoolboy joke..." Before she could ask him to enlarge on this hasty invention, he asked her whether she too was on holiday.

She hesitated before continuing, but Anthony was smiling gently at her, not particularly madly. "No, not really. I've come here to look at a painting. The farmer with the campsite has got a picture he wants to sell, by a painter called Hopkins, perhaps you saw his picture 'Pylons' which was in the newspapers when the Communication Workers bought it? He was one of the so-called Festival painters, after the nineteen fifty-one Festival of Britain, you remember..."

"Of course." *Of course.*

Frieda was Frieda, not a Fred.

"And you must be Frieda Semperdine. I'm so sorry. How do you do?"

Thank goodness. There was no mystery here, at least. Clearly Frieda Semperdine had heard about the cache of Festival paintings which had turned up in a farmhouse not a stone's throw from Lands' End. She would have little reason to be suspicious; uncovering treasures in unlikely settings – farm workers' cottages, terraced houses in Salford, the sweaty games-kit cupboards of bankrupt prep schools in Wales – was one of the romances which kept the public's interest in art and antiques alive. *Titians in the Toilet* and *Granny's Goldmine* were television programmes whose ratings had ensured that they survived all attempts by game show hosts or sex therapists to displace them.

Frieda he knew by name only. He had, surprisingly, never met her at the many sales or exhibitions of Festival paintings which he had attended. She had a reputation for unearthing unusual, and sometimes very fine, examples of many genres of art. Anthony knew that she owned a Pre-Raphaelite portrait of an unrecorded girl representing Browning's Pompilia which seemed to be painted, unusually for the school, with some feeling for both the individuality of the model and the personality, and anguish, of the character portrayed. Not that he, Anthony, would give it house room, of course. Too much Chelsea Flower Show, too many burnished auburn tresses. He didn't know where Frieda got her funds from. She didn't seem to resell much, nor, as far as he knew, did she have a highly paid job, nor was she married. Inherited money, he supposed.

"I know you by reputation", he continued, "and I can understand that you would be interested in the Williams' collection. I didn't know any of them was for sale?"

"Oh, right. You haven't told me your name?"

"Anthony Evans"

"Well I never. How do you do? I'm amazed we've never met before. And you didn't know any of them was for sale."

She looked at him, not so much suspiciously as ironically, over the top of her glasses had she been wearing them.

"Truly. I had only just heard about them, and – the person who told me about them – certainly made no mention of it."

"But you're not going to tell me his, or her, name?"

"I don't think I should at the moment. It's all rather complicated."

As Anthony spoke the last sentence he thought that the whole affair was possibly no longer quite so complicated – extraordinary, certainly, but perhaps explicable. The fortuitous use of the term 'picture' instead of 'photograph' accounted for the entire dreadful shooting episode and its aftermath. Because Anthony had thought that the pictures were at the centre of the affair, he had unearthed the story about the forgery discovered in the Russian's palace, and Maurice's subsequent commission. And it was these rumours of chicanery which had brought him to this crazy place, a farmhouse in the middle of nowhere jam-packed with masterpieces, a campsite whose only other visitor was a pot-smoking hippy from the nineteen sixties, a gastro-pub whose only customers were members of the secret service or millionaire art lovers – so, was Frieda here solely to look at a painting with a view to buying it? Had she, also, heard rumours about forgeries? Of course, such was the essentially speculative nature of the market for fine art and so multifarious the methods used to manipulate it, that somebody might want doubt cast upon the authenticity of the Williams paintings, to discourage buyers like Frieda, probably eventually to acquire them himself?

Anthony embroidered away, mentally stitching together more and more unlikely scenarios one upon the other, some overlapping, some separate. Little stories might have been invented and deceitfully circulated, dropped casually into conversations here and there, at openings or in selected galleries, perhaps by someone close to the Russian collector whom Maurice had visited. There was no doubt that Maurice had discovered a forgery in the oligarch's palace. Or – no, he found this too painful to consider; Maurice was one of his oldest friends, and the thing about Maurice was that he was totally honest, even priggishly so. But it was Maurice, wasn't it, who had first mentioned counterfeiting in connection with Festival paintings? Anthony's memory of their conversation in the roadhouse was hazy now. Why had Maurice thought it might be relevant? Why should anyone try to steal what he knew to be counterfeit? Not, of course, that anyone was trying to steal a painting – but neither he nor Maurice knew that at the time. *What had happened to Maurice?* So, maybe some pieces of the patchwork fitted together, but there were still a lot of gaps and cloth of the right colour to be found.

He continued, "No, I'm sorry, of course I can tell you. It was Maurice Symes-Franton. He had heard from a local art dealer – don't know his name. How long have you known about them?"

"Only a few days. Probably from the same chap as Maurice. He put me in the way of a good quality Nicholson once. No, Winifred, surprisingly. It was propped up in the corner of one of those net loft studios, only uncovered when the last tenant had drunk her final mug of scotch and turps. I was quite grateful, and so, I imagine, were the executors. He's called Henry Edwards, actually he calls himself Hank, he runs a gallery in St Ives called the Red Porpoise. I think he paints a bit himself. How is Maurice, I haven't seen him for ages? Do you know him well?"

"Yes, we were up at Brasenose together. He's fine – I think. Tell me, what have you heard about these Hopkinses up the hill at the farm?"

"Nothing at all, except that they're there. I presumed Edwards had seen them; all he said was they would be worth the journey, because they're Michelin three star. Out of his league, he said. I wouldn't be surprised if he gets a commission, though."

"He didn't say anything about Wallises?"

Frieda looked surprised.

"Wallises? No, have they got Wallises as well? That would be strange – I mean, that would be a really local connection, but Hopkinses are, what should I say, *international* art; they often come up in Paris and New York. They're much more valuable. You pay half a million at least for quite a tatty Hopkins, and small Wallises – they're tatty too, of course," – she smiled and he smiled back, acknowledging her little joke about the painter's style, and choice of materials – "they start at about twenty five thousand."

"Easier to forge, though."

"Why do you say that?"

"Oh, I don't know. But they are, aren't they? Maurice said he thought his contact – this Edwards, you say? – had mentioned Wallis. I might ask."

Anthony felt calmer. It only took a simple chat with another ordinary – well, not extraordinary, at least – person, and one who inhabited the world with which he had been for a long time familiar, to suppress his anxiety about the photos, the repercussions of his law-breaking rampage, and the possibility that Smith would murder him merely as a precaution. He was glad now that he could see this particular worry to be irrational, and he realised that his mood was bound to be volatile considering the events of the last few days.

They chatted for a while, Anthony recounting his meeting with Emily and his pleasure at seeing the paintings. He was slightly worried that Frieda might ask what he was really doing there; or perhaps she thought that he might be considering buying a Hopkins for himself. He had often found that seriously rich people had difficulty empathising with those who were only trivially rich. They just failed to understand budget constraints. In any case, she didn't ask.

Smith returned to the bar and did not attempt to conceal his surprise that Anthony was deep in conversation with a woman who was now sitting next to him.

"Hello," he said to Frieda. "My name's Fred. You've just met Tony?"

"And mine's Frieda. Yes, I've just met – Tony – but we've heard each other's names mentioned here and there for quite a while."

She explained. Smith smiled and nodded, mentioned the countryside and the weather.

"Fancy Anthony – Tony – staying in a camper van!" she said, "I'm sure Maurice told me that you were quite a byword for soft living at Brasenose? Something about candles and apricot brandy?"

She turned to Smith.

"There was a story going around about Anthony that at Oxford he..."

"Not now, please Frieda. Mr Smith and I have only known each other for a short while. But – why don't you come up and see the van, it'll amuse you I'm sure. It's only just up the hill a quarter of a mile or so – the cliff path is pretty, but much longer. I've got some fairly unusual slides from the Tretyakov, you might be interested. Shall I see you here this evening, then, Fred?"

"Oh no, I think I should come too, don't you? I'd love to see your camper van. And my arm's giving me gyp, perhaps you've got a couple of aspirin and a band-aid, if it's not too much trouble?"

For a moment, Smith had actually looked quite cross, but quickly recomposed his features. He turned to the man standing by the bar, who had been within earshot.

"Bert, why don't you get the car and take it round the road to that farm up there. Bill can walk up later. I'm going to have a cup of tea with my new friends."

"Right you are, Fred." Bert might have grinned if he had been that sort of person, but he wasn't.

As they climbed the hill, Anthony turned to Frieda and asked her if she had heard any rumours that the paintings might not be authentic.

"Not at all. Is that why you mentioned forgeries just now? I don't know who has actually seen them, apart from Edwards, that is." Her expression changed, briefly showed resignation, even sadness, but then she smiled and continued in a light-hearted way, "Are you playing some sort of deep game, Anthony?"

Anthony answered her, initially matching her tone but attempting to show her that he knew her worry to be genuine.

"No indeed. Shallow as a Chinese saucer, that's me. Seriously, Frieda, I don't act for other people, or give advice – I'm a systems analyst, not an art dealer. I buy things if I like them, not to sell them on."

He would have added, "And I certainly can't afford a Hopkins," but that might have prompted her to ask him why he was there. Then he wondered whether it was really true that he had bought the second Bradley just because he liked it, and not because the bidding had stopped at a bargain price? Might he have sold that one to the Scandinavian man had the offer been made for the paintings separately? He probably would have. That counted as dealing, he supposed.

The path up to the campsite, although not more than about four hundred yards long, was steep and rough, bordered and in places obstructed by gorse and blackthorn. It crossed four or five small fields, and the gateways in the thick stone walls between them were slick and green with mud and manure. Stiles were offered as alternatives, awkward granite steps with no handhold except the quartz-sharp edges of the stones, or the occasional lichen encrusted branch of an overhanging tree.

"Well, Anthony, this is not quite what I expected," said Frieda, "I thought you would be more of a Winnebago sort of person. Does this – Dormobile? – have a washroom? Sink? Plastic bucket?"

"Of course. Certainly the first two. There's a loo, but there's one up at the farmhouse as well."

"No, I only want to wash off the mud, and bathe my scratches, after that entertaining stroll. Mr Smith here doesn't seem to have suffered at all, despite his sling; I won't be long in the cupboard."

"I'll switch on my notebook and I can show you those slides of the Russian exhibition at the RA."

"Oh, er, yes, that would be nice."

She edged into the tiny lavatory.

"Please find the camera for me, and then, when Miss, Mrs? Semperdine has gone we can see about putting an end to this farce." said Smith quietly. "Bert will drive the van back to its angry, puzzled but compensated owner, I will drive you back to Broadharbour and that will be the end of our brief but incident-packed acquaintance. Obviously, you must speak to no-one else about these events. Mr and Mrs Baxter and Mr Symes-Franton – who has been returned home with a vague promise of consultancies and public patronage – have already been informed that you suffered a short mental breakdown brought about by an unexpected reaction to a painkilling drug which you were given while being treated for pleurisy. You will receive two thousand pounds as compensation for the assault upon your amour propre. Unlike myself, I might add, who will receive no compensation for my flesh wound, nor indeed for my ruined clothing."

What is there about this man, Anthony thought, that he feels entitled to order me around like this? He, and his equally anonymous friend, broke into my house, were quite prepared to rob me, caused me to break God knows how many laws, terrified my sister, and is now treating me like some poxy subordinate. Like one of his Bills or Berts. I don't feel particularly subordinate, no I damn well don't – out of my depth, yes, but that's not the same at all. And in fact, perhaps after all there is a 'picture' connection – painting, not photography. Why were they watching Armstrong? He was just by the auction rooms. Did they recognise Phillips? How many galleries has *he* got now? I need to stay here. I need to find out more about the pictures; I need Frieda to look at them too. And I damn well will copy the flash card.

He replied. "Actually, I need to stay here this afternoon. I'll ring my sister, and then go straight to meet them in – well, where she is."

"No, I'm sorry, that's not in the game plan at all. We want things cleared up asap, and that includes you back at home with your Walter. Good God, Evans, your sister must be going spare, and you want to mess around here talking about bloody pictures?"

"You know where you can put your game plan. My sister and son are fine. I saw them, when I went 'off your radar'. Frieda and I are going to look at some paintings first. Just over there, in the farm house." He added, slowly and with considerable emphasis, "These pictures are very valuable. They were painted by a British artist called Hopkins, who's as important as..." he tried to think of a painter with whose name this policeman, spy, whatever, might be familiar, "...Francis Bacon. You've heard of him? So it's quite surprising to find them stuck out here in the sticks."

Smith realised that he had struck the wrong note; he had been surprised that Anthony had jibbed at a straightforward proposal of the best way to clean up the mess, and he wanted to get to the bottom of Anthony's overriding interest in the paintings. What was this Frieda Semperdine doing here? Were she and Anthony – no, it would have been on his file. Anthony was fidgeting and looked nervous; Smith stepped outside the van to see if his phone had a signal.

Anthony took his notebook from the case and switched it on. It started its noisy and in the circumstances irritatingly slow boot up. But it was a while before Smith returned, slipping his phone back into his breast pocket.

"Did you find a signal?" Anthony asked. Smith was looking thoughtful, almost undecided, only fleetingly, but it was an expression Anthony hadn't seen before.

"Yes, just, thank you. Now, may I have my gun back, please."

"Willingly." Anthony pulled it from under the mattress and relinquished it. Smith broke out the chamber and counted the bullets.

"Not fired it again then?"

"Hilarious. What do you want to see the photos for?" Anthony asked.

"I wondered when you were going to ask that."

"Yes, well, I've been thinking about it. There was a new boat in the harbour. Perhaps it was the latest independent nuclear deterrent. A guided missile platform disguised as a small container ship, nicely distressed with a lot of rust and an Estonian registration?"

At this point Frieda extricated herself from the lavatory. Smith was irritated with Anthony and showed it.

"Don't be facetious. And I'm not going to tell you. Just find the damn camera and give it to me."

"All right, keep your hair on, I'll get it." He pointed at the cupboard over the sink. "Fill the kettle, will you?"

As Smith was looking in the cupboard for the kettle Anthony bent over his notebook computer and slipped the flash card into its slot. It was set up to auto-copy, but not, thank goodness, auto-delete, and Anthony shielded the screen from Smith with his body for the few seconds until he was able to clear the 'done it' box. He retrieved the flash card.

"I can't find your kettle."

"It's on the shelf to your left," said Frieda. "Why do men always ignore what's in front of their noses?"

Anthony winced. "I'll get that camera now, if you like."

"Yes, do, there's a good chap."

Anthony edged to the back of the van and, turning his back, pretended to find the camera among the jumble of clothes and general impedimenta littering the area behind the toilet cupboard, which was not in Smith's line of vision. He slipped the flash card back and returned, handing over the camera.

"Can I see those slides from the Tretyakov, please, Anthony?" said Frieda. "What are they?"

"Um...Kandinskys, Korovins...and, um, Grigorievs."

"Really? Grigorievs? At the Tretyakov?"

Anthony hurriedly opened his explorer and pretended to examine the folders in the pictures directory.

"Damn, they must all be on a disc. I haven't got it. I'm so sorry."

Smith, meanwhile, had been looking at the photographs on the camera. He smiled at Anthony.

"Yes, it's a nice little job isn't it. I might get one myself. Thanks for letting me look at it."

He handed it back, and Anthony put it into a drawer, checking the card slot which was, of course, empty.

Frieda turned to Smith. "Are you interested in art, Mr Smith?"

"Please call me Fred."

"All right. Actually, some of my friends call me Fred. Are you a Frederick?"

Before Smith had had time to decide whether he was a Frederick or an Alfred, Anthony interjected, "No, he's actually got a very unusual name, it's Ethelfred, some of his friends call him Ethel."

He gave a little hysterical giggle, which he tried to disguise with a cough, turning aside and spluttering into his handkerchief.

"Anthony, you have got a weird sense of humour," said Frieda, embarrassed.

"Yes, I know, I'm sorry," said Anthony, wiping his face with his handkerchief. "But he insists on calling me Tony," – turning to Smith – "don't you?"

"I'm sorry. I forgot you didn't like it."

"Oh God," thought Anthony, "Am I losing it, after all? I felt better half an hour ago ..."

Frieda, meanwhile, was wondering what the relationship was between these two men. She had always understood that some men could indulge in banter – a sort of impromptu pantomime exchange of gross insults, with a lot of bad language but no bad feeling – and that this was a knack which, as Ishiguro's butler found out, was difficult to learn. She thought that on the whole, women didn't do it. She may have been right. In her circle of female acquaintance friendships would most definitely be sundered by the sort of imputations about honesty, strength and above all sexual performance which were said to fly around freely during male banter. But, then, neither she nor her friends had ever worked on the crimping line of a pasty factory.

These two men didn't seem to know each other very well, and surely a well-established friendship was a prerequisite for the casual exchange of insults? Perhaps they were not friends. Why had Anthony been so keen for her to come to see the van? Slides of a few Russian paintings? It was a bit thin.

Turning to Frieda, Anthony said, "We must go up to the farm and look at the Hopkinses. Then Fred's going to drive me into St Ives, aren't you Fred, and we're going to have a chat with Andrew Bond at the Saline. Do you want to come too? It's not the Saline's kettle of fish, of course, far too figurative, but he's an academic, isn't he, he's bound to know something about them, surely?"

Anthony glanced quickly at Smith, expecting an objection to what he'd almost thrown out as a challenge, but Smith was surprisingly silent. Silent and, again, thoughtful. Then to Anthony's surprise he replied that he would quite happily fall in with such a plan.

Anthony had had no time to consider why it was of national importance – which seemed, even as he thought it, a grandiloquent or hackneyed term, but what else could explain the involvement of all these secret policemen, what were they called in popular television programmes, spooks, and their willingness to pay him money 'for his inconvenience'? – that he should not recognise Armstrong? Perhaps it was the people who had been with him? Anthony had recognised a couple of them, not famous, not OK or Hello celebrities, but well known in art and curating circles. Once again he thought there might be a real art connection, not just an absurd misunderstanding caused by the use of the word 'picture'.

Frieda replied, "Well, you never know. How long have the Williamses been at Boselloe? Not much more than a year?

Some of these academics have tunnel vision; it's not surprising. It must be difficult enough keeping up with all the new movements these days, without having to remember their old Courtauld stuff. But yes, I mean, four or five Hopkinses must be worth a fortune – you'd think he'd want to have a squint at them, wouldn't you? How far away is St Ives?"

"Only about eight miles along the coast, but I think Andrew actually lives in Camborne. St Ives rents are through the roof."

Hank the hippy accosted them as they walked across to the farmhouse.

"Hello Frieda, so you decided to come and have a look for yourself?" he said.

"Of course. I wouldn't be likely to ignore your call, would I? Especially after the Nicholson. Anthony, this is Hank Edwards. I told you, he has the Red Porpoise gallery in St Ives."

"Yes, we've met. Hello again."

"Well hello Anthony. So, you know Frieda. Just here for a little holiday, then? Sea and scenery, I believe you mentioned? Might as well pop in and have a dekko at the Hopkinses while you're here? Why not indeed. I'm sure Emily will be delighted to give you the tour, and Peter may well entertain you with a little background, if he's finished mowing the cabbages."

Introduced as a friend, Smith smiled, was briefly acknowledged, then ignored. Edwards continued to chat to Frieda as they walked towards the house. Smith took Anthony by the elbow and they walked on a few paces. He spoke quickly to Anthony. "I have suddenly acquired an interest in the paintings of Hopkins. I think I should join you in the farmhouse and afterwards, perhaps you could tell me a little more about them. And him. I know very little about art."

Edwards had turned away towards the barn, making for the door which had been locked in the morning, and which was now half open.

At the farm, Emily seemed delighted to see Anthony again. She was wearing gardening gloves and an apron, and had been weeding and raking the gravel beds in front of the house and setting out small alpines. Empty pots were neatly stacked, newly washed and glistening with moisture, upon a table constructed from oak slats standing close to an outside tap. A brush was hanging from a metal hook set into the granite. Anthony didn't attempt to account for Smith and Frieda, beyond saying that Frieda was an old friend, and leaving Emily to guess that there was some connection between Frieda and Smith. Emily said that she would summon her husband from the fields because he would be upset to miss the opportunity of telling his Hopkins stories, especially to Frieda, she said, with a smile which was hard to interpret because she didn't seem to Anthony the sort of person who would make even slightly suggestive remarks. Her husband answered his radio immediately – he was in the barn, not up the field – and he said if they would just give him a minute or two to wash he would be right with them.

He looked different off his tractor, and, Anthony thought, could he be behaving differently also? Perhaps these huge machines, with their giant wheels and hermetic cockpits, give their mahouts confidence which they would lack grounded and un-armoured. Is there such a thing as field rage? On the prairies of Norfolk do combine harvesters cut one another up? Peter Williams seemed, if not anxious, certainly less comfortable than when he had joked about turnips with Anthony early that morning; possibly this impression was associated with the slight change in accent and dialect which Anthony noticed – less bucolic, less peppered with flowers and me'ansoms. He was particularly attentive to Frieda, who, it transpired, had left a message on his answer-phone the previous day.

"Yes," he said to her, "I would be delighted to show you the pictures. Emily tells me that your friend here", he indicated Anthony, "is quite an expert. I suppose it gets round in a place like this – Cornwall, that is, with St Ives and Newlyn, and what have you – these pictures, I mean, and to be honest with you I've been expecting that chap from the Saline, Andrew Bond, to give me a bell, but he hasn't yet." He carried on like this for a minute or two.

Anthony and Emily had stopped in the front garden because Anthony had been admiring the swirling pattern which she had raked in the gravel, which he knew from an exhibition held at Kew, and from a series of black and white photographs in some book he had seen, probably at Maurice's, to be a Japanese style of landscaping. Peter called to them.

"Emily, could you put the kettle on? And, Anthony, could you bear to hear how these paintings came to be in the family? I was just going to tell Frieda."

Cups of tea – English, that is to say Indian, not Japanese thank God, thought Anthony – in hand, and, could he believe it, little lotus buns awaiting them on a side table, they stood in a polite semi-circle around 'The Overseer'. It seemed that Peter had very little in the way of artistic explanation or insight to impart. He clearly knew next to nothing about the Festival school, and was not particularly interested in the position of this work in the artist's canon. He was only vaguely aware that the 'Overseer' in the London showed one fewer women on the production line, and relied on Emily's quiet interjections to flesh out his own shallow but longwinded appreciation of the picture.

"That's really very interesting, isn't it Anthony?" said Frieda, despondent that each painting in turn, and there were five more, might be introduced and explained in the same insensitive manner. What she wanted to do was to get close to one or two of them and have a careful, uninterrupted look, and she wondered how to contrive this. Peter Williams must surely have thought of her as a possible purchaser, although she hadn't made that explicit in her phone message. And she didn't know which were for sale. She had often encountered the self-consciously casual, take it or leave it manner of owners hoping to offload hundreds of thousands of pounds worth of artefact – nothing in the way of a sales pitch, nothing vulgar like praising the article or saying how nice it would look above the fireplace. But Peter's behaviour was slightly different, as though he was enacting a preliminary ritual which he knew must precede the real business, a ritual which he thought fairly pointless but was determined to carry out to the letter. So she was relieved when he suggested that they sit down, finish their tea and have a bun, while he told them about his father and the painter Hopkins. This story he told with much greater ease than that with which he had introduced the paintings.

Ted Williams had been in the second year of his National Service, quite looking forward to returning to his father's farm, nevertheless enjoying the relative freedom, and predictability, of army life, and the opportunities it offered for friendship and conviviality which were lacking – despite the obscene suggestions of the other squaddies – on the hill farms of North Lancashire. His mates thought he was a bit slow, a bit agricultural, but he was popular because he would often do more than his fair share of the trivial, tedious, deliberately pointless tasks set by the platoon sergeant. He would grab a mop out of the hands of some underweight townee, who was dabbing it ineffectually around the iron legs of his bedstead, shift the bed, mop the floor, which was spotless save for cigarette ash carefully scattered by sergeant and corporal, replace the bed and move on to the next one. He was a big man. He ate large meals, mainly potatoes, and drank only moderately. Although not particularly clever, nor well educated, he had a talent for drawing quick sketches, which would sometimes capture the essence of a subject by means of slight emphasis or distortion. He could have been a cartoonist if he had been mean or impassioned, but he was neither.

The battalion was sent to Cyprus. The colonel explained the role they were to perform to the company commanders, who explained it to the young lieutenants who commanded the platoons. They explained it to the sergeants, who explained it to the men. Ted understood that they were to stop two kinds of poorly differentiated foreigners from killing each other. They weren't to fire their own guns unless they had to, and then they could. Some of the foreigners were reasonably well disposed to the British, but most were not. It wasn't always easy to tell which were which. The main enemy was called Eoka, its commander General Grivas, but he wasn't a real general, like Brooke or the Auk.

One burning August day, under a different sun from the one which shone over the moors of Lancashire, part of the platoon was patrolling farmland towards the north of the island. The land was poor and dry, the air pungent with the scents of herbs which needed only rocks and sunshine to survive. There were goats, olive trees. The barns and eyeless cottages, the walls which enclosed the tiny fields, the squat domed churches, were built from the stones of the landscape, roughly assembled.

The soldiers picked their way along the dried-out course of a stream. The conscripts were nervous, some of them exhausted. The regular soldiers, one or two of whom had fought in Africa, were fitter, but they too were quiet and wary. Everyone was very, very thirsty.

Lieutenant Hopkins, who must have been four or five years older than Ted, turned and signalled to the sergeant that they should rest for a moment or two. He pointed to a crumbling barn a little way up the hillside, where there would be some shade, and gestured that three soldiers, Ted among them, should take up positions as sentries. Ted curled his body in the narrow crescent of shadow cast by a withered tamarisk, and took a long pull from his flask. The water was as hot as he was, possibly hotter. Possession of his rifle was taken, the moment he put it down, by a column of ants. They marched up the stock, over the bolt. The first few paused to assess the nature of the grease and to investigate the magazine, but they decided it was of no use or interest and communicated this almost instantaneously to the file of followers. The ants continued along the barrel, over the foresight, across Ted's boot and back into the scrub.

The sound of the machine gun came from the other side of the barn, out of his sight, a noise compounded of the sharp rattle of the gun itself – which Ted only faintly recognised, having heard it just once before, on Salisbury

Plain – and the thuds, cracks and whines as the bullets struck and ricocheted from the barn wall. He supposed, afterwards, that he must also have heard shouts and screams, but if so they had been elided from his memory. He could see a few puffs of dust, but nothing to give him any clue where the gunfire came from. He crawled towards the barn, pushing his gun ahead of him – paddling himself forward with it in the dust, as he had been taught, and keeping his bottom pressed to the ground. A few rifle shots, recognisably from the old Lee Enfields with which the patrol was equipped, a couple of bursts from a sten, pistol shots, then silence. He paused, flattening his body as best he could among the rocks and thorns. He had no idea what to do. Minutes passed, then three more shots. A foreign voice sounded loud from the barn, now about forty yards away, followed by others. Then a sharp command, and silence.

Five men, dressed in makeshift camouflage, edged round to the side of the barn, and when they saw no British soldiers they relaxed and started to talk again. One was carrying a light machine gun over his shoulder, and one was festooned with its ammunition belts. Another seemed to be giving orders, so Ted presumed that he was the leader.

Ted estimated that he was between fifty and sixty yards away. He had never been convinced by the army's rules of thumb about range – face definitions, eyes and suchlike, and on the firing range had used his own system, based largely upon the distances run in school races, fifty and a hundred yards sprints, two-twenties, four-forties. He had used a shotgun on the farm, of course, but the distances were usually much shorter and aiming was more of an instinct. He set the sight on his rifle, and wedged the barrel firmly between two rocks. Pulling the bolt back slowly, covering the breech with the thumb of his left hand to prevent the cartridge clicking into position noisily, he slowly eased the round into the chamber. Equally quietly he locked the bolt down. At this point the leader turned so that he was facing straight at Ted. Like a target at Aldershot. Just a target. Ted aimed at the heart, held his breath, squeezed the trigger. The leader was slammed against the wall, his legs crumpled and his knees gave way in a manner impossible for the living. He fell like a beast at the knackers.

But his men seemed to take no notice. One was staring at the ground, pointing and shouting. Ted saw the Mills bomb a second before it exploded. The machine gun crew were lying inert, one of the others was rolling in the dust, screaming, and the fourth was leaning against the wall, bleeding from a wound to his head, and clutching his thigh. The leader was dead. Ted knew he was dead because he had shot him through the heart. Blood now covered his chest.

Another man came round the corner of the barn, dressed in shirt and trousers and holding a revolver. Ted instinctively aimed, but he did not fire because the man was Lieutenant Hopkins. Instead he jumped up, shouted "I'm with you sir!" and ran towards him. Hopkins registered his presence with a wave, but limped straight up to the screaming man on the ground, and shot him twice in the chest. He pointed at the machine gunners and said, "Make sure they're dead, Williams."

"What do you mean sir?"

One of the gunners moved. Ted had turned aside to look at the other, half of whose head was missing, when Hopkins suddenly barged him against the wall. The gunner's first pistol shot missed completely, his second scraped along Ted's forearm. Hopkins kicked the pistol out of the gunner's hand, Ted held his rifle by the barrel to use the butt as a club, but the gunner jerked both his hands out, palms up, in a hopeless gesture of surrender.

"Christ, thank you sir."

"Shoot the fucker, Williams."

Ted reversed his three-o-three and shot the man point blank. The heavy bullet travelled through his body and dug itself about a foot into the stony soil.

"What about him, sir" – pointing at the man leaning against the wall, whose trouser leg was now saturated with blood – "and did they set a sentry?"

"Don't know about a sentry." He walked up to the man, now lying on the ground half propped up by the wall, and spoke in what Ted assumed was Greek. The man said something, not satisfactorily, and Hopkins kicked him hard on his bleeding thigh. He screamed a response, and Hopkins turned to Ted.

"No sentry. Why should they? They've been trailing us for hours, waiting for the moment. Bastard partisans. Go round the other side, look."

Every British soldier was dead. Two had their arms tied behind their backs.

"They were going to be taken prisoner, but the one you shot said no. So that one" – he pointed at the man who had been screaming – "shot them in the head."

"What about you sir?"

"Well what about me, Williams?"

"I mean, why did you ...?"

"I had my fucking pants down, Williams, I was having a shit, OK? Over there. And like you, Williams, I didn't throw myself screaming into the fray. If we had, Williams, we'd all be fucking dead, wouldn't we, not just those poor sods. We both chose our moment, and we were both right. We were careful but not over-cautious. Say it, Williams."

"We were careful but not over-cautious. But, sir, I just ..."

"So did I, Williams. As soon as I could."

"We should take that one back with us, shouldn't we sir? We're supposed to take them in for interrogation aren't we?"

"How, Williams?"

"He's not big, sir, we could rope him and I could carry him easy. Tie up his wounded thigh?"

"No, Williams, too risky."

"Leave him then, his mates might find him?"

"Williams, I'm tired, just do what I tell you, for Christ's sake. Yes, tie him up while we go and find the other sentries."

The sentries were, of course, dead, their throats cut.

The partisans had pulled the field wireless from the body of the signals lance-corporal, but the machine gun bullets which had perforated his body had also shattered its mechanism. On the hard, hot ground lay broken valves and coils of wire, sticky with coagulating blood. There was no way to contact Company headquarters, and it was not certain that another patrol would be sent out the minute they failed to make the next routine radio contact – which was not, in any case, scheduled for three quarters of an hour.

They would have to return, the way they had come, as quickly as possible. They removed the bolts from the rifles and smashed the barrels against the rocks. Hopkins collected the men's identity discs, knifing them off, making no effort to wipe away the blood. Ted hoisted the trussed partisan over his shoulder, but the man groaned and struggled.

"Dump him, Williams", said the lieutenant, "just drop the bugger."

"We'll have to gag him, sir, or he might shout on the way back, and ..."

"Yes, obviously. Untie him." He took his revolver from its holster.

"Sorry sir?"

"Untie him, Williams. Untie his hands and feet, take that field dressing off his leg."

Ted understood. But he was certain that this was not right. A captured partisan was enormously valuable and it was surely their duty to make every possible effort, to take every risk, to get him back to Company HQ. And in any case, would it be *right* – he searched for other words, but none came. He had been given an order, and his entire training had been designed to ensure that he obeyed orders, all the stupid, pointless, unnecessary tasks imposed on conscripts, the interminable polishing the brilliant, cleaning the spotless, right turning, left turning, about turning, facing your front, no your front you pathetic little worm, had been directed to one end, that Private Williams should afford Lieutenant Hopkins unquestioning obedience. Well, it hadn't worked, and, looking at Williams, Hopkins realised this.

175

"Remember, Williams, I saved your life. Now, I'm telling you, we have no choice."

They did have a choice, Ted thought, but which of them would make it?

Lieutenant Hopkins continued, "That other one had surrendered, you know, he had his hands stretched out, empty. He was looking at you. You shot him all right."

Yes, it was true. But it had been a split second, he had had no time to think.

"I thank you for saving my life, sir. But I can carry him, he's not too heavy."

By now, Hopkins was desperate to get back to Nicosia, more than five miles stumbling along the rocks of the watercourse, or pushing through the hostile scrub. Every rustling branch was a partisan creeping up to ambush them, every bird call was a coded signal. They left the stone barn, the men where they had fallen, the growing stink of drying blood, and set off the way they had come. Ted carried the bound and gagged prisoner over his shoulders, like an injured sheep on the Bowland moors.

For a mile or so they sought concealment among the prickly bushes of the maquis, forcing a path through the thorns and malevolent bush. All the shrubs, even the wild olives and the lotus tree, had spines, designed by God to protect their leaves from the hungry beasts of the field, and to test the patience of His chosen species, and their skins were soon covered in scratches and lacerations. The worst affected must have been the prisoner, who was the most exposed and the lightest clad. Hopkins ordered them down onto the watercourse, and they trudged along its stony bed until, after about half an hour, Ted missed his footing on an unstable rock and fell. He pulled himself up, sat down again and grasped his right ankle. Hopkins stared at him, his face showing no expression; no sympathy, no anger.

Ted said, "It's OK, sir, it'll be all right in a while, I've just twisted it a bit." He sat still for a minute or two with his elbows on his knees, head in his hands, then pulled out a handkerchief and wiped the sweat from his face, unscrewed the top from his flask and drank most of the warm, unpleasant water.

"You can wait, you bastard," he said over his shoulder to the prisoner, who lay behind Ted, where he had been tumbled in the fall. The lieutenant was leaning over him, and straightened up as Ted spoke.

Lieutenant Hopkins cleaned his knife by plunging its blade once or twice into the sand. "He won't need a drink at all now, Williams." He untied the ropes and removed the gag, avoiding the blood trickling onto the rocks, "perhaps they'll think it was the Turks. I don't give a tinker's. Can you walk on your own, or have I got to bloody help you back? I can't carry you, that's for certain."

"I don't think you should have done that, sir. My ankle's fine now."

"Don't be insubordinate, Williams. Time to go home."

Hopkins bounced along happily for a while, but his elation gradually subsided and, after about three miles of struggle through the thorns he called a halt. Ted looked at him for orders, but could sense that he was unlikely to receive any. Again, he searched his mind for the appropriate word, and this time found it. Hopkins was lost, lost like a little boy in the darkening forest trying to find his way back to Scout camp. Hopkins carried no rifle and his pack was small, so Ted swung it over his own shoulder, and they set off, once more along the stream bed. Hopkins grumbled and dawdled like a child, and eventually Ted pushed him in front, and shoved him forward whenever he stopped. They were not attacked again by partisans, and in this manner they reached Company base that evening.

The next day they were interviewed at length by the battalion adjutant and by a captain of military police. Afterwards Ted was sitting in the NAAFI tent, even he finding it difficult to remain good-natured as the questions were repeated over and over again by the other off-duty soldiers, and as brimming glasses piled up in front of him. A corporal pulled back the flap and called him over. He was to go over immediately to the adjutant's office, why, the corporal did not know.

Well before he reached the office, he heard his name called softly from an open doorway, and Lieutenant Hopkins beckoned him in.

"You needn't bother the adjutant, Williams. Come in and sit down."

The room was a store for household items, and they sat among mops and toilet rolls. It was not clear to Ted whether Hopkins had regained his confidence, but he knew what question Hopkins would ask, and Ted couldn't bear the thought of any tentative preliminaries, so he spoke first.

"I said he was weak from a bayonet wound which he got in the fight, and that he died on the way back, so we left him."

"Thank Christ. I just said he died. They're sending one of the Sikorskys and God knows how many soldiers." He smiled nervously. "It was either a court martial or a medal."

Peter beamed at his small audience. "That's it, really. Neither of them got a medal, but Dad was made a corporal. I think Hopkins saw one of Dad's cartoons; at any rate he went to stay with them at the farm after his short service commission. He did some sketches of my sister on our new Field Marshall."

They looked bemused, as Peter had hoped. "It was a tractor. Made during the war by Marshalls. Engineers' wit." He took a couple of sheets of rough cartridge paper from a drawer. "Here, look."

"Good lord!" Frieda passed them to Anthony, who inspected them reverently. They were just sketches, in soft pencil. They were good, naturally. Were they obviously Hopkinses? Of course not – although Anthony knew some experts who would pretend to detect a master's touch in even such simple work.

Peter continued, "and he drew Dad as well, captured his look exactly. I framed that one – it's hanging up over there, above the little table."

Simply framed, a charcoal sketch of a burly, good looking man in his thirties, with a calm expression possibly betraying to the unfriendly an element of self-satisfaction, even perhaps smugness.

"And they were friends from then on. Hopkins was bipolar, you know," – they did – "it was called manic-depressive in those days. Dad latched onto this as an excuse for Hopkins' brutality, cowardice, or whatever it was, on that awful afternoon. Hopkins would actually have given Dad more pictures, even when he became famous, but Dad said no."

"You mentioned your father had a talent for drawing," said Frieda, "did he carry on with it – did Hopkins give him any encouragement – did he help him at all?"

"Well he did, yes. In fact, they used to go out sketching together. Dad did a few line drawings of Hopkins; actually, Hopkins passed one of them on to Brotherton for the biography, but he didn't use it. I think Hopkins was a bit starry eyed about Dad, and it probably clouded his judgment. It was one of those friendships which may seem odd but are actually quite common; him so mercurial, so sharp, often miserable, and Dad so stolid and contented. I loved it when Hoppy came to stay. He teased me like hell and he was quite rough. He would pick me up and spin me round till I was dizzy. God knows why I enjoyed it."

"Did you draw or paint at all?"

"Me? Good Grief no. Hoppy tried to show me how to draw people, but he gave up. It was the shoulders, you know. They don't stick out at right angles, I knew they didn't, but that was the only way I could draw them. And full face. So I couldn't draw the nose."

They smiled politely. Smith was becoming restless, but asked a question.

"Did you keep any of your father's work?"

"No, Mum threw it away when he died. She didn't rate art, thought it was daft. She was jealous of Hoppy, I think. None of it was framed, just kept in an old suitcase. And she was going to sell his paintings, I think, but she died too, quite shortly after Dad."

"Which is your favourite painting, then, Mr Williams?"

Funny question, thought Anthony, what on earth is Smith up to?

"Definitely the Overseer." He glanced at Emily, then back to Smith. "You can, um, appreciate it on a number of different levels, if you see what I mean."

He then asked Frieda if she would like a closer look at it. It was well lit, and she gladly accepted. Anthony sidled up to her, and together they examined it and discussed it quietly. Peter Williams was chatting with Smith and Anthony joined them while Frieda took a quick look at the other Hopkinses. He had remembered Maurice's story, that their Oxford friend Ratcliffe had come here in search of Wallises, and found the walls bare. Smith and Williams were actually talking about the military action in Cyprus, rather than the paintings, and when this conversation flagged – Williams couldn't remember whether his father's regiment had been the Lancashire Fusiliers, or the Lancashire and Cheshire Light Infantry – Anthony mentioned that he had heard that the Williamses used also to own a number of paintings by Alfred Wallis?

Confusion was followed quickly, surprisingly, by a spark of anger, which coloured his reply.

"Not us. Our friend; at least he used to be our friend. Thompson is his name, Robert Thompson. He borrowed our house – this house – last year when we went to Japan. The idea was that he would look after it and keep an eye on the lad that our neighbour would send down to keep the farm – well, it's a small-holding, really, isn't it? – keep it going. We stored the Hopkinses, of course. But he used the house for a bloody art gallery, sold all sorts of stuff for himself and some shady London dealer. Local stuff like Wallises, and a Wells or two, and a couple of small Hepworth drawings, so I was told. Impersonated me, once, as well. We still paid all the bills, including the insurance and security firm, and the place looked as if it had been used for a rugby club party. You should have seen the carpet, filthy, we had to have a new one.

Ask Emily, she'd just decorated this room. You think it makes me angry, you should ask her!"

He looked at his watch. "Good Lord, five thirty. Time to hit the bottle. Gins OK? Tonic? Or there's Scotch?" There seemed now to be no rural timbre to his voice.

*****

The Saline gallery in St Ives closes to the public at five o'clock, but it was remaining open that Wednesday evening for a lecture on the artist Peter Lanyon, and they were meeting Andrew Bond, a Professorial Fellow, after his talk. They – Anthony, Frieda, Smith and one of the Berts – had driven some eight miles along the northern coast road, through villages originally built to house miners, and little improved, and through farms where the road suddenly twists and turns and is choked to a single vehicle's width by judiciously sited granite obelisks and enormous trailers filled with slurry. Hens, cockerels and ancient sheepdogs guard the road, cars and charabancs drive slowly. They drive slowly, in any case, because between the villages the road swoops and wheels, like the gulls and buzzards above it, through scenery matchless in England, long reclaimed by gorse and heather from the tin and copper mines which scarred it for three thousand years. The only reminders of mining times are a few square, ruined engine houses, with crumbling brick and granite chimneys, some clinging to the sides of cliffs in places where no-one except, presumably, a mining engineer could imagine it possible, let alone sensible, to construct them. At the base of the cliffs the Atlantic breaks against the rocks, and every bend in the road, every rise and fall of the downs, yields a different view of the cliffs and the sea.

Between the road and the shore lies a network of stone walls which enclose and protect small fields of pasture and the cattle grazing them, a hardy breed uniformly patterned in jet black with a broad white band around the belly. The boundaries and walls of these fields were constructed while Agamemnon was besieging Troy, Anthony reminds Frieda, and the bronze of his sword was forged with tin dug from these moors. Frieda looks out of the car window and remarks that if they took a boat westwards, along the fiftieth parallel of latitude, they would pass the Scillies then sail for two thousand miles before seeing land. "Ah," murmurs Anthony, "my Newfoundland," then blushes. Frieda, thankfully, does not pick up the allusion. Soon they descend into St Ives and drive optimistically straight to the Saline. Half an hour later, their pockets emptied of all loose change, they reach the gallery on foot, having followed the signed paths through the pleasant centre of the town, past the high old walls of Barbara Hepworth's garden where her sculptures are now displayed, up and down steep narrow roads lined with fishermen's cottages, all turned into holiday lets, suddenly emerging at a wall overlooking the surfing beach of Porthmeor, a stone's throw from the gallery.

They entered by means of a low passage underneath the grand circular sweep of glass which formed the inside wall of the atrium – between side pillars the outer wall was open to the elements, an architectural decision usually described as 'brave'. The design reminded Smith of nineteen thirties' Odeon cinemas, but he was told that it was a reference to the storage tank of the gasworks upon the derelict site of which the gallery had been constructed – the sort of reference which, according to Bond, was dear to architects but puzzling to others, especially since the few indigenes who remembered the gasworks did so with little affection.

The entrance, more or less a tunnel, had an awkward feel about it, like the way in which aristocrats usually admit the public to their houses, through some insignificant opening in the rustic, leading to kitchen or domestic offices, seldom up the grand steps and in at the front door. They climbed four flights to reach the exhibition floor, then two down to the curved and glazed display area under which they had entered, then two up again to the far end of the exhibition where Andrew Bond was waiting for them. He was very young for a Professorial Fellow, surprisingly bubbly and enthusiastic, which was all to the good, Anthony thought, since the painting which he was explaining to a small group of Friends of the Saline was a dark and gloomy study of what may have been gargoyles, possibly on a monastery. He came over and introduced himself, mentioning that he of course knew of Frieda and Anthony as collectors, and was also delighted to welcome their friends, whom Anthony briefly introduced as Smith and er-um Bert. Anthony recognised the signs of a man who intended to go places; he was certain that Bond would never have heard of him before Frieda's phone call. It was probably true, however, that he was familiar with Frieda's name; Anthony remembered that she was a trustee of the London, and that might easily have explained Bond's willingness to meet them so expeditiously.

"Shall we go and have some nibbles and a drink? Or would you like to come and have a quick look at these paintings? Morgan was a brilliant painter, he worked here for ages, you know, before he moved back to Lampeter. And of course," he smiled towards Frieda and Anthony, making a small inclusive gesture, "now he's got the appreciation he deserves."

They admired the paintings, then followed him up more stairs to the cafe where he offered them a violent sauvignon, probably from New Zealand, and an assortment of vegetarian pasties. They nibbled in silence for a moment, captivated by the panoramic view of the beach and the tiny black figures of wet-suited surfers catching the evening waves.

"Well now," said Bond, "You mentioned some Hopkinses at a farm in Boselloe. I have heard of them, actually, one of the curators lives out at St Just, and was telling me about them in the Brig a couple of days ago. It's only a farmhouse, I gather, and apparently a foreign chap, Australian I think, rented it last year and used it as a sort of gallery – he even had a Wallis or two, so I was told. I never got round to going out there. There was gossip floating around – well, there always is, isn't there, especially round here, my goodness I've learned to keep my trap shut and my opinions to myself this last three years, slightest word of criticism of something, you know, at a private view or a party, and who do you find standing behind your shoulder but the artist's mother, father, wife, cousin, you name it. Where was I, oh yes, apparently he did a flit or something, left the house in a hell of a mess. But I don't know whether the present chap, Williams, is that right? is after selling them. There's some sort of family connection, apparently. This curator friend of mine knows a dealer who's seen them, he's got the Red Porpoise gallery, mixed quality stuff, but you've got to make a living?...and he rates a painting called the Cherry Picker very highly. It's a Festival painting, he says, one of the Industrial series, why it should be called the Cherry Picker I couldn't say. There's an airport and one of the people's cars series as well, apparently. I'm not very well up in the Festival school, you know; they are supposed to focus rather on the local talent down here, but they're scraping the barrel a bit at the moment, there are only so many angles you can cover. I've arranged to pop over to Boselloe next week, Tuesday I think.

Anthony said, "Yes, we liked the Cherry Picker too. His 'Overseer' is in the London, isn't it? Do you think you could tell us something about it?"

Andrew Bond may have disclaimed expertise in the Festival school, but in fact he knew considerably more about the history of the Overseer than Anthony or Frieda would have expected. He was, after all, a Professorial Fellow. He chewed his pasty for a moment while he organised his thoughts, then, moderating his ebullient manner, told them the painting's history, including a detailed account of the arrangements made with the owner of the factory, an old established firm of agricultural tool manufacturers in the Black Country. There had been a mild disagreement between Hopkins and the owner of the firm over the painting's subject. The present owner's Victorian ancestor had installed, around the middle of the century, one of the very last large steam powered trip hammers. For over a hundred years this enormous machine had been forging spades and hoes to designs which had hardly changed. The massive shaft of the hammer was formed from the trunk of an oak tree, some fifteen feet long, squared off and tied round with iron bands. The operator sat in a sort of shallow metal bucket, suspended like a swing from an overhead gantry, and he pushed himself around the head of the hammer, itself weighing half a ton, by kicking a metal rail attached to the floor. This man, Albert, in his late sixties, was immensely proud of his skill, as was his employer, and they had hoped that Hopkins would be able to use the trip hammer as the focus of his painting. Hopkins had jotted down some of his thoughts in his diary – the subject was fascinating, the lighting very poor but perhaps something could be made of the shadows, and the workman was never still – and (he wrote this in capital letters) it was damned dangerous, no safety precautions at all; then he added, "for him, I mean, not me!" Then he scrawled in the margin of his diary, "And for me too!!"

He had, in any case, wanted to paint one of the new, modern, production lines installed at the behest of a famous international garden tool manufacturer for whom the Black Country firm was a sub-contractor, and whose notions of engineering tolerance were somewhat more exacting than those of Albert and his steam hammer. Their technical Director had visited the previous autumn and quizzed Albert on a number of points, including how many 'thou' he worked to. Albert had smiled, and held up his left thumb, pulled the fleshy ball down to leave the thumbnail projecting, and placed his right index finger on it in such a way as to show the approximate tolerance he considered acceptable. The visitor had blinked a couple of times, smiled back, made a note, and moved on.

After Hopkins and the owner had discussed the subject matter of the proposed painting over what Hopkins recorded in his diary as faggots and mild beer, – although, after Hopkins' death, when the factory owner, still in the saddle at seventy-four, was interviewed for the Dictionary of National Biography, he had suggested that this may have been a joke, and it was more likely to have been grouse and malt whisky – they decided finally on two pictures, one of the new production line and a smaller one of Albert with the trip hammer. The factory owner was going to buy the second picture if he liked it, and they agreed a price in advance, but what that price was, no-one knew. The foreman of the factory, a man who did not hide his authority, featured in the main picture, which was why Hopkins called it 'The Overseer'.

Anthony was surprised and grudgingly impressed by Bond's command of detail, as was Frieda. Smith had been listening intently, Bert had slipped over to the counter and was trying to charm some meatier food from its youthful guardian.

"How did Hopkins work when he was actually painting the Overseer?" Smith asked; Anthony stared at him in surprise, Frieda glanced across to Anthony because they were both aware – he had told them – that he was no expert in these matters. What was he getting at? He picked up their reaction immediately, and expanded his question. "I mean, would he do sketches, take notes, that sort of thing and do the painting in his workshop?" Anthony's lips silently formed the word 'studio'. "...studio, I should say, thank you Anthony, or would he set up his easel in the factory and do the oil painting there?"

Bond had registered all the nuances of the interactions between his visitors, and was particularly courteous in his reply to Smith.

"That's a very interesting question. You would think, wouldn't you, that it would be sensible, especially in what I expect was a cramped and mucky factory, to make sketches and notes of colours, and do the painting in the studio. But actually he hardly ever made sketches, and almost always set up his easel and painted on site; when he did resort to sketches and notes of colours and shading he was never really satisfied with the eventual painting."

Anthony had been impatiently waiting for an opportunity to drop his own twopenn'orth into Bond's torrent, and before Bond could start telling them where Hopkins had bought his paints, and who stretched his canvases for him, he drew attention to his own familiarity with Hopkins' diaries by mentioning a passage where the artist bemoaned what he called his poor visual memory.

Bond screwed his face up in a frown and drew breath. Oh Lord, Anthony thought, perhaps it wasn't Hopkins' diaries, perhaps he was confusing him with some other painter. But Smith spoke first.

"Can a painter really have a poor visual memory? I mean, wouldn't it be like a musician saying he couldn't hold a tune?" Smith asked, directing his question to Frieda, who replied before Bond could start up again.

"I don't know about that, but painters – figurative painters, that is, – and visual memories; no, of course they can't. But Hopkins was comparing himself with Turner and one or two other landscape painters who had outstanding visual memories. Hopkins actually liked to paint in the open air, and possibly he was using the poor memory claim as a bit of an excuse to be out and about with his paint box."

"Why the sudden interest in techniques?" Anthony asked Smith, in a fairly challenging tone. Smith just shrugged and said nothing. Anthony suddenly realised that Bond had only talked about one "Overseer" – with his apparently encyclopaedic knowledge of the painter's oeuvre, surely he would have mentioned that there were two versions? And, of course, that was what Smith must have been getting at, trying to find out if Hopkins might have made another version in the studio. But what was that to Smith? And Smith continued with another question. This was really too much; Anthony had some carefully prepared and perceptive comments to make to Andrew Bond, and this philistine policeman, or whatever he was, was monopolising the conversation quite ruthlessly.

The question was about Hopkins' car paintings, and was along the same lines as his previous questions. But Bond's knowledge of the subject, or his present interest in the topic, had been exhausted, and he gave a fairly meaningless and anodyne response. Perhaps he had been distracted by the approach of a statuesquely beautiful, fortyish lady, dressed with ridiculous success in an artful melange of nineteen fifties sixth-form schoolboy's uniform and Grayson Perry haute couture. Descending upon the group like Artemis from her chariot she linked her arm with that of Bond, who took a moment to regain his balance.

"Andrew dear, you must introduce me to your friends. Are they Friends? New Friends, perhaps? Has he been dazzling you all? He does know a lot, doesn't he?"

She squeezed his arm while demonstrating to the company that as a dazzler Andrew Bond had a lot to learn. Anthony blinked, Smith returned her smile, Bert, about to take a bite of his ham sandwich, temporarily forgot that his mouth was open. Frieda smiled, in a brief and noncommittal sort of way.

Andrew made the introductions. She was called Alison, and was the Chair of the Friends. She was also, apparently, a Romanian Countess; Anthony assumed that she and Bond had been performing in some local light opera, or amateur dramatics, but he was wrong, she was a Countess; however, she never used the title. But, Anthony thought, isn't averse to having it mentioned. She was explaining to Frieda that her husband's surname was just impossible, all 'c's and 'z's and 's's; and he was a Count, but she was just Alison, Countess sounded so absurd!".

"Alison paints herself, you know, she's very good, she does rock pools, don't you, her sea anemones are unparalleled."

This was obviously some old joke between them.

"I sold one the other day, I'll have you know. It had starfish as well, and a blenny."

"Well, jolly good. Where was it?"

"In the Red Porpoise, you know, Hank Edwards. I think he was doing me a favour."

"Surely not," murmured Bond.

"Well, we bought that Hopkins off him, didn't we, so one good turn ..." she said, and, turning to Frieda, "I'm sure we've met; possibly at the Courtauld? That series of talks last year, on forensics, given by Charlie Salterton's bluestocking daughter?"

Frieda nodded, they chatted about common acquaintances. Bond had been buttonholed by a Friend, or had put himself in the way of the Friend, a middle aged man who managed to look both prosperous and artistic. Anthony approached them and hovered, smiling politely at one and then the other, making it obvious that he wanted to join the conversation or speak to one of them, or ask where the lavatory was.

"We were discussing the Howard," said Bond to Anthony, pointing at a bold pattern of hard curves and lines, all red black and yellow.

"Oh" said Anthony, who thought that the works of this distinguished and successful artist would have made attractive curtain designs for nineteen seventies coffee bars.

"You were explaining it to me, more like," said the well-heeled gent, "haven't got the jargon, myself. Can't really see its link to Pinter, sorry."

He waved, possibly to someone the other side of the room, smiled at Anthony, gripped Bond briefly by the arm, and departed. Before Bond could spot some other member of the gathering who might be more important, or more advantageously cultivated, than himself, Anthony quickly took up their previous subject of Hopkins' mode of working, a discussion which had been interrupted by quasi-philosophical musings upon the role of memory in the production of different types of art, by Smith's subsequent interjection, and by the advent of the Countess, who was now munching celery with Frieda. The doubts concerning paintings by Hopkins, of course, which Maurice had passed to Jane, and which she had in turn passed to David by phone in the pub, had first been shared with Anthony on the long, drunken evening at the roadhouse, and David's interjection, although it had annoyed Anthony, had brought up an issue which he thought worth pursuing. He now asked Bond whether, considering Hopkins' preference for painting on site, he often produced more than one version of the same subject. Bond thought not.

"It's possible, I imagine, but he's not known for it – unless my memory – no, I'm fairly sure not."

They agreed that it was a pity that the Catalogue Raisonée of his work was such a poor effort, compiled during the retirement, and gradual mental failure, of a once eminent critic and historian. At this point Alison the Countess, who had given up on the celery and was now eating a sandwich, almost certainly filled with smoked salmon, and which Anthony therefore inferred had been procured for her by Bert, joined them as they were shaking their heads and tut-tutting at the perils of academic procrastination.

"Well," said Anthony, who could hardly have failed to pick up Bond's unspoken signals at her approach, "I mustn't keep you. In the light of what you say, though, I think you should definitely go and have a look at the Hopkinses at Boselloe. I might ring you later."

"How mysterious! Do explain," Anthony heard Alison say to Bond as he sidled through the throng to re-join Smith and Frieda.

David was ready to leave now, he had found out enough to be going on with, and perhaps he would phone Bond later, after Bond had managed to visit Boselloe. Charlie Salterton's bluestocking daughter; that rang a bell; Alan Green's name came into his head – why? Was it important? well, you never knew, it might be worth a phone call. But later. Now, thank God, they could all go home.

Chapter 9

June 26, evening   Henry   Jennifer

"You know, Jennifer, when I was a lad I wouldn't have been able to find you nearly so easily."

"Really?"

"Yes, there would have been smoke everywhere. It seems strange, a fleapit with air conditioning, no cigarettes and no men in macs."

"What would you call that, then?"

Henry was wearing a thin waterproof coat with a belt.

"It's a Burberry. Surely you can tell the difference. I don't expect you can buy mackintoshes these days."

Dame Jennifer had chosen their rendezvous wisely. They sat in a rear corner of the cinema where they could see the entire auditorium. There were, as Jennifer had expected, few other patrons, and they were annoying no-one with their subdued conversation. But why were they there, such senior people?

The present Director General had initiated a policy of random checking, and any member of staff might find him or herself the subject of a vetting procedure which included a week's log of movements. An entire Security Committee meeting had been devoted to the randomisation procedure, and advice had been taken from the Pro-Vice-Chancellor of the University of Westonbirt. This lady was the only person whom the cabinet secretary thought fulfilled the various criteria specified by the Director General. She had started her university career in the Operations Research department of the Warwick Business School, and could be expected to know something about quality assurance methods, she had been vetted (and signed the Official Secrets Act, a legally pointless procedure but one designed to impress the impressionable) and emerged fault-free, and she was known to covet an appointment to the House of Lords (or a seat in the ladies, ha ha, as she joked to weary but career conscious academics in the senior common room).

She had made a number of suggestions. First, in accordance with Quality Assurance theory, if a member of a batch ('team, perhaps', murmured the Second Permanent Secretary of the Ministry of Defence) were to fail – be observed pinching bottoms on the Tube, or passing secrets to the French – then the whole batch should be rejected, or, in this case, vetted individually. This suggestion went down well with the Deputy Assistant Commissioner (Special Branch) who could see an immediate expansion in his empire, but he was a policeman so the mandarins ignored him.

Her second suggestion concerned the DG. If he were privy to the selection procedure then he would know if he had been (randomly) selected and would be able to modify his behaviour accordingly. The DG had been taken aback, but suppressed his annoyance, for which in any case he knew he had no justification. So she suggested that the DG would be vetted about once every – what, three? four? years – they agreed three – but that the selection of which week would be random, and controlled by the Cabinet Secretary.

"So, Professor, will you write the appropriate software for us yourself?" asked the DG.

"Software? You don't need software. Get a tombola drum and keep it in your cupboard. Names on screws of paper. Much more secure than a computer, Good Lord yes."

The DG and the head of Human Resources exchanged glances.

"Do you know how many staff we're talking about, Professor?"

"No, perhaps I should have...about six or seven hundred? I suppose that would be quite a paper twisting exercise!"

"Multiply it by ten, Professor," said the Personnel Director.

The professor recovered quickly and offered to write a simple random selection procedure, but even as she was explaining the rudimentary principles she realised that no useful results would be achieved without an enormous, quite unrealistic, commitment of staff to this internal policing exercise. After a weary discussion they decided to limit the new vetting procedure to staff with a high security clearance in certain 'sensitive' sections.

"That was a fudge, you know," said the Professor to the Director of GCHQ as they were walking across Waterloo Bridge afterwards.

"Yes, of course," he had replied, "but we tend to call it a sensible compromise."

The upshot of all this was that everybody in Henry's and Jennifer's sections had started to behave like spies again, especially when, like Henry and Jennifer, they were balancing on the cusp of transgression.

"Henry," said Jennifer, as a naked Swede crunched across the snow in the twilight, from sauna to log cabin, "cast your mind back to lunchtime today. I'm sure you remember the two young ladies who joined us?"

"Of course."

"I presume you found them attractive?"

"What!"

"There were two young ladies, one straight out of, I can hardly use the term, *you-knee*, and the other rather more mature, quietly dressed, dark hair, mixed ethnic background. Now I infer from the way you were staring at the blonde one's bosom that you found her appealing, but I would like to make sure that the other lady was also attractive to persons of your sex, orientation and, ah, ethnicity. Incidentally, I'm sure the blonde one knew who you were."

"Yes, of course she did. Yes, she was very pretty. Attractive. So was the other one, if not quite so obvious. Ethnicity? This is a very non-PC conversation, Jennifer."

"We are above such matters, Henry. You would agree then, that the dark haired lady, who has only this very afternoon joined my little team, would be found attractive by the majority of your gender?"

"Yes, I would." He sighed. "Oh dear, I've never got used to it, you know."

"Do you really mean, Henry, that you would expect them to put their lives on the line, but not their fannies?"

"Well, Jennifer, put like that, it does seem somewhat illogical, I agree."

"And, goodness me, Henry, it's Armstrong we're considering, not some randy Serbian colonel. I merely wish her to use her quiet charm to insinuate herself marginally further into his household than were she to resemble a Bulgarian weight lifter."

"How will you get her in?"

"Armstrong has a protection unit of six officers, two being on duty at any one time. I propose to substitute Jane Ryan for one of these. She can always work with the senior officer – Armstrong gets an inspector, most of them only have a sergeant – and Armstrong can be informed that she is in training. Clearly, we can't take the risk that harm might come to him when Ryan is on duty – because, you know, she might not quite understand exactly how to throw her body in the way of an assassin's bullet – so we must arrange additional protection. I'll naturally leave all these details to one of your departments, but I suggest that pro tem she reports directly to me. I'll brief her; I think that as far as she's concerned you should remain a shadowy figure in the background, don't you?"

"Haven't you anyone else with more experience?"

"What makes you think she's inexperienced? Just because she was lunching with the very young lady *au grand décolletage*? Why do you think she's been attached to my branch?"

"What's she done, then?"

"Come along Henry, Davies's one of yours. The Breezeblock affair? Rather advanced ordnance finding its way via East Africa to nasty-land? Davies's outfit winkled our intel on that in an exceptionally traditional manner. But, of course, Breezeblock is – was – an Arab, and might have had somewhat different...and we had taken pains to learn that he was not very discriminating in his..." Her speech tailed off, and Henry quickly replied.

"Yes, of course. Davies kept that one rather close to his chest. Until I had to authorise Oliver's involvement, of course."

"You did a spell in South Wales, didn't you?"

"Short spell. Oliver and I came in together, he stayed. I got out. They're barmy, you know."

"Oliver too? Now he's a general? I've always found him most amenable."

"Barmy enough. They're not all barmy, I was exaggerating. I don't mean barmy. I mean exceptional. David, for example. But you know that."

"David was involved in Breezeblock wasn't he?"

"Only at the end. Very involved, you might say. But – I remember Simon's report, he said the officer was relatively inexperienced, I don't remember her name. So it was Ryan?"

"Yes"

"Jennifer, I may notice whether a lass is pretty or not, and I can assure you that Ryan is, but as I have just mentioned I have always found entrapment very distasteful. Sorry to sound pompous."

"Not at all. I do pompous all the time. It makes for clarity. Simon doesn't share your views, neither do I."

"Lie back and think of England?"

"Well, you know, I don't enquire; perhaps, in the Breezeblock case, perhaps not – I'm not even sure that Davies knows – but it will be neither necessary nor indeed permissible in this operation. Good heavens, Henry; Armstrong!"

They both took a short time to mull over the possible, appalling, ramifications if an unauthorised project should result in a liaison between a secret service operative and the Deputy Prime Minister.

Jennifer broke the silence. She looked at Henry, almost as if she was concerned to have his good opinion.

"They're instructed always to use condoms, you know, it's in the manual," she said.

"Yes. Very caring."

"And girls aren't so fussy these days".

"How do you know? You haven't got a daughter, have you?"

"No, Henry. Women in my position didn't go in for AI and babies thirty years ago."

"Well I have," said Henry, but he sighed. "I'm probably being both sexist and hypocritical. When have we ever given a damn for the women in relationships made by the *men* we have in deep cover? Left high and dry when we call the men in? Pregnant once, I think. He didn't use a condom, did he? Did we look after her? No, we didn't. And do we offer the *men* counselling at the debrief? I can't remember; it's a long time since I did one; I don't think I've ever seen it referred to in a report."

"Yes, Henry, we do, but as far as I know the offer's never been taken up. By a man."

An old memory, a little vague, rose to the surface of Henry's mind.

"I seem to remember, Jennifer, that a member of Five, as it then was, formed an attachment to a well-known ban the bomber after Thatcher beat Callaghan in 1979? In fact..."

"Yes, Henry, I remember that too."

"Was it useful? Did it help? Who broke it off ? Or did they just drift apart?"

"Really Henry! The reports were made, as instructed. I don't know how useful it was. I was very junior." She frowned, irritated, not just with him. "We all know now that CND was a spent force in the eighties. Most of us knew it then, too. But Jefferson had just taken over as head of the civil service, we didn't know much about Thatcher, but we were damn sure she wouldn't like to learn that any threat was being downplayed; Sir Joseph would get it in the neck and then so would we. It was all a bit futile. The lady in question knew nothing much, because there wasn't much to know. She kept doing silly things and getting sent to prison for a week or two, that's all. And they didn't drift apart, our officer was pulled out and spent the next six months in Paris and then put on a tedious internal security rotation. Perhaps they thought she might fall in love; go native."

"She?"

Jennifer frowned. "I think, Henry, that you know damn well who we're talking about."

"Well, yes, but I wasn't quite certain. I'd only just joined."

"The Met SDS does it all the time; they don't have any silly scruples."

"Yes, of course I accept it may be necessary. I've been behind a desk most of my life, you see, you're much more au fait with realities in the field."

"Falklands, Henry? Desert Storm? Had a *desk* in Kuwait in '92, did you?"

"That was different. Boy's Own stuff."

"Come off it, Henry."

"Well, there it is. Back to Armstrong. When I spoke to the Chief, I mentioned his Bridget Riley. He's only acquired this quite recently, I believe. But he's apparently got quite a collection, Modern British, generally speaking, which he could have bought before they went stratospheric – well, tropospheric – but he's also got a small Turner. When did he buy that? How much did he pay? I think your Jane will have to acquire a passion for art. Could she have a crash course with the Met art squad, do you think?"

"Good idea. Can you fix it?"

"Of course."

"At what stage, Henry, will you seek authorisation from Richard?"

"Maybe at a slightly later stage than is customary, do you think?"

"I take your point. I imagine you've touched on the issue with him?"

"Oh yes."

Henry explained about the note from Winterbottom. Jennifer looked slightly surprised when she learned that the discussion had taken place at an off the record meeting, since such meetings were supposed to be confidential between the participants, but it was clear that she understood C's arm's length approach.

"Watching his back?"

"Exactly. So we must be very careful. A cover story ready for every occasion."

"At least one. Possibly even a fall-back."

"What shall we call it?"

"Typewriter?"

"Very apt."

"Jennifer, why has the screen gone black?"

"It's one of their dogmas, Henry – Dogme films, you've heard of them? No artificial lighting. Good job too, from the sound of it. Not very decorative, were they? Bibi Andersson, now, she was my idea of a Swedish beauty."

"Still is, Jennifer, I believe."

"Yes, indeed."

As the bleak Scandinavian dawn slowly illuminated the lakeside cabin, jerkily revealing the expected scene of rumpled sheets and breathy congress, Henry crept from the cinema. Jennifer stayed; her partner was out somewhere that night. Henry had left his car nearby, and its windscreen had collected a parking ticket. He tore it off and threw it into a litter bin. He never received any demands for payment; his registration mark had a little flag in the DVLA computer. At home in St John's Wood he settled down to watch Newsnight, with a Famous Grouse and his wife of thirty years.

June 28   A security officer   Jane   Jennifer   Sophia Adeleke

"Sit down please."

The man from Internal Security, or some such organisation which didn't feature in the staff list, indicated a straight backed chair on the other side of the desk. He held a small notebook computer, and the desk was bare. This room was clearly not his office. There were two chairs, which looked reasonably comfortable, either side of a table above which hung a dark engraving of a bearded man with a ruff.

"We have, as you are of course aware, followed up various items of information which you gave us at your induction. And I have here the various questionnaires" – he pronounced it kestyonair – "which you have completed. I also have your report upon the Breezeblock affair, and a memorandum, almost completely favourable you may be pleased to learn, from Mr Davies concerning your involvement. Let me see – if I can grope my way through this fricassé of metaphors, Davies writes for the Police Gazette, you know, under a pseudonym, of course – here it is, – *in at the deep end – swimming strongly*, – *emerging intact* – well, really, I feel that this was a very sensitive business to immerse you in so early in your career." He looked at her and asked sharply, "Were you *comfortable* with the Breezeblock business?"

"Not to start with. I was nervous. But it all happened in Lille and Munich, not Egypt, and Simon had arranged the fall backs, so I don't think I was physically scared. It was no big deal."

The man blinked. "No big deal. Really. Is that how you've decided to describe it, or do you really mean what you say?"

"Both."

Jane's report on the operation had been terse; no more detail than necessary, except for the accounts of the conversations which had revealed the information the Service wanted, which were given almost verbatim. Her debrief had been similar, her interview with the shrink a formality.

"Not to put too fine a point on it, Miss Ryan, if necessary, would you have..."

"Yes of course. But I shan't always be twenty-seven, and I wouldn't like to think that my career will fade with my figure."

The man delayed his response. Most young female field officers usually replied "If necessary" and didn't interrupt his question. He was also wondering whether, even if she meant what she said now, she would be so clear about her duty in the field. Luckily, he thought, this was a judgment he didn't have to make, he just had to ask the questions. Perhaps now was the time to stir her up a little, dent her composure.

"I see that Simon has noted that he was very good looking."

"Is that supposed to have made a difference? What a very... what are you smiling for? I know; he didn't write that, did he? So why did you..."

"Just checking."

Jane felt annoyed, as she was meant to, and she realised this. It didn't take too much effort to regain a calm appearance, but she was still irritated, mainly with herself.

"Why don't we sit over there?" she said, "This chair is very uncomfortable."

"Yes, I know" he said, but didn't move. "Can we talk a little about your background?"

"What else do you want to know? It's all down in that file."

"Perhaps a little more detail. After all, you are going to work in Temporary Initiatives. Quite a lot of prestige attached to that. Worth answering a few personal questions, don't you think?"

"Yes, of course." Why did he want her to be uncomfortable? Was he going to needle her, see how she reacted? Should she keep cool? And indeed, would she actually *feel* any genuine anger? These situations, so artificial, could produce surprises, one way or the other. After the Breezeblock business, she had undergone routine counselling from the Department's shrink. She had been recalling the progress of their relationship and had been asked how she had reacted to a suggestion from him – how did you *feel* about that, Jane? – and she answered, truthfully, what her response had been. She expected him to nod wisely and say "Yes, yes, I see" or something equally anodyne, but he rocked back in his chair and said "You didn't, did you? Bloody hell!" quite puncturing the sympathetic little balloon he had so gently inflated.

The internal security man's next questions were simply answered, with more details about her upbringing and education, then there followed questions about what he called her 'perceived ethnic identity and cultural heritage'. Did she have a chip on her shoulder, she thought was the issue here. These questions were also easy to answer. She spoke of her childhood in Oxford, where her mother, who was single, and her mother's friends, and their children with whom she was at school, had obviously been her strongest cultural influence. She felt no loss because she didn't enjoy rap or diddley diddley.

"Diddley diddley?"

"Irish fiddle music. You know, Guinness and weddings."

"But isn't 'cultural heritage' a rather wider concept? Morals, religion?"

"Table manners, bedtimes, drugs of choice?"

"Yes, if you like"

"Honesty? *Patriotism*?

The man spoke carefully. This was of course the central question. He would have preferred to have raised it himself. "But surely all cultures value honesty?"

"Only to a degree. You know fine well that some cultures put blood ties first. But you can take it I do – value honesty, that is, and that I see that as a moral issue. Transcending culture, if you like. When are you going to get round to patriotism? The great cricket-team question."

"Now, if you like. In fact, let's use the concepts you have brought up yourself. Would you be dishonest, tell lies, in the interests of Britain?"

"Yes of course. I don't believe in moral absolutes. And I already have done, as you know. Perhaps the commonest lie a woman can tell, mind you."

He seemed satisfied. They discussed different interpretations of honesty; she dredged up some rather jumbled memories of the philosopher Hume's thoughts on the matter – she had forgotten most of the ethics module of her degree. He was easily convinced that her background, mixed race and mixed nationality had left her with no psychological scars. She spoke, indeed, of hybrid vigour; he blinked again, then laughed. This was all plain sailing, she felt. Then he said,

"Why are you called Ryan?"

"What do you mean? It's my name; my father's name."

"Your mother's name is Adeleke."

"But my father's name was Ryan."

"Your father's name was Morrison. Patrick Morrison."

"What do you mean? It was Ryan! He died when I was eighteen months old! My mother kept her maiden name because she's an academic, they almost always do because that's the name they've written under, but I didn't, obviously. My father's name was Cormac Ryan. Wasn't it?"

"No Jane. It was Patrick Morrison"

"I've got a passport. I've had one since I was nine. This is ridiculous. I don't understand what you're saying."

"Have you got a birth certificate?"

"No, my mother must have it. I've always used my passport. I only just managed to be born in England, you know that, my parents came over from Ireland when Mum was six months gone. My mother was naturalised, she says it took her eight years to become British."

"So you think that your father died in England after eighteen months or so?"

"No, he died on a trip home to see his parents in Roscommon, he had a heart attack."

Jane was very shaken. She asked him, "What do you – what makes you think that my Dad was called...?"

"Patrick Morrison. We think that your mother has, for some reason, concealed your father's identity from you."

He waited for her response. Eventually she asked, "How do you know any of this – if it's true?"

He didn't reply immediately. For a few seconds they stared at each other.

"We always investigate the families of field officers, and especially carefully when they are likely to be assigned to, how shall I say, delicate tasks."

He continued, speaking quietly, and carefully.

"At the relevant time, only two Cormac Ryans lived in or near Wallasey, where you stayed until your mother moved you both to Oxford. They are married, and live there still; neither could be your father, one because he is too old."

"What about the other?"

"DNA testing, of course."

"How on earth...?"

"Quite easily. Routine, really. We already have yours, of course. Well, having established that, we looked for but couldn't find his grave or any trace of his parents in Roscommon. We rather ran out of steam when we searched the Irish records, and your mother told us that she seemed to have lost his death certificate."

"My mother! When did you see her?"

"Only a phone call. She wasn't surprised we were making more inquiries about you. She seems very – assured, no, authoritative, rather?"

"Of course she is. She's the Duke Humphrey Professor of Letters."

"Well, she couldn't help us much. Gave us the name of the street in Wallasey where you lived, and would you believe it, it was all redeveloped ten years ago. Not a brick standing."

"So, what about this Morrison? How do you know he's my father? Why should Mum lie to me?"

"After we'd failed in Ireland we asked – well, I won't tell you whom – to pay a visit to Wallasey Hospital to look through Maternity records just in case anything relevant turned up."

"Are you allowed to do that?"

"*Greater good* argument, Jane. Like the DNA sample. Usual subterfuge, youngish chap, white coat, stethoscope, tale about some GP worried a condition of one of his patients might be linked to a delivery problem."

"Surely they'd realise he wasn't a doctor?"

"Who said he wasn't a doctor?"

"Good God. I know nothing, do I? But why not use DOR 34/7?"

"Ah, Jane, DOR 34 is a precious jewel, guarded from the public eye and only brought out on very, very special occasions. In any case, it usually takes longer and it's not such fun, is it? At any rate, he eventually found the file, and in the ante-natal notes a midwife had written "Sophia accompanied today by baby's father, v. young, Irish from Culcenny (??), Patrick(?) Morrison, said it was his birthday, left before Sophia. S wouldn't talk about him."

"Did this man die, then; die less than two years later, like I was told? Is he still alive? Why did Mum change his name – give it on the birth certificate, too?" She sat quite still for a moment, biting her lower lip and blinking. The man also sat still, as if waiting for her to continue, but since she remained quiet he answered her questions.

"We don't know why she changed the name. No, he is not still alive. Patrick Morrison, from Kilkenny, moved to Newry in 1974 and died, stabbed, in a bar fight in 1977. He was 26. I'm very sorry." The man leaned back and waited.

Jane had mastered her emotions – exactly what emotions they were she would have to work out later, she decided – but now she was suspicious and becoming angry.

"Why should you be sorry?"

"Because I've had to tell you of your father's death, of course."

"But I already thought he was dead."

"Raising your hopes – dashing them again?"

"Shall I tell you what I think? You thought – think – that I knew why my mother registered a false name; that I knew about my father and...well, what then? It was just a bar fight? He hadn't... upset anyone, any..."

"Group or other? In Northern Ireland? In the seventies? What can you be thinking of?"

"Is that your idea of humour? – I'm sorry, I apologise; surely, there's no... why did he move to Newry?"

"Just a job, we think."

The man waited, to make sure that Jane's expression, and changes of expression, were captured by the video camera located behind the left eye of the sixteenth century gentleman in the ruff.

"So why should Mum change his name? How old was he when I was born?"

"Twenty two"

"Same as my mother."

"Yes"

"Do you believe me? That I didn't know about him? Will you take the risk? What is the risk? That he was killed by the loyalists and I'm after revenge?"

Jane was angry now, and didn't conceal it.

"I could get a normal job, a sensible job, earning a damn sight more than I'm ever likely to in this miserable circus. Why should I bother? Or will I be marked now?"

"That's not for me to say. You *want* to work here, don't you?"

"Of course I do. You must know that by now. But it's obvious that you're wondering why. I've told you the truth, I thought my father died soon after I was born. I shan't say it again. I presume that you can't do anything as unguarded as to tell me whether you believe me?"

"Your presumption is correct." He smiled, a little, with no artifice. "Perhaps we shall meet again, in corridor or canteen. Not, alas, in Paris or Rome. I have a depressingly parochial role."

"When will whomever you report to make a decision?"

"I can't tell you that, I'm sorry"

They left together. As they passed in front of the painting, Jane asked who it was, and why it was there.

"Francis Walsingham."

"Oh God, whose clever idea was that? It's a bit the worse for wear, isn't it?"

"It's only a Victorian etching, nothing valuable. What a man though. The very first C."

*****

They had watched the video of the interview twice, on both occasions pausing and re – running the moments after the first use of Morrison's name. Jennifer turned to Hardwick Reynolds, a psychiatrist, among other things their body language man, and asked him for his opinion.

"I believe her," he said, "Cunning questions. Got under her skin, all right, no feigning there. She's OK."

"You couldn't be influenced at all – now don't take this the wrong way – she's very attractive, isn't she?"

Reynolds did not take this question the right way, whatever that might have been, was not pleased, and told her so.

"I'm sorry, Hardy. I've got to be sure about her."

"She'll go straight to see her mother, bound to. She's probably phoned her already."

"She has, yes. But she hasn't said why, just arranged to see her in her rooms at Jesus."

"What if she rings again? Goes into more detail?"

"She won't get through, or her mother will be busy. The Master of Cranmer has asked her to go and see him urgently about a problem on the Examination Committee they both sit on. It's a storm in a tea cup, of course, but I expect he'll wine and dine her afterwards, and keep her late."

"Convenient. How do you know? Ah, silly me."

"The Master of Cranmer is one of our favourites. Now, he's kosher if you like. Hardy, I would like you to eavesdrop on, observe even, the meeting between our Jane and her illustrious ma tomorrow morning."

"Short notice, isn't it? Can you set it up so soon?"

"Arranging the audio is trivial, but I would naturally like you to have vision as well. It is Oxford; as you know, we have a number of talented friends there. Cambridge too, of course, for the more off-piste occasions. I'm sure we shall manage something."

*****

Jane arrived earlier than her mother had expected, just as the Junior Dean of Laud, who had called to ask her opinion on a paper he was hoping to submit to the *New Pedant*, was leaving. He smiled and made a little 'I'm in a bit of a hurry' gesture as they crossed on the staircase. Jane and her mother embraced, more briefly than normal, and as Professor Adeleke poured coffee she asked her daughter how she was faring in the Foreign Office. She had naturally inferred from the abrupt way in which Jane had spoken on the phone, and her obvious anxiety now, that all was not well. She half hoped that the problem concerned her work, or her rent, or mortgage; she didn't know anything about her daughter's finances, and when she had handed over a large sum of money, the amount of which she couldn't remember now, she hadn't asked what it might be used for. (It had, of course, been a difficult time for her, what with that disappointing portrait for the National, and the undignified television spat with Amis *père*.) She would have been more comfortable with a practical problem than an emotional one. After she had discovered Morrison's deceit, and had run from him, six months pregnant with Jane, she had been careful to construct an image of the cool aloof intellectual whose career would only be impeded by personal attachments. Jane understood this, and secretly treasured the contrast between the poise and gravitas of her own mother and the chirruping gossip of her school friends' parents. Jane had tried hard, and had been on the whole successful, to conceal this opinion, because she was a sensible little girl, and knew how important it was for a single parent to cultivate and cherish a network of friends.

But Jane would have been amazed, then and later, to learn of Sophia's worry that her protective shell might also to a degree have excluded her daughter. Sophia had actually always been a perfectly normal, good mother, caring and loving. She just worried that she wasn't. When she was tired, bad tempered or cross with Jane she tended to attribute her mood to what she saw as her self-imposed chilliness of character, instead of ordinary features of life, like a week's hard work and the unrelieved care of a clever, talkative girl who was not especially naughty but no Little Nell.

Jane felt that she had no reason to soft pedal, to lead up gradually to her question.

"Mum, who was my father, and why am I called Ryan?"

For a long moment Sophia did not answer. She thought, why in God's name did I do this to her? And then, why didn't I tell her? Well, I know why, it never occurred to me she'd find out; of course I should have realised these FO people would poke around. How angry will she be? What was I thinking of, I must have been deranged.

"Your father was not called Ryan. He was called Morrison. Patrick Morrison. You never knew him. I left him three months before you were born." She used language now to her daughter, the only person in the world whom she loved, language of a sort which she had only ever referred to, read in poetry, written, discussed with her students, but had not used herself, for nearly thirty years. "I loved him, Jane, I loved him more than I thought possible, I was consumed by my love. You've never felt this, have you, Jane?"

Jane shook her head.

"And I thought he loved me, the same. But I found out he didn't. I followed him, I stood in the rain outside their house and I saw their shadows against the curtain of the upstairs window. I heard their voices. In my mind's eye I could see them, naked in bed, and I still shiver at the memory of my pain. I went home, it was only a bedsit, I picked up my purse and I left."

Jane said, unguardedly, "What about all your things?"

"What things? We had nothing. I stayed with a friend for a night, I took a boat to England, rented a room in Wallasey, got a filthy job in a canteen, and I managed. He found me a bit later, came to the clinic with me; but anyone could see he didn't love me. He probably never had done – and to my amazement I felt nothing for him. How such intensity of feeling could just have vanished I find it difficult to understand. But it had. He left the same day and I never saw or heard from him again."

She stood up and walked to the window. Undergraduates were already queuing at the buttery for sandwiches, noisy rowing men drinking beer and clustered round their dainty coxes. The Senior Tutor fluttered, black and bat-like, through the screens passage to the inner quadrangle. Sophia had written her dissertation at night, during the hours when Jane was asleep; precious, precious few hours for the first year or so. During the day she earned a pittance as a child carer herself; she was always exhausted, often hungry. She lived on bread, milk, tinned beans and potatoes. But she had sailed through her doctorate, surprised only by the poor quality, the general lack of sensitivity, of her university teachers. She found that she could perceive immediately, intuitively, layered rafts of meaning in literature which she often had to explain, carefully and methodically, to her own supervisors. Her thesis, on aspects of twentieth century American poetry, was published with a famous imprint and she had not needed to apply for a job in her entire career.

"But – do you know what happened to him; my father? Please tell me what you know."

"I don't know anything. I stopped myself wondering about him, then I just stopped wondering. I never went back to Ireland after my DPhil."

"But why aren't I called Morrison? Or Adeleke?"

"Yes, I'm sorry, you should have my name. I was so angry, I wasn't going to let you have his name, and then, well, they asked who the father was, so..."

"But why Ryan for God's sake?"

"I'm sorry, it seems childish now. But you see, Patrick behaved just like a character in a poem by Elizabeth Bishop, you know – no, you don't, do you – an American poet laureate who wrote some poems from the point of view of blacks, 'colored', she called us, that was the term then. In one of them a man called Leroy does the dirty on his woman, and she leaves him.

"Please, Mum, I read economics, not literature."

"Isn't it obvious? Leroy, French; Ryan, Irish. Both mean King."

"Yeah, well Mum, I dare say it was a very stressful time for you. Still it doesn't really have any significance, does it? It's just a name."

"Just a name, dear. No person, no connection. Just your mother, angry and stupid. Do you wonder I never told you? All I feel now is embarrassment."

"Mum, come and sit here."

Jane made room for her mother on the small settee, and then, when her mother didn't move, she stood up, went over and took her hand.

"Mum, sit with me, please."

They sat together in silence for a while.

"Mum, why don't we go and have lunch by the river? Can we buy a picnic?"

"That would be lovely, yes, really lovely." She started to get up, then paused. "Why did you come, Jane, why was it suddenly important? Oh, I'm sorry, of course it was important, and I should have told you ages ago, but when I hadn't, then it just seemed, how shall I put it, its importance seemed to fade with the years. But now I'm so glad you have come. And you don't seem angry – are you?"

"No, no I'm not. You're right, it doesn't seem so important, really. But I'm having an interview at work, and they're asking all sorts of questions. Look, I'll go down and get something from the buttery."

"That's a good idea darling, thank you. I've got a seminar at two, but we'll have time to go to the Meadows."

Her visitor, the Junior Dean of Laud, had forgotten his briefcase, so Sophia picked it up and said she would drop it in for him after lunch. Jane took it from her; it was heavy with books and, presumably, essays.

Down by the river they sat on a bench and watched the rowers. Sophia, her spirits lifted, felt close to her daughter. She giggled.

"Gorgeous, aren't they?"

"Mum! Yes, of course they are."

After a moment, Jane said, "I've something to tell you now, about my father. Patrick Morrison."

"Have you? How can you? Yes, yes, I should have realised. They must be vetting you very thoroughly."

"You know about vetting?"

"Of course. I've often been interviewed about past students. I think most of us have, one time or another. I suppose it's because he's Irish?"

"Yes. They found out about Morrison from the antenatal records."

"Good heavens. Are you going into the PM's office, or something?" She beamed, momentarily delighted at the thought of her daughter's career advancing.

"Or something. But Mum, they gave me bad news about him."

"They actually found him? What's happened to him?"

"Mum, I'm really sorry. He died fifteen years ago."

"Oh. Oh dear. Oh, that's terrible. Oh, Jane."

She held her daughter's hand tightly. She bit her lower lip hard, but could not prevent her tears.

"How?"

"He was knifed in a bar fight. He'd moved to Newry."

"Good God. He was a bit of a drinker, but still... Newry. His woman came from the North."

"Mum, did he ever have anything to do with the Fenians?"

"No, of course not. Why, are they worried?"

"You mean the vetting people?"

"Yes"

"I don't know. Yes, I think so."

"It's inconceivable. He used to make jokes – he was never really serious about anything, he danced and fiddled through life, he found someone else when he realised that being a parent was going to be serious. Well, I suppose that's why he did it, it's what I always thought. I remember what he said once, he said that Ireland would be a wonderful place if it wasn't for the politics, the church and the rain. It was the music he liked, and the drink, of course. We were miles from the border, he never had anything to do with the Fenians, or any of them. He used to sit in a bar, play his jigs and drink stout."

"You said you didn't feel anything for him, when you last met?"

"That's right, it wasn't the same... you've got to let me have a little weep, darling, it wouldn't be natural..."

"I suppose I feel sad, but I think it's just for you, Mum. It was a long time ago."

"You're right, it was a long time ago. He was very good looking, you know. Dark and thin, with a light in his eyes. Not like those, those pit-props over there."

June 30   Henry   Jennifer   Charles   David

"Hunky blokes, Jennifer", the Deputy Director said, predictably, to the Policy Adviser.

"Not quite my *tasse de thé*, Henry," she replied, to humour him. "Still, at least we got the sound. We were lucky she lugged that case along, we could hardly expect her to line up the lens. What did you think, Dr Reynolds?"

The psychiatrist was quite happy. He had observed the interaction between mother and daughter in the college room, and he felt that neither was concealing anything significant.

"You can discount an Irish link. It's not important. You needn't bother to trace the man who knifed him, if you haven't already done so, that is. But, I mean, all that Leroy-Ryan stuff. Potty lot on the whole, academics, wouldn't you say?"

"Come on Hardy, you've got an honorary something-or-other at UCL, haven't you?"

"Yes, but I'm a *medical* doctor, that's different."

Jennifer found this rather annoying, but forbore to reply. He might have been joking. She asked him to write a short note for the file, and they went their various ways.

As they walked down the corridor together, Henry asked Jennifer whether she had, in fact, traced the man who had killed Morrison.

"Yes, of course we have, what *do* you take us for? No political connections at all. Just a blackguard, Henry."

"It's nice to be sure."

"It is indeed. I am."

In her outer office Jennifer told Charles, her personal assistant, that Jane Ryan would be joining them shortly; would he please ask David MacMaster to step in when he had a moment? Oh, and by the way, could Charles ask Resources to find Ryan a computer and a coffee mug?

"And a bunch of flowers, Jennifer?"

"No, Charles; perhaps a small pot plant? What a nice thought."

Damn, thought Charles as he took the five pound note, would he never learn? Now he would have to waste time buying a wretched plant in his lunch hour.

David MacMaster found that he did, in fact, have a moment to spare for Dame Jennifer, and hurried to her room. He had been expecting a summons since the previous afternoon, when she had stopped him in the corridor and intimated that a new, short term, project was on the blocks, and that he should temporarily clear his desk. His physical desk was usually clear, because most of his paperwork was stamped secret and a modicum of official disapproval attended the practice of leaving such documents in full view of the unwashed. Not that there was much paper these days. His computer files were as secure as the in-house IT department could contrive; secure, as the Deputy Director was prone to complain, from everyone except teenage hackers in Hartlepool and the entire Chinese nation. Upon David's virtual desk lay an unsavoury urologist in Kiev who was treating a senior member of the Ukrainian government in complete confidence, and one or two less productive sources in the fissile mess of the old Yugoslavia. One small project would be completed later on that day. There were odds and sods, of course, badly fraying loose ends, mistrusted intelligence, but nothing of importance. Like a number of his colleagues he was learning Arabic, and hoped soon to be transferred to more exacting, and exciting, duties in the Middle East, or North Africa. For the time being, therefore, he transferred the relevant files to a caretaker, together with a few tips upon how to deal with the individuals involved.

Jennifer's new project surprised him. His first reaction was annoyance. Why the Service? Why not the Branch?

"I can understand," she said, "that you might think this work, on the face of it, demeaning. It should be an easy enough exercise, and will probably turn up nothing more than a legacy received by his wife, or some very clever investments he made some time ago. The reason that Henry wants us to do it is, simply, internal secrecy. If Armstrong is squeaky clean, but finds out what we've been up to, then gibbets will be erected, and bowels drawn. I expect the Branch could manage the task, could find out the facts, but I'm honestly not confident that they could achieve this in complete secrecy. They're not bad at what they do, we know that, but fundamentally they're plod. In any case, if they bungled I doubt if they would be prepared to walk to the scaffold unaccompanied. And I've asked you because Henry and I feel that you'll work well with Jane Ryan, who's very professional, just been double vetted, and showed extreme discretion in her handling of the Breezeblock affair."

"Ah, that was her, was it? But Jennifer, if this project is so risky, and I detect from your demeanour that it doesn't exactly have Sir Richard's explicit approval, let alone the PM's, why are you putting yourself – and us, I dare say – on the line for it?"

"David, why don't you answer that question yourself?"

David thought for a moment.

"Well, Jennifer, I live in a fairly scruffy flat in Notting Hill. My neighbours think I'm on grade C in the Foreign Office. I imagine that's my salary equivalent. I drink, occasionally, in the Dog and Bucket, and I can usually pay my round, but I have to make my excuses when the accountants and solicitors come in. I drive a five year old Volkswagen, and I don't often take girls to posh restaurants. If I were married, and had kids, we would definitely have to move out into the sticks. I can never get drunk – not that I particularly want to – and I can never talk about, moan about, my work, to anyone, ever. I shall never have much money; my father, as you know, is a retired clergyman. Maybe, perhaps, I may gain a small mention in the Honours list in twenty years time. So I must do it because I think it's worth doing? Is that it?"

"Yes, David, that's it. Ah, Jane, come in and meet David MacMaster. You'll be working with him to start with."

"I can see why Jennifer's group is called Ticklish Issues," said Jane as she and David walked back to the large open plan office where Jane had been allotted a few square metres. "I'm still not quite sure who'll get it in the neck if it all goes wrong. Jennifer seemed to be warning us that the entire section would be bundled into a cart and towed off to Tyburn. D'you know David, that hardly seems fair, does it?"

They both laughed. Fairness was a concept of limited value in their line of work.

"I think she was laying it on a bit thick, actually," said David, "In my experience we tend not to go in for scapegoating; Henry and Jennifer would, theoretically, carry the can, but I'm sure that Henry has cobbled together a fire escape. We'll just have to be very careful. When did Jennifer say you get seconded to Armstrong's protection unit?"

"After my week with the Art squad at the Met. I'm looking forward to that. I can't quite visualise arty farty policemen."

"Or policewomen. I wish Jennifer wouldn't talk about the plod. They're not all Territorial Support Group heavies. I've worked with some very good coppers; Branch and Serious Crimes. Alan Green – he fixed up your visit to the Art Squad – told me that he met some seriously bright types when he was working on the Case of the Duke's Vermeer."

"The what?" She laughed. "That sounds like Conan Doyle."

"Yes, well, we thought so too. We got involved because the cousins asked us. Reading between the lines, they were worried that Hinfangle had somehow arranged the theft. He hadn't, of course. It was a sudden panic of the Vice-President."

"Hinfangle's a collector, isn't he? Hasn't he set up a gallery in Wisconsin, a bit like the Getty?"

"Yes; and he's a crook, and he's one of the White House's biggest contributors. Still, it was nothing to do with him. It was an insurance job; the Duke of Redgrave got his Aquarium back, Moon Mutual paid the ransom, and the thieves, well, who knows?"

"Look," said Jane. "Someone's put a cactus on my desk. On the laptop. That's new."

"You haven't met Charles yet? Jennifer's PA?"
"No; should I?"

"You will. Best to keep on his right side. Bit of an old woman. Person. Sorry."

"I know what you mean. It never works the other way round, does it?"

"Hmm. 'She's a bit of an old man.' No, it doesn't conjure up any image, does it? Certainly not Jennifer."

"Jennifer – and Henry – are almost a generation older than us, aren't they; what were they doing at our age?"

"Cold war and Ireland. Very hairy. Jennifer did a bit of infiltration at home, hated that, did a spell in Paris, then ended up in Belfast, Henry played havoc with the STASI – Scarlet Pimpernel stuff, I've been told. Then Henry was dropped into Argentina in '82."

"Wow. That's impressive. And now …"

"Tell you what, let's put the old warriors out to grass. I'll be Director, what do you want to be?"

"Actually, I've always wanted to be an opera singer. Can I be Renée Fleming?"

"We'll give the canteen a miss, what do you think? We could go and feed the ducks."

*****

They sat in the Park eating their sandwiches, and Jane told David about her recent meeting with her mother, and their lunch by the Isis.

"As you're lead officer, do you get to read the report that Internal Security made?" she asked.

"Good Lord no. I suppose Jennifer sees it, but I'm not even sure of that. It's a sort of grey hole, Internal Security, but they obviously gave you a tick or you wouldn't be on this job. Why did they need to double vet you?"

She told him about her father, and her mother's convoluted choice of surname for her. He laughed and suggested that a lot of learning was possibly quite as dangerous as a little. Then he thought that maybe his response had been too flippant.

"No, not at all. I don't think I care what I'm called. My mother and I seemed very close after she told me, and this really pleased her. I've always felt close to her, mind you; I think she's been worried that she hasn't always been a proper mother to me. I think she was a great mum. I mean, look how I've turned out."

He glanced at her; she rolled her eyes up. Then she said,

"Am I allowed to ask you anything about yourself?"

Talk about jumping the gun – but he could only say no, and she was by now sure he would say it nicely. They were much the same age, David perhaps a few years older, they seemed to have the same sense of humour, to be getting on well, in fact. She had known that she would be working closely with another of Jennifer's officers and had hoped that their relationship would be an easy one. But he was still her boss.

She need not have worried.

"Why not? One or two things I can't tell you of course, a couple of need-to-know forays into badland..." she started to laugh..." what is it?"

"I'm sorry, I still haven't quite got used to the Ticklish Issues jargon. Does, let's think, Bulgaria, count as badland?"

"Oh no, not for some time. It's a fluid category, badland. Iran is, obviously, but so is Switzerland now."

"Switzerland? Unbelievable. Oh, money laundering?"

"Spot on."

"So we have people in Switzerland trying to..."

"Shh. Ducks have ears."

"So come on, tell us a bit about yourself. Did you do any other job before you joined the Service? Did you have a happy childhood?"

"Of course. My father was Archdeacon of Littlehampton, and we lived in a rambling Georgian manse on the banks of the River Arun. We would scull on the river, my er my sister and I, when I was home on holiday from my public school, naturally."

"Which was?"

"Chiddingfold, unpretentious, favoured by the clergy. I studied Latin and Greek, as you might have expected. We would take a picnic up to the water meadows at Arundel, read poetry to each other, disturbed only by an occasional swan and her trail of cygnets. At home, in the orchard, we played games among the ancient pear trees, and hid from each other among the sloe bushes." He continued, wistfully, "I remember the warm autumn sunshine, the golden light, the rustling leaves. One July we asked the gardener if he could mow the croquet lawn – it had got into a terrible state – and we found the mallets and things in the old tumbledown orangery. I seem to remember that the Bishop was there, and the Rural Dean, of course. There's nothing like a friendly game of croquet of a warm summer evening, is there?"

Jane felt, and looked, a little puzzled. She also had played croquet, at St Anne's and Trinity. Well, perhaps the games sometimes started off friendly. And – Littlehampton was on the south coast, wasn't it? *Scull*, on the river, he had said, and *summer*. School, she had heard, for a second, before he continued talking about the river, and, definitely, soomer. Ah. The blackthorn.

David continued.

"We would play plum bob together

"What? Plum bob?"

"You know, where you put the fruit in a barrel with water, and duck your head under to get them out?"

"That's apples, David. A plumb bob is something – "

" – damn – decorators use to put wall paper up. I know, I'm sorry, I was running out of steam."

"Well?"

"I had a very happy childhood. My father was a clergyman, but not an Archdeacon, just a vicar in Preston."

"Is there a Chidding – whatever it was?"

"I think there's a village. No school as far as I know. We didn't have enough money for posh schools, but Preston Grammar was very good."

"Which University did you go to?"

"Oxford, but that was later."

"Oh?"

"After Sandhurst."

"Yes, of course. Did many boys go to Sandhurst from Preston Grammar?"

"More than you might expect. But most went to Liverpool or Manchester, or Lancaster."

"Why the story about Sussex? Was that impromptu?"

"Yes – it wasn't very good. Not convincing, obviously. I thought I might see how long I could keep it up. Occasionally we have to improvise; cover stories are never a hundred per cent watertight, and I'm not naturally fluent. And I was laying it on a touch thick for fun. Do you mind?"

"No, of course not. It was a bit purple, and that soppy look you put on, it just wasn't you. And, hiding in a sloe bush, not a brilliant idea."

"Oh. Why not?"

"A tad prickly. You haven't got much of a Lancashire accent. Just the odd ploom or soomer."

"I know, it sort of dropped off in the army. I imagine that you *are* naturally fluent?"

Jane ignored this.

"I should have thought of the army. You've got that sort of smartness about you."

"Well, that depends on your standards. But I can do scruffy if necessary. Not shaving is quite important."

Jane thought he might look quite good with a bit of a stubble and jeans.

"Your creases are like knives. Do you iron your own trousers?

"Well, as a matter of fact I do. You're very inquisitive."

So she was. She wondered why.

"It goes with the job, doesn't it?"

"Ah, the job. Jennifer outlined it to you, but she left a couple of blanks for me to fill in. Procedural things. By the way, was that your first meeting with her?"

"Second. I had an embarrassing lunch, not with her exactly, but at the same table. The DD(O) was there, and the girl I was with more or less offered him her body in return for promotion."

David laughed. "Well she won't get very far. Henry doesn't play away. He's been monogamous for God knows how long. However, to continue. It's about procedures for Typewriter."

He became serious, and explained to her.

"Your cover is simple. You go in as a member of the protection unit, and this is represented as part of your normal training. The Met might send someone else in as well, or if they grumble, we might. The reason why you are undergoing this training is that you may be assigned a security role at one of our embassies. This is a very good cover because it is consistent with your age and seniority on the FO staff – indeed, it may be not too far from the truth, now that 5 and 6 have joined forces. Because this is such a sensitive project..."

"Ticklish?"

"...exactly, you will need what we call a secondary cover. If Armstrong, or indeed your new Protection Unit colleagues, discover that you are not what you seem, you will be provided with another false reason for your presence, which you can admit with a proper show of embarrassment."

"What is it?"

"Jennifer is working on this. It'll probably be something to do with information leaks, or possibly activities by the rivals. We would hope that the operation could continue, but we may have to terminate. I'll brief you within the next week or so.

"Keep normal records on the secondary cover, if it's decided that you can continue. You can follow up contacts made by Armstrong, and you can request surveillance through the customary channels. You can expect Armstrong to get access, one way or another, to this level of information.

"But, whether you are operating under primary or secondary cover, you must under no circumstances enter any data which might alert him that it is his own activities and relationships which we are investigating. These records must not be kept on a web enabled computer. Buy an early notebook without connectivity from a junk shop, pay cash. Keep it hidden. Encode all names – properly. Commit key information to memory. That's about it. Shall I run through it again?"

"No, but I will, if you like?"

"Good idea."

Jane repeated her instructions, comprehensively and succinctly. She then asked, "I shan't be starting for a while, shall I? It'll take a week or two to set up with Protection, and I've got my art-for-philistines course first. Will you be doing the obvious things, like finding out that his wife isn't a secret zillionaire? And if she is, or he won the lottery, it will all be called off?"

"Yes, and yes. But Henry is suspicious. That means a lot. Have you done a firearms course recently? You could do that while you're waiting."

"Firearms? On this job?"

"Come on, what's your primary cover?"

"Well, yes, PU carry guns, but they don't use them, and I certainly shan't."

"The coppers you'll be on with will – we hope – take your primary cover seriously. They might put you in for a half day's training. You've got to be at least familiar with the bloody things."

"Like that J-frame 38 that you're trying to conceal in the small of your back? Just there." She prodded his back just below his right kidney.

"It's a 357."

"There's posh. Buy it yourself?"

"I did. You might consider one. You have to keep your own, you know, and the standard issue 38 is a bit boring. Alan – you'll meet him soon, he'll probably pop in from time to time to see you at the Armstrongs', make sure the PU lot aren't getting in the way, that sort of thing, I wouldn't put it past them to put another pretty girl, damn, woman, in as your oppo – well, he has a 357 as well. Before you ask, I'm not going to tell you why I'm carrying now. But tell me, do, are you actually wonder woman? Can you fire these things as well as spying them with your x-ray eyes?"

"I think that I'm possibly not wonder woman. But I can fire them, and occasionally hit the target. Which is surprising since of course I squeeze my eyes tight shut and squeal when the gun goes bang."

"So, no firearms course?"

"Don't mind. Up to you, boss. But look, what happens if, for example, the wind blows your jacket back and some outraged citizen causes a bother? Like, calling the police?"

"It doesn't; I'm careful."

She wasn't satisfied, and persisted. He replied,

"That's where the Portuguese Ambassador comes in. Or Venezuelan, or Puerto Rican, sometimes. But as I say, I've never really needed him – or her, of course."

"If we are going to work together, David, you are going to need to adopt a less enigmatic tone."

"I'm sorry, I thought perhaps they might have covered this manoeuvre in your firearms course."

"No, they didn't. It was just firing procedures, and shooting practice."

"Well then, if you have to explain away a sidearm, you claim to be protecting an important diplomat who's just over there" – he pointed towards a man who was turning off the path ahead of them – "you see him – no, he's just out of sight now. Here's my ID" – he took a Diplomatic Protection Unit card, complete with photograph, from his breast pocket – "and there's the phone number. Before you get round to explaining this, of course, you find yourself lying flat on your face with your hands on your head, three policemen dressed up like extras in a Bruce Willis movie pointing submachine guns at you and screaming their heads off. In London, at any rate, where Armed Response Units seem to be round every corner. Then you get one hell of a rocket back at the office. It's happened to me twice – but it turned out both were exercises, dummy runs, tests – once of me and once, would you believe it, of the Response Unit."

"That all sounds good fun; there must be a course for field officers that's different from the one I went on. That was just types of gun, and firing them. I didn't have one on the Munich operation."

"Yes, I imagine that you wouldn't have been so successful with him if he'd found a revolver in your knickers."

"As for that, you must have read my report," she said waspishly."And I've no intention of letting Armstrong anywhere near my undergarments." She was not particularly pleased by the turn the conversation had taken. "You want to watch it, you know, you're a good looking enough lad; perhaps there's something fishy about Pauline Osmotherley? Perhaps Jennifer will send you after her?"

"Lady Osmotherley is a very reliable and effective chairperson of the Joint Security committee. And rather older than my auntie. However, I apologise for the inappropriate comment."

They had passed the bandstand, and approached the bridge to the accompaniment of rhythmic music, possibly an arrangement of Mozart, played by a military band. David straightened up. So did Jane, and they both stepped out in time to the music. David wove his right hand and flicked his fingers as if he were a nineteen sixties off duty guards officer with an umbrella.

"Do a good spot of lunch at your club, do they?" he asked.

"Be careful with Dalby, Palmer. He hasn't got my sense of humour" she replied, after a moment's thought.

They both laughed, and started to walk normally again.

"There's something about that film, isn't there?" he asked.

"Yes, well, it was different; Harry Palmer isn't posh."

"It's old though; do you watch old films?"

"I used to, at University. You had to say that you were interested in film. It was naff to use the plural."

"Yes, I remember that too. We used to have such serious discussions. I think we had just discovered metaphor;

everything had to have a double meaning, every image had to be a symbol."

They walked for a moment in silence, negotiating a route through a group of lunch hour saunterers. David continued, "I used to like the evening meetings of the film club in Michaelmas term, when it got dark early, because they were held in a room off the Pitt Rivers museum, and to get to it you had to creep through the dinosaur hall without the lights on."

"I don't remember that. It was held in a room in Trinity, as far as I remember, but I'm, what, five years younger than you? Which college?"

"Corpus. You were Jesus. And I'm six and a half years older than you."

"Oh dear. What don't you know about me?"

"Lots. What sort of music you like, are you a gourmet, do you do crafty things?"

"What?"

"You know, embroidery, tatting, whatever?"

"That sort of crafty, I see. No, not at all, and I can't cook much, either. I like some music. I love Billie Holiday. And Bach."

They chatted for a while, trying politely to find common areas of interest where potential disagreement would not threaten the friendliness of the occasion. It was very pleasant, strolling in the leafy Park in the June sunshine, in the undeniably impressive heart of Empire, they wryly agreed, and it would be easy to be seduced by its history and glamour.

"A bit like the last night of the Proms," David said.

"Do we have to beware of it then, sentimentality, emotion?" asked Jane. "Isn't that what it's all about, really, patriotism?"

"I hope not," replied David, who thought that perhaps their conversation risked becoming more serious than he had intended at his first meeting with a new colleague. After a while David looked at his watch.

"Back to base for you. I'll start on Armstrong's wife's money, do the banks and check out the gambling. Have you got any housekeeping to do? Leave you could take?"

"A couple of days' leave would be nice. Can you set up the Art course as soon as possible?"

"Sure."

Jane set off to walk back to Thames House, but changed her mind and turned along Birdcage Walk, intending to catch a bus to Wandsworth at Victoria.

*****

There was something happening at Buckingham Palace as David took the path round the lake to Constitution Hill, on his way to Knightsbridge. An investiture perhaps, or some sort of official visit. Soldiers stamped around, and were photographed by foreigners. Some of Her Majesty's subjects waved paper flags, craned their necks and stood on tiptoe to peer into the black limousines which were passing through the gates. Some of the passengers waved back, but most stared straight ahead. A voice from David's past boomed in his ear.

"Major MacMaster, upon my soul! I thought you'd disappeared into the forests of the Marches. Well this is very jolly!" The speaker paused and lowered his voice. "Oh I say, you're not *on duty* are you; don't tell me I've *blown your cover.* No, no, I'm sure they would have told me. In any case, nothing out of the ordinary today, just a reception for" – the vast and outrageously uniformed figure extracted a slip of paper from his tunic pocket – "God Almighty the chief executives of the twenty largest firms in the food processing industry. Having their ears bent by Wales I imagine. Well, how are you? Looking a bit, um, down market? No problems I hope!"

"Chubby, how delightful to see you again. And if I can shield my eyes for a moment from the glitter of your epaulettes, I do declare that I see more stars twinkling beneath those crowns. Many congratulations, I hope the job that goes with them suits?"

Chubby looked a little downcast. "Much of the time, much of the time. And of course it's back to the regiment after a year. Although I doubt if they'll want me running around dodging snipers in the Rugova. Getting a bit long in the tooth for all that. Not sure I want a desk job, though – but what are there except desk jobs for old soldiers like me, eh? What about you, what are you up to – if you can tell me, that is? When you left us you were off to join the elect in South Wales. I wouldn't have minded doing that, but I was never as fit as you. And you were a clever blighter too, as I remember."

"I stayed for a while, did a couple of tours in the desert, then I got fed up, Chubby. I'm in the FO now; I think it was a good move, still get to see the world. I'm sorry you think I look a bit scruffy."

"Oh no, no, no, not at all, I mean, you look fine, of course. Depends on expectations and all that. Oh, forgive me, try to ignore me."

This was difficult. So impressive a figure was Chubby that some tourists were already pointing their cameras, manoeuvring to obtain a picture with at least a Union Flag, preferably the Royal Standard, in the background. David turned away until the photographers moved on.

"Ah well, Chubby, I'd better be off. Time and tide, you know."

"Indeed, indeed. I say, are you a military attaché somewhere? Somewhere interesting?"

"Not really. Just mainstream FO. Give my best wishes to Amanda, won't you?"

"Ah, Amanda. In the past, old man. On my own now."

"Oh, I'm so sorry."

"Thank you, David. I'm over it, I think. Possibly not. It was terrible. Just this little pain she had, didn't do anything about it, I woke up one morning and there she was, or rather, I should say, she wasn't. Heart, just like that."

"Chubby, how awful. How long ago?"

"A year. Think about her all the time, of course. Function OK, though, now. Well, must go and make sure the courtyard detail's up to the mark. It will be. I'm just window dressing here, really. How about a drink sometime?"

"Yes, where do you suggest?"

"Black's?"

"I'll leave a note there for you, one evening next week suit?"

"Excellent, we can have a good old chin wag. Fare thee well."

He gathered himself up and marched dramatically to the northeast entrance. Video cameras followed his passage. David walked briskly along Constitution Hill, to keep his appointment in Knightsbridge which was, he hoped, the wrap of a case he had been working on for the last three months. In the furniture department of Duncan's there was, unusually, a second hand, but hardly used, arm chair, made of leather and ply, veneered with rosewood. One of the shop's money-no-object customers had been refurnishing his apartment, and had asked Duncan's to get rid of – possibly at an auction – the existing furniture. Duncan's buyer had spotted this chair, identified it as one of the first Charles Eames lounge chairs, and was exhibiting it on the floor. Whether or not it was actually on the market David didn't know. His contact, a diplomat from the embassy of Murdistan, one of the ex-soviet states, had asked for a final meeting there. David presumed that he was interested in interior design. He couldn't say that he had himself ever heard of Charles Eames. They would pretend to argue like a couple of bargain hunters over a coat in a sale – this was to allay the suspicions of any security staff from the embassy who might have been following the diplomat. In fact, they would be finalising the details of his defection. Unnecessarily elaborate precautions occupied too much of his section's time, David thought, especially when, as in this case, they were at the insistence of the client. Rules stipulated that all officers should carry side arms when undertaking activities which might – even with a stretch of the imagination – result in a confrontation with rival firms, or when the task fell under the elastic heading of combating terrorism. David had no problem with this ruling – his spell with the covert forces had accustomed him to carrying concealed weapons – but he was aware that some staff would have preferred to use their own judgment.

The meeting went smoothly. A salesman pointed out the chair, and gave David the impression that he should sit in it to test its comfort. David made a mental note that in future, when expected to try out furniture in the line of duty, he would wear a shoulder holster. He sat gingerly on the edge of the front cushion, but the expression on the salesman's face led David to believe that he had misinterpreted the initial gesture. He stood up – awkwardly, because it was that sort of chair – and was pleased to see that his contact was approaching. The salesman moved away to assist another couple. David and the Murdistani had their mock quarrel over the purchase of the chair, which was probably unnecessary because the only other customers were the elderly couple, greeted as old friends by the salesman; agreed some final conditions of the defection, one of which was, surprisingly, that the entire family would be eventually rehoused in Blackpool; shook hands and left by different doors. A useful piece of work, David thought. The Murdistani, who had been listed as a trade attaché, was, among other things, an industrial spy. His intimate knowledge of the Murdistani industrial base was what he had offered David in return for cash and, apparently, a large house in Blackpool. He would soon learn that Murdistani industrial secrets were of little interest to HMG, but that his familiarity with the sites and conditions of the ex-soviet nuclear armaments in Murdistan, and those of its larger neighbour, certainly was.

*****

Obsolete laptops were two a penny in Wandsworth's small computer shops, run on shoe-strings by bunking-off schoolboys for ageing layabouts who had once known their way around operating systems with names like CPM86. Jane allowed a delighted lad in such a shop to sell her one, together with a dusty box of ten floppy discs. He sold the discs to her cheaply, he said, because some were probably no good by now; she said that would be OK, she would only need two or three. An old copy of Word was already installed, and there seemed to be directories full of documents, with names like *Xmas cards* and *to Linda.*

"Haven't you cleaned the disc up?" she asked.

"Haven't a clue. Obviously not if there's stuff still there."

"Well, I'll delete it then, shall I?"

"Not the programs, that'd be daft. It hasn't got any connectivity, no-one's going to find out."

She paid cash, as a matter of course, and left.

At home, a small flat in a Victoria mansion block, she prepared to make notes on her conversation with David, thinking that she would write directly to the floppy. Encryption was going to be a problem. She couldn't use any of the office facilities; that was clear from David's instructions. She decided to write in clear to the floppy, which she would then hide, and each day she would run an overwriting program on the partition of the hard disc used by Word for buffering. How would she know which that was? How would she get the security program onto the computer? Would it work with the ancient version of the operating system which she presumed lay under Windows? This was ridiculous; what a stupid problem to delay her at this stage. She was out of her depth. Returning to the shop, she arrived just before the helpful young assistant was about to leave, to eat his tea and do his homework. She explained – somewhat lamely – what she wanted to do, and how she thought it might be achieved. He cut her short, and asked, not what she wanted to *do*, but what her *objective* was. She explained, concocting a plausible story about competitors, hacking and industrial espionage. He loved it.

"Leave the machine and come back tomorrow? About half four? It'll cost you ooh, say twenty five?"

"Twenty five; oh dear, I'm not sure"

"Well, let's say twenty?"

She felt like cuddling him, except for his spots.

"I was joking. Look, thirty five for a failsafe job, OK?"
"Great."

Chapter 10

July 3   Jane   Harriet

On occasion Jane had visited Contempo!, once to slide down the back of a giant centipede, and once to trip over an artfully uneven floor tile. A year or two previously she had enjoyed a couple of days in the National Gallery, but that was probably because she had been taken there by a boyfriend; nevertheless, she could remember some of the pictures quite well, but now only the faintest image of the boyfriend remained. The entire world of the visual arts was obviously far too large for a comprehensive exploration. She would have to concentrate on one or two areas which interested Armstrong; he would hardly expect her to be an expert – indeed, that would itself be suspicious – she should just know enough to keep a conversation going and not make a fool of herself, while demonstrating a real, or possibly pretended, appreciation of his own collection.

A few fairly guarded telephone calls to the art correspondents of broadsheet newspapers gave Jane some of the pointers which she needed. The terms in which this information was cast seemed slightly and perhaps unnecessarily opaque – no sooner had she mastered one jargon, she thought, than she was expected to learn another. She realised that her course with the art squad would have to start with a language lesson. But the gist of the information she had received was that most of Armstrong's collection centred upon a theme, rather than a school, or an individual artist. The theme was work – labour; in factories, fields, shipyards, mines. Paid labour or slave labour, but real labour, not a prettified, romanticised version. The man from the Custodian had mentioned that Armstrong had recently acquired a small, exquisite watercolour by Turner of a sunset over the beach at Granville, but on the beach eleven or twelve women, their backs to the artist, were bent double, scraping in the sand for cockles or razor clams. No, the man from the

Custodian had said, the sunset was not romanticising this picture of grinding toil, it was emphasising it by contrast – a romantic view would have arranged the labourers differently, some standing, perhaps talking, facing the artist. Hmm, she had thought. No, he didn't know how much Armstrong had paid for it. What was exquisite about it? It was small, and by Turner.

She had taken two or three works of art criticism out of the library, and read a chapter which explained the influence of Gainsborough on Magritte. At least it taught her who Magritte was. She ate a cold meal of assorted leftovers, switched on the television and watched some economists playing competitive guesswork. Her flat was not particularly cosy, although warm enough. She was dissatisfied with it. Other people's dwellings often just seemed *right*, in a way she couldn't define. Their untidy piles of books, their musical instruments propped up beside the dresser, created an air of comfortable informality. Her mess was just a mess. She had thought she might improve her sitting room by replacing the central pendant light with table lamps, and maybe buying a new carpet, but had never quite got round to it. Perhaps, after her art course with the Met, she might hang up a few pictures, not necessarily exquisite ones. She switched off the television, washed the dishes, tidied a bit and went to bed.

Monday morning dawned bright and sparkling, even in Victoria. At this time of day beams of light dodged the offices and apartment blocks and streamed through her living room windows to illuminate parallelograms of dust on her surfaces. Sunday mornings were the best, of course. She set off, as usual, at half past seven. Electronic communications, their use and abuse, were at the very centre of her job, but she had often resorted to personal contact when phone and email negotiations had dragged on tediously. In this case she hoped to persuade the art team at the Met to arrange her visit quickly, even to start it straight away. She couldn't think what form it might take; their induction course for new members, probably. What were they like, these artistic coppers?

Perhaps it was her curiosity which impelled her to eschew the normal channels.

The Met Art and Antiques Unit had moved recently to a warehouse in Homerton, one of the remaining ungentrified parts of East London. These premises were rented by the police at a peppercorn rent from a group of insurers and art dealers who had financed the move, and subsidised its running costs, because they had been upset by the rumours that art crime was being given a low priority by the new Commissioner. Jane did not often travel on the North London line, which seemed to have a somewhat different character from other London railways. There was a girl sitting opposite her, reading the Thames Book Review, with an extraordinary hair style of ribbons, beads and tight plaits which Jane thought she might just get away with herself. How on earth could the girl plait it so neatly?

"My mum does it for me, hun, only takes her an hour, bless."

Her mum. Oh well.

They chatted for a while. Jane had never seen the TBR before, and tentatively asked whether it was a good read. The girl grinned. "I wouldn't call it a page turner. It's essays really, they use a book review as an excuse. It's often the same contributors. I read it for the politics, usually."

"Is it very committed, then?"

"That's a difficult one. Some of its authors are off the radar lefties, Marxist even, but they're critics as well. Writers. Or historians. All obvious bright guys, know what I mean? One of these days some MP is actually going to read it, then I expect it'll lose its grant. I just like the idea that it's getting cash from Tory taxpayers."

"Perhaps I'll stick to Tolkien, then."

For a moment the girl looked disapproving. "That's fantasy, you don't want to be reading that now, there's too much serious stuff going on in the real world. Are you a student, too?"

"No. I was. I know life's serious. I just like a break now and then."

The girl with the stunning hair and the serious outlook on life left the train at Hackney Central. At Homerton station, overlooking the track, a man was standing on a makeshift platform constructed from nothing much more than a scaffolding plank with a rope attached to each end, suspended from the brick chimney of a blank gable end. Gripping one of the ropes and the handle of a paint pot in his left hand, with his right he had reached the last word of a slogan *Decent housing is a right not a pr.*

The entrance to the Art and Antiques Unit's new home was an airlock affair, all cameras, pushbuttons and intercoms. The inner door was opened by a woman about Jane's age, wearing white overalls and the sort of crinkly green translucent hat worn in hospitals, who asked politely in what way she might help, in the precisely modulated tones of the career academic, underneath which Jane thought she detected a hint of the oddly pronounced vowels and elided gutturals of the hereditary ruling classes. Jane introduced herself, and apologised for her unexpected arrival. She didn't know whether her visit had even yet been requested, but the woman didn't seem particularly surprised. She introduced herself, Harriet something which Jane did not catch.

"From the FO, I believe? Something to do with the British Council and a touring exhibition? Theme of men at work? Sounds most interesting, I wonder if the Imperial War Museum will let the big Stanley Spencer out again."

"Yes, well, you expose my ignorance. I shall have to bone up quite a bit so that I don't annoy them too much."

"Oh I'm sure you wouldn't. Still, if you're arranging the visits, I dare say it would be a good idea to ah..." she waved her arms vaguely in the air, and continued, "I do apologise, but I feel it would be remiss of me not to ask for some sort of...oh look, I'm sorry, can I see your identification?"

Jane had brought the appropriate documents.

"Let me take you through to see Ronald."

They walked through the warehouse; shelves of large cardboard boxes, racks of paintings, a library of art books and sale catalogues, and a table which resembled a white elephant stall at a jumble sale.

"Penny, please don't touch any of the allsorts, I'm boxing and cataloguing them. Ronald likes me to wear SOCO uniform, goodness knows why. Policemen are rather controlling, I find. Ronald, this is Penny North from the FO, I was just telling her you were the boss. Penny, Chief Inspector Harrison. I'll carry on with the knick-knacks, Ronald."

"OK duchess. Pleased to meet you Penny, I hadn't expected you yet, I didn't know liaison had firmed anything up?"

"I don't expect they have, but I've just finished a job, and thought I'd come and make contact. Just to say hello, you know."

She gave him her warmest smile.

"And you'd like to start straight away and bugger the formalities, right?"

"Oh, well, no, I wouldn't expect that at all, I just...came to say hello."

She smiled again, with rather less confidence.

"You can start tomorrow. There's no problem, we've got a standard induction course for young coppers who are doing a stint here, and for our part-timers. We used to do it at Hendon, but it's easier here. We'll trot that out for you. The AC said you were mainly interested in men at work. Persons at work. Do washerwomen count?"

"I'm sure they do. I don't need to be an expert, you know, just not to make a complete fool of myself."

"Look love, the only experts here are the scientists. The ones who use chemicals and spectroscopes and suchlike. Take Harriet. She's filling our boxes because she likes to keep busy. But she's a chemist, on sabbatical from Imperial College. She's brilliant at paint layers and paper age. We've only got a couple of in-house scientists, young girls – women – who we put through degrees ourselves. No, the rest of us have just picked up a bit of savvy here and there. Like most art or antique dealers, really." He called through the door, "Duchess, can you show Penny around? She can start proper tomorrow. Find her some books or show her a film after lunch."

"Thank you Penny, you've rescued me from the old curiosity shop. We do get some dross. Here's the cloakroom, I'll just disrobe. You'd like coffee? I'll introduce you to the others."

Three middle aged men occupied grey metal desks in a corner of the warehouse. Their computer screens were large and high resolution. A small cubicle was set up for photography and a nondescript (so it seemed to Jane) painting stood on an easel in front of a camera with an elaborate tripod. Jane was introduced, and another chair was found. Harriet sat in a vast all-encompassing wing armchair, which had, apparently, been dragged along to each of the Art squad's various homes from its inception. Two of the men were police officers, the third a civilian photographer. There were others, but they were out and about – some were special constables, staff loaned by insurance firms, museums or the larger auctioneers.

"The specials are very well behaved," said the older of the two policemen, "and I'll say this, they do their share of the cataloguing. They love making arrests. We let one of the girls – sorry, women – arrest a fence last week. She can't stop talking about it."

Jane was sitting at the end of the row of paintings. Because of the way they were stacked she could only see the end one, which seemed to be by an artist familiar even to her.

"Isn't that a Lowry?" she asked.

The older policeman didn't move.

"Go and fetch it Rob," he said. The younger policeman pulled it out of the rack and brought it over. He held it up so that they could all see it.

"You go first, duchess" he said to Harriet.

"I think it's a Lowry. But what do I know? I've never scoped it. Is the paint right?"

"Oh yes, but it would be" said the older policeman. "Only a real berk would get the paint of a Lowry wrong. What do you think, Rob?"

"I think it's horrible. So it's probably a Lowry."

"Well I think it's a fairy. What do you think, Penny?"

"Good God, how should I know, I don't have to know about forgeries, do I? What do you mean, a fairy?"

"Like, you know, cup, or wedding, know wo' I mean?" said the younger policeman, probably a constable, in a Dick van Dyke chimney sweep accent. Jane cottoned on quite quickly.

"Or Madeira. OK. But surely there must be a list, or something, of his paintings; isn't there a Lowry gallery in Manchester, couldn't the curator help?"

"Answering in order," said the sergeant, "No; it's in Salford; she's no idea, we emailed a photo." He continued, "Painters don't usually know that they're going to be famous, they paint lots of stuff, sell it privately, give it away, leave it in a cupboard, repair their shed with it. What they don't do is catalogue it."

"Where did you find it, then? Why has nobody claimed it?"

"Oh, in a run of the mill raid, after a tip off. There may have been an insurance claim, but not recently, because we would have known – so, why hasn't it been claimed? Your turn, Robbo."

"Almost certainly because it hasn't been missed. There are other reasons, but you'd be amazed how often people forget things after a burglary. Of course it doesn't help if the theft was ages ago, and the owner hadn't liked it, or known it was valuable."

"Very good, Rob," said the sergeant. "Now stick it back, there's a good lad." He turned to Harriet. "Has the boss asked you to look after Penny this pm, then?"

"He has. We'll watch a couple of your films after lunch. I don't think she wants to know about spectroscopy. It's something for the British Council isn't it, Penny, some touring exhibition about men at work?"

"Yes, I'm not sure it's been firmed up yet. They said something about paintings of the Clyde, would that be right? Just men at work, I think."

"English painters, then?" said the sergeant.

"Well, British, certainly."

Clyde, she thought, Glasgow, Scottish painter, surely?

"Which countries are you visiting?"

"South America, mainly. It's not exactly a plum job, but it shouldn't last long – it's a sort of secondment, really – and then perhaps I'll get something a bit more substantial. Still, I've never been to South America, it should be interesting."

This was terrible. Worse than David schooling up the Arun in the golden sunlight. *Always prepare your lies in advance*, she had been told. *If you try and wing it, you will stall, and then you will crash*. She would have to clam up now. With a bit of luck they would just put her down as some brainless twit from the Foreign Office. Not that there were many of those, not that she'd met, anyway.

"You must think I'm very unprepared," she said, with a quick ditsy smile.

The younger policeman spoke.

"I think I can help," he said, "One of my university friends works at the British Council here in Holborn. I'll give her a bell and find out exactly what's going into this touring exhibition of yours. No, no, it's no trouble at all."

Jane sat quietly while he walked over to his desk and picked up the phone, her face expressing something like friendly anticipation, she hoped, which was far from what she felt.

He returned quite quickly.

"Yes," he said, "*The Dignity of Labour* it's called. She didn't know about South America, that wasn't on the file, but she said that most of the stuff would be reproduction, like the *Shipbuilding on the Clyde*, but they hoped to take a Joseph Wright of Derby oil."

"Thank you so much," she said, and thank you too to Henry, Jennifer or David.

After coffee Harriet suggested that Jane should settle down with a couple of relevant books while she finished her stint of dross-cataloguing. Jane looked at the items lined up on the table. Most seemed to be pottery or silver.

"It's not really all junk, is it?" she asked.

"No, of course not. About half and half."

"How on earth do you know what they are – that, for example," she said, pointing to a vaguely Chinese vase.

"Some I do. The porcelain has marks, and I've got a crib, so has the silver. So has a lot of the silver plate. I can fill in some of the fields in the database straight away, naturally, like where and when found – just like an archaeologist's hoard, only instead of 'layer three, grid F6' I'll have entered 'Bill Sikes' room under the bed'. Then I put in whatever identification I can, then Len photographs it front, back, top, bottom, against a scale. Photos are digital now, of course, they go straight on the database. Then, from time to time, as we accumulate, let's say, a lot of Chinese vases, we send the data to our Chinese vase expert – who is actually a dealer in Broadway – and he fills in the blanks."

"Do you keep it all? The real rubbish? For ever?"

"I don't know." She called over to the desk area, "Rob, what happens to the rubbish?"

"Boss takes it to a car boot sale every week. And the silver. We've got a flat in Marbella, didn't you know?"

"Thank you Rob, you might find Ebay more rewarding."

"Too much effort, duchess. We keep it, natch. Guess how many pieces so far." He pointed at the shelves and boxes.

"Ten thousand?"

"Sixty."

"Good God. Well Penny, that's a question I've never asked before. Rob, do we have a decent book on Stanley Spencer? One that covers both wars?"

"Should have. Yes, top shelf, on the left."

July 3   David

The old man in a grey scarf, wound twice round his neck and tucked into his unravelling pullover, also grey although in its youth it might have been brighter, had so far paid the fruit machine seven pounds and twenty pence and even David was hoping that he might soon be rewarded with at least a small tumble of coins into the hopper, if not the bar-rousing, floor spilling clatter of a Las Vegas jackpot. A breathless messenger, announcing a six-nil away win for Liverpool against Manchester United, might, David thought, just possibly stir some of the ancient boozers, maybe to lift their glasses to their lips or even to hazard some limited communication. A couple of these silent creatures, a man and a woman, sat together on hard chairs at a cast iron table. 'Together' did not seem quite the right word. They gave no indication that they had ever met before. They stared impassively at different stains on the wallpaper and ate crisps from separate packets. But David knew that they were husband and wife, because he had followed them to the Ormskirk Arms from their semi in Garston. Twice in the last ninety minutes the man had approached the bar. They had drunk, between them, one and a half pints of Guinness and a whisky with ginger ale. They had each been to the lavatory once. David knew their name. They were Mr and Mrs Connolly and their son in law was the Prime Minister's closest ally, the Treasurer of the Hundred Levels. David was quite certain that they were not rich. Nevertheless he would have to speak to them, make a few enquiries up and down the street. It would normally have been easy for him to get hold of their tax and social security records, but in this operation he could take no risk that Armstrong himself might be alerted that it was taking place. In a run of the mill investigation, like that into Jane's Irish connections, or if a particular foreign business man or diplomat were being targeted as a potential agent, David would have the entire administrative, security and police apparatus of the state at his disposal. But the personal network of Armstrong, a fairy ring carefully nurtured over well-nigh ten years, had insinuated its mycelia into every branch of government service. Suspicious or even unusual questions about Armstrong asked of authority anywhere – especially of those branches of Government such as the Inland Revenue which were supposed to hold their information in confidence – could easily lead to his being alerted to them, and then there would be the devil to pay, and no pitch hot.

This would effectively put an end to the project, but Jennifer had exaggerated the risks to their own positions, possibly to impress upon Jane the delicacy of the task. David knew from Charles (in Jennifer's office, he upon whose right side it was advisable to be) that a dummy operation had already been set up, supposedly triggered by intelligence received from an agent in Lagos, to the effect that Armstrong was being targeted by a group of business men hoping to obtain a mining concession in an African country which received aid from the British government. Possibly – the fictitious cable reported, and so it had been minuted in the case file – some approach might be made to him or his family; what sort of an approach was not described. In an emergency, if a clumsy or unlucky move were to set the Treasurer's antennae aquiver, the pretence would be maintained that David and Jane had been working on this operation. Another fictitious report would soon be received to the effect that the first had been mistaken. But then, whatever misconduct – if any – of which Armstrong might be guilty would remain unexposed.

When the old couple settled down with a third drink, and half each of a local newspaper which a customer had left on the bar, David returned his glass, left the pub and retraced his steps to the Connollys' house. He knocked, waited a moment for the answer which he knew would not come, and walked round to the front door of the adjoining semi. The door was opened before the Westminster chimes had finished sounding, and he waited for them to stop before speaking to the little girl who had answered.

"May I speak to your Mummy or Daddy, please?" he asked, smiling. The television could be heard from the back room.

"Mum, there's a man." the little girl shrieked, loud enough to be heard over a noisy row between Debs and Dev.

"Ask 'im worry wants" came an answering shout.

"Worrier want?"

"I've got something for her."

"E's got something for yer."

"Ask im worrit is."

"It's a bank cheque for twenty five pounds."

"Something for twenty five quid."

"Tell 'im to sling it, I ain't got twenty five quid. Silly bugger."

David had had enough of this. He shouted into the hall, tried to explain. The little girl shouted also. For a second or two the volume of the television also increased, as her mother presumably tried to drown out the noise from the hall. Then it was switched off, and a woman emerged from the front room. She advanced on David, young, burly, full of anger and menace. He held his hands up, with an Ayrshire and Borders cheque for twenty five pounds between the thumb and first finger of his right hand. She despatched her daughter into the kitchen with a sweeping movement of her arm and peered at the cheque. She hesitated for a second, long enough for David to ask her why she didn't want it. He managed to convince her that he was giving her something, not selling it, but she remained suspicious.

"Woddier want then? Worruveye gorrer do?"

"Just tell me what sort of tea and coffee you use – and a few other things, you know, soap and J-cloths and things like that. It'll only take ten minutes, and you can have this cheque. You use Cutcosts, I suppose?"

"Sometimes. Sellgood's nearer. But – can you spend it on anything?"

"Oh yes, anything at all. The Post Office'll cash it for you."

"I druther av the cash now."

"Well – perhaps – " David took twenty five pounds from his wallet.

"I'm not supposed to do this, but – oh go on then, I'll make an exception. Can we do the interview now?"

She took the cash."Orright"

As David filled in his fake market research form, he gradually started to chat. He wove in a few compliments, about her housekeeping, the brightness of her daughter, how sensible her shopping pattern was, how he preferred this that and the other as well, and soon they were sitting in the kitchen drinking tea. The daughter was sent off to watch television. David folded up his papers and asked whether Margery thought her neighbours would be willing to answer his questions as well. Margery was not on speaking terms with her neighbours on the left – the other side, not the Connollys – for a number of very good reasons, mainly concerning their Jack Russell, which she would have to tell David about or he'd think she was daft. After ten minutes or so of deprecating the unsavoury behaviour of this animal, he managed to manoeuvre her to a consideration of her other neighbours, the Connollys. She dealt with them pretty smartly. They were as poor as church mice and would pull his arm off for twenty five quid. Honest, mind you, as honest as the day was long, but he didn't have a pension from his work, did he, just had to rely on the old age, couldn't even afford a dish for their telly."

"Jelly?"

"Jelly? Eh? What you on about? You know, Sky."

"Of course. Sorry."

"And e won't take a penny from is daughter. She's married to that MP, you know, Armstrong, but old Conny's a real old die in the woods lefty, can't stand is guts. Don't suppose anyone can. They're all crooks, ant they? She never visits. I think she sees 'er mum sometimes, think they do a bitter shopping in town. Look, why don't we aver spotter something stronger?"

The Connollys were indeed poor but honest. They had returned from the pub by the time he had extricated himself from Margery's house – having inferred, from her not particularly disguised suggestions to him, that she was, at least at the present, unpartnered – and he used the same ruse, posing as a market researcher with an unusually deep pocket. Their house was tidy and clean, but meagrely furnished. They showed no influence of Guinness or whisky, unsurprising considering their modest rate of consumption, they accepted his payment and answered his questions. Their lifestyle was very economical, they usually bought cheap brands, they never ate in restaurants, they went to the pub once a week. After the interview was complete he asked them the name of the people with the offensive dog, and continued, "Look, I'm in a hurry, I've got to get back and I'm supposed to do another interview this evening. You know Mr and Mrs Mattison, don't you, you could give me some answers for them, and you can have their twenty five quid. How about it?"

The Connollys were outraged. They didn't ask him any questions about the viability of such a procedure – which genuine market researchers would, of course, never have been able to employ – they were obviously shocked at the suggestion, and asked him to leave. He could see that Mr Connolly was debating whether or not to hand back their own twenty five pounds, so David left in a hurry, walked quickly back to his car parked round the corner, and started the drive home.

July 10   Jane   David   Alan

On the Monday morning after Jane's art course had finished, she and David met in a café, almost empty at ten o'clock, to discuss progress. They would continue, if necessary, in her flat. His report was succinct; no evidence at all of any family sources of money; none of Armstrong's relatives had inherited money, won the lottery or robbed a post office. Jane had started to tell him about her own, clearly more enjoyable week, when the café door opened and a youngish dark haired man, not tall but lean and wiry, dressed in loose jeans and a leather jacket, came in. He made a brief gesture of acknowledgement, and sat down at their table. David said hello, and introduced him to Jane.

"This is Alan Green; I've mentioned him. He'll be working on Typewriter with us when he's finished a couple of things. Alan, meet Jane. She's just done the Met art course."

"Hi Jane. Yeah, I did that too; has David mentioned the Vermeer affair?"

"Yes, I did. The friends got their knickers in a twist because the Veep wanted to spread vicious rumours about Hinfangle."

"That's right, dirty business, American politics."

"Shocking."

"Hello Alan. David, do you want to know what I learned about Armstrong at Hackney?"

"Jane, could we go to your flat? Straight away? Would you mind?"

"No, no, not at all, it's quite close."

"Good. Alan will need coffee, will you be able to manage that, do you think? Shall we go?"

Alan apologised to Jane for David's bossy manner, attributing it to his military background.

"He's OK when you get to know him, providing you can keep him off Charlie Chaplin, and that Russian battleship bloke."

Jane was going to make a joke about the sharp creases in David's trousers, but decided that despite their friendly chat in the park she really didn't know him well enough yet; she had concluded, when she thought about it, that David had quite deliberately contrived its light hearted tone; and she didn't know Alan at all. It was true, though, that David dressed just as she imagined an ex-army officer would; in warm weather she could imagine he would discard his jacket and tie, and roll up his sleeves neatly. Alan was much more fashionable; she noticed his shoes which were a sort of slub grey, not quite suede, and looked expensive. And they had very different hair styles.

Back at Jane's flat, before she could even find the cafetière, let alone the remnant of real coffee which she hoped was stored somewhere towards the back of the fridge, David asked her whether she had acquired a suitable computer to keep her notes and records. She pointed out the ancient laptop.

"Have you put anything on it yet – I mean, anything identifiable as Typewriter?"

"No, I've just experimented with it a bit – the encryption, and cleaning up the hard disk. I keep everything on floppies, including the system. Nothing at all about work so far."

"Floppies? Can you still get them?"

"Yes. Not fresh from the factory, though."

"You're sure there's nothing left on the hard disk when you've finished?"

"Yes, of course." She was about to enlarge on this when there was a knock on her door. David said that he would get it, and two women appeared, with aluminium suitcases and what appeared to be miniature metal detectors. They were sweeping her flat. Of course they would be sweeping her flat; they had probably done it before, perhaps during Breezeblock.

"All clear, sir," said one of the women, who then turned to Jane. "Where did you get that computer? V and A would like that, you know. How on earth can you keep it secure? Maggie – " she turned to her colleague – "get something off it, will you? Anything that's supposed to be protected."

Jane glanced quickly at David.

"Are you happy with this – sir?" she asked.

"Oh yes," he replied, and looked away, smiling.

Maggie picked up the computer, and Jane assumed she would switch it on; instead, with magic-circle speed she had removed about a dozen screws, taken out the hard disk, and attached it with a ribbon-like connector to a device within one of the cases.

"It's a tiny hard disk," she muttered, "that's bad."

Jane looked worried. "Bad?" she asked.

"Bad for us ma'am," she said, "good for you."

Within a very short while she had confirmed that there was no readable content. There was nothing, no trace even of the operating system, and she seemed disappointed.

"What scrubber did you use?" she enquired.

"It's called Dinkywipe, I think. It's on the floppy."

"Your system's on a floppy?"

"Yes, and the encryption is called Haystack."

"Never heard of either of them. How does Haystack work?"

"I don't really know. It's based on a book cipher, but three different books. E-books, obviously. The books are on floppies, and I know a code word which apparently provides the parameters of an algorithm to combine them."

"Blimey." Maggie said. "You're Patty's lot aren't you? Always something different. Dinkywipe seems to work. It's not easy to scrub a disk properly. As you know, I'm sure. And it takes ages usually, but this is a tiny disk, so it's much quicker."

"Based on the – Goodman? – system, I think."

"Near enough. Right you are then." She turned to the other technician. "All done."

"Put it together again for them, Maggie."

"Oh yes, sorry. I'll just..."

David picked up the laptop pieces, and the screws.

"Thanks very much, we're not totally incompetent."

"Despite your gender, sir."

"Yes, that's right, and my age."

The two women left and David pushed the bits and pieces towards Alan with the sort of gesture which a Brahmin might make towards a steak pie. Alan re-assembled the computer, Jane prepared coffee and they made themselves as comfortable as was possible in Jane's unlovely sitting room.

"Well done, Jane" said Alan.

Jane asked Alan whether he had found the art course with the Met useful – or perhaps he wasn't such a philistine as her to start with? She had enjoyed it; especially meeting the part time special constables. She had had no idea, and thought that this was probably true of most of the public, that civilian experts were employed – attached, rather, because they weren't paid by the police – to help the Met art squad, for example in searches of galleries and store rooms, sometimes belonging to quite reputable firms, for stolen or counterfeit work. Alan agreed; in the early stages of the search for the Duke's Vermeer he had moved in social and artistic circles where the air was so thin that he had found breathing, let alone conversing, quite difficult, but his course with the Met had restored his self-confidence. He had enjoyed their matter-of-fact approach, and absorbed the sergeant's warning that anything, whatever any expert said, or provenance purported to prove, might be a fairy.

"Did you meet the duchess?" he asked Jane.

"Harriet? Yes, she was lovely, very friendly. She more or less mentored me; she knew a lot about everything, but she seemed to like late eighteenth century British best. We went to the London; they obviously knew her there, the Director actually came out of his office to say hello. Why do they call her duchess? I didn't think it polite to ask."

"She does know a lot about Turners, doesn't she? Four of her dad's are hanging there. That's why the Director smarms around her."

"So she is a duchess? I didn't think she was married."

"No; it was probably the witty Constable Reynolds who started calling her that. But her dad's the Earl of Salterton. Nice gaff; bit smoky in the hall when they're roasting an ox."

"Oh, you visited, did you?"

David cut them short. He had dropped the light hearted, casual tone of their walk in the park before she had gone on her Art for Beginners course. In fact, he looked ever so slightly put out. Jane noticed this, and wondered.

"Jane, you're off to join the Met Protection Unit tomorrow. As far as they're concerned it's part of your training, because you might be posted abroad to do some sort of security job in an Embassy. Don't start nosing around for three or four days, just feel your way in. Remember, the PU are trained to be suspicious – you have to be just as careful with them as with Armstrong – more so, probably. Armstrong has a team of five, two on most of the time, sometimes just one when he's at home. The leader is called Ken Foster. He'll introduce you to the others. I can't guarantee they'll be particularly friendly. Report to Holland Park police station, that's where PU is based, at oh seven hundred and they'll kit you out. They know you can fire a gun, but you'd better take your PSA/6 with you."

"Wilco."

"Sorry, I sometimes forget we're civilians. Seven o'clock. In the morning. The certificate they gave you after your firearms course. Any questions?"

"If there are problems I presume that I liaise with you – not Alan here?"

"Of course. Use the secure mobile number. But I don't expect you'll need to."

As they left, Alan allowed David to walk on ahead, and told Jane that he would be quite interested in Armstrong's art collection; in fact, that was why he'd asked David if he could join them this morning.

"Anything in particular?"

"No, not really; just wondering whether he's got it all hanging up; it's not a very big house, is it?"

"You'd like to know if he's got the odd Raphael in a bank vault?"

"That sort of thing, yes."

"Well, that's partly what David wants to know, isn't it? By the way, Alan, why did David insist on you putting my laptop together again? I meant to ask him."

"There are three other Deputy Directors as well as Henry. Two ex MI6, one ex MI5. Henry is an old mate of Sir Richard, and gets on very well, as we know, with Jennifer. The others can be a trifle envious."

"So we're not all one big happy family?"

"We rub along quite well, really. But people like to know what's going on, don't they?"

"You think – you really think – they might have been going to bug it?"

"You just never know."

"You're paranoid."

"Thank you, it's very kind of you to say so."

Chapter 11

July 17   Armstrong   Jane   Danny

Patricia and Christopher

Armstrong was in a meeting with the PM and assorted advisers. Sergeant Danny was there, wearing his baggy suit, light blue M&S shirt and regimental tie. He had been a soldier in Bosnia before he joined the police, but didn't talk about it. He took very seriously his task of preparing Jane, whom, of course, he knew as Penny, for her potential role in security at an embassy abroad. Jane liked him; she thought him trustworthy, understood and approved the instructions which from time to time he gave her, and felt comfortable in his company. In fact, the various training courses she had attended in the past three years had covered most of the ground already, in some cases in greater depth, but she took pains not to reveal this. In her FO and SD career so far – not always in her private life – she had encountered neither sexism nor racism, and she had wondered whether working with the police might be different. It hadn't been so far. Quite a few of the PU were female, although she was the only woman on Armstrong's detail. The race thing just didn't seem an issue either. Perhaps she had been lucky.

"Hello Penny. How are you today?"

"Fine thanks, and you?"

"Mustn't grumble. Armstrong's off to visit his aunt in St Egbert's this pm. But we think," – he indicated the Cabinet Office aide who was fidgeting in the recess between the umbrella stand and a bust of Robert Walpole, arranging and re-arranging papers in a buff folder. He caught Jane's eye and smiled briefly. Danny continued, "we think that the PM is just asking him to have an informal word with some of the staff, possibly a couple of the consultants, gauge their reactions to the White Paper. Then he'll have to say hello to the Chief Executive, but the idea is that he gets to the nurses and doctors first. So he's just going to go up at visiting time. His PA will ring the hospital, but late, accidental on purpose. We'll have to go with him, of course. What do nurses and doctors think of these new ideas? Do you know?"

"Hate them, I should think. They're just ideological, aren't they?"

"Search me, love. I'm just wondering whether we'll have to get him out the back way."

"Down the mortuary lift, you mean?"

"Well, that would be fun. On a trolley, covered with a sheet. Will you push me or would that upset the porters?"

They had been overheard by Armstrong, who was walking briskly towards the front door. Jane grinned, and they followed him out, together with the aide, who spoke to him as he bent down to get into the car. Whatever it was he said, Armstrong answered that he'd just have to cancel it, or why couldn't Archie go instead, for heaven's sake? Then he shouted to his protection officers, "Get into the car, we're not going in convoy, when we get there you can make sure that bad men haven't been following us, then you can go and have a cup of tea with Sister. See what she thinks."

"About what, Minister?" said Danny, heavily, as they accelerated down Whitehall, leaving the aide behind looking exasperated.

"About the White Paper, of course. Desmond's baby. Step-child. Foisted on him, poor blighter. Continuous change, I ask you." He shook his head. "Ironic, really, because it was that Trotsky who invented continuous change – Daniel? Penny? "

Danny looked blank, so did Jane.

"Well, Trotsky liked armoured trains and he just loved the rattle of machine guns, and Desmond's a gentle soul. And not exactly on the left of the Party. As for continuous change, it may be all right for oil companies or banks, but I'm damn sure... well, we shall see."

So, thought Jane, that's your cards on the table. Who's for the ice pick? Not gentle Desmond, surely?

"Minister, with the greatest of respect," said Danny, with even more weight than before – Armstrong looked as if he was about to interrupt, but changed his mind – "we are not allowed to take any role which appertains to your political or civil service staff."

"I know, Daniel, I know. Thought you might be interested in what the NHS staff think of all this turmoil about to be thrust upon them, that's all. It doesn't matter, though. Just make sure she doesn't stick a needle full of insulin into me."

"We will keep you quite safe, Minister."

"That appertains to our role, Minister," added Jane, who received an old fashioned look from her colleague.

"I keep forgetting you're Foreign Office, not straight police. How's she getting on, then, Dan, am I safe in her hands?"

"I'm sure you would be, sir, but at the moment you have two pairs of hands protecting you from vicissitudes, and, sometimes, like yesterday, buying you a newspaper and a bag of toffees."

"Well, so I do Dan. You put it very nicely. I met your boss the other day, Penny, he asked how you were getting on. It was at one of these interminable security meetings. He was talking to Dame Jenny, I don't expect you've come across her? SIS. SD, I mean."

Christ. "No, minister, um, I hope you..."

"Oh yes, said fine, I thought. But the point is I said to myself, God, he's posh for a copper, before I remembered." Then he winked at Danny.

One of Patty's FO cronies, Jane presumed, adding a bit of colour to my cover.

Armstrong continued, "Alice, drive up Bond Street, would you, I want to dash into Dowland's."

"That'll make us very late, Minister, the traffic's terrible. It's not on our way."

"I know that. But I haven't got an appointment, remember, I'm just turning up."

"Very well sir."

The driver pulled down her sun visor, which then displayed a large badge which would indicate to any traffic police that they should give her priority, and neatly performed a u-turn to the indignant surprise of the oncoming cars. They had to drive slowly along Bond Street because taxis and chauffeured limousines would stop and start abruptly as, presumably, their occupants spotted the very shop which they needed. There should have been a sign at the end of Clifford Street, she thought, which read 'No entry except for the filthy rich. No coats except mink, no wrist watches except Rolexes, no semi-precious or costume jewellery.' Jane was mentally enlarging upon this theme as she watched a woman in fur and lizard dart across the pavement from Asprey's into the safety of her Bentley. The men were easy. No coats except cashmere, no shoes except thin brogues with little tassels, no untidy hair. No hats – their car was drawing to a halt, pulling in front of a taxi, ignoring signs which promised especially high parking fines, stopping outside the deceptively modest frontage of the famous auction house. Armstrong jumped out, Danny said quickly, "You go in after him, Penny, it's a bit posh for a copper."

Alice the driver and Danny had a bit of a moan about their boss, but it was only half hearted. Danny actually found him quite friendly and considerate, not at all arrogant – "There's no *side* to him," he would say to his friends in the PU, and they would know exactly what he meant, because they encountered plenty of VIPs who were all side and very little bottom. Alice, in fact, who was an excellent driver and seemed to know all the back doubles not only in London but in half the big cities in England, rather liked the privileges afforded her car by virtue of the status of its passenger. She also found him very attractive, and envied her younger colleagues who would sometimes flirt with their bosses.

Armstrong was immediately recognised by the young lady in the foyer of Dowland's, who had indeed been expecting him, she confessed, to view the upcoming sale. They walked along a short corridor and up the stairs to the gallery where the paintings to be included in the sale were hung. There was no great press of people viewing, and many of them seemed quite ordinary – they must have acquired special permits, Jane imagined, pursuing her previous train of thought, to visit the saleroom, on condition that they didn't try to enter any of the shops. Armstrong was chatting to one of the other viewers, a school-masterly looking chap in his middle years; they appeared to be discussing one of the pictures. Jane had surveyed the room and clocked two of the punters who had come in shortly after themselves, and who clearly recognised Armstrong, a slightly shabby couple in their late forties, she guessed; they seemed to present no immediate threat and were in any case intent on examining a beautiful painting of race horses exercising in the early morning mist on the South Downs. She was sure she recognised the style – this was one of the painters to whose work she had been introduced by Rob in Hackney – but she couldn't for the life of her remember the name. The picture had a number, and there was a list on an easel. Alfred Munnings, of course. The man turned to her, and asked her if she liked it.

"Of course I do," she replied. "But I'm just here with a friend, I'm not a collector or anything."

"Yes, I think I saw you with Jim Armstrong just in front of us?"

"That's right; do you know him, then?"

"Oh yes, don't we dear?" he said to the lady who was with him, introducing her as Patricia, but not waiting to hear Jane's name, "we quite often bump into them at sales, but I don't think I've ever seen Jim buy anything?"

"No, I don't think so. Lucy likes modern British – and Sebastian was telling me that they've acquired a very good late Hopkins. We went round once, some time ago, wasn't it, Chris, with Leonard – they didn't have it then. I'm sure Lucy would have shown it to us."

Chris leaned towards Jane, and spoke to her in the sort of tone commonly used to confide information about a person's illness, or prison record. "They say she's got a very good eye. Can spot a bargain, too."

Patricia said, "I think he's coming over. Oh God, he's got Reg with him. Shall we have to talk about that bloke who wets his bed and exhibits the sheets?"

"It isn't real urine darling, it's orange squash, I think. Or is it tea? Let's ask. Oh, missed my chance, he's off. Jim Armstrong, how nice to see you. Are you going to bid against the London for that Nicholson, then?"

"You jest. And the London isn't interested in it either, Reg was very cagey about what he was doing here; he's got enough Nicholsons of his own, I imagine. What's he looking at now?"

"Oh, yes, it's the Freud, we wanted to have a look at that too, it's relatively modest, isn't it?"

"Modest? Not a term I would use. It's a *Freud*."

"Not too big. Not life size."

"Oh, I see what you mean. I like Freud. He's got a vision, hasn't he?"

"Yes. He's extraordinary. Have you met him?"

"Once, at Cheltenham actually, Robin Cook and I were having a bit of a flutter and so was he. I must say, I like that painting. What's its estimate, Penny, can you see?"

"It's up on the easel over there, Minister."

"Yes I know, Penny, but I've got the wrong glasses on. Be a dear, will you, thank you so much."

When Penny had called Armstrong 'Minister' Patricia and Chris had caught each other's eye and looked slightly surprised.

Penny went to find out how much the auctioneers wanted the prospective purchasers to think the Freud might fetch – usually a deliberate underestimate. She noted this figure, and reported back impassively.

"Is it now? Upon my soul. How many BCs have got Freud, Tricia?"

Chris whispered to Jane, "BCs – big collectors. If a lot of them are in to Freud, the prices will probably rise when the old rascal pops his clogs – not that he's ill, or anything, but he must be in his late seventies."

"Let's think...I can think of about ten straight off. Plus the rock stars, of course, but they don't count – probably forgotten they bought one. Yes, I expect prices will hold."

"Hmm. I wonder. I don't know, though...what do you think, Penny?"

Jane was startled, but contrived a polite and sensible reply, relying mainly on what Harriet had told her about this most eminent modern representative of a distinguished dynasty.

"Yes, but do you *like* it?"

"Well, yes, I do. A woman, not a sex object? But why does she look so, so...grim?"

"She's probably been sitting for hours and hours. It's a strain sitting for Freud. Unless he lets you go to sleep, of course. And, as for not being a sex object..."

Jane knew perfectly well what people said about Freud and his models.

"As a matter of interest, Minister, does he ever paint black women?"

"I don't think so. He wouldn't be able to use his customary palette – the colours he likes to mix, that is."

Patricia and Chris had been patrolling the room, stopping occasionally to inspect a painting more closely, and they had now re-joined Armstrong and Jane. They had seen a few things they liked, but probably not enough to want to attend the sale. There were a couple of Festival paintings, and a Ravilious, but they weren't inspired.

"I agree. Apart from the Freud, that is, and there's one over there – oh, I'm sorry, I haven't introduced you. Penny, Chris and Tricia. They've got a marvellous collection, their own gallery really."

"Hello, Penny. You're in Jim's private office, I imagine? Destined for great things?"

Jane didn't know how to reply. She was fairly sure that Armstrong would not have included any of his other PU staff in this sort of encounter. She tried the simplest response.

"No, I work for the Foreign Office, but I'm seconded at the moment."

Chris had, meanwhile, been playing his little private game of matching Jane to a character in a picture. The ladies in the paintings from Dominica which came to his mind all had nipped in waists; Penny was wearing a loose jacket. Hang on, he thought, what's that?

Armstrong, noticing immediately what Chris had noticed, and having also noticed that Jane had been momentarily at a loss, explained.

"Penny's here to protect me from assassins. But she does work for the FO. It's some sort of training secondment. Her partner's in the ante-room, I think, watching the door."

Chris asked him whether it was usual for Cabinet Ministers to go about with two bodyguards.

"No, but the PM thinks I might be particularly unpopular for some reason. Perhaps it was the uproar over the Lightship deal which made us – me and the Foreign Secretary, that is – more than a few enemies in North Africa. And the Daily Shield campaign didn't help."

He asked Jane whether she had been given any special instructions – any particular types, or individuals, to look out for.

She replied that he was of course always privy to whatever brief had been issued to his protection staff.

"Oh yes; that's right – and that's what we say, Chris, 'Protection Officers', not 'Bodyguards'. We're not pop singers. Now, let me ask your opinion of the ravishing little Gwen John watercolour over there. That might be more to Lucy's taste, I fancy. And my price range. Just."

The drive to St Egbert's was as slow and tedious as Alice had predicted. She asked Armstrong whether she should ask SB Ops to whistle up a motor cycle escort, and he answered that his visit to Dowland's could not be called official business, – but his visit to Auntie in hospital was less obviously private, since he would be using it to gain some insights into how the changes to the Health Service which had been foisted on his friend Desmond were viewed by nurses and doctors on the wards, not just their unions or colleges. Alice explained to Jane the arcane accountancy rules which determined the payments for the use of cars from the Government car pool. Apparently each department had to pay for the use of these vehicles, and whether or not they paid the extra for the armoured cars was a matter of negotiation between at least three sets of civil servants. The computer billing system, not quite up and running, was a standard refuge for Government programmers whose departmental IT schemes had been scrapped. (Alice screwed her face up and winked at this point, but Jane thought that what she said was probably true). Armstrong himself would probably pay for half the afternoon's excursion at a standard rate of – and here Jane's concentration once again wandered. She was watching pedestrians and the other cars, as she was supposed to, and could see that he was occasionally recognised in traffic jams, but there were neither friendly waves nor obscene gestures. Armstrong himself noticed nothing; he was now working through papers in his red box. The cultural interlude was over.

At St Egbert's, Armstrong told Alice to pull up under the shabby porte-cochère, ignoring the clear signs which indicated that only 'permitted vehicles' and ambulances were allowed to stop. He walked briskly up the steps followed closely by Danny and Jane. The grand mahogany doors with which the nineteenth century benefactor had equipped the hospital's portico had been replaced by modern glass ones, which hissed and puffed as they slid open. Inside he looked around him. Jane pointed out the Enquiries desk, but he explained that although his visit to Auntie was private, he wanted to have an impromptu chat with medical staff about the White Paper. He had spotted a very tall man dressed in what appeared to be the trousers of an expensively tailored chalk stripe suit, and a short sleeved shirt from some chain store with a gold Mont Blanc fountain pen in its breast pocket. This man also had an entourage, two presumably junior doctors, wearing similar clothes but with cheaper trousers, and carrying the tools of their trade more conspicuously than Jane and Danny were carrying theirs.

"Good afternoon," said Armstrong to this man. "Could you direct me to Agnes Ward, please?"

The man looked more bemused than annoyed. "The Enquiries desk is just behind you."

"Yes, so it is, but there's a bit of a queue. Just the briefest of directions would be fine."

The older of the two junior doctors, noting the expression on the consultant's face, hastily answered that it was two floors up, then turn left and follow the signs. "But no visiting until four o'clock" she added.

"Thank you so much," said Armstrong, giving all three doctors his nicest smile, "Come along, chaps."

As they took the stairs, two at a time, he said, "That was about right, I think, that tall guy knew that he knew me, he'll be putting a name to the face now, I shouldn't wonder."

This recognition did not in fact occur until the consultant was explaining to his trainees in clinic, some ten minutes later, that they really must learn not to put all their faith in biochemical tests and that a patient who was showing obvious clinical signs of thyroid disease should not be discharged just because her chemistry appeared normal. He told his houseman to re-examine the patient, and walked quickly down the corridor to the office.

"Get Sister on Agnes on the phone straight away please. Yes, immediately."

"Crosby-Hunt here, Sister. Who have you got on the ward with a famous relative? Or friend – do you know?"

"Well, Doctor, there's Flo Meredith, says she's some politician or other's auntie, but she's eighty two and she has got a slight UTI. She's got three people with her now, we stretched the visiting rules, they seemed very nice, Staff said."

"Thank you Sister, I'm afraid you may have one or two more visitors. Who's Flo Meredith under?"

"Professor James, Doctor. He's got a round at five thirty."

"I suspect he may be early, Sister."

*****

Armstrong had introduced himself to the Staff nurse as Flo Meredith's nephew, and apologised that he and his friends had come outside visiting hours, but it would be his only chance of seeing Auntie before her operation.

Oh, she had said, but they can't operate until her infection's better, and it's only a minor op, could be done as a day case in someone less frail. But since they'd made the effort – and it would cheer her up. So in they went.

Danny and Jane agreed afterwards that he was lovely with her. She was very pleased to see him, and laughed with delight when he introduced Danny and Jane as his bodyguards.

"It's ever so hot in here, isn't it?" she said after a moment. Of course it was hot, with the temperature designed for lightly clad, immobile people, not for the well and vigorous, dressed in outdoor clothes. But they both refused, as nicely as they knew how, to take off their jackets and show her their guns.

She wasn't very ill, but as Armstrong said afterwards, she was over eighty, and he hadn't seen her for quite a while, and you never knew. They had talked a bit about current matters, about Flo's health and what the Queen was really like, and why England couldn't ever win the Eurovision Song Contest, but soon reverted to family stories, mainly centring on Christmases past, and a famous holiday together on Anglesey. In a little while Armstrong told his Auntie that he just needed to pop out and see Sister, or she'd think him rude. Penny would stay with her, but Daniel had better come along with him.

Danny tapped on the Sister's office door, put his head round and asked if it would be convenient for 'The Secretary of State' to have a word with her. She looked momentarily puzzled and Danny added, "Mrs Meredith's nephew?"

"Yes, yes, of course." Oh dear, she thought, and we wondered whether Flo was a bit... and who is this, what was it, Secretary of State? Aren't there more than one? At any rate, no procedural short cuts now. "I'll just come and see if

Mrs Meredith is happy with this," she said, "and who did you say the gentleman is?"

"Mr Armstrong"

No wonder Dr Crosby-Hunt thought Professor James might come up a bit early. With all his firm, no doubt, and half the bloody administration too. She stood up and came to the door, which Danny held open for her. She squeezed past him, saying, "And you are...?"

"A member of his staff, Sister, as is the young lady."

The sister recognised Armstrong at Auntie Flo's bedside, and the three of them chatted easily for a few minutes. What a charming man, she thought, not a bit like the Daily Shield makes out. The woman with him kept in the background. Armstrong asked what arrangements had been made for Auntie's care while she was recuperating at home – she wouldn't be able to cook, with her right hand in plaster, or even wash easily. The sister assured him that the aftercare team would draw up a plan together with Mrs Meredith and... who had Mrs Meredith named as carer? she asked one of the three nurses who had by now found jobs to do in Flo's four-bedded bay.

"My niece, dear," Flo answered for them, "Jimmy's cousin. But she lives in Guildford, and can't come above twice a week, and that's an effort. But I've got lovely neighbours, they're always popping in."

"Hmm," said Armstrong, "perhaps we ought to have a word about that, Sister."

"You mustn't worry about her aftercare, Mr Armstrong, it'll be properly coordinated with Social Services."

And on this occasion it certainly will, she thought.

One of the nurses brought in a tray of coffee and biscuits, chocolate ones on a paper doily. The sister rolled her eyes up and Armstrong grinned. He picked up the plate and offered a biscuit to Sister and then to the nurses, and asked her how the impending reorganisation might affect people like his aunt.

"Your auntie would be just the sort of person they'd economise on," said the youngest nurse, who started to explain just how the system worked at present, and why it would change. Danny, who had been listening intently, seized on this point. It emerged that his mother had recently been discharged from hospital earlier than he had expected; his father had explained to him who was responsible for what, but Danny hadn't really understood, so he asked the nurse to explain, and to tell him why it might get worse – scrappy, she said, after these daft changes. Armstrong listened attentively. By the time Professor James, his registrars, housemen, and students, arrived, and they had all except Jane moved through to the day room, he had learned from the nursing staff, who had rapidly gained the confidence to tell him what they really thought, the strength of opposition to the changes. Moreover, it seemed that the cooperation, the link, between hospitals and social services, a bridge between two quite different philosophies, laboriously constructed over the last decade and still a precarious structure, was about to be torn down and replaced by a system of competition, with all the secrecy and questionable marketing which that would involve.

More medics arrived, followed by an indeterminate group of managers; on the whole the doctors opposed the changes but – and this surprised Armstrong – some of the lay staff seemed quite enthusiastic. Armstrong, despite his long experience of political antagonisms, was almost embarrassed by the patent contempt in which the senior doctors held these managers. Jane meanwhile, who was listening to Flo's opinions on afternoon television game shows, the extended Royal family, and immigration, was smiling as much as she could, and becoming rather bored.

"So, where are you from then, dear?" asked Flo.

"Cheshire originally, but I was brought up in Oxford."

"Oh. That's nice."

On the way back, as the Jaguar inched its way along the Euston Road, Armstrong thanked Danny for the extremely useful way he had started the conversation about the new health service policy.

"Obviously I couldn't start it myself – that would have been quite out of order. Mustn't tread on Des's toes. But, no harm in listening. And you're jolly well informed about the NHS. Very helpful indeed, thank you."

"Oh, well Minister, I didn't actually, I mean..."

"Yes of course, it doesn't appertain, sorry, I was forgetting."

Armstrong winked at Jane. At least she thought – it was the merest flutter of his eyelid, perhaps she was imagining it – and, how was Danny with teasing?

Danny was all right. In fact, he was quite pleased.

Alice had decided to make an attempt to avoid the jammed dual carriageway by looping through Regent's Park, and had made momentary use of her siren to cross the stream of east bound traffic. She left the Hampstead road and cut through Robert Street, intending to cross Albany Street and make her way to the Inner Circle. Half way along Robert Street a length of the road had been coned off, and a gang of men were lowering pipes down a hole. There was a small digger, and a yellow diesel compressor. No temporary traffic lights had been erected, nor were there any workmen with stop/go signs. A tortuous pedestrian way through the works was roughly marked with red and white tape. Two workmen had seen the Jaguar, and it was clear to Jane, by the way that they were staring, that they had recognised Armstrong. One of them was gesticulating and talking excitedly to his mate.

The Jaguar had halted to let two cars through, and then, before it could carry on, this man stepped out in front and walked straight at the car, stopping a dozen or so yards from the bonnet. He was white, thickset, and bare armed. In his right hand he carried an iron bar.

"Whoops," said Danny, and, to Armstrong, "don't worry sir, the car's well armoured. But we'll have to see to him. Stay with the Minister, Penny."

But Jane was already half out of the car, probably failing to hear Danny who called, "You have to shout 'Armed Police'."

"Damn," he said to Armstrong, "She'll have to use an aid; I wouldn't, I'm big enough."

"An aid?"

"A weapon sir. PAVA spray, in this case."

Hope to God she doesn't lose it and get her Glock out, Danny thought.

"Well, go and help her then."

"Can't now sir, got to stay with you."

"What about the other guy, what if he joins in?"

"He won't, sir, just look at him."

The other workman indeed looked scared, glancing nervously at his mate, the car, and the shop doorways, perhaps searching for somewhere to hide.

Jane had quickly decided that the man approaching the car was not angry in the sort of over-excited, uncontrolled way of rioters in a mob; rather, he appeared determined to do harm, merely pausing to work out exactly how to use his weapon.

"Get out of the way, love," he said, as she walked towards him.

She put her hands up, palms towards him, in the standard placatory gesture.

"You know that I can't do that. Don't come any closer, please don't come any closer. Why are you so angry? Tell me the reason for it. Tell me the problem, please. Tell me the problem first."

"It's got nothing to do with you. Just fuck off, will you?"

In the car Alice spoke to Danny. "Go and help her now, for God's sake."

Armstrong said, "Yes, you'd better go now, Dan."

Danny had been watching the confrontation intently. Alice was right; if the man got much nearer, could Penny get her spray out in time? If not – it didn't bear thinking about. He started to open his door.

They appeared to be talking. The man had been angry at first, shouting at Jane, but now he seemed to be listening to her replies, and speaking to her in a more normal tone of voice. As Danny prepared to get out of the car the man's right hand, holding the crowbar, gradually dropped to his side. Danny became still, and gently pulled the car door shut again. The man turned abruptly, and walked away. He let the bar fall to the ground and leaned on the side of the digger, no longer gazing intently at the car and its occupants.

Jane returned, and Alice drove quickly through the roadworks and away.

Armstrong said, "Well done Penny, that could have been nasty. It upsets me, you know, to see the hatred, the open hatred ..."

Danny said nothing, but they all sensed his anger. Alice murmured that she'd switched the video on, of course, and the local police could take over.

After a moment Armstrong asked Jane how she had managed to alleviate the man's anger, and, in any case, what had caused it. Jane, who seemed to Danny to be surprisingly calm for a trainee – not even one with police experience – told them the story. It was simple, and tragic. Two years ago, a Trade Department enquiry had established that a British armaments manufacturer had been gaining contracts with unpleasant regimes abroad by means of immense bribes. This was illegal, but it was well known among exporters that in those countries gross bribery was a prerequisite of any business negotiation. It had been up to the Government to decide whether to cancel the contract, the Prime Minister had been conveniently obliged to attend a conference in Paris, and the cancellation had been made, and announced, by Armstrong. The workman hadn't had to explain this to Jane – it had been all over the newspapers. Most commentators berated the Government for putting international law before British self-interest. A factory closed, workmen were sacked, in a depressed town in the North East. The man's brother, after a year on the dole and the break-up of his family, had killed himself with whisky and paracetamol.

"I didn't do anything special, I just spoke to him, said the obvious things. Just got him talking, that's all."

The drive through Regent's Park passed in silence. Jane wondered why she had taken it upon herself to jump out of the car before Danny. What did she have to prove? She was, after all, only playing a role here; she wasn't really a trainee protection officer. On the other hand, she supposed that it didn't matter what sort of report might reach David. He might raise an eyebrow at 'precipitate behaviour', – if he read it, and why should he? It just didn't matter how good a protection officer she was.

Danny was still silent. Jane feared that he would show his anger when they both went off shift later. She would have to use her newly discovered talent for calming down furious men. Danny was, in fact, employing a technique of self-control taught him by the counsellor to whom he had been referred some time before, after an incident in which he had used improper language to a badly behaved younger member of the Royal Family. He was supposed to imagine himself spooning all the words, or phrases, which he wanted to use, into a large jar of treacle, then stirring thoroughly and screwing down the lid. After a while the worst expletives would sink, and he could open the jar and carefully spoon the top layer, of lighter and less offensive terms, from the mix. By the time he would be able to speak to Jane on her own his words would be measured, if still appropriate to the enormity of her transgression.

Armstrong, also silent, had been deeply upset by the story of the workman's brother; like all statesmen he could accept that in a fundamentally unfair world no decision would be without its costs, but where these costs were exemplified in terms of acute personal suffering he was unable to accept them with equanimity. In this respect he was unlike many of his cabinet colleagues.

"Alice," he said, "what did you mean when you said that the local police could take over?"

"I give them the video recording, they trace the assailant and prosecute him. He'll plead guilty. The video's quite clear."

"The assailant. Is it just a disk?"

"Yes, there's a slot in that bit of kit," she pointed at a bulging affair between the top of the windscreen and the padded roof of the car. He could see it now – he'd never noticed it; the front of the car seemed to have controls, dials and switches all over the place. He spoke to Danny, who was sitting next to Alice.

"Let's have a look, eject it for me, Danny."

Danny frowned, but did as he was asked.

"Thanks. It just looks like an ordinary DVD. Do you keep others – blanks – in the car, Alice?

"Yes, in the glove box."

"Good." He dropped the disk into the foot well of the car, and scraped his foot across it. "Damn, how clumsy. You'd better put another one in, Danny."

Danny shut his eyes and took a deep breath, but again did what he was asked.

Armstrong continued, "You didn't really feel threatened, did you, Penny? He just wanted to tell you about his brother? You handled it very well, I thought; you thought so too, didn't you, Danny?"

"I think we get the point, sir," said Danny.

"Good. Now, Penny, which of those paintings would you have liked to take home with you?"

*****

Back at Holland Park police station, Danny did indeed tell Jane that she had behaved recklessly, and that quick reactions were pointless when the action taken was incorrect. She readily admitted her failing, displeased with herself not because she had put herself in a situation which she might not have been able to handle – she thought this to be untrue, – but because in the heat of the moment she had allowed her cover to determine her behaviour. Going native, it was called. Again, she put it to herself bluntly; she was here not to protect Armstrong, but to spy on him. It had turned out well, Armstrong had praised her, and it would probably make her job easier. But she couldn't deceive herself that she had worked this out in advance. She had jumped out of the car to protect him, that was the long and short of it.

"Well," said Danny, "we'll let it rest then. Mind you, I don't think I've ever seen such a cut-and-dried case of threatening behaviour. The police are supposed to enforce the law, you know, and we leave sympathy to the magistrates, or the jury. At least, that's the theory. I don't suppose you see it as a policeman would, because you're not one, are you? You must admit, an iron bar, that's pretty bloody aggressive."

"But," he added, "it was quite something, the way you handled it. If there is a next time, wait for my instructions, OK?"

"Yes, Danny. Sorry. And thanks."

Chapter 12

July 22   Jane   Lucy

Saturday morning, and a shift at Armstrong's house. Jane would stay there, and if Armstrong were to go out for any reason the other PU officer would accompany him, and Jane would remain behind. She was supposed to make it obvious that the house was protected by standing outside some of the time, but she would also have to patrol the interior – not that it was a particularly large house – and watch the monitors of the CCTV cameras. She relieved one of the night shift officers at half past seven; changeovers were staggered and she was briefed by the officer who would remain until nine o'clock. The night had been quiet, Armstrong working on his boxes until midnight, and Lucy reading or listening to music. Only one of their three children still lived at home, but she was away, staying with friends. The Protection Unit had been given the use of a small room facing east, which had probably been called the breakfast room when the house had been built a hundred years or so ago. There was a view through trees to Victoria Park, and the early morning sun streamed in, almost killing the images on the monitors; but it was a nice room to work in, well-proportioned, with bookcases, pictures and a worn oriental carpet. The armchairs had been moved out to make room for a desk and small filing cabinet, but a sofa remained, with a sand coloured loose cover and a faded Indian cotton throw, which Lucy Armstrong hoped might protect it from the boots of tired policemen. Her Maltese cleaning lady had in fact made it quite clear to the policemen that dirt on the sofa would be about as acceptable as ring-marks on the table top, but despite her representations to Lucy some pottery items, fairings, and Staffordshire figures, had been left on the shelves. It was the sort of friendly room which Jane liked, while being doubtful whether she could create. Most of the other rooms were less intimate, cooler; mainly, she thought, to afford the most favourable setting for the art collection. She hadn't been on this duty long enough to talk to Armstrong or his wife about anything except Protection Unit affairs; she thought that the previous day's visit to the auction house, and the incident with the workman and the iron bar, might now give her one or two opportunities for conversation.

Armstrong was collected by Alice in the Jaguar at about half past nine. The diary showed that he would be spending most of the day at Number 10. Maria, the cleaning lady, only came in for a couple of hours in the morning on Saturdays and before she left she put her head round the door and asked Jane if she would like a cup of coffee. They chatted in the kitchen for ten minutes or so, mainly about Maria's cousin who was struggling to make a success of a small restaurant near Homerton hospital. Maria had quite taken to Jane, partly because she always made an effort to tidy up the kitchen properly – the use of kitchen and bathroom was often a source of friction between PU officers and their clients, or their clients' staff; however painstakingly the training course might deal with this issue, there were always officers, of both genders, who could not see the difference between a tea-towel and a hand towel, or between a mug swilled in cold water and plonked on the draining board and one washed and dried properly and left hanging from its own hook.

After Maria had left, Jane entered various diary items on the database and checked the CCTV. The movement read-out showed nothing except Armstrong, the protection officer, and then Maria, leaving. Nobody lurking in the shrubbery. Her own notes, kept at home, were so far sparse. She stood in the porch for a minute or two, looking up and down the street for anything unusual, then she walked round the house and checked the back garden, peered in the tool shed and rattled the sitting room French windows to make sure they were locked. She was returning to the breakfast room through the front door when she heard Lucy shouting, wailing rather, "Penny, Penny, where are you?" The call had a certain quality, not exactly desperation, nevertheless it caused Jane to hurry into the hall. The call came again, "Penny, *Penny*, – oh, for goodness sake – " her cry tailed off, but it had clearly come from the dining room. Jane ran to the door, unclipping the flap of her holster because that was the routine. When she entered the room she saw Lucy standing at the end of the long table with her back to the door, gripping something; a skein of wool, some sort of bundle of threads? At the other end of the table seemed to be a complicated wooden frame, with wheels and a handle, and the cords which Lucy was holding stretched the length of the table to this contraption. Lucy turned round to her, and burst out laughing.

"I'm *so* sorry, I didn't mean to alarm you, I've been calling for ages, well, not ages, you know... "

"I've been checking outside."

"Yes, of course... could you *please* help me... I've just bought this thing, it's from New Zealand, it's a loom and I've got to wind these threads, the warp, onto that roller, but it's taken me all morning to get it ready and if I let go they'll all go into a tangle again, I think. It's my new toy. I'm trying to run before I can walk. If you could just hold them – like this, yes," – she moved quickly round the table to the loom, and started to wind the handle.

"Keep them straight, yes, and tight... that's great."

Jane was now bending right over the end of the table, which was about nine feet long.

"I think you'll have to creep along the side."

So Jane manoeuvred herself round the corner of the table, holding the bundle of warp parallel with the table's edge, and shuffled crab-like towards Lucy. When the warp was completely wound onto the roller, Lucy put the brake on and stood back with an expression of extreme relief.

"Thank you *so* much. I've started a weaving class at the William Morris centre in Hoxton, and we have to have a little table loom set up at home. But I don't think it'll do here, do you? I'll have to put it up in one of the bedrooms. We must have a spare table somewhere. That's enough for now. Come and have a coffee. I made a ginger cake yesterday – you were out with Jim, weren't you? – and you must have a piece. You don't look as if it'll do *you* any harm...whereas I, well...but I think I deserve it. Do you know, I started on that warp yesterday morning?"

"Very nice cake," said Jane as they sat by the French windows in the sitting room. The sun shone on the early summer flowers in the garden, the roses and geraniums, and various plants which looked to Jane like big daisies, but the room itself faced north. Jane had checked it twice a day, as part of her routine, but had spent no time looking round it beyond registering the five pictures, the painters of four of which she could not identify. The walls and woodwork were white and what furniture there was seemed to Jane a sort of cross between post-war utility and modern chain store Scandinavian. There were some very heavy pots on the floor, and today there were only four pictures; one wall was completely bare and there was a mark in the plaster where presumably the picture hook had been, and where now the end of a Rawlplug could be seen just proud of the surface.

"Thanks," said Lucy. "It's a dead easy recipe, would you like it?"

"The recipe?" said Jane. As far as she could remember no-one had ever, in the whole of her life, offered to give her a recipe before. Her expression must have betrayed this, because Lucy smiled and said, "No, I suppose you don't have much time for baking. And I don't expect you eat cakes very often?"

For a while they chatted about nothing in particular. Lucy had recently embarked upon a diet as well as a weaving course. Jane had never really given her figure much thought – a fact which had sometimes annoyed her girl friends in the past, although she was unaware of this. It didn't annoy Lucy, who was twenty five years older, and not in any case given to envy.

"I never used to cook, either," she said, "and weaving, that's completely new. Have some more cake?"

"Yes please. Why these new things?"

"Ah. You know what they say – how long have you got?"

"Me? Oh, I see. Let me just go and check the screens, I shan't be a minute. Then I can have that cake?"

She returned very quickly.

"Nothing untoward. No suspicious characters loitering. You were saying?"

After a short discussion of the virtues of fresh food, Jane thought that she could turn the conversation towards the art collection. She asked about the paintings; said that she wasn't familiar with the style of three of them, but was the fourth by Inchcape?

"Yes it is; do you know her work, then?"

"I've seen some; aren't there one or two in the London?"

"Yes, there are. They've only just dusted them off and brought them up from the cellars – there wasn't much interest until that girl – can't remember her name, friend of Emma Brockridge, publishes feminist tracts – did some research for a monograph and found out that she'd actually taught Hopkins in the late forties. He'd written around to his friends saying what marvellous stuff she produced. Well, as you probably know, Hopkins is all the rage now, bandwagon rolling all right, so the London has hung up these Inchcapes. Never misses a trick, does old Reg. Reg Nicholls, dear, Director of the London. Has rather a rude nickname. You have heard of Hopkins?"

"Oh yes; founder of the Festival school?" Reg. The Mr Chips character in Dowland's had been called Reg, hadn't he?

"They do debate that, you know, these art historians. I'm not sure how important it is, but you should hear them argue! I tend to go for the zeitgeist theory."

"Where? I mean, where would you hear them argue?"

"Lectures, mainly, at the London, or the Courtauld, sometimes at Farrier's. People actually interrupt, you know; it can get very heated."

"But Inchcape's work isn't like Festival paintings, is it?"

"No, not a bit. In any case she produced her best work two or three decades earlier. Very influenced by Sickert."

Jane laughed, because the painting on the wall was a Sickert-style nude, but in this case a male figure, supine, in a pose as revealing in its way as any of Sickert's. Lucy smiled back.

"It was never exhibited, of course. It was a private commission for Peggy Guggenheim, but she can't have liked it much, well, it was obviously far too figurative, what did she expect, and it emerged at a sale in New York in the early fifties. The buyer wrote to Guggenheim and got a brief letter back saying it had been excess stock at the Art of This Century, never displayed and sold off in 1946."

"Wow. Have you got the letter then?"

"Oh no."

"How do you know all this?"

Lucy sucked at her bottom lip, and said, "Our friend Axel told me, I think; I might have got some of the details wrong. How long have you been interested in art?"

"Not long. My boyfriend has been trying to educate me."

"Well he seems to be making quite a good job of it. Is he an artist?"

"No, he's, well, in the same line of work as me."

"Really?"

Lucy realised that her intonation had verged on the rude, and she blushed. Jane didn't particularly feel like easing her embarrassment, but decided that she ought to.

"I mean, he's in the Foreign Office. I am too, you know, hasn't Mr Armstrong told you? This is a sort of work experience I've been sent on; I'm thinking of going into the security arm. I'm supposed to be supernumerary, but they let me do routine stuff here on my own. And I had to do a firearms course. But I'm never on my own with him when he's out and about." It sounded a bit thin, but Lucy grasped its tone, which was all that really mattered at that moment.

"Yes, I think he said something. Of course; I thought there were more police around than before. Look, if you're on duty here on Monday, we've got a really marvellous Michael Harris coming to fill the space," – she pointed at the blank wall – "and it's actually got the Skylon in it. You can't get more Festival school than that. And another one, I think, another corker, a Hopkins."

Jane knew that she was scheduled to spend the day with Armstrong, wherever he needed to go. There was a Cabinet Committee meeting of some sort in the morning, when, of course, Cabinet Office security took over, but it probably wouldn't last more than an hour. She would have to get the rota changed.

"Yes, I'm here Monday. How exciting for you! Is it big?"

"Enormous. It'll fill the wall. Jim has got to drill it tonight and put about six plugs into the bricks for the hooks."

Jane was surprised. Amazed.

"You mean he'll do that himself? After work? After his boxes?"

"Yes," said Lucy, "yes, he's a bloke. They have to do that sort of thing. I'm not going to. I've never used a hammer drill in my life, have you?"

"So," said Jane, "was taking up an interest in art like the cooking and now the weaving – carving out a space for yourself independent of Mr Armstrong?"

"No, not at all. I've always been passionate about art. You can't be *passionate* about cooking, can you – unless you haven't got much upstairs, that is – damn, I shouldn't have said that, I don't mean people who do it for a living, obviously, I don't know what I did mean, really – and perhaps the weaving is a sort of attempt actually to *do* something vaguely artistic. Just like the piano was, but that didn't work, I've got a lousy ear. At any rate, everybody thinks that Jim and I met through local politics, when we were teachers in Liverpool, but in fact we met by the Bratbys in the Walker art gallery. The subjects appealed to us both; muck and poverty."

Later, Jane checked the rota. Danny was the house day-duty officer on Monday; today was one of his days off so she phoned him on his private number and left a message on his answering service, asking him to ring back.

His phone call woke Jane at half past ten on Sunday morning. She denied a hangover, told him that she had been watching a late film on television, which was true but he didn't really believe. Yes, he was quite willing to swap duties. If she wasn't doing anything special, would she like to come round for tea?"

"Oh. Tea. Right, umm..."

"Well, high tea really, we have it together before the kids go to bed. They'd love to meet you, and so would Ruth."

High tea. The kids. Well, why not?

"Thanks, I'd love to."

"Six thirty, 7 St Mawes Rd., Lewisham. The neighbours call it Blackheath, but it's SE13. Train to Lewisham, walk up the hill towards the Heath. Third turning on the left. Ring if you get lost, I'll pick you up. OK?"

"Yes Danny. Thanks, I've got an A to Z. How many kids?"

"Only three. The oldest has got a party."

"Look forward to it. Thanks very much."

"Bye then."

July 23   Jane

She had intended to make herself lunch that Sunday, and, influenced no doubt by her conversation with Lucy, had bought a piece of fresh fish at an actual fishmongers on her way home on Saturday. It had looked like a big plaice, but was labelled Brill, and was more expensive than she could have believed possible, more expensive than an entire meal at her local Indian, including a bottle of Kingfisher and poppadums. She was going to cook oven chips and frozen peas, and had thought that it would be a gourmet touch to mix up some mayonnaise with parsley and squeeze some lemon juice into it. The fishmonger had sold her a lemon, and given her a handful of parsley. But could she manage a substantial meal at lunchtime – she supposed you could put the fish in the oven, she certainly wasn't going to try and find a recipe – and then ham and salad, scones, cake, jelly – what *did* you have for high tea – at half past six? She decided to cook the fish and peas and forego the chips.

After her lunch, which turned out quite well but left her doubting whether it justified the expense, she set her player on random and started the weekly housework. Never very adept with her double duvet cover, she was more or less enveloped in its folds when she heard her mobile's ringtone, slightly louder than the Enya track on the stereo. David was on the line, and he asked her out, for a drink and dinner, that evening, if she wasn't doing anything else of course.

She explained about the invitation from Danny. She thought, maybe a drink afterwards; no, she would never get back from Lewisham in time. She didn't suggest it. She apologised, said it would have been lovely.

"Good Lord, don't apologise; stupidly short notice. Just thought I'd give it a shot. Some other time?"

"Yes of course."

"Have a nice tea. See you next week, probably Tuesday."

"Yes, thanks, see you then."

She put her phone down, dreadfully disappointed, much more disappointed than seemed reasonable. For a moment she couldn't understand why, but the moment was very brief. She hoped that he would ask her again, that some other time would be soon.

July 24   Lucy   Jane   Axel

"So, did you enjoy your evening round at Daniel's?" Lucy asked on Monday morning.

"Oh, did he tell you then?" asked Jane.

"Yes, we were chatting earlier on, just before Alice arrived. Daniel said that his youngest, what's she called?"

"Monica."

"Monica was well impressed by your cartwheel. Actually, I can't remember whether she was well impressed or gobsmacked. Whichever it wasn't is what she felt after you scored 66 with axolotl."

"Well, I'm glad I made a hit. I thought she was a darling. I had a really nice time."

Jane would have liked to talk to Lucy about her own upbringing, and how different her home life had been, but she had always to remember that she was Penny North, not Jane Ryan, and her cover included few details of Penny's background, certainly not that she shared Jane's lack of brother, sister or father.

Two small but obvious piles of masonry dust left by the skirting board on the wooden floor of the sitting room caused Jane to wonder whether Armstrong's attitude to the Hoover was much the same as his wife's to the electric drill. Lucy went to fetch the dustpan and brush. Shortly afterwards the Michael Harris arrived, brought in by two men, obviously acquaintances of Lucy, who tested the hooks carefully before hanging the picture. It was huge, perhaps nine feet by five. The Inchcape had gone, along with one of the others.

"We're going to hang two small paintings by Hopkins as well," said Lucy, "provided they're not completely overshadowed by the Harris."

"That's a wonderful painting," said Jane, indicating the Harris. "I can't really cope with abstract." She glanced questioningly at Lucy, hoping to elicit a sympathetic response. When Lucy said nothing she continued, somewhat lamely, "I haven't learned very much about art yet, I suppose."

Before Lucy could respond, if she intended to do so, Armstrong put his head round the door, said, "My God, that looks wonderful, I wish I could stay. But I shan't be late tonight, God willing; goodbye darling, cheerio Penny. Tell Lucy what you think of the pictures." He left, together with his PPS and a young girl from the Private Office who had just 'popped in, if she might, to use the loo.'

"Where are the Hopkinses now? I mean, have you got somewhere else?" Jane knew that Lucy and Armstrong owned a small semi in the Mossley Hill area of Liverpool, where they went for Jim to hold his surgery most weekends, and although Jane had never been on duty there she thought it unlikely that the Armstrongs would leave such valuable paintings in an empty house. She would nevertheless check with Danny. Hopkins was on the list of artists given to her by Harriet whose works never fetched less than half a million. And the Harris, so large, in such marvellous condition, might easily be worth ten times that. It certainly seemed as if the Armstrongs were more than comfortably well off; but only in the last few days had she felt that she was acquiring some modest degree of familiarity with them, certainly not the level of intimacy which Henry and David had intended. And if either of those two had thought that she would get anywhere by fluttering her eyelashes at Armstrong – and by now she hoped that David hadn't – then they would be disappointed. She could tell that with no shadow of doubt. One of the instructions which she had been quite surprised to hear given to male PU officers was that they were to resist any advances made to them by their assignee's female relatives, usually wives, sometimes daughters – or, of course by the assignee her or himself – and in this last case the assignment would be immediately changed. Naturally, officers were forbidden to initiate any such liaisons. Despite the rule, some officers regularly bedded their charges. Most officers, after all, were young, fit, strong and they often wore uniform. Jane found that wearing uniform enhanced sexual attraction. She knew that this was a cliché of hen parties and stag nights, but what was a cliché if not a truth universally acknowledged? Maybe not universally, she thought, but perhaps seventy per cent? Perhaps more? By herself, certainly. Surprisingly, no-one seemed to object strongly to a bit of hanky-panky here and there. Cuckolded ministers were often unfaithful themselves, and daughters, well, girls did what they wanted these days, didn't they, another TUA. Even *very* highly connected young ladies were not above a bit of rough and tumble with the help. Nor, come to think of it, had very highly connected ladies ever been. These antics, or relationships, were usually an open secret among the PU staff. There was no hint of any such involvement with Armstrong or his family. Jane was relieved; this may not have been a particularly professional attitude, but she was beginning to like them. Where, however, did the money for the pictures come from? She would have to be patient, and continue nurturing her embryonic friendship with Lucy.

Before Lucy could answer, Jane saw, through the open door of the PU room, the front path warning light flash, and moments later the doorbell rang. The screen showed a large car which she couldn't immediately identify and two men, one, good looking middle aged Nordic type, well-dressed with an expensive overcoat slung over his shoulder, the other in working clothes carrying a painting protected by bubble wrap.

"Do you know them both?" she asked Lucy, who peered at the screen and answered that of course she knew the well-dressed man, he was her friend Axel, but not the man carrying the painting, the man wearing a rough brown cotton protective coat, known in the portering and warehousing business as a cow gown. When Jane let them in she stopped this man just inside the door, and told him that if he wished to enter he would have to submit to a search. There was a set formula for what was known as a 'code 2' search, which included the wording of her request. Axel answered for him, making a couple of jokes to gloss over what he presumably thought might be an awkward situation, but in fact if anyone was embarrassed it was Jane when the man – and Jane, it must be said, was expecting something of the sort – said she could run her hands over him whenever she liked, luv.

The two Hopkinses were not overshadowed by the Harris. They were sombre representations of industrial processes, centring upon the operatives more than the machinery and illustrating clearly the difference in status of the various workers portrayed. This, Jane thought, was their striking quality; the workshops, the shining new equipment, were incidental, the paintings were about relationships. In fact, the paintings were about domination. The Harris was extraordinary, yes, and it, too, elicited an immediate response; but its meaning, if it had a meaning beyond the scene depicted, was opaque, whereas she could interpret the Hopkinses, they might have been called allegories long ago; she could read them, as well as see them.

"You like the Hopkinses, officer?" asked Axel, and Jane realised that she had no idea how long she had been looking at them.

"Yes, I do," she replied. She looked round for Lucy, but she was no longer in the room. "The Armstrongs have some marvellous paintings, haven't they?"

Axel agreed, and explained some of the background to the three pictures, and some of the allusions which Jane had not yet picked up. Her familiarity with the school of painting, and one or two comments she made, obviously surprised him, and he complimented her, in a rather old fashioned, heavy handed way, on her knowledge. He spoke with the grammatical precision of a foreigner; Jane detected a slight accent, and wondered whether he was perhaps Danish. Lucy brought in coffee, Jane drank hers quickly and, with the diligence of a neophyte, checked the bedroom and bathroom windows, and the Velux in the attic. Axel and his assistant were leaving when she came down, and she accompanied them to the door. The car was possibly the largest coupé she had ever seen; its roof sloped straight down between the rear wheel arches, just like most fast cars, she thought, but it was about three times as big. It was a beautiful, shiny, dark green monster. She had never been much interested in cars except in her later teenage years when sometimes, if they were fast or noisy or unusual, they might just add enough glamour to turn a boy into a boyfriend. She still liked speed. But this motor was beautiful, no argument. Axel was quite a dish, too. She briefly imagined him, ten years younger, asking her out for a spin.

"What sort of car's that? I've never seen one like it. It's gorgeous."

"Yes, isn't it. I'm afraid it's not mine, it belongs to a friend. He is kind enough to let me use it from time to time. It's a Bentley."

"Not a new one, surely?"

"Good heavens no; do you wish to guess how old it is?"

"Oh, I don't know; fifteen years?"

He smiled. "Fifty."

She was impressed, and looked it. The assistant put the bubble wrap and brown paper which he had removed from the pictures into the boot, they said their goodbyes and drove off.

"He let us go away for the weekend in that car, last year," said Lucy as they cleared up the coffee cups. "Jim loves cars. Like most men, really. He built his own once, when he'd just got his first job at Childwall Grammar. He did love that car. We called it the lawnmower. We've got a Jag now; nice car, but they haven't got the cachet they used to have."

"Why not buy one of those Bentleys yourselves then?"

Lucy burst out laughing. "They only made two hundred. Parkers in Shepherd Market had one for sale last year. A bit knocked about. Just over a million pounds."

"Wow. And he lets you borrow it – of course, it's not Axel's is it. Who does it belong to, then?"

Damn, she thought, too abrupt, too familiar – rude, in fact. But Lucy didn't take offence.

"Oh, just a friend. Do you think you could give me a hand with these chairs? They need to go back in the kitchen." She gave Jane a sly glance. "Of course, I know it doesn't appertain..."

Armstrong had obviously told her about the way he had teased Danny for his rather pedantic use of the word. Or possibly Danny had told her. Jane was not going to collude in any sort of humour, even gentle, at the sergeant's expense, so she smiled, said, "Yes of course I will," and picked up the nearest chair.

"I expect Axel talked to you a bit about the pictures?" Lucy asked.

"Yes, he's very well informed, isn't he? Does he have a gallery?"

"No, nothing like that. He's a sort of posh – very posh – gopher for a foreign business man. In fact, more than one, I think. He always reminds me of ... that chap who played Lawrence, very famous, damn... "

"Peter O'Toole?"

"Yes, of course. What a nice man he is."

"Have you met him then?"

"I've met everybody, Penny, from the Queen to Gordon Ramsay." She looked at her watch. "Which reminds me, I must check the caterers, they should be here soon. They should be here now, actually. We're having Turkish, so you'll have three Turks – don't know what sex – to cope with."

"Having Turkish?"

"Food, dear. For my ladies' lunch party. It should be in your diary?"

Hell's teeth, what with all the art and the chatter she hadn't checked the schedule. Still, not to panic, it was still only ten thirty. It was a bit much, this job, being a bodyguard and a spy. Lucy was still talking.

"We're just having mezze. There are only five guests coming. No-one'll eat much except for Martya; she never stops. I should sneak a glass of wine if I were you, it's delicious. And free."

Martya. Jane hurried into the PU room, and examined the schedule. Yes, Martya Zabliskya, who was singing Lucia at Covent Garden, was there. She'd recognize her all right. The PM's wife and the latest sporting dame – she knew what they looked like. She would not, however, recognize the Director of the British Museum, nor the editor of *Couture*. She followed the links given in her schedule to sites which showed pictures of these two members of the nomenklatura. They were both women in their forties, quite different in appearance. The PM's wife would have protection, usually a woman Jane knew, called Sheila, who could be difficult at times, partly because she was trying for promotion, so far unsuccessfully. Jane would stay in the kitchen, if Sheila would cope with front of house. First, however, she would need to check the Turks. The schedule described them and gave pictures; two women and a man. He was the cook. Wasn't mezze cold finger-food, things like boiled rice wrapped in leaves, or little pastry bags of mince? Hoovering up pastry crumbs definitely did not appertain to her role. And why was a cook needed? To make perfect coffee, perhaps? The thought of a free lunch and, perhaps, Turkish coffee, cheered her up.

Sheila explained the etiquette before the guests arrived, all likely to be punctual except Zabliskya. Jane and she would stand at the side of the room, after being introduced generically, or, as in this case where the hostess was polite, individually, and would smile without making any eye contact while quickly drinking a non-alcoholic aperitif. No, definitely no wine. Then they would slide away, one to the hall, and one to the kitchen.

"Why no eye contact?" whispered Jane?

"Because then they might talk to you, and they're so *boring*, they can't talk about anything."

"Nothing at all?"

"No. You'd think the telly had never been invented."

Jane did as she was told. From the kitchen she heard Zabliskya arrive. Jane had rather hoped she would make an operatic entrance, but she joined the group in the living room quite normally. She was, however, a satisfactorily imposing figure, in whose presence the others, apart from the athlete, lost a little of their colour. Jane could see changing vignettes of the party through the door to the kitchen, which was left ajar. The PM's wife was a lecturer, and the three professional ladies were clearly uneasy with each other; no-one had laughed yet in any sort of genuine way; each time she glimpsed them they had changed their stances and expressions. Perhaps, Jane thought, they should play scissors, paper and stone. Or there should be a net and a spear and a sword for them to choose hanging up inside the front door. A waitress was trying to top up their glasses with the wine, from the Loire, which none of the guests knew was from one of the smallest, oldest and best appellations in France. Each was wary of being the first to accept a refill. Zabliskya's heavenly talent protected her from observing the failure of the professional ladies to establish their status relative to each other; of their status relative to herself she had no doubt.

"Tell me, darling," she said to the editor, in a voice the timbre of which made it difficult to believe that she also had the sweetest top F in the trade, "tell me, you are fashionista, yes, are these clothes you wear the latest in fashion? Do I say *retro*, is the right word? I have not seen it in Milano. Look," she said to the athlete, "do you read this magazine, shall you wear these clothes?"

"No, not my style. I just go to Bloopers. Most things seem to suit me; nobody says they don't."

"With your figure, my dear, you could wear a bin liner and look stunning," said the PM's wife. This was not an entirely successful compliment.

The editor, whose habit it was to dress down at parties where there would be no photographers, partly because she didn't wish to upstage the other guests too dramatically, partly because she had not got the figure to compete with Anna Wintour, muttered something to the effect that the editor of Motor Sport didn't always drive a Porsche. The museum Director, beautifully coiffured and wearing understated Nicole Farhi, wondered whether she should talk a little about the Museum's recent acquisition of the Medici Manuscripts, but decided against it. Zabliskya, who abhorred silences, turned to her with a look of triumph. "I have *seen* you; I have seen you on the television, with I think dear

Melvin. They call you, yes, they call you thinking man's crumpet. Crumpet, that is big blini, is not so?"

Lucy made a sign to the waitresses, and the Turks brought in the lunch.

After the guests had gone, Lucy asked Jane if she would like anything more to eat. "You did manage to get something, didn't you?"

"Yes, thanks, it was excellent. Delicious – burek? – is that right? And I hope you don't mind but I did manage to get hold of a glass of that wine. Largely because Sheila told me I mustn't. I've never had anything like it. Sort of honey flavour, but not sweet, if that makes sense."

"Yes, it certainly does. And you can't have been reading about it in the Sundays because they've never heard of it. Or if they have they've been keeping it to themselves. Which is possible because they don't make much. Jim and I found it when we went to the Loire to see the chateaux, oh, fifteen years ago. The Duc de Louresse tried to sell us a case of his Anjou red. I mean him, the duke, himself, in his own dripping dungeon under his own castle. Isn't that marvellous? Have some more."

"No, no, I can't possibly. I shall get sent back to the FO in disgrace. But thanks all the same."

"I'll give you a bottle to take home, then. Would you like a cup of tea?"

Lucy then decided that first she ought to clean and tidy up those areas of the house which the lunch time staff had overlooked. Maria would be coming in for a couple of hours later on, she said, but it wasn't really her job to clear up after parties. In the light of her brief meetings with Maria, and some words of advice from Danny and the other PU officer, Jane interpreted this to mean that Maria would be forthright, probably politically incorrect, and possibly racist, about the qualities of the employees of catering firms, especially ones providing Middle Eastern food, and that Lucy was hoping to avert this. She felt obliged to help, and for the next twenty minutes they polished glasses, rearranged furniture and swept up crumbs. Lucy did the vacuuming.

They sat with tea and a bottle of wine, three quarters full, left over from lunch, on a couple of folding chairs in a pool of sunlight between fuchsias and a strawberry tree, where the lawn was bordered by a bed of prostrate, weed suppressing evergreens. Daisies in the grass, spikes of unsuppressed willow herb poking up through the juniper, and a scatter of withered petals under the standard roses would have told the tale to any horticultural enthusiast, but Jane was no gardener. Nevertheless, she established that Lucy had no help in the garden, except for a lad who came sporadically in the summer to mow the lawn.

There was a kind of subdued background drone which filled in any gaps between the various topics of their conversation, and that was a series of gentle moans from Lucy about the difficulties which beset her entertainments. They were almost always during daytime; usually women only. There was never enough time, or alcohol consumed, for guests who were strangers to each other to relax. Penny had probably observed that the only two of that day's guests who seemed quite at ease were the two Olympians?"

"That's only because they didn't talk to each other," said Jane, "I remember my mother telling me once that the Greek Gods spent most of eternity bickering about precedence."

Her mother had also told her to remember not to confuse the mountain with the stadium. But she had forgotten this, and Lucy didn't notice, or if she did, was too polite to point it out.

"Not just bickering either. That's the trouble with important people." Lucy sighed, and refilled her glass. Jane drank her good strong Co-op tea.

"It's awful sometimes," Lucy continued in the same vein, "when I've got a Minister's wife here, because no-one's usually got the face to ask the only sort of questions which really interest them – I mean, what can you ask the PM's wife that she can actually answer? Like, were the SAS really told to assassinate that Australian in Cairo, or is it true that the Trident launch-button suitcase had been left in the Grand

Metropolitan cloakroom overnight? So they dredge up some boring rubbish about one or other of her charities, and since she's patron of about two hundred, unless her secretary is super-duper efficient she won't know what they're talking about. And they're afraid to ask me anything, because Jim's been built up by the Shield as a sort of cross between Cardinal Richelieu and Don Corleone."

Jane was relieved that Lucy had ignored her indirect, nevertheless transgressive, reference to her mother's education. She asked Lucy why, if, as she had told her last week she was becoming eager to insulate her life from her husband's job, she put up with these boring demands on her time. Lucy replied that she was only just starting to scramble out of the pit she had, over the years, dug for herself. In any case, this administration could hardly last forever. When Jane suggested that a man of Jim's abilities and experience wouldn't be content to spend the rest of his life wandering around art galleries, and would probably become an ambassador, or a bigwig in Europe, Lucy shrugged and said that she would just have to do her best. She didn't want to leave England, because what she really wanted to do was to open a gallery of her own, not in London, of course. Maybe somewhere along the South coast, perhaps in Brighton? She would prefer Devon or Cornwall, but that would be too self-indulgent, she'd never make a profit there; in any case, she would never see Jim, he would be in London all the time. Jane asked what sort of art she would like to sell in her gallery, although by now she realised from Lucy's wistful and slightly unfocussed expression that she was sketching out a daydream, not making serious plans for the future.

"I'd really like to sell post-war British. But I'd never be able to build up a stock of my own, so it would probably mean giving exhibitions to promising newcomers." She explained, "that means artists who've sold a few paintings somewhere in the sticks, to friends and relatives usually, and who want to show their stuff in a gallery. Then you have to get some publicity. Get a review in the Standard, something like that." She looked gloomy and emptied the bottle mainly into her glass, partly onto the lawn. "It's all marketing, you know. PR. Advertising."

Jane had never really given much thought to the economics of the legitimate retail art market. The subject had hardly been addressed by Harriet or anyone else at Homerton.

"So, then it's all sale or return, is it?"

"Almost always, yes."

"And, you wouldn't be able to ..." Jane was uncertain how to continue, but Lucy took her meaning and answered immediately.

"No, I certainly would not. I mean, how could we? Do you know how much even a little water colour sketch by, oh I don't know, John Nash, costs?"

"Five thousand?"

"And the rest. Sorry, that sounds vulgar. But you see, don't you, without money to start with you've got no hope."

She fiddled morosely with her glass, trying to make it hum by rubbing the rim.

"Come and see my vegetable garden."

She led Jane round the side of the shrubbery to a rectangle of earth, bordered by what seemed to Jane to be railway sleepers, and covered with a varied and apparently random collection of plants. Some canes supported thin plastic netting, whether for protection or support it was impossible for her to tell. Jane screwed up her eyes and tried to make some sense of this unfamiliar profusion of greenery. A normally dormant part of her brain picked out some plants relatively similar to each other, and determined whether or not they would fit along an approximately straight line. It ignored the intervening plants, defining them as weeds, and as it gained experience it found that by eliminating these it could identify more patterns of presumably deliberate growth. This process itself yielded more plants to be defined as weeds. And so on. Soon it had given her a map of at least some areas where the planting showed purpose – about six rows of similar vegetables, and a couple of square blocks. Her memory was summoned. Did any of these vegetables remind that deeper organ of anything encountered in Sainsbury's? Lettuces, there were lettuces. And, of course, peas, growing up through the net. Jane had felt herself, her inner self, somewhat, somehow, divorced from this process of ratiocination, as if she had asked her brain a favour and it had, on this occasion, obliged but wouldn't like her to think that it would always be so accommodating; but she complimented Lucy on the lettuces, and asked when the peas would be ready.

"It's a mess, isn't it?" asked Lucy, sadly, "but I try to be organic. The peas are over, they're meant to be mange-tout."

"I wish I had enough space for a vegetable garden," said Jane untruthfully.

"Jim won't let Mickey help. He says not as long as he's a Minister." For a moment, Jane thought that she was talking about the garden, but Lucy had lost interest in the vegetables.

"Axel said that he'd make a sort of informal arrangement with Mickey, so that I could sell some of his stuff instead of him sending it to auction. We'd split the profit, and eventually I'd have enough to buy some stock myself. But Jim wouldn't hear of it. He'd have to get it past Billy Boy, and he couldn't bear the idea of that.

Jane knew who Billy Boy was. He was Sir William Buoy-Dodd, Cabinet Secretary. Now he *was* a blend of Richelieu and Corleone, with surprising notes of Savonarola in the farewell, but journalists knew nothing of this. Jane felt that she was on the brink of a revelation. Lucy was more than a little tipsy, that was clear, and she would probably regret this conversation, in which she was becoming more confidential, treating Jane as a friend. It was Jane's duty to encourage her, although she couldn't prevent herself feeling mean as she did so.

"Billy Boy?"

"You know, Bill Buoy-Dodd, the Cabinet Secretary. Jim thought he might even make tutting noises about borrowing valuable pictures in the first place. These bloody Sir Humphreys, they think the sun shines out of their sea green arses."

Her speech was becoming indistinct, Jane didn't like this business at all, but she had to press on, it was obviously pay dirt time.

"Borrowing pictures?"

"You know, the pictures, the Harris, Mickey's. You know? Oh, of course, you don't, do you?"

"No. Should I?" asked Jane, slightly disingenuously, because there was a Russian listed in her briefing paper as an occasional acquaintance, dating from the time when Armstrong was at Export and Trade. His interest in art was noted, but not emphasised – all Russian oligarchs collected paintings, just as Arab sheiks collected race horses. She couldn't remember his name.

"I expect you've heard of him, haven't you? Michaelov? He owns a fleet of tankers – and most of the oil wells in Kazakhstan, I think. And Lewisham United. But he's most interested in paintings. He bought the Goya Bonaparte – you remember, surely; the Marquess of St Helens was going to sell it to the Louvre, but Mickey bought it and put it on permanent loan to the National Gallery?"

"Oh yes, I've seen it, yes, of course, it hangs near the Duke of Wellington, doesn't it? I wasn't aware that it belonged to, who did you say, Malenkov? I thought it was, you know, ours. There was a great crowd when I saw it, but it didn't look much like Napoleon to me."

"Not Malenkov, Michaelov. Malenkov was someone else, one of Stalin's crew, wasn't he? Or was that Molotov? No, that's a drink – isn't it? Tennyrate it isn't Napoleon, it's his brother Joseph."

"Oh," said Jane, her complexion darkening with embarrassment, "actually, I have heard of this Michaelov. Didn't he just promise to give all his money away to the Bill and Melinda thing before he dies?"

"Yes, he did. Jim got to know him when he was at Export, and we're best mates now..."

How irritating, Jane thought, that she had confused the two Bonapartes. On the other hand, it squared with her cover. So why should she find it irritating? God forbid she was becoming kulturny. But what was that about borrowing the Harris?

Lucy frowned and pulled a couple of pods from the overripe mange-touts, split them open and handed five little peas from one of them to Jane. She fumbled with the other, and the peas fell onto the railway sleeper where they rolled together under the eye of the attendant pigeon in the ash tree.

Lucy continued, "... at least, I think he's a genuine friend. It's so difficult to tell, Jim being what he is. You know what he says to me, he says that old thing, keep your friends close..."

"And your enemies closer?"

"That's it. But the point is, Penny, he thinks he knows the difference but I don't think he does, half the time. Everyone thinks he's such a Machiavellian character, just because he works his balls off for the PM, has done from the start, when the other lot were fucking things up years ago. Not that we're doing much better. He tries his best for me, too, though, I'll say that. He knows I want to open a gallery, but we haven't got enough money. He says there's still a possibility, oh, I don't know, some sort of partnership. Look, I'm tired, I'm going in now. Need a bit of shut-eye. It's been nice, this chat. Next time you can tell me about yourself."

She turned round before she reached the garden door. "Whatever have we been talking about? I hope I haven't spoken out of turn. You'll trick it all, treat, treat it all in confidence, won't you?"

Jane found she couldn't answer that, so she asked about the car.

"Mickey owns the big green Bentley, then, does he?"

"Yes. Sorry, I really must go in now. Have a little lie down."

Chapter 13

July 30   Maurice   Alan   Jane

The pretty Wessex countryside flashed past the window in the rear passenger door of the BMW, but Maurice was in no position to enjoy it. For one thing he was scared to death, and for another he was more or less immobile, trussed up at hands, ankles and knees by the sort of plastic cords which he himself used in the garden to tie up his rambling roses. He was facing into the car and his nose had the choice of rubbing against the car's arm rest, or the elbow of the large man called Fred. He no longer doubted the truth of Anthony's story. He had no information to give these people, he had been told little about the pictures. But he knew about the attack upon Anthony; he knew more than anyone else – except, perhaps, their friends Paul and Anne. Would they also, then, be abducted? Was he going to die because of this knowledge? His captors remained silent. Initially he did not, for he was not gagged, but after a while he gathered his wits, realised that there was no point to his entreaties, and lapsed into silence. The car, having been driven extremely fast for the first ten minutes or so, had slowed down, and it eventually drew into a layby where it stopped. The man Fred, who had been in the back with him, got out and lit a cigarette. The woman who had been driving turned round and asked him if he smoked; he shook his head and she told him that they would stay there for a little while; she might get out to stretch her legs. He closed his eyes, and waited. He heard, and then saw, a motorbike draw up and park in front of the BMW. Its rider stepped towards the car, removed his helmet, opened the back door, but when he saw Maurice, started in surprise and stood for a moment still and silent. He waited to observe Maurice's reaction; would Maurice remember him?

Of course Maurice did; had he not already recognised him in the hotel bar?

"Green, thank God! Why didn't you stop them? Watch out, that big bugger's just behind you! The woman's one of them, look out!"

"Mr Symes-Franton. I'm sorry. This is very awkward. I had no idea. Jane, please cut those ties off. Bert, Fred, what's-your-name, get Mr MacMaster on the secure line. Mr Symes-Franton, er, Maurice, I must ask you to bear with me for a moment. Please don't worry, we mean, I mean meant, you no harm, I promise you. Let me just speak to my colleague, and then I'll explain."

Alan had a brief conversation on his mobile, and something he heard obviously annoyed him, but his expression quickly reverted to normal. "Jane," he said, "this gentleman and I have already met. You remember the Aquarium – the Redgrave Vermeer? Mr Symes-Franton has a gallery, and I picked his brains one afternoon. Fred, why did you tie this gentleman up? Did he? You surprise me."

"Surprise you! What would you do if some..." Maurice shook his head and vibrated his lips for a second, "damn chit of a girl and this great ape manhandled you into the back of a car and told you to keep still and you'd be OK and then drove off at a hundred miles an hour? What would you do, just sit there and admire the scenery, not that I could, dammit?"

"Well, at any rate, I'm very sorry. We were only concerned for your safety. The man you were with is dangerous. We needed you well out of the way before we could arrest him. The, um, vigour of your struggles surprised them and they over-reacted, I'm afraid. We'll get you back to your car as soon as possible. In the meantime let's go and have some coffee, or a drink if you like, and then perhaps you wouldn't mind telling me why you went to meet Mr Evans?"

Maurice was very quiet as the admirable scenery of the Wessex countryside, now easily observed, slid past his window and he spent the ten minutes before they reached a small country inn arranging his thoughts and deciding what he could share with the Chief Inspector. He would try to tell as few lies as possible, but he would deny any knowledge of a gun. Presumably Anthony had been arrested; without,

Maurice fervently hoped, any further recourse to firearms. How had the police tracked him down? Perhaps they had in fact followed him after his visit to Paul and Anne. Were the pictures in some way the link? But hadn't he been told that Green had moved on from the Art Squad? In the end he decided to say as little as possible; that he and Anthony were old, and close, Oxford friends – readily verifiable – that Anthony was totally distraught, hardly coherent and completely exhausted, and that they had intended to talk more in the morning, after Anthony had slept.

As they entered the pub, Alan caught Jane's eye, and indicated that he wanted a private word. They waited for Maurice to take himself off to the lavatory, and Alan told Jane about the debacle at the hotel.

"Got away?" she said incredulously, "From Jack and Jill?"

"Beginner's luck."

"He's not a beginner, is he? Shoots David with his own gun, then lays out two K branch heavies? Who the hell is he?"

"Calm down, will you?" There was a definite edge to Alan's voice, which betrayed his own anxiety. Almost immediately, though, with what Jane thought was unsettling efficiency, his tone, and mien, returned to normal. This quality of his struck Jane as something important to remember. He explained the precautions which had been taken and reassured her that Evans would be quickly captured.

Over coffee, and in Maurice's case a large *fine*, the two soi-disant police officers (the bulky Fred having taken himself away on Green's Suzuki) seemed reasonably satisfied with Maurice's simple explanation of his meeting with Anthony. Maurice mentioned the names of some of their friends in common at Oxford, one of whom, knighted, was now Second Permanent Secretary at the Ministry of Defence, a couple of quick phone calls were made, a couple received, and Maurice promised to make himself available to Green again in the near future if necessary, which they thought it would not be. When Maurice asked them what had actually happened in Anthony's home, they reacted as stuffily as he might have expected, nevertheless they managed to give Maurice the impression that Anthony had been a victim of circumstances, and would not necessarily be treated as a criminal. Nor did they continue to claim that he was dangerous, despite Jane's reservations which she kept to herself. Gunplay was not mentioned, neither by Green nor, certainly, by Maurice, but Maurice guessed that the involvement, and of course the loss, of the revolver was an important factor in the seriousness with which the authorities were treating the affair. But why the police should have been armed in the first place he could not imagine. It struck him then; he only had Anthony's word that the gun had been the policeman's.

Maurice presumed that Anthony had been arrested, so was surprised when they asked him whether Anthony had told him of any plans he might have made, and whether Maurice knew of any of Anthony's close friends, or relatives not too far away. Maurice told them what he knew, which was very little; he didn't know where the holiday cottage was, so did not mention it; he decided that he had forgotten the story about the paintings in Cornwall, and he actually had forgotten most of what Anthony had said to him; all he remembered was Anthony's obvious stress and incoherence. And, of course, the gun.

They set off to return Maurice to the hotel. Green drove, and Maurice sat in the back and chatted with the damn chit of a girl, who introduced herself as Jane, and although not quite still a girl even Maurice could see was very attractive.

When they arrived back at the hotel, for Maurice to gather his wits and his suitcase, there was no indication that anything out of the ordinary had occurred. The lounge was dotted with business men having coffee after their lunch; the dining room was being prepared for a conference. Maurice intended to go straight home; he tried to assure Alan that he was quite composed enough to drive himself safely, but Alan said that they would drive him and deliver his own car later. Without making too much fuss about it Maurice also acknowledged that the police had behaved quite properly in the circumstances, and that he had no intention of involving lawyers or newspapers.

He found that his bill had already been paid; it had been paid in cash. He was not aware that his name had been changed in the hotel information system, an alteration effected, unknown to the manager, while the police were looking through the booking records as a matter of routine, they explained.

"Do you think he meant what he said about not contacting any newspapers?" Jane asked Alan as they also drove away. "This would be quite a story for somebody like Alf Grisham at the Herald, wouldn't it?"

"I don't think it matters, to be honest," replied Alan, "the pantomime at the pub will get out, obviously, but I'm sure the cover will hold. I dropped quite enough hints, let the manager overhear part of a conversation with Fred; he'll think it was a fairly run of the mill arrest of a drug dealer, which we cocked up."

"Bear in mind that Symes-Franton doesn't know Evans got away. What happens if Evans tries to phone him?"

"Yes, Jane, I have borne it in mind. Maurice will ring me I hope, he's got the number. I can't imagine what else he might do. We'll get Evans soon, in any case. Just hope the silly bugger hasn't driven into a ditch and killed himself. Henry is liaising with the police."

"Not bringing them in, surely?"

"Keeping them out, I sincerely hope."

Alan, who had been running various thoughts around in his mind, asked Jane a question.

"Jane, you told us, David and me, that Armstrong refused to tell you why he was taking you on a trip to Broadharbour. Think really carefully; no hint at all? Nothing on the journey there?"

"He was working, they call it 'at his boxes', most of the journey. He sits in the back, the Protection Officer sits in the front. He did tell us the meeting itself was private. There were five minutes or so after he'd finished his boxes when he did chat for a while, mainly about a present he was buying –

no, actually he said arranging – for Lucy, his wife. Then he talked a bit about art; I'm very glad Henry sent me on that course, because it really is what he's interested in. He'll go on and on about some exhibition or other he's been to, and they're often in small galleries, Danny says he goes to lots of private views on the spur of the moment, even when he hasn't got an invite, but they always let him in. Well, they would, wouldn't they? He never talks politics – I suppose he wouldn't, especially about other politicians and he doesn't talk about sport, or television. Well, sometimes newsy things, usually foreign though. I think he's very careful. No, I didn't get any clue, really, why we went there."

"You're sure the reason he talks to you about art isn't that he thinks art is what you're interested in?"

"He wouldn't bother, would he? Why should he?"

"You tell me."

"Oh, I see. No, he's never come on to me, not once, not an iota. No interest at all."

Alan laughed. "Does that annoy you?"

"No! Of course not! Well, I don't know, should it?"

"Ring David, we need to speak to him, if the poor old bugger hasn't succumbed to his wounds, that is."

She rang David on the secure line. It was answered, but the code was not entered so the connection was terminated.

"Try his ordinary number."

This was answered by a woman with a foreign accent. "Sorry, he cannot speak to you, he's just being stitched up. By Mr Ali. We don't know why, it's usually the houseman. Does Mr Peterson know Mr Ali?"

"Thank you, I'll try later."

She relayed the message to Alan.

"He can't talk. He's just being stitched up."

"Literally, I hope. Better ring in. You're supposed to be back with Armstrong this pm, aren't you? Ask if Jennifer wants me to join the chase for Evans. I hope not, I've got enough on my plate in Suffolk."

"I'm surprised they put you onto the bunny huggers. Or is it one of your back-burner jobs?"

"I'm not on animal rights. Jennifer doesn't do animal rights. That's mainly the Branch."

"But I thought – David told me – you'd had some sort of crisis? At Chik-Pak?"

Alan replied, "For Christ's sake Jane. Look, I asked you to ring the office and see if they want me to join in the search for Evans. D'you mind doing that now, please?"

Jane was expected at the Cabinet Office at half past five. Alan drove fast, ignoring speed limits and taking advantage of any other driver's hesitation to overtake. Jane was mortified that she had not read his character correctly – she had registered his quick changes of expression after the phone call in which he learned about Evans's escape, but she had not been at all prepared for his show of temper. He had always been very pleasant with her; nice guy, is how she would have described him. Now, well, she certainly didn't want *asks too many questions* in any report he might be asked to make. She was, in fact, quite upset; when was the last time someone had actually snapped at her?

So instead of a simple reaction like 'moody bugger isn't he?' she began to wonder whether she had underestimated the degree to which people who worked in this most devious department of what was in any case a secretive service would be careful to protect their personalities; responding, talking, painting the colour of their behaviour differently according to the nature of the commission given to them – not necessarily always to blend in, but always with some end in mind. She was quite clever enough to assume different roles and identities. She had become Penny from the FO quite easily, but that was not quite the same. She had still behaved in her usual manner, maybe showing interest in different things, and in the Munich affair simulating an attraction which she did not feel, well, certainly not so strongly as she pretended, but without changing her underlying character; she had just been doing a different job. In effect she worried whether the word 'underlying' was relevant; maybe in this job you just had to choose who you were being.

She may, of course, have been wrong. A simpler explanation would have been that Alan was tired, bad-tempered after a clumsy operation, and that he might have felt challenged by her recent preferment; but this did not occur to her, she was still too much in awe of her new colleagues. She tried hard to remember the details of the conversation which she had had with David that first day in the park – surely that had been straightforward, light hearted and friendly? Or had she made a fool of herself in some way? Was David just being 'nice chatty David' instead of whatever other persona he might have chosen? This seemed much more important to her; Alan's irritability was temporarily sidelined. In any case, she would herself try to be more careful in the future. Perhaps it just came down to cutting down on the chatter.

At Holland Park police station Alan waited for her to change into her civilian protection clothes. She preferred full uniform because of its tight belt, even though she felt her balance diminished by the weight of the low holster, almost strapped to her knee, containing a Glock pistol with its full complement of fifteen cartridges, as heavy as the hardback edition of *Fowler's Modern English Usage* which her mother had bought her for her last birthday. But she had had hardly any opportunity to wear it, and she hated the baggy suit which was her civilian outfit. She liked to wear clothes with a strong waist line but she was obliged to wear the opposite, the wide shouldered, double breasted jacket needed to cover her belt holster and Kevlar vest.

"What excuse did you give?" he asked.

"Just the mussels. Bound to feel better tomorrow"

He dropped her in Whitehall, drove away, and Jane walked up Downing Street to the door of Number Ten where she was delighted to be let in by a smiling policeman in a traditional helmet, who thought that she looked lovely in her new jacket and said so.

*****

Maurice was soon handed over to another policeman, in another car, and driven home. They had hardly communicated; Maurice had fallen asleep in the car, and when he got into his house he made himself a cup of tea and drank half of it, then dozed in front of the early evening news.

By half past seven, after he had re-lived the events of the last two days half a dozen or so times, attempting to remember everything Anthony had said to him and he had said to Inspector Green and the policewoman, he changed his shoes and jacket and wandered for a while in the drowsy warmth of the summer evening along the lanes and bridle ways around his cottage, ending up, as he was bound to, in the garden of the village pub.

Chapter 14

July 31   Maurice   Jennifer   Charles   Armstrong   Alice   Danny

Maurice woke at half past three, his heart thumping and his mouth parched. He went to the lavatory, drank a glass of tepid bathroom water, swallowed three or four random painkillers and went back to bed. Of course, he couldn't get to sleep. His mind was a pin table of catastrophes, his thoughts ricocheting from spring to spring, accumulating a monstrous score. But when he managed to get his thoughts back under control, however he assembled the facts or twisted the logic, whatever explanations he concocted for his own behaviour, it was still true that the police were holding Anthony, that Anthony would be interrogated and tell them he had shown him, Maurice, the gun, and that this would contradict his story that Anthony had told him nothing. The attitude of the police would change; at the moment they seemed to more or less trust him. He still didn't know what Anthony had actually done; he had believed Anthony's story when he thought he was himself being kidnapped by thieves, but this belief dissolved when he learned who his captors really were. What he would call loyalty to a friend, the police would call concealing a serious crime. He reached the stage of four-in-the-morning despair when, thankfully, he fell asleep. When he woke it was quite clear to him that he must confess all. Before the plunger had even sunk on his Blue Mountain he phoned the number on the card which the Chief Inspector had given him.

Jennifer had come into the office early. She had spent most of the three days before the week-end out of the office, in a series of excruciatingly tedious meetings with the entire range of security amateurs, persons who had never had to give serious, sustained thought to the practical and ethical issues which daily confronted her officers. These amateurs:

judges, peers, members of parliament, cabinet ministers, soldiers, policemen, diplomats, journalists, oh Christ, journalists, and God knows who else, all sat on committees of this and that, and almost all came to their seats with a firm preconception of how she should do her job. Some were extreme libertarians, some were almost fascist, some were bound by tradition, some by precedent, some only saw threats from particular beliefs, like animal rights, or religious extremism. On the whole, their common problem was moral absolutism. None of them was faced, every day, every damnable day, with the need to choose the least bad from a hopeless set of options, pretty well every one of which would contravene some legal or moral principle, but where the do-nothing choice would be the very worst. So, somewhat frayed, Jennifer had come in early to cope with any problems which might have cropped up, and had not been pleased to learn from Charles who was always an early bird – he lived a bachelor existence and had little to stay at home for – about the debacle in the South West.

"And your new little Lara Croft came bouncing back all chipper, thought she'd saved the day with her snap."

"How did she get it to MacMaster?"

"He was *there*, Jennifer, Ryan thought the whole trip so odd that she'd already phoned him. He took Davies with him.

"Mr Anonymous, eh?"

"He can't help his style, Jennifer. I'll just pop into my room and make us a coffee then, shall I?" he asked her, offering her the opportunity to fume a little in his absence, "and I've got some minty Penguins?"

"Yes," she said, "bring me a coffee but you can..." he does his best, the old tart, she thought, I mustn't take it out on him "... get Green for me on the scrambler, please."

"Alas, Jennifer, he's incommunicado until tomorrow pm; he's had to go and pack chickens all day, he has to be hygienic, no mobiles allowed. *If* you can believe that. I've already had to field three of his calls, one from some new boy he must be running? *Said* his name was Maurice Symes-Franton. Very likely, I thought. Most agitated, quite beside himself when he couldn't speak to Alan. He didn't use any of the sesames, so I left him to fester until tomorrow."

"Is MacMaster in yet?"

"I fear not."

"I want to see him the minute he steps through the door. Yes, I dare say his arm is sore. No, actually I want to see him now. Find him. Bring him in."

"So let it be written, so let..."

"Oh, get out."

David, summoned peremptorily from his breakfast table and driven to Thames House in a fire engine, (which was the name given to the vehicles used to transport SD staff when they, or their boss, were in an unusual hurry – one of which actually was a converted fire tender) found Jennifer, now joined by Henry, in the sort of mood which he might have expected. He carried the can, he ate humble pie, he gestured towards his injured arm with the uninjured one, he reminded them that his aged mother and crippled father had no support beyond the allowance he made them from his meagre salary, he abased himself like a Chinese revisionist before the Chairman himself.

When this formality was complete, and his dress gathered in a heap around his ankles, they sat down, over more coffee with Penguin biscuits sneaked in by Charles, and discussed the way forward.

Henry suggested that David should give a report upon Typewriter, to date. They would then decide what changes, if any, might be necessary; if Typewriter was in effect complete, and if so, what were their conclusions; if Typewriter should be closed down incomplete; if it should continue.

David had known that he would be called to account, and had mentally prepared a brief report. He wasn't particularly nervous, nor shaken by his reprimand.

"OK. A competent journalist believed it possible that Armstrong had corruptly acquired funds which enabled him to live beyond his apparent means. Henry persuaded C that a low key investigation was appropriate, in case the suspicions were true, and especially since the Shield would be digging away at the story with every spade in its shed.

"I have failed to uncover any legitimate source of wealth. Ryan has now been under cover for over three weeks, and she has discovered that there are explanations for some of the signs of apparent wealth, in particular Armstrong's friendship with a Russian billionaire, Mickey Michaelov, although Ryan has only so far met this man's gopher, a Scandinavian called Axel.

"Jane, Ryan, that is – the name she is using at the moment is Penny – took the number of the Bentley Continental that the man called Axel said belonged to the Russian, but DVLA said it was registered to a carpet shop in Warrington, who told us, I should say the teenager who was managing it told us, that the shop was owned by a textile firm in Denmark, or so she thought. Some of the paintings apparently belong to Michaelov. The paintings are valuable, some of them very. The rumoured Turner is not in evidence.

"Ryan says that she has become quite friendly with Lucy Armstrong, and that Armstrong himself is quite unlike his reputation – quite charismatic, but not dangerous, is how she put it. And he doesn't flirt."

"Pity," said Jennifer.

"Predictable," said Henry, leaving it unclear to whose comment he referred.

"Now, to the Evans debacle," said David, bravely. Neither Henry's nor Jennifer's expression changed. They were no longer interested in fault, nor blame, merely in the facts.

"A man was observed by Ryan..."

"For heaven's sake," said Henry.

"Ryan saw a man taking some photographs, one of which almost certainly showed me taking a video of Armstrong and the men he was meeting. She immediately realised that if the photographer recognised Armstrong he could easily think that at least the local paper would publish it. The sequelae, sorry, the consequences would be dire. Ryan took a photograph of this man.

"What with?"

"Her pocket camera."

"Lucky she had it."

"Not at all. It's standard."

"Carry on."

"Meanwhile, Davies himself had arrived. The man was located, followed home. He had been drinking, and fell asleep, so we entered and started to search for his camera. He woke, refused to cooperate..."

"And we know the rest. Have you found him yet?"

"No, we haven't. But there's a good lead. As soon as we lost the beacon..."

"Under the spuds?" said Henry.

"That's right. As soon as we lost it, we got on to South West police again, and it seems he's left a trail of chaos, at least they presume it's him; they found his car burnt out, then a van was stolen opposite an ATM he tried to take money from – they should pick the van up before too long. In fact...may I?"

He indicated Jennifer's phone, and within a minute he had learned that Anthony's Dormobile had been picked up by one of the automated cameras just north of Brighton, but had been lost again.

"Well, I'm sure you'll catch up with him," said Henry. "You're getting all the feeds from the cameras? I don't want the police involved again. Use K division if you have to. As soon as you track him down, get him somewhere quiet. You've got his file, thank goodness he's got one, persuade him that he won't be held for murder and arson. I'll leave it to you. Then I think we should bring Ryan in, debrief her, find out some more details about the relationship between the Russian and Armstrong – or Mrs Armstrong, of course, – and in all probability call it a day. Jennifer?"

"Agreed."

Henry would himself act as cleaner; this operation was too sensitive to delegate. He had already arranged a second meeting with the South West Chief Constable, and had postponed one with Alan Green which, in a burst of nostalgia, he had proposed to make in the field, although 'the field' was neither so far away nor so foreign as in the halcyon days of the cold war. Nor was Green's present adversary powerful in the way that the Soviet Union had been, but he was different; in those days the enemy had just been the enemy, for nearly two hundred years the great game had been played with little thought of right or wrong; now, if the word *evil* had any meaning at all, which in fact he often doubted, then it should be applied to this particular enemy; sociopathic, psychopathic, *evil* would suffice. But that was a different operation, Green could look after it himself for another day.

After David and Henry had left, Charles brought through the various routine items which Jennifer had to deal with. The raison d'être of Ticklish Issues was to deal with problems which were not routine, but that didn't mean that Jennifer could avoid the responsibilities of administration; dozens of memos to read, expenses and expenditure to authorise, personnel matters handed back to her by the jobsworths in Human Resources. She worked through the pile of paper, then called Charles back in and gave him one or two instructions. As he was leaving, she remembered that someone with a name unfamiliar to herself or Charles had phoned for Alan Green on one of the secure lines.

"Charles, I think you'd better get in touch with that Morris hyphenated doodah. Find out what he wants. Try and put him off again. If you think it's urgent, if it's the chicken packers, come and tell me. Try and be discreet."

"Oh Jennifer, really!"

"Pop along now."

Charles returned almost immediately. "I think it probably does count as sort of urgent, Jennifer. He's the character that our Mr Evans met. The one we lifted. Alan was sure he'd soothed him down with Ryan's help; apparently not. He's not angry though, he sounds extremely worried."

"Oh for God's sake. Jane will have to handle him. He'll just have to stay extremely worried for a day or two. I'm extremely worried, we all are, that's life. Our life, at least.

Signal her, tell her to ring in, she can go and see him on her next day off from the PU."

*****

Jane was in the car with Armstrong, Alice and Danny when her phone rang. Armstrong had asked her straightaway if she felt better; she said yes, it had just been a twenty four hour thing, she should have known better than to eat mussels from a sea-side kiosk. Danny shrugged, they hadn't done him any harm. She was sitting in the back with Armstrong, and apologised, asking him whether he minded her answering the phone; he said of course not, but Danny looked disapproving, because messages to the Protection Unit were meant to come to the senior officer present, which was he. She recognised Charles' voice; this was obviously not a routine call. She quickly told him where she was, and with whom; he answered that there was a problem with her next posting, and would she ring the chargé at Madrid as soon as her duties with Armstrong permitted? And please give his compliments to Armstrong, and he hoped that she was protecting him satisfactorily. Charles had used his Leslie Phillips voice, which Jane detested.

Their present destination was a horticultural research establishment; neither Danny nor Jane knew anything about horticulture, and they suspected that nor did Armstrong, before, that is, he had read the briefing document prepared for him by the Ministry of Agriculture. But they were wrong; he glanced at the brief, tut-tutted, and turned to Jane. "Who do they get to write these things? Some fool with a classics degree? Or do they think I'm just a politician and don't stand a chance of understanding anything as complicated as genetics? I don't know, this isn't even correct, he's...never mind ..." He sighed, and tut-tutted again. But then a new thought struck him. "Oh dear, you didn't read Greats, did you?" he asked Jane. She reassured him, but he didn't give the impression that he thought philosophy, politics and economics was that much better.

The visit to the research centre did not turn out to be the walk in the woods which Danny had expected. It turned out that the technicians and field workers – in effect, farm labourers – had been refused a pay rise but the scientists had received theirs; press and television were everywhere, pointing their cameras at the demonstrators and their placards instead of the rather unphotogenic Director who was trying to explain to Armstrong and the BBC news crew the various improvements which her team had made to fruit and vegetables, and who had chosen to compare two apples which may well have differed substantially in terms of taste, sweetness and shelf life, but unfortunately not at all in appearance. She cut them up and offered them to Armstrong to taste, but confused the slices so he had more or less to guess which was which. Danny and Jane not only had to keep jostlers and camera-wielders at bay, but they were both – they discovered when comparing notes afterwards – nervous about the displayed and accessible heaps of produce, especially the tomatoes. They had met some Civil Service staff at the research centre, and when at last they left, having avoided, or prevented, any newsworthy fracas, they were to part company, the mandarins returning to Whitehall, Armstrong to a meeting with the CEO of Honda at Swindon. But as they drove back to the motorway, Armstrong told Alice to radio the other car to stop at the nearest layby. They all got out, except Armstrong, who instructed the senior civil servant to join him in the back of the Jaguar. The car window was open, but Jane could not hear what was said, merely that it was spoken in an ordinary tone. After a minute or two the car door opened and the man emerged. Jane thought he was going to stumble. She had previously put his age as mid-forties; he looked a bleached sixty as he bent down to get back into his own car. She looked, wide eyed, at Danny.

"Oh yes," he said, "that's the effect he has on people, if he's angry."

"Will we get it in the neck too?"

"Probably not. You didn't see a briefing about a demo, did you?"

"No, of course not, in any case, you'd have seen it as well."

"Well, fingers crossed."

The drive to Swindon passed uneventfully, Armstrong even making a few humorous comments about the dangers averted at the research station. Danny tried a joke of his own, about avoiding egg production units, but it fell rather flat. Then he asked whether Armstrong thought he might have been 'set up'?

"By whom?"

"Well, the press, I suppose, sir."

"Look, Dan, you take a bunch of twenty-something lads, give them a grievance, let them near a pile of tomatoes, a politician and a tv camera, and they really don't need to be told what to do by some hack from the Shield. In the circumstances – avoidable circumstances, as I mentioned to that prat from Ag and Fish – you both did extremely well to avert, well, I don't know what, a dry cleaner's bill at least. You did splendidly to calm down those guys over by the bins, Penny, you seem good at that."

"She's got an advantage there, Minister," said Danny, not altogether good-naturedly.

"I can't imagine what you mean."

He smiled at Jane, a broad and charming smile which she had never seen before. Danny was looking out of the window.

"Ah well, the Nation's business calls," Armstrong said, opening one of his red boxes. Jane settled back beside him, wondering when she would get a moment to return Charles' phone call without the risk of being overheard. She realised then that Armstrong was waving a piece of paper at her, obviously something out of his box, and he started to talk. The issue was a Europe-wide controversy concerning the rights of Muslim working women, for example school teachers or doctors, to wear clothes which concealed all their bodies except their eyes. Jane and her mother had talked about this recently, and at some length, on one of their late night phone conversations, so she found no difficulty in following his arguments, discussing them, in some cases disagreeing with him, and more or less maintaining the position which she and her mother had reached. Armstrong nodded. "Yes," he said, "I think you're right." He scribbled a note on the paper, and crossed out the final paragraph.

"Thank you, Penny." Again, the charming smile, the frank eye contact.

Jane, who had recently found her thoughts dwelling to a surprising extent on David MacMaster, found this very disconcerting. Perhaps her report that Armstrong was 'not dangerous' was a bit wide of the mark – but it was certainly true that he didn't flirt.

Alice and Jane chatted while Armstrong, guarded by Danny, negotiated some investment deal with the Honda board. Alice's son was 'going through a difficult phase' which apparently meant that he would rather play computer games than do his homework. The boy's entire career had been mapped out for him by his parents, on the strength of a casual comment by a teacher that he was quite good at biology and chemistry, and unless he got good grades at GCSE he would never... Jane stopped listening, and didn't find out what the child would never do, because she was very anxious to make contact with base. She made tautologous but comforting noises to Alice about the temporary nature of phases, and excused herself to phone the chargé at Madrid.

Charles, who had been waiting impatiently for her to return his call, told her that she had to handle Maurice and whatever his problem was. When was her next day off? Wednesday, the day after tomorrow? That would be fine. Go and see him, no messing around, no inconclusive phone calls. Meet wherever he wanted – *just sort it, Jane. Jennifer's very words.*

A curl of smoke from the other side of the Jaguar showed Jane that Alice had taken the opportunity of a quick cigarette, so she phoned Maurice immediately. He answered the second of the numbers Charles had given her – it turned out to be his gallery in Exeter. He sounded nervous and worried, he would have preferred to meet Inspector Green, but of course he remembered her, and certainly she could come to his house. Wednesday! Surely she could... tomorrow morning would be best... oh, very well then, but if anything happened... anything, um, if Anthony... would she make a note that he'd phoned... oh good, he was only trying to do what was right... yes, he did find what she said reassuring... had to be at the gallery in the afternoon on Wednesday... half past eleven, yes that would be suitable. At this point, Maurice realised that she was putting herself out for him, and that she probably had some distance to travel, so it behoved him to remember his manners.

"You'll stop for a bite of lunch, I hope. I can't promise you anything too elaborate, but there's usually some smoked salmon: I'll see what's lurking in the freezer. And perhaps a glass of gooseberry from New Zealand, if your parotids can cope, of course." This practised patter, tripping off his tongue so easily, served to restore his self-confidence. She was quite young, after all, – attractive too, he remembered, – funny, he thought, how he preferred girls to be pretty – so it was a positive advantage that she was coming instead of Green. He could admire, instead of pining. What was she, a sergeant, perhaps? His mood had lifted. A cup of tea now, he thought. Definitely, a cup of Lapsang and a small slice of lemon sponge.

August 2   Jane   Maurice

Jane owned a car, of sorts, but she kept it in her mother's garage in Oxford. She used one of the pool cars, unfortunately the small underpowered saloon almost into its second decade. One of their inconspicuous cars. She had been hoping that the Subaru would be available – after all, she was still in her twenties (just) and cars with a bit of poke still held their appeal. So the following morning she turned up at Maurice's house a little late, after a noisy journey, and desperate for coffee. His welcome was courteous, perhaps slightly nervous, a pot of coffee was ready, and they sat down to drink it. They stayed in the kitchen, but it was the sort of kitchen where rich people entertained their friends to supper, not at all like the utilitarian galley in Jane's flat. Jane had glimpsed his sitting room; it seemed rather overblown to her, but she felt this probably reflected more on her taste than Maurice's. There was plenty of art around, and she thought she could at least make a sensible guess at some of the painters' names. But she really didn't like the gilded plaster putti, blowing their slender trumpets at each other over the (presumably faux) renaissance tondo above the mantelpiece. Was there a Mrs Maurice? No, no, she realised, obviously not.

They had only met briefly, and in unusual circumstances, so Maurice hadn't formed much of an opinion of her. He presumed that she was a policewoman, junior to the man he knew as Chief Inspector Green, but in his anxiety he forgot to ask her to show him her warrant card, which saved her the trouble of choosing one from her selection. They finished their coffee, Jane said what a delightful house he had, was that a John Piper, and yes, her journey had been no trouble. Maurice pushed his cup away, drummed with his fingers on the table for a moment, tried to reconcile her demeanour – and her accent – with membership of the police force, but then thought of Green again; obviously, all sorts of people became coppers these days – well paid, good pension, start again when you're forty, just like officers in the army.

Well, she hadn't started by bullying him, or interrogating him, she was just sitting there, smiling – what a smile – and sneaking glances at his pictures. It *was* a John Piper, a rather colourful tapestry design.

She said nothing; she knew that he would start the conversation, or the monologue, she was even fairly sure what he would say. She was right.

"I expect you're wondering why I asked for a meeting?"

She just smiled.

"Well, you see, I was obviously very upset when you, that is, Mr Green, was asking me what Mr Evans – Anthony – told me about the, um, events which had, er, occurred on Saturday morning. I..." he paused, waving his hand around helplessly, as if completely lost for words, " that is, he said..." again he paused; it was time, Jane thought, to offer him a formula which he was probably too embarrassed to use himself.

"You've just remembered, haven't you, some things he said on Saturday evening, which in your understandable anxiety you forgot to tell the Chief Inspector on Sunday."

He exhaled a trembling, thankful breath. She continued,

"And you were obviously anxious to tell us what you remembered as soon as possible. Am I right?"

"Yes, yes, that's exactly right, yes, just that, spot on! I say," he added, after a slight pause, "did he come away with you all right, you know, quietly, not like me, I hope?"

Again, Jane just smiled, inscrutably, she hoped.

"I think you and he probably had quite a conversation that evening," she said, "Why don't you tell me what you remember now?"

"Yes. Let's go and sit in the conservatory. Chairs are comfier. More relaxing. Sun's over the yard-arm, isn't it, what would you say to a snifter? G and T? Martini?"

"Just a juice, please, anything, but you go ahead, I would if I weren't driving."

In the small dining room through which Maurice showed her, two places had already been set with more cutlery and glassware than were necessary for a scratch meal of smoked salmon from the freezer. The chairs in the conservatory were definitely more comfortable, planters' chairs, perhaps even real ones from Malaya. Maurice brought drinks through on a tray with coasters, little saucers of cashews and olives, a tiny earthenware flower pot for the stones, and a porcelain hedgehog with wooden toothpicks for spines. She had clearly been staring at this, because Maurice said,

"Isn't Norman cute? I found him in Southend."

"Norman?"

"Spiny Norman," he said, surprised, "you remember, he terrified Dinsdale?"

Jane did not seem to remember.

"Never mind." Maurice had regained, or more than regained, his bounce, and Jane was sure she would be able to comfort him and convince him that as long as he didn't breathe a word about their escapade to anyone else he would have nothing to fear from the – *authorities*, perhaps she would say? More encompassing than *the police*. She moved her small handbag with the miniaturised recorder onto the table.

On her journey down from Victoria that morning, as the tinny little car vibrated along the middle lane of the motorway, flashed and hooted by vans that couldn't overtake because the fast lane was a continuous stream of Mondeos and Vectras, while the slow lane was a crawling blockage of lorries and caravans, she had gone over and over in her mind the purpose of her visit, rather, the purposes; what might Symes-Franton want from the meeting, and, whatever this might be, what did *she* want? Clearly, Maurice and Anthony must have had a longer talk on Saturday evening than Maurice had admitted to Green. The crucial issue was, had Anthony looked at the photographs he had taken? Well, he'd been tracked down after God knows how many cock-ups, so David would soon know the answer to that. And, if he had looked at his photographs, had he told, or shown them to, Maurice?

But she soon learned that Anthony had made no mention of photographs. Maurice's only concern was the gun, David's personal, expensive, Smith and Wesson J frame 357 Magnum, which, Jane remembered, fitted so neatly above his taut and undeniably attractive buttocks, and which Anthony had apparently been waving around in the restaurant of the road house where he had the following morning escaped the botched clutches of Jack and Jill from K division. Maurice was really worried that he ought to have told them about the gun. And, in normal circumstances, he would have been quite right to be worried. He could have been accessory before and after, if not during, depending upon what his unreliable friend did, deliberately or much more likely accidentally, with the weapon. Not that circumstances were ever normal, really, cause and predictable effect, that sort of thing, not in her line of work they weren't. More like the butterfly flapping its wing and causing a tsunami. Was that correct? Well, chaos was the word, all right.

She was allowing her mind to dwell on such matters because Maurice had relaxed after he had learned that the police (and by now he was calling Jane 'Inspector') couldn't give a flying fuck whether he knew about the gun or not. Jane had reassured herself that he knew nothing about any camera – he looked very puzzled when Jane mentioned this; genuinely, she was sure, she was looking very intently at him, watching for any of the movements that she had been taught signified lying, and observed none, no revealing eye movements, no tightening of the left index finger (she had checked that he was right handed), nothing at all. Maurice had, in his relief, drunk almost the entire contents of the cocktail shaker into which Jane had noticed that he had poured about a quarter of a pint of gin, and possible a dessertspoon of vermouth, and was consequently in full flow. He had, it seems, been telling Anthony about some fake paintings which he had come across in St Petersburg – St Petersburg, is that really what he said? – and Jane, with her new interest in art, should, she thought, have been listening more closely, but the account was so disjointed, and, as he became relaxed and intoxicated, so full of asides, and meaningful little glances, and arch references to personalities no doubt eminent but completely unfamiliar to her, that she had given up trying to follow him, and was waiting for an opportunity to suggest that they attack the oysters and game pie with truffles or whatever, and then she would be on her way. Then she heard him say,

"...of course, he would have loved to have been able to bid for the Hopkins – if that's what it was, of course, dear..." said archly, with raised eyebrows, doubtless referring to his tale of forgeries on the Baltic "but he'd already spent three hundred grand on the Bradleys hadn't he? Well, so he said, God knows the truth of it..."

"Sorry, what was that? When did he ..."

"At the auction, you know, just before he went home and found – well, whoever it was, I ask no more questions, I take your word..."

Jane interrupted. "So, he actually attended the auction? Bought something?"

"Yes, of course, well... so he said. I mean, I've only got his word for it..."

"What did he buy?"

"Two little oils by Quentin Bradley. You won't have heard of him, he was one of the Festival group, they..."

"I know about the Festival school. I think I've heard of...Three hundred thousand?"

"Yes. They're on the up and up, I can hardly afford to show any, my own stock, that is."

Only a month or so previously Jane would have been astounded. When she first went on duty as part of the Protection Unit in Victoria Park she had known from her week in Homerton how valuable many paintings were; the Lowry which Constable Rob had hated, for example, providing that it wasn't a fairy, well, Harriet had said that a dealer would ask at least half a million, and there were dozens of artists, even live ones, whose work would have price tickets like that. But knowing this had not been quite the same thing as accepting it; accepting that fairly ordinary people, people whom she might meet at a party, or share an office with at work, would spend such an enormous amount of money on something to decorate their living room wall. Her quarry in Munich had probably spent millions on his mansion and its furnishings, but he had not been an ordinary person; he had been extraordinary in so many ways, completely egocentric, utterly violent, charming of course, but – and why should she try and think of any other word for him – the enemy; she would expect him to do extraordinary things. If she had seen the Ashmolean Cézanne on his sideboard she would have taken it in her stride. But that was a year ago; she had heard that after the accident at Klosters his castle had become a private clinic, and his yacht had been acquired by a Saudi prince.

She had been half expecting something approaching the same sort of lifestyle, if not at the same level of opulence, when she went to work at Armstrong's house near Victoria Park, but she found it to be very little different from that to which she had herself been accustomed in North Oxford, and it was considerably less luxurious than the style her mother enjoyed in College. Mr and Mrs Armstrong were ordinary people – he was of course in an immensely important position, and she could not deny the force of his personality, but he was not of another world. Mrs Armstrong, Lucy, kept house, painted a little, gardened a little, and entertained her husband's many guests. She dressed neatly in clothes from shops like Jaeger, never wore gold jewellery, and her only diamonds were the small ones in her engagement ring. Their shared passion was a love of art, and they seemed to know a great deal about it. Jane had heard them talking about exhibitions, and sometimes the pictures hanging on their own walls, both together and with guests who she knew from the PU logs were from the professional artistic world – artists, gallery owners and directors, art historians and television pundits. This was their private enthusiasm, above all else, and almost immediately it seemed quite natural to Jane that they should spend whatever capital they might have accumulated on works of art. Prosperity in middle age enabled other people to buy farmhouses in the Dordogne, Mercedes cars and Rolex watches; if Evans chose to buy art instead, then why should the Armstrongs not spend similar sums on paintings and sculpture? Why had this seemed suspicious?

Evans. Yesterday he had been heading south west on the M5. Had they – had David – caught up with him yet? She had quickly scanned an extract from his file; owner of a successful business which had apparently supplied useful advice, sometimes under contract, to more than one Government department, moderately rich, one child, wife dead from a late diagnosed ovarian tumour. She had wondered why he had a file; perhaps because of some of his work for the defence departments? Then she found a note that the intelligence liaison officer from the Russian Peripheral Independencies section of the Foreign Office had on occasion debriefed him after some of his work in the Caucasus. A tick and two rough hand drawn asterisks on the file at this point indicated to her that his information had been deemed both reliable and useful. She frowned at the recollection of the hurried briefing which she and Alan Green had received over the phone, in which Henry himself had instructed them to get Evans's companion safely out of the way so that Evans could be detained with a minimum of risk to others. Maurice was an art dealer; well, it was natural that a man who would spend over a quarter of a million on two paintings at a provincial art sale would be friendly with art dealers; what was the name of the artist? Bradley, that was it. Evans hadn't had a couple of paintings tucked under his arm when they had followed him in Broadharbour.

Maurice had paused, not in order to fill his lungs for the next effusion but because he needed to lean forward from his awkwardly angled chair in order to spear a couple of olives, and this movement compressed his diaphragm and temporarily silenced him. Jane took advantage of the lull.

"So where are the paintings now?" she asked.

"The conservator's, he said, Prowley's in Guildford."

"Ah. And you said something about a Hopkins?"

"Yes, that must have been the star of the show, that's Festival too, he didn't say who bought that. But," he added, winking at her, actually screwing up his face and winking, not going so far as to tap the side of his nose although that wouldn't have surprised her, "I could tell you a thing or two about Hopkinses – they're best avoided, if you ask me."

So was this why Armstrong had dragged Danny and her off to Broadharbour, for 'a little private business'? Thoughts raced through her mind; she felt that a tangle of threads was being pulled apart and woven into a pattern. Had Armstrong bought a picture? He hadn't gone into the sale room – but he had made a long phone call – who were the men he had met, had research identified them yet? Why did Evans take the photographs? What did Maurice's sudden little obiter dictum *best avoided* mean? She sensed that he might backtrack if asked directly, so she would try and talk around the topic for a while, approach it indirectly. She could always listen later to the recording of what he had already said about fakes in St Petersburg.

She asked him about the type of work which he sold in his gallery, which, he said, was mainly twentieth century British, although he carried one or two of the less well-known French surrealists, because he found they sold reliably if he wasn't too greedy. Sometimes he had managed to get hold of some St Ives School paintings, but prices had risen so fast recently that he could really only afford to keep minor examples in stock – small gouaches, or the odd watercolour. Occasionally an Alfred Wallis. And then, of course, there was the problem of attribution – sometimes he thought that a provenance was more valuable than the painting.

Jane smiled, and said, "Journalists just love the idea of some embittered genius fooling the entire art establishment, don't they? And then it usually turns out that forgeries are just so dead obvious that if any real expert got near them they'd be rumbled straight away. It's not the art establishment that's fooled, it's the poor ignorant punter who really wants to believe that he's got a Canaletto on the cheap." She was repeating, not quite verbatim, a couple of sentences from one of Harriet's little homilies, this one, Jane remembered, delivered in the tea room of Harvey Nichols.

Maurice was not so sure. He thought that the 'art establishment' was frequently fooled, partly, of course, by trusting its own judgment instead of employing Harriet's battery of scientific tests.

"Well – sometimes, yes. Not always the completely ignorant punter, sometimes the slightly ignorant curator. Look at the Eastwich Constable. And himself, he had come across one or two more, very suspicious they were."

They sat in silence for a minute or two, Jane sipping her pomegranate juice, Maurice almost absent-mindedly pouring more Tanqueray into his shaker. He was thinking again about his trip to St Petersburg. Of course, abroad was jam-packed with forgeries, mainly classical antiquities, or the continental masters; he had to admit to himself that if he were a gifted but indigent Italian, or Dutch, or German artist, the British Festival school wouldn't be the first place he would think of exercising his talents. A thought then struck him about the two Hopkinses – one probably genuine, the other definitely wrong – which the Russian billionaire, Kuznetsov, had shown him. The good one was an Auto Union – a model first produced in the fifties, he thought – but the bad one was a Volkswagen. Would Hopkins have included a German car, developed before the war at Hitler's instigation, in his series? Probably yes, if he had actually called the paintings his 'People's car' series – but did he? This was the crux, really; if the series of paintings had been named by Hopkins, it would have contained a Volkswagen – the original people's car. If, for one of a number of possible reasons – he had been a soldier, hadn't he, but later than the second world war, surely? – he had not painted any VW pictures, he surely wouldn't have chosen that name. Maurice made a mental note to check the Catalogue Raisonée, without much hope of enlightenment as it had been produced by a retired art historian, Hopkins' executor, in his dotage. Maurice didn't remember any VW paintings. Would a forger choose a different make of car, or would he paint another version of a model already in the series? Hopkins had painted two A30s, Maurice was sure. Or perhaps...?

Maurice realised that although he had been voicing some of his thoughts somewhat at random, the girl Penny looked really more than quite interested. Had he mentioned Kuznetsov's forgery? The wrong VW. Perhaps he had. Well, no harm done, nothing to do with Anthony and his revolver. He put the top back on the gin bottle, pushed the shaker to one side, and said, rather lamely, "I don't expect you knew that paintings of old cars could be so valuable?"

"Not as such, but it's not really surprising, is it? I mean, didn't Monet (damn, was it Monet or Manet?) paint trains? And boats, lots of painters painted boats. And, (this was a good point, she thought) horses were like cars are now, and there are hundreds of valuable pictures of horses, aren't there?"

On an easel, in the window of the sale room, of course, a small green saloon, a meadow, a picnic hamper, some trees – she had seen this as she ran past, to the entrance of the small shopping mall where they had first lost Anthony. It must have been the Hopkins, or perhaps a large reproduction.

"Have you got a catalogue?" she asked Maurice, who looked bemused.

"What of?"

Off guard, imagining that Maurice was privy to her own train of thoughts, and therefore slightly irritated, she replied, "The sale in Broadharbour, of course, when Mr Evans bought the Bradleys."

"No need to snap, dear. It's all on the internet now."

She apologised, cross with herself, Maurice stumbled off to fetch his laptop and they found the picture, which had been sold, to the agent of an anonymous principal, for eight hundred and fifty thousand pounds – high, but not a record.

"Look," she said, "It's one of those old Morris Minors! One of my friends, at – she was going to say, 'Jesus College', but substituted, 'Police College' – had one, it had a hole under the accelerator pedal, and you got mud up your jeans."

"No," Maurice replied, "Look closer, look at the radiator, it's a German car, an Auto Union, that's an Audi, you know. Just like the one in..." he managed to stop himself, and Jane did not notice, because she was trying to work out the actual subject of the painting.

"Oh," she looked closer, "Well, if you say so – those blokes in tweeds are in the way. Yes, perhaps the bonnet is too rounded? What a strange picture."

Maurice was thinking the same, but for a different reason. He knew why Jane – Penny, to him, – thought it was strange, because she didn't know that Hopkins would often turn a painting into an elaborate joke; the joke in this one was presumably that the girl in the blue bonnet, who appeared to be adjusting her shoulder strap, was actually preparing to strip off before eating her picnic lunch naked with the tweedy blokes, while her friend was going to plunge into the stream in her slip. It was a sneaky reference to a painting which was itself half parody. But he couldn't be bothered to explain all this to Penny. No, he thought it was strange that Hopkins had, once again, chosen an Auto Union. There were no other foreign cars. No 2CV; surely, if he was painting foreign cars that was the people's car par excellence? And was Hopkins still producing car pictures at the end of the fifties? It was possible, he'd had that break in the army; he could have taken the series up again, they sold well. Maurice discounted the title – possibly that had been changed from Auto Union to Morris Minor by some dealer in the sixties, to make it more saleable.

In Maurice's bathroom, whither she had excused herself, (surprisingly plain, she thought, because she had not yet learned that gold plate on the bathroom taps is not necessarily concomitant with gold leaf in the sitting room) Jane phoned David's mobile, but was immediately patched through to Charles.

"He's lost his signal, I'm afraid, but we've had a call on a land line from Evans. David's made contact. Evans was checking up on him. They're at a country pub in, let's see,

West Penwith, that's near St Ives. The Cornwall one. Well, it's all right for some. Is there anything we should know?"

"Yes, but later, David first, urgent."

She telephoned the number he gave her. She asked to speak to Mr Smith, a man with an injured arm, hoping that the receptionist, or barman, had noticed this. He had, the gentleman in question was sitting in the alcove talking to a friend. No, his friend was middle aged, not large at all. The large man had come in with the injured gentleman, and was standing at the bar that very moment.

"Hello Jane," said David, after the barman had handed him the phone, "I know, I know. Yes, quite a surprise. No harm done, just tell Jennifer, please, *so far so good...*"

But Jane continued speaking. There was a pause as if David had taken a moment or two to assimilate the information. Then he said, "Yes, sure, bye now," and ended the call.

Jane drove back even more slowly than she had driven there in the morning. She had drunk only one glass of the champagne which had accompanied the foie gras (it was a *sec* which surprised her, although it shouldn't have done) and to Maurice's chagrin had accepted only a taste of the Chablis which he brought in with the turbot. His murmured *grand cru* had meant nothing, and she only knew the species of the fish because she asked him. But she enjoyed the meal, although she noticed that there was a dish of potatoes on the sideboard which Maurice had forgotten to put on the table.

Before she left, she said,

"It was Monty Python, wasn't it; Doug and Dinsdale Piranha? The Kray twins? Or was it the Richardsons? They were only scared of the hedgehog?"

Piranhas? The hedgehog? Maurice knew there was some connection he should make. But at the moment he wasn't up to it. He blinked and gazing vaguely in her direction smiled and waved goodbye, but she noticed that he was clinging tightly to the door jamb.

August 4   David   Jane

"Well," said David, "So that's how the little jaunt to Broadharbour fits in. But you say he didn't actually attend the sale? Perhaps someone bid for him? We'll have to sort out the details. Mrs Armstrong's bound to know. You'll have to have another little chat with Lucy.

"Then there's this forgery business that you learned about from Symes-Franton. These were paintings by the same artist Evans went to Cornwall to see, where he dragged me off to that party at the Saline, and I'm sure that he was suspicious as well. Do we think – do *you* think – that some of Armstrong's or Michaelov's paintings are counterfeit? This we shall have to take upstairs; it might be a very ticklish issue in all sorts of ways. What do you think of Armstrong? I mean, do you have any feelings about him?"

"I haven't seen him as you might say in action, except for the hospital visit, but I do get the sense that he's always on the ball. He's very decisive. You've read my note about the episode with the builder. He's not in any way overbearing, David, but he has, after all, effectively been deputy PM for nearly ten years. I suppose people think that to be successful you've got to be ruthless, and I suppose I don't know enough of his history, but he seems, well, quite kind really. Although," – she paused – "he was very sharp with that principal after the veg station visit. But I'll tell you something that I found amusing, Lucy made him drill the holes for the new pictures. Somehow that surprised me, I don't know why."

"Just like any old husband, you mean?

"Ok. But he's not, is he? Come on."

"Mrs T used to do the washing up."

"When the photographers were there."

"What about the painting that Winterbottom was on about? A Bridget Riley?"

"No sign of it. He's just got some more pictures in. Just as valuable. Hence the hooks. I'm sure I can find out more about the art; I just about managed to keep my end up at Dowland's. Give me a day or two."

"Perhaps Lucy will have another boozy lunch. That would help. Or maybe she drinks in any case. Have you noticed? Little pick-me-ups from time to time?"

"I don't think so. I hadn't noticed before. But one doesn't always. People can be nearly blotto, can't they, and unless you've actually seen them tipping back the Teachers you think, well, that's just their way, a bit loquacious, old so-and-so?"

"Well I don't know about that. Alcohol can be very useful. What other points are there, your items seven and eight." He referred briefly to the green and white screen of Jane's antique computer. "Ah, we've dealt with this, what is Mickey Michaelov's involvement? Can we confirm that he's just lending the pictures, quite frequently, I gather and apropos of that, who is this Axel character, and, of course, there's the forgery issue. Next, and I'm glad you phoned me about this, is there friction between Armstrong and the Cabinet Secretary? What are the problems which Armstrong is having with Sir Bill? Well, Jane, the first of these is your pigeon, obviously, but you'll have to wait until I – we – have spoken to Henry. The second, equally clearly, is not. Please don't pursue this; you are supposed to have only the vaguest acquaintance with the Cabinet Secretary – your boss, remember, as far as Mr and Mrs Armstrong are concerned, is the Head of the Diplomatic Service. I'll speak to Henry. He'll enjoy a private tête à tête with Billy Boy."

He smiled at Jane to point up the irony of his last comment, but the smile faded quickly. David had an uneasy feeling that he, Jane, and the team, were creeping along a benighted path which others had trodden, if not in the midday sun, at least with the aid of a couple of Maglites and a map.

Jane, meanwhile, was pursuing her own train of thought. She had, over a year ago now, enjoyed her first independent assignment – her baptism of fire, in-at-the-deep-end, operation in Munich with that handsome, courteous, hospitable, gun-running psychopath. But he was part of the game, he was the opposite team, he was the enemy, and if push had come to shove she would have handed over without a qualm to the mechanics, or, if necessary, dealt with him herself (so she imagined). The shock she had felt when she learned of his recent accident had subsided quickly and had left her relatively unmoved. But she found her deception of Lucy very distasteful. To encourage the poor woman to drink in order to loosen her tongue – this was David's implicit suggestion – seemed a cheap trick. Poor Lucy, she thought, not at all insulated by her prosperity and social position from the conventional angst of the middle class, middle aged, unemployed female, the *kept woman* was the derisive term which had been used by many of her friends at Jesus; indeed, her husband's importance and success could only make the contrast more obvious. Her bloke more or less runs the country, and she paints wishy-washy water colours. As for herself, Jane certainly wasn't going to fuck up her career with a husband or children. Sex was a different matter. Where was she? She shook her head and reassembled her thoughts. Of course David's instructions must be carried out, and carried out efficiently. She and Lucy could chat without boozing; women could do this, perhaps it was only men who needed the stimulus of alcohol to talk about matters more personal than football or Formula One? In any case, although she had struck up a sort of friendship with Lucy, she had to remember that her role in the household was not much more than that of a police constable. She could hardly suggest a quick gin and tonic in the pub at lunchtime.

"I think we should aim for a wrap quite quickly, Jane," continued David. "Here's a potted biography of Michaelov. You're looking very serious? I don't feel we'll find any chicanery, I think that for once Henry's gut feeling will turn out to be just a touch of the wind. However, that doesn't mean we can stop, not until we've got enough evidence to convince him. As far as the body politic is concerned, a negative result is the best conclusion; we mustn't forget that, in what Henry would call our zeal to unmask heretics. And now, I think the sun's over the belaying pin, as Maurice whatsit would say. How about a drink?"

It had been late afternoon when they had met in David's flat, the first floor of an early Victorian house on Ladbroke Road. No woman lived there, she knew; there was no hint of the horrible bachelor smells of unwashed towels and stale antiperspirant, but on the other hand there were no signs of distaff domesticity, no pot plants, no south sea island shells on the lavatory windowsill, and, more to the point, the only shampoo in the bathroom was a cheap one from CutCosts.

David had made tea and had put milk in her cup, and had made no fuss about replacing it when she told him she took her tea black; indeed, he apologised that he didn't keep any Earl Grey. She had offered to help, or make it herself, in consideration of his injured arm, but he said that he could manage, and did so easily. But he thanked her nicely, not at all brusquely. When they had finished work, he opened a bottle of supermarket Sancerre and they soon found themselves chatting easily, with a sort of intuition about what would interest each other. And if there was a gap in the conversation they smiled, and that was all right. It wasn't particularly late when Jane left, because David had to finish a report, and Jane caught herself humming and even making little pop-pop musical noises, vaguely following the tune of some crummy advertising jingle, as she sat on the tube. This was very unusual for her.

Chapter 15

August 3-7   Anthony   Helen   Walter

Dorset is the very epitome of rural tranquillity, unrivalled now that Herefordshire has been covered with polytunnels, and Anthony looked forward to a few days holiday there, trying to unwind after the frightening events of the past few days. That his sister and son might also deserve some comfort, some comforting, had of course occurred to him, but after his wife had died he had tended to pay rather more attention to his own needs and problems than he had before, possibly because Amy had done much of the attending unobtrusively but effectively. This was more obvious to Helen than to Walter, who rubbed along all right, really, most of his pressing needs – karate lessons, guitar club, junior chess club, the latest film and a burger afterwards at the multiplex – satisfied; he missed out on none of the activities which his two-parent friends enjoyed. He missed nothing, Helen thought, only because he was too young to understand what he was missing – the blanketing, security-inducing warmth which she thought, not necessarily correctly, only a mother could give. Anthony was, as it happens, more loving with Walter than Helen knew, but his cuddles tended to be in private – also one of Walter's requirements. Nevertheless, Anthony sometimes became inward looking, if not blind to the interests of others, certainly seeing a diminished image of them.

Anthony's phone call to Helen in the Brighton hotel had of course come as a great relief to her. She paid no attention to his attempts to tell her about the paintings and the gallery, nor to his garbled references to Mr Smith, and this, on reflection, was a great relief to Anthony, since in Brighton he had spent some time and, he thought, no little ingenuity, in convincing her that Mr Smith had been a phantom, a druggy hallucination. Helen and Walter had taken the next train west, travelling first class and eating lunch in the restaurant car. Helen fully intended to get the money back from Anthony, plus some extra to buy a carriage clock for her mantelpiece. And, possibly, a new food processor. Or a vacuum cleaner with the new hurricane design. Something, at least. Something quite expensive. She wasn't at all poor, but she had been more than a little annoyed by Anthony's matter of fact manner, smug almost, on the phone, as if she and Walter had had an enjoyable little holiday while Anthony had been on a work trip, for a project which had turned out quite well, all things considered. Walter, of course, was perfectly content now, had enjoyed himself enormously in Brighton, and was at the moment nagging his aunt for a Coke and a microwaved bacon and egg bap from the buffet. Walter's equanimity exasperated her, whereas in fact she should have been congratulating herself on the way in which she had avoided transferring her worries to him. When she did realise this she cheered up considerably, and decided that she too could cope with a flabby bap but first, why not, a vodka and orange.

When they met in Exeter, Anthony suggested they should all three return to the Anford cottage for a couple of days. Helen had had no time to mention the vacuum cleaner, nor the food processor, and since Anthony, unprompted, took her into a jeweller's and bought her a new watch with a gold bracelet and diamonds round its face, she decided that would do instead.

"Will you come with me to choose a new car?" Anthony asked Walter, later.

"Can we have a Hummer, Dad?"

Walter was trying to wrong-foot his father, but Anthony knew about the Humvee. He knew *all* about the Humvee. He actually knew its advantages and disadvantages relative to MRAPs, Jeeps, JRRVs, Ridgebacks and several other British military vehicles in the series named after large aggressive breeds such as mastiffs, long before it was discovered by the press that such dogs can bite and sometimes kill non-combatant children. In fact, he also knew that a young captain in the Royal Army Logistics corps had, as a poorly calculated joke, suggested the name Pit-bull for the latest such vehicle, and that this name had passed in paper over the desks of colonels and a brigadier before it was eventually noticed by the Second Permanent Secretary, who substituted the name Foxhound.

Walter was puzzled, then irritated. Did his dad really expect him to listen to all this? Why were grownups always showing off?

"Ok, Dad, OK, let's have another Merc then. But please not the one that looks like a banana?"

The Anford cottage was of the common terrace design with a narrow entrance hall and staircase, two small living rooms off the hall, scullery/kitchen at the rear, three bedrooms, two small and one tiny, with a bathroom later built over the kitchen. Anthony and his wife had not changed it much beyond modernising the heating, bathroom and cooking arrangements. But they had sold the tiny, inefficient, ugly, cast-iron and tile fireplace to a man who was restoring his house in Fulham, and replaced it with an unobtrusive but effective log-burner. Being able to lie on his tummy in front of this fire, indulged with a little snack – a Mars bar cut into slices, a packet of smoky bacon crisps, or a couple of peeled mandarins – placed conveniently close to his right hand by his aunt, while reading a comic or playing on his Nintendo or even watching Disney cartoons on the small TV setup in the corner, was one of the things Walter particularly liked about staying in the cottage; the other was his bed, in the tiny room overlooking the meadows on the other side of the lane. He liked the bed because its mattress was stuffed with duck down; it was a real feather bed, and had belonged to his grandmother, even, almost certainly, his great-grandmother. Walter's mother had pulled this from the skip into which Anthony was piling most of his mother-in-law's chattels, the old girl's rubbish, he said, betraying, at last, to himself indeed rather more than to his wife, an element of his feelings towards the argumentative old lady. This slightly smelly, yellowing and stained, giant overstuffed duvet affair had then been cleaned, sanitized, re-stuffed and generally restored for something like twice the price of a new top-of-the-range pocket sprung royally appointed mattress, partly as a punishment for Anthony, not for his feelings but for his thoughtlessness in showing them. Walter, who had hardly known his mother let alone his grandmother, loved it. It cocooned him, it was like the glowing warmth of the evening log fire stealing up to his bedroom.

They didn't stay long after breakfast on Sunday since Anthony had promised to take Walter to see Warwick castle, and was expected in his office on Monday; there were three projects under way at the moment, each perfectly competently managed by his staff, who had not expected to see him in the office the previous week, but it was not in his nature to indulge in random, inexplicable absences. In any case, surely the Affair of the Misunderstood Picture and the Resurrected Spook was over now, as far as he was concerned; he would lay it to rest at the Armstrong house on Tuesday afternoon.

On the way home Anthony and Walter stopped in Sidmouth for tea. Walter spotted, in the window of the shop two doors down from the café, among the tea towels and the cross-stitch Corfe Castle sewing kits, a cylindrical tin with a Union flag curved round one half of its surface and a picture of three grassy feather-duster things round the other. In this tin, point up, were *two dozen* fat colour pencils, beautifully sharpened. Welded upon the top of the lid, which was displayed leaning against a small resin crusader, probably a member of the Order of the Knights Hospitaller, sat a brass plated, double hole pencil sharpener. Walter's best friend Perry had an upright cylindrical pencil tin, and it had a picture on it, an ancient old buffer in a dressing gown with a dirty white cloth hat – which was a million times more boring than the flag and feathers, – and it held only twelve pencils and its tin lid just had a knob. Walter had nevertheless envied Perry his pencil case. But no longer; the pencil case in the window had supplanted it, this total triumph of the stationer's art with which he dreamed of drawing pictures with colours more varied and vivid than his art master had ever seen before. He wouldn't boast or show off, of course, but the other kids were bound to notice it – especially Perry, who sat at the next desk. The great question was, when to ask his Dad to buy it for him? He coveted it so much, he thought about it so often, that it never for one moment occurred to him that perhaps to his Dad it would be no big deal – that it might not even be very expensive. So, ten minutes later, outside the shop, clutching with both hands the plastic carrier bag which bore the same design of feather dusters as did the pencil case inside it, he could hardly believe that his father had, almost absent-mindedly, handed him the money and said that he would wait for him outside the shop. Anthony's eyes appeared rudely fixed on a bald and bearded pensioner in the bus queue but his mind's eye was ranging over vignettes of the recent past, snapshots of his great adventure. Ah, the pictures, the photos. He had forgotten until this moment that on the hard drive of his computer lay the photographs of Broadharbour High Street, including the one in which appeared Armstrong. Surely he could now wipe them off and forget about it all; forget about it, not in the sense of *forget* about it, obviously impossible, and a good story for the pub when he was retired, but put it out of his mind for the present.

But of course when he opened the folder that evening, he thought that there would be no harm in having a final quick look before he erased them. He had been right that only one was interesting, the one with Armstrong. There was Smith, again, whatever his name really was, stooping with his camera. And the attractive mixed race woman, where had he seen her before?

What would Maurice be thinking about it all now? He must give him a ring, take him out for dinner at least, no, something much more, perhaps another weekend in Florence? Bloody good idea. They would spend a quiet afternoon in Santa Croce with the Giottos, then rare steak and Amarone at the Bronzino. Umberto Eco had been there last time; they had talked, of course, about signifiers. Maurice would certainly want to go to the Bargello to see the David, or Mercury, as he insisted on calling it. But however. The photograph. The Director of the London, well, not too unexpected; and there, sitting in the car, he had spotted before but forgotten, Martin Phillips the great expert, the expert's expert and gallery owner. Who was the sixth man, standing behind Phillips? He knew him, surely; of course, of course, it was the Scandinavian, he of the insider dealer topcoat and expensive wine. The Scandinavian and Armstrong; that there was a connection was clear; he had an appointment for tea-and-pictures as evidence. The Scandinavian hadn't quite left him with the impression that he was, himself, on personal terms with Armstrong. Possibly he wasn't; it was only a small matter. Oh well, he would delete the photograph now; why should he keep it? What advantage to himself did it bear; what protection did it afford? It carried information, yes, and information which Smith, Green and co were prepared to go to considerable lengths to protect. Protect from whom? How could it possibly be significant or damaging that Armstrong, who was well known to have an interest in art, should be spotted in exalted art world company near an auction room in Broadharbour? But why was Smith taking a surreptitious photograph – no, not a photograph, it was a video camera he was holding?

    He knew that he should dismiss these considerations from his mind and destroy all the files, but he found that he couldn't. His training, superstition, neurosis; whatever it was, it would not allow him to destroy the photograph. On the other hand, on his computer it was vulnerable; he must make the image secure. He quickly printed the picture, folded it and slipped it into his wallet. Then he wiped the pictures from his hard disk – unlike Jane, he knew how to do this; he had written a program for his own office in machine code which gave the location of all his files and the various caches, and he overwrote them all seven times with random characters. Even the most sophisticated machinery available to the engineers at Cheltenham or Langley could not delve deeper than that into the shadow memory of the hard drive. It took a surprisingly long time; perhaps his code wasn't as efficient as he had thought. Perhaps he had deleted more than just the pictures – that didn't matter, everything else was backed up. Nevertheless, the job was now complete. He had switched his own router off, but noticed that he had picked up his neighbour's service; he made a mental note to pop next door and explain internet security to Austin and Mary. The print itself he would hide between the leaves of the seventh volume of the sermons of the Rev Adolphus Binns, privately and beautifully printed and bound, then donated to the Chapter House Library of Exeter Cathedral in 1876, where it had remained, dusted occasionally but otherwise undisturbed, ever since. This, at any rate, was his intention; the idea had probably been prompted by something like a Father Brown story, read in his youth.

*****

In Cheltenham, a young lady working the twilight shift felt much the same about her job as did the temptress on the Thames who wanted to stop cross-referencing previously undefined but possibly suspicious activities. Unfortunately, at Government Communications Headquarters, Directors of the Security Services were generally unavailable for eyelash fluttering at lunch time, and in any case she was happily married. She had become reconciled to her task which involved monitoring various hacked computers and implementing pre-defined protocols. Her activities were possibly legitimised by arcane sections of the Defence of the Realm Act, but she seldom paused to worry about the strict legality of the operation, which had of course never been tested in the courts. One day she would be promoted; even as it was, she earned more than her husband who was a school teacher. A red light started to flash, an activity code and a reference to one of the monitored computers appeared. The activity was unusual; a machine code procedure. Damn, there was no specific pre-def. She quickly patched it through to one of her own screens and interpreted it – the operator of the monitored computer was implementing a Guttman procedure to erase data. What on? The data patterns – they were photographs, large ones, surely. Could she insert a command to upload something, anything, from the same folder before it was overlaid – the first time round, it would have to be, of course, she couldn't read the latents on a remote disk. She was partly successful, and acquired a number of data blocks; it would have slowed down the erasure but it probably wouldn't seem significant to whoever was doing it. The procedure on the remote – the monitored computer – had been terminated, and the machine was now switched off. She tried a pattern recognition program on the data blocks; they were simple JPEGs, photographs downloaded from an ordinary digital camera, probably incomplete. She could top and tail them, and open them with any media package. First, she picked up her loose leaf general-instructions manual (never digitised, never let out of the department) and flicked through the pages until she found the section, *Procedures appertaining to non-indexed occurrences*. Tut, she thought, how pompous.

However, it seemed that she had to telephone the answerable officer, who in this case appeared to be a David MacMaster.

Mr MacMaster was unavailable – this didn't surprise her as it was nine o'clock – she left a brief message, logged the acquired data files, and wondered whether she should look at the photographs. Perhaps she would wait until MacMaster returned her call; on the other hand, it might be interesting – but at this point two more red lights started to pulse, and she turned back to her routine.

Anthony climbed the stairs quietly, and put his head round the door of his son's bedroom. Walter was asleep, sharing the pillow with Eeyore, whom he was protecting from Megatron with his new Frontier Colt. Anthony carefully eased the gun from Walter's grasp, blew him a kiss and retreated downstairs. After tidying up for a while, unloading the dishwasher and fishing the Fat Controller from underneath the sideboard, he went to bed with a good book, where he fell asleep with the light on before Jack had fired a single cannon, or Stephen once confused larboard and starboard.

Monday August 7   Anthony   Jane

The following morning he made breakfast, walked Walter to his primary school and took himself off to work. He had, thank goodness, an undemanding day, meeting, or, rather, fronting meetings with a couple of generally satisfied clients in his own office. Before he left, he made a telephone call to Dowland's, the auctioneers where he had bought the Bradleys. Yes, they told him, the Director of the London had been shown some paintings before the sale, but he had apparently been there in a private capacity. Yes, he had a couple of people with him, no, certainly not Armstrong. The people who were bidding by phone? Dealers, or agents, couldn't remember who at the moment, in any case, probably confidential. No, no trouble, hope to see him again, soon be offering a lovely little Laura Knight, quite sexy, tasteful of course. He put the phone down, looked up a number in the office on-line Directory, and dialled again. After explaining the purpose of his call to three officials in succession he found that he was speaking to a Penny something-or-other who asked if she could give Mrs Armstrong a message for him. Then, however, she was able to confirm that they were expecting to see him at four o'clock the following day, along with a gallery director, a Ms Frieda Semperdine and possibly others. Armstrong was unlikely to be at home, but Mrs Armstrong would be delighted to show them their own collection, as well as the Hopkins and one or two others which they had on loan.

So, thought Anthony, that explains my invitation. The Scandinavian has got his eye on Frieda as a customer for the Hopkins. I'm being presented as the competition. Or, maybe, the other way round? How rich does he think I am? Perhaps – yes, that's what all that offering me money for the Bradleys was about. Was it? To see how rich I am? God knows. Well, all will be revealed tomorrow. I jolly well hope so.

In Victoria Park, Jane stared at the computer screen, where the appointment had been entered, presumably by the overnight officer. This man Evans again. The man who had shot David. And, surely, this Frieda Semperdine, she must be the woman, the art collector, who had met Evans and David in the Cornish pub. She took out her mobile and entered David's secure number.

Chapter 16

Monday August 7   Henry   Richard

Henry and Sir Richard stepped carefully into one of the shining aluminium pods of the giant Ferris wheel which had just been constructed on the South Bank of the Thames, and which was designed to afford tourists a bird's eye view of the city. There were more passengers than seats, but it had been correctly predicted by the designers that passengers would stand, and move from point to point of the capsule as different vistas were revealed, and the two spy-masters easily secured seats in the corner of a bench. On their walk from Horse Guards they had conscientiously employed a couple of little tricks to lose any shadow, but since they had advance tickets to the Eye to avoid the queue, and queue jumping was not tolerated in the centre of Town, any opportunistic agent of a foreign power hoping to acquire some crucial intelligence would have been frustrated by the popularity of the attraction. Sir Richard had quite taken to Henry's suggestion of a meeting on the Eye, had in fact responded to it as gleefully as his Hebridean origins permitted. They both intended to pause their conference when the pod approached its zenith, and stare around pointing things out to each other.

"So Henry, what news of our important friend?"

"Squeaky himself, Richard, but has a friend with a friend with friends who aren't."

"Who is the friend of our friend's friend? I mean, no, for the good Lord's sake, list them in order, start with Armstrong's own friend."

"Mr X, first name Axel."

"An excellent start, Henry. Mr X. Distinctive, don't you think?"

"Actually, Richard, I'm afraid this is rather difficult. Have you noticed most of these tourists have got cameras?"

"That's all right, Henry, we're not celebrities, and why shouldn't we be talking to each other? We may be caught on film and appear anonymously on a computer screen in Japan next month – so?"

"Visuals aren't the point, Richard. Most of these video cameras capture sound as well."

"Ah."

"It's my fault, Richard, I'm so sorry, it was my idea. I'm getting rusty, I'm afraid."

"How long does this infairrnal ride last?"

"Half an hour, I think."

"Well, I suppose that's not too bad. Cricket?"

"I think so."

After a quarter of an hour Henry intimated to Richard that the pod had attained its apogee. They called a temporary halt to their analysis of Mark Ramprakash's outstanding performance in the West Indies, rose and edged to the west extremity of the capsule. The view to the east, over Waterloo Station towards Elephant and Castle, held little of interest to them. Even the sights to the west proved disappointing. The view of the Palace of Westminster was familiar from dozens of aerial photographs, and they weren't high enough to see round the bends in the river.

"Interesting to see Horse Guards from this angle, over the MOD."

"Yes, that's true. Good view of the Abbey."

"Yes."

Their seats had been taken, so they had to remain standing during the descent, frequently obliged to move from one side to another in order to afford the tourists the best views of the London roofscape.

They alighted – "Disemcapsuled, might one say?" said Richard, who had been put in a good mood by being able to give Henry a ball by ball account of Graeme Hick's latest test innings. "I think, Henry, that we should continue our meeting in the Park. We'll take a cab. Incidentally, I shan't mention this little contretemps back in the office, so you need have no fear of embarrassment. No doubt you feel the same?"

"Indeed I do."

The same ducks which had eavesdropped on Jane and David a month previously were still shovelling their beaks through the mud at the water's edge as Henry and Richard circumambulated the lake in St James's Park.

"You were about to tell me of Armstrong's friends. Starting, presumably, with the pseudonym used by Mr X?"

"No, we just don't know his surname. We haven't any information on him yet. We've only had twenty four hours to check."

"Next."

"Michaelov."

"Ah, well, yes. Clean, I suppose, as any billionaire."

"Yes indeed. But he has a wide circle of acquaintances of a number of nationalities including, I may say, our own, some of whom are about as fragrant as a baboon's backside. My senior case officer, David MacMaster, and his operative, think that there's something fishy somewhere along the line. It seems to be connected with the world of investment paintings, but almost certainly stops at, or before, Mrs Treasurer. David's plant thinks it centres on a certain type of painting, a group of artists called, I believe, the Festival school."

The DG stared with alarmingly mock admiration at Henry. "So that's why you planned the meeting on the South Bank?"

"Do you know, Richard, it never occurred to me. Subliminal, I suppose. So you know about the Festival school?"

"Of course. I may not have immediately picked up your reference to Bridget Riley of Op Art fame, but I've always found representational art, even of the allusive variety, much more ..."

"Yes, Richard I take your point. But David's operative seems to think that Mr and Mrs Armstrong are very close, not altogether unusual you know, and that any scandal touching her will be bound to touch him too. No, no, Richard, she's not exactly making a *judgment*, she knows that would be quite inappropriate, she's just, well..." – his voice became an inaudible mutter.

"One of Jennifer's, is she? I imagined you'd bring Jennifer in on this."

"Yes; she's the young officer who delivered the goods on Breezeblock."

"Good lord, Sophy Adeleke's girl?"

"You know her, C?"

"Sophia? Yes, indeed I do. Dined with her more than once. At high table, I mean, not tête à tête. She still thinks her girl – Jane, I seem to remember? – works for the FO. I'm not even one hundred per cent sure she approves of us. Not that that matters. Now, Henry, can we be sure that Armstrong himself is unaware of our efforts so far on his behalf?"

Henry would have dearly liked to tax Sir Richard with this blatant re-formulation of the objective of the last six weeks' work. But he let it pass; at some stage, quite soon, he would have to hand him a report which included David MacMaster's brush with death. He hadn't quite decided how to smooth out – no, that would not be possible – to minimize the impact of the regrettable incident. Oh dear no, he could not call it a 'regrettable incident', not in a report to Richard, who would first be derisive and then scandalised. Perhaps a verbal report first. MacMaster would have to be present. Perhaps, just perhaps, someone could have another word with this Evans. He had, after all, it seems, been known to them before the debacle, had cooperated from time to time with Dougie Blantyre, one of their FO liaisons. There was no problem with the police forces and their own department's mechanics; the Chief Constable had made no waves; Henry had spoken to him again in unctuous terms, apparently unnecessary, he'd been quite happy with the little chitty absolving him from responsibility, especially since, as he said, a firearms chase would have been damned expensive and involved one hell of a lot of bumf.

"Quite sure, Richard. Jane Ryan, that's her surname now, no, she's not married, it's a long story, no significance I assure you, Jane Ryan is attached to the Met as an FO security trainee, sexy uniform, guns and all, and it would appear that she has struck up a rapport with Mrs Armstrong. There are simple – well, fairly simple – explanations for the show of wealth. The Bentley, for example, belongs to Michaelov, and Armstrong gets a go in it once in a while. Nihil nisi notwithstanding, it looks as if that arsehole Winterbottom got it wrong this time."

"But something isn't quite right?"

"You're right, it is a bit odd. Ryan went on the Met art crime course, which Alan Green also went on – you remember that flap, when the CIA were all over us? Well, she knocked on his door a couple of days ago and asked him what he knew about Hopkins, because Armstrong was going to hang one up in his front room but the point is it actually belongs to Mickey Michaelov. Yes, C, unusual, but not in any sense corrupt."

"Now, Richard. Here is the issue. Whether it is in fact an issue, whether we should pursue it further, is a matter upon which I must ask you for direction. It seems that Alan Green had become aware, through a recording made of a conversation with one of the contacts which he made on the Redgrave Vermeer case, that someone is forging Festival school paintings, and, for various reasons which will be detailed in the report you'll receive, it is possible, even probable, that the Michaelov Hopkins is one of these counterfeits. The question is, do we stay involved? Do we tiptoe away and close the file? Do we pass on what we know to the Met?"

Henry realised that he should not have mentioned the recording – he hoped that Richard would not ask questions about it; who made it, and why – but the DG was anxious to answer Henry's last question.

"Goodness gracious no. Involving the Met, I mean, of course not. How could you possibly imagine it?"

Henry had not, of course, imagined it, he had considered it quite out of the question, but he had needed the DG to say that first. Otherwise, were the whole affair to prove no more than a mare's nest, misguided and, worse, expensive, there was in his mind little doubt that the DG would castigate him for retaining the operation within the Service. He could, in fact, hear C's Anglicised but still prissy Western Scottish tones taking him to task for wasting resources which the Department could ill afford in these strrraitened taimers.

"Very well. Should we just walk away, then?" Henry guessed, and hoped, that Richard would disagree. He was correct. The DG was consolidating the new position which he had adopted, and addressed Henry in much the manner used by William Ewart Gladstone to Queen Victoria.

"Our over-riding aim, is it not, is to protect the interests of the United Kingdom, her Government and people. If – *since* – we have uncovered information concerning a potential threat to the, ah, stability – stability, would you say, Henry?" Henry extended the fingers of his left hand, waggled it about in front of him while nodding, blowing out his cheeks and making a quiet puffing noise, by which he intended to convey that stability might not be quite the word he would have chosen, but it would do for the time being – "thank you, stability, of a Principal Secretary of State, then it is incumbent upon us to take appropriate measures to investigate, report on and if necessary neutralise any such threat. In pursuance of which – " he raised his index finger and opened his eyes wide, staring towards the golden memorial of the great Queen herself, glinting through the branches of the London planes; he was already addressing Sir William, the Prime Minister and, possibly, the Privy Council – "*in pairrsuance of which* the Service has taken immediate steps to introduce extraordinary protective procedures – I like that, Henry, I hope you do – to guarantee the integrity of the essential work carried out by the Treasurer and his staff." He stopped addressing his meeting and resumed a normal tone of voice. "Then we'll stick in a précis of your chaps' reports. How's that?"

"Just the ticket, Richard. I particularly like the integrity of the essential work. I don't imagine we need place too much stress on our ferreting around among Armstrong's friends and neighbours?"

"Ye – es, Henry, I think you might have overplayed your hand a little there. Still, no harm done. I agree, we don't want the Committee bogged down in too much detail."

"So I take it we proceed?" Henry was quite happy to accept the not unexpected and only very mild criticism.

"Yes, Henry, I think so. It can have a name and a file now. I'm much happier with *accountable* work, you know; Jennifer's little off-shore forays always make me nervous. What shall we call it?"

"Jennifer has provisionally called it *Typewriter*."

"*Typewriter* – ah, I remember, the deceased Winterbottom's note. Any more news about the motor accident?"

"No, we've rather shelved that for the moment; we'll pick it up again, tomorrow perhaps, but I don't want anyone else involved in this one, in *Typewriter*, and Jennifer's quite stretched at present."

They ambled on, and C took the opportunity of asking Henry whether he had any experience of the new heating boilers, the condensing ones, because his own central heating was giving him no end of trouble.

"I've got something called a combi. I don't know what 'condensing' means."

"Nor I. By the by, Henry, I had Bill on the phone this am, Flying Fish is on the cards again, possibly quite hot."

Bugger me, thought Henry, you've been playing that close to your chest.

"Ah. So that explains our, um, re-alignment, of Typewriter?"

"Well, yes, you see the point. Without Armstrong and his rapport with the President, we – that is, Bill and I – feel that the fish will certainly not fly."

"I'm glad you passed that on, C; it does put a different light on things."

"Yes, doesn't it. Lunch?"

"Meetings all pm I'm afraid. Green's nearly ready to wind up the Chik-pak show"

"Ah. I rather fancied a tandoori. Never mind."

Monday August 7   David   Jennifer   Jane

David was taking tea with Jennifer, and keeping her up to speed on *Typewriter.* She asked whether Jane was performing satisfactorily.

David assured her that she was. He thought that Jennifer seemed, unusually, to be distancing herself from the details of this operation. He wondered whether some other flap was brewing – he nodded once or twice, and she continued.

"For the moment I'm handing you, and Jane, and your little team, over to Henry on Typewriter; obviously I need to know if there are any problems, I'm sure there shouldn't be. It's not quite so sensitive now; Richard has had a discreet word with Buoy-Dodd – changed the emphasis, rather; we're protecting Armstrong from any fallout from this I may say highly unlikely forgery business. I think that must be your phone."

"Excuse me," David answered his mobile, which was playing some very rhythmic piano music, probably Bach.

"MacMaster."

"David, an odd thing has happened. Just a minute. Yes, of course, should I come now, no, Lucy, that's all right, this call isn't urgent."

"Okay, understood, when does your shift finish?"

"Seventeen thirty."

"I'll call at the house."

"Roger that."

Jane ended the call, and went to see what domestic task she was required to share.

David finished his Hobnob and after the briefest of courtesies left Dame Jennifer to her red files.

"Madam is a little preoccupied at present," said Charles as David passed his desk in the outer office. "A certain well known Serbian general is proving tiresomely difficult to locate."

"Not the Nairobi bombers, then?"

"Always the Nairobi bombers, David."

"Well I'll get on with the trivial round, then."

"I hope it furnishes you as per Ancient and Modern."

David left as quickly as he could.

David, being of considerably lower rank than Henry and Jennifer, did not merit his own Personal Assistant. He shared a clerk and typist – neither called by those titles, of course – with two other officers of his own seniority, both of whom were in the field, one in Northern Ireland, the other in the Balkans. David was at least allowed his own office, reasonably large, furnished with a sort of civil service compromise between the polished wood and conference tables of his seniors and the metal-and-melamine of his juniors. His walnut veneered desk, nicely aged, had first been supplied to the old Ministry of Transport in Southwark. There were a couple of carver-style chairs, and an indeterminate item which looked like the kind of breakfast table the base of which slides under a bed in the room of an invalid or film star. His modern computer had its own table, and he had three colour-coded telephones. On his desk stood a framed black and white portrait of an elderly couple, while an elaborate curved sword, with jewels set into its hilt and gold tooling on its scabbard, hung on the wall. David returned to his room to clear his desk before setting off to meet Jane in Victoria Park, and found a note from one of the staff who had returned the phone call from GCHQ, where the young officer had said that she could speak only to David MacMaster. She answered his call and told him the story. The computer monitoring had been authorised at Deputy Director level – obviously by Henry himself – but David couldn't at first understand why she had been alerted by what seemed to him to be normal computer housekeeping.

"Surely, he was just clearing space, getting rid of old files? I do it almost every day."

"No, this was a special program, take it from me, it erases every trace of a file."

"All the same..."

"They were photos. I managed to download and tidy up some very small parts of two of them. I've checked that you can view them in more or less any standard program that handles JPEGs. There's a bit of a man's leg, showing his shoe, and a car door I think, and maybe the corner of a shop window in one of them, and the other's just something like a bit of dark green clothing with what looks like the flap of a pocket – perhaps a woman's jacket? I mean, why should he be making such a fuss about deleting them?"

"Goodness knows, better stick to the routine though, log it but no flag, I think." As soon as the GCHQ officer had used the word 'photo' David had understood. How prescient of Henry – but David should have expected no less. Another cock-up, good God, where would they send him next, Riyadh was the current destination employed to punish fallen officers. He continued, "I suppose you'd better email me the bits of the photos you salvaged. And – smart work, very well done, um..."

"Mandy."

"Very well done, Mandy."

"Thanks. Do you want them emailed direct, then?"

"Is there a problem with that?"

"Not if you've got Linksafe implemented."

"What's that?"

"Have you got a yellow phone?"

"Yes."

"Good. You have to disconnect it and then make sure your computer is plugged into the datalink socket. Could you do that please?"

"I'm not quite sure ..."

Mandy carefully explained the way in which his computer should be connected to the multipoint terminal behind his desk.

The pictures arrived before David had dusted off his knees.

"Good they've arrived, let me just check..."

They were as Mandy had described. David recognised Armstrong's shoe, and Jane's green waistline-concealing jacket. But nothing would reveal their identities to an inquisitive member of GCHQ staff. Not that they ought to look, of course. However, that was a marginal consideration. Anthony had seen the pictures. Certainly he had destroyed them – by using some fancy technique, it seems – which maybe implied that he knew they might be harmful, that he ought to forget about them – but he wouldn't be able to, like the donkey's tail, or Hitler's moustache. And the probability that he had not recognised Armstrong was well-nigh zero.

"Well, goodness knows what these are. Still, you did right to alert me. Thank you Mandy."

Mandy was buttoning up her coat in the cloakroom after the end of her shift when one of her friends came in and they started to chat. Mandy didn't say anything about the incident which caused her to phone the Security Services HQ, but she asked her friend whether her husband knew how to connect up, for example, the video recorder and the television.

"No, I don't think so, he leaves that sort of thing to Tom, that's our son. Or me, of course."

David waited in his car a little way along the street from Armstrong's house. Jane emerged, shortly after half past five, looked for him, spotted him and joined him in his car. She told him that Evans was expected the following morning, to look at Armstrong's collection, including the recently hung Hopkins. David did not, at that stage, tell her about the photographs which he now knew Anthony had seen – presumably he had copied them in Cornwall, perhaps in the Dormobile, but David didn't know how. He asked Jane whether she needed to report back to Holland Park police station, but she said no, she was in her civvies so could go straight home. No detours allowed, not even to pick up a newspaper, certainly not to go for an after-work drink, because she had to lock away her weapon.

"I'm surprised PU police are allowed to take their guns home."

"Only sometimes, if they're on call, which I am tonight. You wouldn't believe the regulations. I've got a special safe, bolted into the wall, made one hell of a mess which they did *not* clear up – " she grumbled about the red tape for a moment or two, while David was extricating his car from a traffic jam on the Hackney Road, then asked him if he wanted to give her any instructions about dealing with Evans's unexpected return to the scene.

"Better leave it till we get to your flat, unless you want to go back to the Centre?"

"I don't think so. No, no, of course not. Well, I can't, can I? I've got to obey their rules."

Jane had been taken aback. She had not expected David to drive her home, and she had certainly not envisaged what might turn into a serious discussion with, perhaps, phone calls to other members of the team, even to Henry himself. She wondered what sort of state she had left her flat in; David's own flat had been quite neat and tidy – and clean, probably, although she wasn't very good at noticing dust on furniture, or dirt on carpets. Well, her bathroom and lavatory were clean. The towels? The only other occasion he had been to her flat, when Alan Green and the technicians had also been there, she had had some warning, and had at least found the time to clear away the dishes from the draining board. Not that she had been particularly concerned, then, what her guests might think about her flat. This time, though; she glanced at David's profile as he drove, and she sighed, knowing exactly why it was different this time. And the backs of his hands, too. Pathetic, she thought.

"You all right?" he asked.

"Yes, yes, just, no, nothing. Fine."

*****

"So, he's in the diary to visit tomorrow, along with three others, all apparently friends of Michaelov. Axel, Michaelov's friend, or agent or something, is bringing them. I don't know any more about him yet, I haven't had any more chats with Lucy. It's quite a coincidence, isn't it, but I don't think it's necessarily sinister? Significant, even? I mean – it's not even really a coincidence, given the original..."

"Cock up?"

"No, David, not at all..."

He had accepted a cup of tea, and they sat either side of her dining table, under the window which gave an oblique view of the entrance to the Royal Mews. The room didn't look too bad in the afternoon sunlight, Jane thought. She had shifted the furniture around a bit, and put a pot plant on the sideboard. She hadn't had time to buy any pictures but she had bought a frame for the photograph of her mother standing with Vaclav Havel at some award ceremony in Prague, and put it on the mantelpiece.

"You're thinking, I suppose," David said, "that if the link, for the want of a better term, between these two, Armstrong and Evans, is interest in a certain school of painting, then that could easily lead to their both being at a sale of those paintings, *and* to an invitation to the one to come and see fine examples in the other's house."

"Yes, exactly, and the misunderstanding about the meaning of the word picture, and its, um..."

"*Consequences* is a good term, I think." said David. "Not too value laden. Much better than, for example, *disastrous repercussions.*"

"Yes, I agree, its *consequences* are irrelevant now, coped with, no longer *germane*?"

"But David," she added, "I should have asked before, I'm so sorry, how's your wound? Is it healed?"

"Yes, more or less. Well, it's a bit sore. Proper stitches, I told them, none of your butterfly bandage nonsense. I try not to laugh."

"But it's on your...oh I see. Bit slow there, sorry. Well, I'm glad it's getting better. Would you like a biscuit?"

"No thanks. Actually, I wondered whether you'd like to go out for a bit of supper later. I expect you know somewhere decent round here?"

Jane made a fair job, she hoped, of concealing her surprise and delight.

"Yes, why not? Good idea. There's quite a reasonable pizza and pasta place on Eccleston Street."

"Oh, right. I was thinking – have you got another computer? I mean, not this one, but one with internet?"

"Yes, of course. Why?"

"I was thinking, maybe somewhere a bit more, relaxing, say?"

"Oh. You're going to look one up? Good Food Guide type place?"

Compose your features, she said to herself, you must stay cool, eager is not the right expression.

David shrugged and looked at her enquiringly.

"Would you prefer pizza and pasta? It's up to you, of course, but if you'd like I could try and book something a bit different, perhaps?"

"Yes, that would be great. The laptop's in the bedroom, I'll just get it, be sensible to book now, wouldn't it, then we can carry on with this?" She waved at the file and ancient computer on the table.

David found a restaurant nearby with a single Michelin star and a fairly interesting menu. He didn't eat out much, but couldn't see the point of eating bad food when he did. He wasn't quite sure how the evening would pan out; he hadn't picked up any signals from Jane, who had been more successful at concealing her feelings than she realised.

David had wondered when he should tell Jane about the information from Mandy at GCHQ. He had not had the opportunity of speaking to Jennifer or Henry, nor would he have before the visit by Evans to Armstrong's house to admire his paintings. He made up his mind fairly quickly; it would be quite wrong to leave her in the dark. She should have whatever information was available in order to interpret Evans's behaviour. She *needed to know* that *Evans knew* that Armstrong had been in Broadharbour at the time of the sale. His, Armstrong's, presence had been no secret; the only secret had been that Armstrong was himself under covert surveillance, but was it likely that Evans had inferred this from the single photograph he took, which surely would have revealed this fact only to followers of their own dark calling?

And Evans had, according to Mandy, taken great pains to destroy his own copies.

"So," Jane said after he had told her, "even if, as a worst case scenario, Evans says to Lucy "I took a photo of your husband in Broadharbour and you'll never guess what happened..."

"My judgment is that he won't say that, or anything like it. He knows who we are, he knows what we are. And he knows – or at least thinks – that we could get him charged with God knows how many crimes he committed last week. And, he's actually worked for the FO in the past, in an indirect sort of way. No, he just has a bit more information than we realised, and you need to know that. I shall keep well away. He doesn't know you, as far as he's concerned you're just Protection Unit. In any case he probably didn't notice you in Broadharbour, you're right at the edge of the photo and looking away from the camera. All the same, keep an eye on him on Tuesday and squeal if he misbehaves. You know the routine. But don't worry, he won't. And he probably just won't notice you. No, that's not right, of course he'll *notice* you."

"Why do you say that? Why do you say it *like* that?"

"Oh, well, um, damn," David looked away, quite embarrassed; he had meant it, if he had meant to say it out loud at all which he probably hadn't, as a very definitely throw away comment, not one to be picked up so sharply, just one for Jane to tuck away and maybe remember later. He felt he had no choice now, that there was no point in prevaricating, but he couldn't find the words to say exactly what he meant. "Well, you were very successful with the Arab, I mean, you're a very pretty g... very good looking, you must be aware of that?" Oh, what an *extremely* cool thing to say, he thought, *you must be aware*, oh please Lord, send a Jehovah's Witness to knock on the door, anything.

But Jane only looked solemn for a moment, biting her lower lip. David was expecting a pretty robust response, but all she said was, "Well, no, I'm not... it's very kind of you to... but I don't think that can be..."

Then it was obviously the thing for David to say that he was sure it was, so he did. She smiled at him, and he smiled back. But she didn't feel quite certain that David had entirely and completely explained what he had meant. Then she said, "I don't think that I will be able to keep too far in the background, I might even be the only PU present. Unless Armstrong himself turns up, but that's very unlikely."

"It doesn't matter," David replied "the only thing which Evans will be wondering about is why a casual photograph which included Armstrong should be worth a visit from the goons; why they were so desperate to get it back. After all, it turns out that there was a sale on of the sort of pictures which Armstrong collects – that would surely explain why he was there? Evans probably thinks that the sale was a cover, that Armstrong was meeting someone – someone with him in the photo whose presence was supposed to be secret. You know who he met, don't you, just the people he told you about? We've got our video, of course, but you won't have seen that."

"No, not yet, I've had no chance. But what about Evans's photograph? Have you compared them?"

"No, we can do that now, I've got them both here, I'll pause the video and put them up together on the screen."

The photograph and the video, because they had been taken from different viewpoints, gave two different aspects of the group of people, including Armstrong, who had stepped out of the car. David took a note from one of his files, and read the names written there. They looked at the stilled video, and were able to identify them clearly. They then turned to the photograph; again, the typed names corresponded to the persons photographed, in or standing by the car. But the photograph also showed, as well as an indistinct image of the agent with the video camera, a slice of the interior of the building outside which the car had stopped. Inside the partly opened door they could make out the three-quarter profile of another man, standing inside; the light was not good, and his features were slightly blurred. "Who's the man inside?" asked Jane.

"Unidentified, it seems," David replied, turning again to his file, "He's probably nothing to do with the group on the pavement. Henry's going to chase it up himself, he's going to show it to Alan, remember, Alan was on the Case of the Duke's Vermeer."

"Henry's doing that himself?"

"Yes, we're only down to about the fourth veil, I think. There's still a lot we should keep hidden. And Henry likes a little outing from time to time."

August 7 Afternoon   Henry   Alan

In Plaistow Public Library, two men were standing by the stack marked 'Military Adventure' arguing about the relative merits of Bernard Cornwell and Patrick O'Brian. "Oh look," said the older and marginally less scruffy of the pair, as he leafed through *The Surgeon's Mate*, "somebody's left their bookmark."

"So they have, it's a postcard, isn't it. Give it here, then"

They returned to the shelves the various books they had been using to illustrate their argument. The library resembled in many ways the reading room of the Athenaeum, but in some ways it did not. Avoiding the old men behind their newspapers and the young children with their minders, they left without borrowing any books.

"Thanks for coming all this way," said the younger man, glancing again at the postcard the other had handed him.

"Not at all. I quite like getting out from time to time, and I gather you've business down the road. I'm not sure that I've ever been to Plaistow before. I might have been. It's not very memorable, is it?"

"I shall remember it. There's a warehouse of traffic next street but one, half of them under-age girls. Have a kebab."

He grabbed his companion by the arm and pulled him abruptly into the doorway of a small café which reeked of alliums and rancid fat. The older man stumbled on the doorstep, but understood immediately what was expected of him.

"No ketchup, bitter salad. Fanks."

The black Mercedes with obscured windows slid past the shop and turned the corner. The two men chatted for a minute or two and then left, walked away past the library and towards the bus stop. They chewed at their kebabs until they had walked a couple of hundred yards, passing three betting shops and a pawnbroker, all heavily protected with metal bars and mesh. They screwed up the remains of the food and both chucked the little packages of grease and gristle into the gutter. Green laughed.

"I see you haven't forgotten."

"Indeed I have not. 'Littering is thought to be uncharacteristic of police or government officials' behaviour. Agents are therefore advised to take advantage of opportunities to litter when undercover.' How about that?"

"Can't fault your memory."

"If only."

Alan stopped by a mean looking pub, little more than a couple of terraced houses knocked together, advertising the next darts fixture and karaoke on Saturdays. He pulled up his hoodie and, to Henry's surprise, lit up a cigarette. Then he examined the photo Henry had given him.

"I do know who the lurker in the shadows is," said Alan, handing the card back to Henry. "He's called Bruno, and he's what they call a hunter – you want a slightly shabby Samuel Drummond, maybe going cheap because it's a bit dubious, and he's the man to track one down for you."

"So, he could have found these, what do you call it, Festival paintings and told Armstrong about them?"

"Not really. Dowland's sales are well publicised, Armstrong's bound to be on their mailing list. No, Bruno finds paintings – and other things, sculptures, fine furniture, ceramics – in private hands, sometimes in proper collections, sometimes on mantelpieces or in the attic, and then he negotiates a private sale. He's making contacts and filling in gaps in his networks absolutely all the time. He's obsessional – he has to be, otherwise he wouldn't make a living. Maybe that's what he was doing, meeting someone at the sale, one of the dealers, perhaps. But I doubt it would be anything to do with the actual sale items."

"Does he sometimes do it the other way round, I mean, find buyers for sellers?"

"Sometimes, I think. He'd be daft not to. But it's not what he's well-known in the trade for."

"Does he have a record?"

"No, he's clean. No significant rumours when I was involved – malicious ones, naturally, but that's par for the course."

"Biography, addresses, contacts?"

"I'll email you. The Met probably keep an eye on him; I'll find out."

"You've been a great help, Alan. I hope you're not running any risks here – how nasty are the occupants of that big black Mercedes?"

"Very. We're nearly ready to wind them up, just need to get the Felixstowe end sorted. We're lifting the next container in a couple of days, as it leaves the docks. Then my little team bows out and leaves it to the Immigration Service."

"And has Jennifer any immediate plans for you?"

"I think I must get back to my Slavonic friends now, Henry, they'll be expecting lots of money and I should hate to disappoint them."

August 7 Late afternoon   David   Jane

"Well then, we seem to be agreed," David continued, returning his files and laptop to his briefcase, "that Evans might wonder why we were anxious to get hold of the photos, but that the most likely explanation which will occur to him was that Armstrong was having some sort of secret meeting. And Evans won't talk about our balls-up, OK, my balls-up, in his house, partly because he's not particularly proud of his behaviour with my gun, but also because he gave me an undertaking that he wouldn't. He has occasionally brought back information, useful to the FO in one or two minor ways, from some of his trips to the borders of badland, and he seems in general well disposed."

"And he didn't speak to anyone else about the photos, because until he met you in the pub he thought you were after the paintings he had bought, not the photographs he had taken."

"Correct. So, tomorrow he will turn up at Armstrong's, admire the pictures, possibly engage you in conversation – and go on his way. A short mention in your routine report?"

"Let us hope so. Do you need to touch base, then?"

"Yes, just Henry, not Jennifer, it shouldn't take long."

*****

"I'm very fond of brill," Jane said to David later that evening, "but do you know what 'harissa' is?"

"I think it's hot, with chillies, and something else. Paprika, perhaps? Tomato?"

The waitress explained to them exactly how Chef assembled and prepared his harissa sauce, "Not very hot, more as a complement to the brill, madam, rather than a contrast. Spiced with a very little chilli, mainly cumin and caraway, and just a touch of fennel and coriander."

"Yes, you mustn't overdo the coriander," said Jane gravely.

The Bellini cocktails and the unusual Lebanese wine which they drank with the brill softened the air of slight constraint which had crept into their conversation and behaviour after the awkward exchange about Jane's noteworthiness. But they didn't drink too much; neither of them thought that would be a good idea.

David's briefcase and laptop had been left in the safe in Jane's flat, so he needed to go back there with her. The apartment building's lobby had a keypad system on the outside, but access to the inner hall was by means of a heavy pair of swing doors. Jane and David reached simultaneously for the left hand door, and their hands touched as they both grasped the handle. Neither moved their hand away. They each had had the same ideas, with complete clarity but speeding through their minds far, far too quickly to be formulated in actual words, which were, first did he/she do that deliberately, and secondly, if not, did I, and thirdly, well whatever, surely that's a start?

"Shall we have some coffee?" Jane asked, and David said yes.

She brought the mugs and milk and sugar through on a tray, and went back to fetch the cafetière. David was standing by the mantelpiece, casting his eyes over the ornaments and postcards propped up against them, noticing the photograph of Jane's mother with Havel, and as she bent to put the jug down on the coffee table, he gently, tentatively, took hold of her free hand. For a brief second she didn't respond, then quickly putting the jug down she withdrew her hand from his light grip, clasped both her hands around his neck, and kissed him hard on the lips.

The coffee grew cold. Two rings formed on the wooden table which, the next time she got around to the housework, Jane did not even try to polish off.

Sometime later that evening, he asked if she would put her gun belt on.

She looked at him and saw that he was serious. Dear God, she thought, men. Then she found, to her surprise, that if he wanted her to do that, well, she wanted to do it too. But she felt it was safe to tease him a little.

"Shall I get the gun out of the safe, then?"

"No, no, just the belt."

So she buckled on her belt, tightening it more than usual. Then she turned round, walked to the window and looked out, stretching up slightly with her elbows on the sill.

He unravelled himself from the sheet, rose from the bed and joined her at the window, then kissed her gently on her neck. He stroked the inside of her thigh, which was smooth and muscular, she dropped the belt and they made love again as she leaned there, feeling him, every part of him, pressed against her, and wanting him never to be further away.

In the morning David woke first. He made his way quietly to the kitchen, found breakfast things, toasted bread, brewed coffee and took it into the bedroom on a tray; Jane had just woken and propped herself up on a couple of pillows, yawning, rubbing her eyes and blinking at the sun as he drew back the curtains. He handed her a plate with a slice of toast, cut into triangles and thickly spread with some dark red jam, which was all he could find.

"Oh, what bliss! I'm sorry there's no marmalade, I don't usually do breakfast, it's blackcurrant I think, no I mean blackberry, Auntie Mill made it."

"Auntie Mill?"

"She's not really my aunt, I've just always called her that, she's my mum's cleaning lady. What's the time?" she asked, leaning over to look at her clock, and when she saw that it was past seven she scrambled out of bed and ran to the bathroom, then ran back again and hugged David and asked him if he wanted to use it first.

"Why don't we have a shower together?" he replied.

"No, no, I've got to go to work, so have you, my shift starts at eight thirty, I mustn't be late." She kissed him, then kissed him again, and he said, "Tonight?"

"Yes, of course, when do you get off?"

"God knows, I'll ring you."

"Mind you do."

Chapter 17

Tuesday August 8   Jane   Axel   Anthony   Frieda   Alison

A decent, healthy, breakfast, with the recommended combination of vitamins, proteins, slow release carbohydrates, and a modest quantity of unsaturated fat, was always Jane's aim. As was a thorough shower, careful use of shampoos, conditioners and assorted ointments, and meticulous attention to the application of unobtrusive and subtle make-up. Unlike the bull's eye at the pistol range, this was a target she seldom hit. She usually managed the shower. But this morning she had had real coffee, toast and jam. She felt great. Buckling on her armament, over her clothes this time, she sped from the flat, leaving her new lover to make free with the remaining contents of her bread bin and fridge, and to make his own decision whether or not to take any notice of the sell-by date on the bacon.

It was now the Tuesday morning of her seventh week, a week after the Broadharbour affair, and Jane felt completely at home in the role which Henry had chosen for her. For about half the time she stayed in or around the house, unsupervised and mostly unaccompanied, except when Armstrong was at home and his close-protection officer came in as well. To start with she had found some difficulty in striking the right balance between security and intrusiveness, but this was soon overcome, partly because Lucy seemed so easy-going and friendly. The house itself soon became familiar, and she felt comfortable in it. It was, indeed, a comfortable, welcoming sort of house, neither extravagantly furnished nor austere. Jane's mother had taken her to see friends who had similar houses in North Oxford, although there were differences; Jane had amused (her mother hoped) the Reader in Semiotics by asking her why she didn't own a Hoover. In a way she would be sorry to leave.

Jane's favourite position in the Victoria Park house was just inside the doorway of the picture-gallery room. There she would sit in an Edwardian dining chair, a carver, with arms and a padded, scuffed, leather seat. From that position she could see into most of the ground floor rooms, the doors of which she would contrive to leave open as much as possible. The other advantage of the place she had chosen to sit was that she could see many of the paintings in the gallery itself. Some of these she had grown fond of even in the short time she had been there. A small oil painting by John Bratby of a woman kneading dough on a kitchen table appealed to her – despite its 'take it or leave it this is how I bloody well paint' style. Part of its attraction to her, she wondered, might have been the fact that she had never made bread, and as far as she could remember had only made cakes under the supervision of her mother. The op-art and pop-art pictures she found difficult to appreciate, because the op-art made her blink, which was annoying, and she thought that the designers who had made the original cartoons and advertisements and labels adapted by the pop artists had been ripped off, and it must only be a matter of time before they sued for, what would it be, copyright infringement?

In her crash course on art appreciation and forgery she had learned about the various types of pictures which she had always just thought of as 'abstracts', but she still had problems distinguishing the separate species. The ones hanging here, she had been relieved to see, were of the "colours/pattern without meaning" variety, with titles like "Red and green with manganese" instead of, thank goodness, "Antagonism – the double sided mirror of deceit, no. 4" which she had encountered on one of her trips to Cork Street with Harriet the Duchess. But there was a new one this Friday evening, a large blurred monochrome picture of a girl's head, although it was impossible to distinguish the sitter's features because it looked just like a photograph spoiled by bad camera shake. Did this count as an 'abstract', she wondered? Below the picture a glossy magazine was propped up against the wall. Surprised, Jane picked it up and saw that it was a Dowland's catalogue, for their most recent sale of modern European art. It had been bent open at a page showing the very picture hanging on the wall above it. The artist was German, there was paragraph after paragraph of what Harriet had been rather sharp with the sergeant for calling guff, and the guide price was – good God – three point five million pounds. Pencilled in the margin was the number 4.75. Jane returned the catalogue carefully to its position underneath the picture.

"Difficult, isn't it?" said Lucy, who had just come in.

"Difficult?"

"To understand the art market, of course. Why nearly five million for this?"

"I thought you did understand it – well, better than me at any rate."

"Maybe. I don't know. Nothing came of Broadharbour, you know."

"What? Sorry, I mean..."

"You know, that little jolly you went on with Jim, when he met those dealers – and Reg Nicholls from the London, I think he was going to be there because of the sale at Dowland's, and even that weaselly little bloke, what's his name, Bruno, he said he might be able to find some stuff – well, it didn't come off. Neither of the gallery blokes would commit to anything, it was a complete frost. Jim was, he was, sort of surprised, more than anything; I think he's so used to pulling things off. Well, never mind."

"I didn't see him in the afternoon, I had a stomach upset, I came back in a police car."

"Yes, of course, he told me. I've never asked you, I'm so sorry, did it get better quickly, are you OK now?"

"Oh yes thanks, it was just a twenty four hour thing."

"Well, you're certainly looking very cheerful this morning. More than I am. God, I wish this afternoon was over, I'm fed up with it all. Shan't do it much longer."

She wandered off, looking disconsolate. Her blouse had come untucked at the back, and Jane automatically took a step towards her, but checked herself, and as soon as she was alone took out her mobile and phoned David.

The morning and lunch hour passed uneventfully. Various set procedures, such as checking every room on the first and attic floors, or patrolling the garden, were laid down for performance at reasonably regular intervals, and she had to make appropriate entries on the computer in the room set aside for the Protection Unit. Often, on days like this when the other duty officer had taken himself off during the lunch break, illicitly to the pub Jane sometimes suspected, Lucy would put her head round the door and suggest they ate together in the kitchen. She had often made some soup, or put together a satisfying combination of items like toast, beans and melted cheese, very welcome to Jane who had seldom provided herself with anything more filling than crisps and possibly a bath bun or a Kit Kat, and who was usually hungry after a hurried or skipped breakfast. Her resolution to eat wholesome fresh food had lasted about a week, if that. But today Lucy was busy in the pictures room, getting ready for the afternoon visit by Axel and his friends.

Maria had come in to help, and was clattering away in the kitchen, being very busy with cups and saucers and other noisy tableware. Jane found her trying, with her determination to make judgments about almost everything, usually unfavourable, but on this occasion her presence meant that Jane would not be inveigled – gently, but with no chance of escape – into passing around the cups and fairy cakes. It remained her job to answer the door bell; she could have waited for Maria to do so, but would in any case have had to vet each guest. Axel was first to arrive, in the covetable Bentley, and he brought with him a tall thin lady with a roundish face, freckled and pretty in a slightly faded sort of way. This was Frieda Semperdine; Jane's computer had told her that Ms Semperdine was unmarried, had lived at the same address in Chiswick for twelve years, had no criminal record nor any county court judgments against her, and had once appeared on TV in a programme about Henry Moore. She had never been observed at CND, BNP, SWP or Animal Rights demonstrations. Lucy and Frieda had, apparently, met previously. Anthony had come by tube from Paddington, and although Jane knew who he was, and that he no longer possessed David's firearm, she nevertheless searched him according to the regulations, partly because it might appear odd to Lucy if she didn't. Anthony for his part had a definite feeling that he had seen her before, but he couldn't remember where. It came to him when she turned round to open the living room door; it was the jacket he remembered more than its wearer – she was the woman in the photograph which had started this whole affair off. That figured; she was part of Armstrong's protection team. But – hadn't she also been at the roadhouse when Maurice had been kidnapped? She had been the BMW driver, surely? There was one other female guest, a startlingly good looking blonde woman in her late thirties or early forties, dressed casually but extremely expensively in jeans, sweater and brogues, who seemed to be an acquaintance of both the Scandinavian, whom he now knew to be called Axel, and Lucy. There were also a couple of male gallery owners. Anthony recognised the woman immediately, although he had to remind her that they had met less than a week ago in Cornwall – she was Countess Alison something or other with 'c's and 'u's in it, Chair of the Friends of the Saline, painter of rock pools and spouse of a Romanian aristocrat. Anthony had meant to research her title but had forgotten to do so.

Tea and cakes – scones, in fact, with jam and cream – were taken in the dining room; Lucy and Jim Armstrong normally ate in the kitchen, and Lucy's weaving apparatus had remained stretched over the dining table. Maria had never approved of this, and she had taken the opportunity, obviously without consulting Lucy, of unfastening its clamps, folding the half-finished fabric neatly and placing it all over the back of an armchair. Jane had an idea that relaxing the tension of this sort of weaving before it was finished was harmful; she glanced at Lucy who was staring at the cloth on the chair, quite ignoring her guests. Axel realised that something was wrong, although he didn't know what, and he more or less took over the functions of host, to Maria's annoyance, although after one whispered remark from him she did what she was told.

As Axel ushered them through to the picture room, Lucy grasped Jane's arm.

"You know how long I've been working on that tapestry, don't you, I'm livid, how could she? You'll help me get it back on the loom, won't you? Please, as a friend?"

Jane smiled and nodded and took Lucy's hand in both of hers.

"Yes of course, whenever you want. When I'm off duty?"

"Oh yes, that would be best, that's so good..." she broke off, because Axel had started talking about the unfocussed portrait. She continued in a whisper, "You ought to listen to him, I suppose he knows what he's talking about. I think it's horrible, it won't be there for long, thank God."

"So," Axel was saying, "we pass on from the undoubted master of modern German photosynthesis, as he jokingly described his latest work to me once in Köln, to a pair of paintings by one of the great British painters of the early twentieth century. As you no doubt all know the Festival School was dominated by Hopkins and Harris, and we are fortunate enough to be able to show you two canvases by the former artist. There was also a Harris, but that is now, ah, hanging elsewhere. The paintings you see here" – he was facing his audience, and indicated the first painting over his shoulder by extending his left hand while smiling at Anthony – "represent a clear attempt to demonstrate that the use of the new automated machinery did by no means favour equality in the workplace. Observe the relative positions of the man, presumably the supervisor, and the female operatives at the..." He noticed the expression of surprise on Anthony's face, glanced round to Frieda who was looking confused. The Countess was frowning. He turned to look at the painting, which was a townscape, showing roads, terraced houses, pedestrians and traffic approaching a roundabout. In the background a railway bridge spanned a wide river or estuary. Grey warships were moored at a dock, and a train – a steam train – was crossing. Considerable licence had been taken with perspective and proportions; elements of the bridge, especially the arched tubes from which the railway line was suspended, and the towering columns upon which the structure rested, were clearly exaggerated. So, too, were the warships, cruisers with great guns, menacing but obsolete. Among the wealth of detail, and at no particularly significant point, a green VW Beetle, seen from the rear, turned in front of an ill-defined vehicle, a van or small bus which was already on the roundabout. There was no doubt that this was a picture of traffic and people; the grandiose architecture and moored battleships were its frame. Perhaps, Jane thought, the success of this composition demonstrated the genius of the artist. Or maybe that sort of thing was easy if you had been taught properly; she just didn't know. However, she knew where it was painted, Saltash, and the bridge had been built by Brunel.

Jane missed the consternation in Axel's expression because it vanished as soon as it appeared, but she saw puzzlement, then understanding, then a return to his previous composure.

"Ah, I see that the Armstrongs have had a rehang. No doubt the production line canvases are now hanging in the study?"

Lucy nodded.

Axel started to give an appreciation of the Beetle picture, but his talk seemed surprisingly lifeless, even shallow, and he soon tailed off, suggesting that such a great work told its own story.

Frieda, the Countess – Frieda found it quite difficult to think of her as a Countess – and the two dealers were admiring the painting from what seemed to Jane a sensible distance, but Anthony was almost rubbing his nose on it, staring intently at the little green car, frowning almost as if he was trying to read the number plate. Frieda was obviously irritated; he was obscuring their view.

"What are you looking for, Anthony?"

Anthony stepped back and apologised, mumbling something about the brushwork. Then he darted back in again, locating the signature and examining that closely. He turned to Axel.

"So it was painted in 1950?"

Axel wrinkled his forehead in surprise.

"Yes, of course, you can see it there, after the signature? Are you surprised? Why should you be?"

"No, no, not at all," said Anthony quickly, "He was in the middle of the series then, wasn't he? Hadn't he just painted that jolly little picture of the picnic? You know it, surely? His Déjeuner sur l'herbe painting? – It was sold the same day we met?"

Now Axel looked both surprised and puzzled. He spoke slowly. Not a Swedish accent. What is it? thought Anthony.

"Surely, Mr Evans, Le déjeuner sur l'herbe is a very well-known painting by the French master Edouard Manet?"

"Ah, yes indeed, but Hopkins painted a sort of, what does one say these days, *prequel* to it. The men dressed in unsuitable smart clothes, getting the picnic out of the back of the car? Those girls – just starting to strip off? Not really in character, you know, not in the early fifties."

Before Anthony had finished speaking, before his rising inflexion had indicated that he expected a response, Axel's expression changed again. In fact, his face had lost any expression; he appeared to be deliberately masking whatever reaction he might have had.

"I do indeed know the work to which you refer. You mean, of course, the paintings of the iconic Morris Minor saloon car. You are very perceptive to have noticed the picture's humorous allusion."

"Not really – it was the girl's big blue hat, I think."

"Ah yes, what a very witty reference. It is clear that Hopkins was not innocent of mischief."

"And, of course, it's not a Morris Minor, it's an Auto Union."

Although Anthony had half turned away, as if to look at the next painting which the other members of the group were now admiring, he had kept his eyes on Axel. Axel had moved not a muscle in his face, but at the words Auto Union his diaphragm had suddenly trembled as if he were engaged in some elaborate breathing exercise. He spoke as if he had not heard Anthony's comment.

"We should, I think, move on now to the next picture, which is, as you can see, a beautiful landscape by Paul Nash, depicting a pastoral scene in Sussex. It was painted in 1919, and is of course intended to provide a telling contrast with the paintings which he..."

Anthony listened for a few moments more. The style of Axel's delivery, this correct but superficial description, seemed so familiar, but for the moment he was unable to place it. He didn't particularly like the work of Paul Nash, so he turned back to the Hopkins to fix some of its details in his mind. He realised later that this was unnecessary, and that he should have paid more attention to Axel's homily. The attractive young protection officer, oh, come on, the stunning young protection officer, who had been in his photograph – but, and he couldn't work this out, had also been involved in the scene at the roadhouse – was standing apart from the group and seemed also to be interested in the Hopkins. Perhaps she came from Plymouth, he thought, or maybe she had owned a Beetle?

"Do you like the painting, then?" he asked, "Do you recognise the setting?"

She was pleased that he had spoken to her; he had, after all, already entered the folk lore of the Service as the old art buff who had disarmed and disabled Major MacMaster, late 22 SAS, Major MacMaster who had taken her to bed and had also asked her to keep an eye on Evans and report back any odd behaviour – behaviour which might mean that he was forgetting his undertaking to keep quiet about the 'incident'. She had been wondering how to approach him; now, she didn't have to.

"Yes, of course," she replied, "It's the Brunel railway bridge over the Tamar. Is the setting really so significant?" she suddenly realised that it was, and continued, "Yes, of course it is; it's contemporary with the Great Exhibition, and the Festival of Britain was on its centenary, wasn't it? So it's perfect for the Festival school. I don't think Mr, er, Axel mentioned that, did he?"

"Blow me down," said Anthony to himself, because he hadn't thought of it either.

Jane was amused at the sudden look of surprise which she had seen cross Anthony's face, immediately suppressed and replaced by courteous interest.

"So you're ah acquainted with the work of this school?"

"Acquainted, you might say, yes, but only that. I'm not very well up in its (did she dare? yes, in for a penny...) ah minor exponents."

"Minor exponents?"

"Bradley, perhaps, De Lascelles, Fisher?"

Anthony explained to her, in some detail, that although he agreed with her about the minor status of De Lascelles and Fisher, she was quite incorrect to include Bradley in this classification; what could she be thinking of? Jane, who had been told by David that Evans had bought two Bradleys at the Broadharbour sale, and who had thought, correctly, that mentioning this painter to Anthony would provide him with a topic to talk to her about, accepted his argument and admitted her error. When he realised that this young officer (who was, he noticed, carrying on her waistband, only partly concealed by her loosely cut jacket, a weapon which looked remarkably similar to that which he had removed from the annoying Mr Smith) had been discussing quite subtle points of art appreciation with him, and although her arguments had been flawed had by no means made a fool of herself, his suspicions that she was more than a run of the mill police bodyguard person were reinforced. He would try an indirect approach. It didn't occur to him to leave well alone, to mind his own business, to abstain from poking his nose into what were obviously deep and probably dirty matters of state security. This was possibly because she was so attractive. Beautiful. Oh, Anthony.

"I know of another policeman who is very well up in art appreciation," he said, "He's called Alan Green. Chief Inspector, I think. Do you know him?"

Jane was surprised, and answered cautiously, "I think I might have met him, I'm not sure; he would be much senior to me. But there are a lot of chief inspectors, you know."

"Then there's David – Smith? But I think he might be Foreign Office, some sort of Intelligence. But I know sometimes he works with coppers – sorry, police officers. He's very interested in the Festival School. I went to a, um, talk about it recently – and that other lady, over by the Paul Nash, the one in jeans, not the one with freckles, was there. He called her Countess, I think her husband must have some tin pot Balkan title; I remember, it was Romanian."

Anthony had forgotten that Frieda had also been present. No doubt she had been excised from his memory by the alluring Countess. Jane answered.

"No, David Smith, I mean, there must be a lot of them. It doesn't ring any bells."

Anthony didn't pursue his question, but Jane was uneasy. She would have to report the conversation back to David – this Anthony Evans was very friendly, didn't seem at all ill-disposed to the police, and he mentioned David in a completely matter of fact way – but he seemed on edge; he kept glancing back at the Hopkins, peering at different parts of it, especially, she thought, at the small car which gave the painting its title. After a moment or two's silence, he asked her, in what was obviously meant to be a casual way,

"Armstrong doesn't own this painting does he? I gather they have a sort of arrangement with a friend of Axel?"

"That's right, I think he's Russian, but I've never met him."

"So you wouldn't know where he got it, the Russian, I mean?"

"Sorry, not a clue. I don't think he's had it long, I seem to remember that Lucy, Mrs Armstrong, I mean, mentioned it. Why, do you recognise it or something?"

"No, no, but it's, I wonder..." he looked perplexed, as much as if he didn't know how to express himself as if he wasn't sure what was wrong with the painting.

They both re-joined the group which had finished with the Paul Nash, and was now trying to articulate some agreement over the meaning of a competent eighteenth century copy of a Van Dyck Henrietta Maria with eyes which had been glued over with circles of sparkly toffee paper, and to which a beard had been added in felt tip.

Someone muttered 'Dada', the following silence was broken by Frieda, who asked the Romanian Countess, or, rather, the glamorous upper class English woman who had married a Romanian Count, whether she was ever going to meet her elusive husband.

"My *dear* Alison," she said, "we are really all *longing* to meet him, we all think he must be so...so ..." What she meant of course, was he must be so devilishly handsome to marry someone as gorgeous as yourself, or, and this would be more likely, and definitely much more satisfactory, he must be so old, fat, and rich.

"I hardly ever see him myself," replied Alison, smiling, "he's a bird of passage, lands somewhere to refuel, visits one of his factories, flies off to a board meeting, takes some politico or other for a cruise on the Med – you know the sort of thing. We get the odd weekend together, not often at the Castle, though, I'm sorry to say, I think he finds Cornwall rather quiet. Axel knows him, isn't he on some board or other with your Mr Michaelov?"

"Yes indeed; in fact I have met him in Stockholm, and other places, a number of times. I would say that I know him quite well."

"There you are, then," said Alison to Frieda, linking arms with Axel, "he's not completely invisible, is he, I'm quite sure you'll meet him soon. He's a sweetie, isn't he, Axel?"

It didn't look as if Axel was in complete agreement with this assessment of the titled Romanian's character. He looked sideways at Alison and with a look which seemed to Jane to show disquiet, made a move to release his arm from her grip. Laughing, she only tightened it.

"You mustn't worry, dear Axel, he knows that you have always been a little bit in love with me, and I with you."

Axel had apparently recovered his sang froid, although he was still tapping the floor with his left foot, a sign of tension which Jane had never noticed before, and responded with some light-hearted comment to the effect that his adoration for Alison knew no bounds. The others in the group smiled, except for Lucy whose endurance of theatrical compliments was tested daily, and they returned to Charles1's sightless queen. They soon gave up on her and moved on to a Laura Knight gypsy, which was much easier to talk about. Frieda, in particular, was an enthusiast and explained with an unusual lack of reticence her own ideas about the reciprocal influences of Knight and Munnings. Anthony had sidled back to the Hopkins, and was once again peering at it closely, then he noticed that Jane was watching him, and, embarrassed, he tried to excuse what he thought might appear rudely inquisitive.

"I'm really much more interested in art from this period than the conceptual stuff, and, well, the detail in Hopkins' work fascinates me."

"Which detail in particular? Something about the Beetle?"

"No, no," he said hastily, "It's the two pedestrians, the ones by the Belisha beacon, it's his raincoat, so carefully, um..."

"Detailed."

"Yes, you know, look at the belt, even the buckle..."

Well, Jane thought, he may have defeated David in single handed combat, but he can't lie for toffee. What was it that he was so interested in? She was sure that he had been staring at the little VW. She looked at it again, committing it to memory.

"The little car is beautifully painted, though, isn't it?"
"Yes, of course."
"And that's what the picture's called, isn't it?"

"So it seems. Odd composition though, wouldn't you say?"

Jane wondered how she should reply to this. At the back of her mind an association had been made – that is, she knew that somewhere, among the variously digested gobbets of art information or appreciation fed to her so assiduously by the duchess (a woman who in every way, to her mind, outshone that brassy, Botoxed so-called Countess the men were fawning over) was a painting, a fact, an idea, which would be appropriate to trot out. Ah, she had it.

"You mean, a bit like Icarus? The Bruegel?"

"The what, oh yes, yes, that's right, the Fall of Icarus, by Broygel, of course, you mean, the actual fall, the splash, is tucked away inconspicuously?"

Broygel, Jane thought, *Broygel*. Harriet had characteristically pronounced it carefully the Dutch way. So we just say *Broygel* do we? Never mind, it doesn't seem to have been a daft comment. Anthony was again carefully examining the painting, so obviously avoiding looking at the car that she was now completely satisfied that it had indeed been the focus of his interest. She remembered Maurice's garbled tale about faked paintings, and Hopkins' apparent, but unlikely, predilection for German cars, but couldn't decide if she should ask Evans whether or not he suspected that the painting in front of them was a forgery. She could, perhaps, ask him something else about the picture – maybe his answer would enable her to judge whether or not he thought it was authentic. Only a fairly banal question came into her mind.

"Do all Festival painters cram so much onto their canvases?"

"Yes, they do – I think a lot of painters did in the forties and fifties."

"Not always successfully, though? Can't it just be confusing?"

Anthony was now looking again at the picture, squinting as if he were trying to take it in as a whole, and to forget his overriding interest in the car.

"Well, not in this case, it's masterly, don't you think?"

His expression, however, was not what she might have expected after such an endorsement; he looked perplexed, as if he grudged the praise. She knew, then, that he was worried about the picture. She would listen again, carefully, to the recording she made at Maurice's house, and then she would report to David as soon as possible.

Wednesday August 9   Tall man   Johnson

The tall man with the expensive coat, predilection for plump girls and variable accent had arranged another meeting, in a North London bar, with his ex-forces partner. Their little scheme, their sideline as they had previously called it, had, he thought, run its course. He had never expected it to last very long; it had been lucrative for four years, and now it should be wound up. There were too many rumours, too much interest from surprising branches of the law enforcement agencies, the stupid mistake of the wrong car model, the Bradley, painted on a modern canvas over some seascape nonsense; too many edges were fraying – risk averse as he was, he always found it necessary to trim frayed edges, and it could not be denied that such scissor work carried its own hazards, however carefully he snipped.

As he expected, he found it difficult to convince his partner that their principal activity was being endangered by their sideline.

"Ok," replied Johnson," the turnover isn't so high, but we've got bugger all costs. A warehouse – a shed really, an old barn – a pittance for Rembrandt, five percent for Miyu and her bloke, another five for fancy-pants and Bruno – and nobody knows who we are, not even fancy pants – compare that with the payoffs we have to make on Mainline, all over East Europe and North Africa, ships' crews, lorry drivers, the gangs of yobs we use over here."

"But Mainline has been running smoothly for nearly fifteen years. Again, nobody knows who we are. None of them, not even in Falmouth or Newlyn. Any problem, we disappear. I don't know where your money is, and you certainly don't know where I keep mine, but there's a lot of it now. And Mainline's well managed – it's got expenses, of course, but the take-home's still much larger. Much, much larger."

Eventually Johnson was convinced. He could pretend from time to time that they were equal partners, but he knew that in reality the tall man called the shots.

"There's some cleaning up, I suppose?" he asked.

"Inevitably," said the tall man, "there's Bruno and Edwards. Cash for Edwards, I don't think he's a problem, but Bruno, now that's a different matter."

"You're sure about Edwards?"

"Well, I think so. I see him often. He brings in all the stuff Rembrandt needs. He's never let us down. If the police start ferreting around, God knows why they should, and I feel that he might say something indiscreet, then I can always deal with the matter then."

"Whatever you think best."

But Johnson was uneasy. The tall man could see that Johnson hadn't been satisfied.

"I'll give it some more thought."

"OK. What's with Bruno, then?"

"You know, of course, that Kuznetsov was quite irritated with him about the Hopkins ah *cock-up?* as we say when we're being foreign. The picture was actually dumped on Bruno's doorstep by a couple of East European heavies, who intimated gently that Mr Kuznetsov would like his money back, plus interest, with approximately no delay at all whatsoever."

"Gently? Really?"

"No, perhaps not altogether. Little Bruno was roughed up and moreover found himself owing a Russian oligarch more money than he could readily lay his hands on. So he went back to Edwards, naturally."

Johnson was now very angry and did not hide it.

"And Edwards came to us, that's what you're going to say, isn't it? How the fuck were you or I supposed to know anything about sodding old cars? That was Edwards' job, that girl of his, let them cough up, it's not down to us."

"Yes, it was a mistake, but doing the car series was our idea. Yours, actually. It wasn't a big mistake, he was just unlucky. Calm down, will you? I haven't finished. And there's no point in going on about whose fault it was."

"Why not, for Christ's sake?"

"Just listen. Bruno is angry because of his bruises; you wouldn't expect anything else. He phoned Edwards earlier on this evening and suggested that he should be more than accommodating. In fact, to cut a long conversation short, he threatened to reveal his identity to the Russian unless we – unless Harry Edwards, I should say – gave him a lot of money."

"Fucking little shit."

"Indeed. Fucking little shit."

"And I suppose Kuznetsov is mates with Michaelov?"

"They are not friends, but naturally they are acquainted."

"Hell and damnation."

"Exactly. So you see, something must be done."

"Why did you let Bruno show the fake bloody Hopkins to Armstrong?"

"I didn't. He did it off his own bat. When I saw it at the Armstrongs' – when I realised what it was – I might say, I had to exercise considerable self control. Evans seemed suspicious; luckily he was distracted by the bodyguard, a female with obvious attractions."

"For fuck's sake..."

"Yes. So, something must be done."

"Well, carefully then."

For the first time, the tall man allowed a note of irritation to enter his speech.

"I am always careful. I do not take risks. For goodness sake, you should know that by now."

In fact, Johnson thought that his partner's elaborate schemes, trying to cover every eventuality, were often a damn sight more risky than just going straight at things, with a few simple precautions like balaclavas. But he had to admit, none of them had gone wrong yet – until now, of course, and even so it was true, the car pictures had been his, Johnson's, idea.

The subdued ballad which they had chosen on the juke box came to an end, and Johnson was about to feed the machine with some more coins and play it again when a couple of young bikers, all tattoos and black leather, pushed him to one side.

"That's enough crap, grandad, we'll have something written this century now."

"All right son, I'm cool with that" said Johnson.

The tall man nodded in agreement.

The two bikers were nonplussed. The big fat bloke was supposed to argue. One of them put on a camp voice, which usually got a result.

"Oooh, grandad's *cool* with that, e's a bit ancient to be *cool*, isn't e, Cyril, stupid old queen. And oo does e think e's calling son, I'm not is son, are you is son, Cyril?" He continued in that vein, but Johnson and the tall man just smiled.

The barman came over.

"Come on Tammy, leave it off. Mind your language. Just put your money in. Gent doesn't mind," he turned to Johnson, "although he might when he hears it, gawd-awful racket. Don't mind these two, gents," he added, "they're harmless really; are you ready for another drink?"

Tammy and his mate took up new positions by the bar, self-consciously drumming their heels on the floor not quite in time to Judas Priest's steam hammer beat, but the tall man could see that their hearts weren't in it; they were glancing back and muttering in each other's ears. He knew the signs, so did Johnson.

"Well then, I suppose we'll have to wind it up straight away. Edwards can handle most of it. Then you can handle Edwards. Poncy little fairy. And Bruno?"

"Yes, leave Bruno to me."

"What will you do with Rembrandt?"

"I haven't decided. He could fend for himself. Do beach portraits in St Ives. He's only met me once, in the dark, he didn't know where he was. I don't think he does, even now. He gets everything he wants, he seems happy enough."

"Gets the pick of the women you take there?"

"No, I offered once, he wasn't interested. Don't think he understood what I meant."

"More fool him. So he only saw you in the dark, eh? Bet he was scared. Did you have your teeth in?"

"Your sense of humour gets subtler by the day."

"By the night, you mean." replied Johnson, doubling up with laughter, then, recovering, added, "those two rockers have just left. They may be waiting for us outside. I think we might have to..."

"Yes, I know."

The rockers were dealt with expeditiously, left in a shop doorway, gasping, unable to follow, one with a cracked rib but neither with any serious damage. Johnson had been all for giving the mouthy one a good kicking, but the tall man dissuaded him.

Chapter 18

Thursday   August 10   Richard   The Prime Minister Armstrong

Buoy-Dodd (Cabinet Secretary)

"That disappeared pretty damn fast, Richard," said the Prime Minister, leaning over with the decanter. Sir Richard laid his hand over the top of the cut crystal tumbler.

"No more for me, thank you Prime Minister."

"Bill?"

The Cabinet Secretary took a quick sip and held out his glass. He glanced at Sir Richard. If Sir Richard had not been a Coldstreamer, Sir William might have thought that he looked nervous.

"Jim?"

"It's too peaty for me, Douglas, thanks all the same."

"Peasant. Grab us a bottle of cooking, will you Sandra? Will this do?"

"Bang on."

"Now then, Richard, tell us all about it."

"Well, Prime Minister, as we all know, Armstrong has been for some time at the heart of the negotiations with Cameroon concerning rights to explore for rare earths, and possibly to sink mines, in parts of the Adamawa province. There is a foreign consortium, a group of mining companies, under the wing of, er, largely influenced by..."

"The French."

"Yes, Prime Minster, the French. Now these negotiations have reached a delicate..."

"We all know this, Director General. They've been delicate for eighteen months. You know, Bill here knows, every Tom, Dick and Henrietta knows that our Government – that is, I – give all the shittiest jobs to the Treasurer because he's better at them than anyone else. It's nothing new."

Armstrong intervened.

"Nothing about Campa Fidela, then?"

Sir Richard looked nonplussed, and looked down at his notes.

"No, no there's no mention..."

"Hmm. So, just tell us, what have you been doing, and why?"

Sir Richard wasn't quite sure what, or how much, Sir William had told the PM, and what, if any, gloss he had put upon it. Nor was he certain that Henry and Dame Jennifer had given him, Richard, the whole story. Nor, of course, whether the field officers had held anything back from Henry and Jennifer... he ploughed on.

"We received information that led us to believe that sairrten..."

"As short as you can, please Richard."

Armstrong cut in, "Look, Douglas, someone, some journalist, probably from the Shield, has cottoned on to the arrangement I've got with Mickey Michaelov; you know, he lends me pictures from time to time, the sort I couldn't possibly afford. You saw one of them when you came round last month? That Gainsborough?"

"Oh, yes, possibly," said the PM, who had no interest in art, "I think I remember – why does he do that – do you know? Just because he's a friend?"

"Yes, and they're very safe of course – guarded day and night."

"C?" said the PM.

"One small amendment, sir. It is not in fact the case that the journalist knew of the arrangement. Nor... nor... "

"... did the Security Service?"

"That is correct, Prime Minister," said Sir Richard, wishing that he was back in the Bogside, at risk from snipers, but among soldiers who were his friends.

"Ah, I see. So, you planted that nice girl Penny in my house to see if I was up to something?" said Armstrong.

"Not at all, not at all," said Sir William, smoothly. He had decided that to express shock would arouse suspicion, or amusement, in this worldly audience. "The Service had evidence that there might be a scheme afoot to discredit you;

they did not know what stories had been fed to the journalist. The operative in your house was merely the junior member of a team – is that not so, Richard? – which was making comprehensive enquiries, focussed upon the contacts of the journalist who was, who was..."

"Digging up the dirt?" said the PM.

"Indeed. Trying to. But the Director General has not mentioned that this journalist no longer presents a threat. He subsequently met with an accident, a fatal car accident, and..."

"What? What on earth... Good God, Bill..."

"No, no, no, Prime Minister, no *of course* not, we would never... no; but we do think that he was murdered, and this has imparted a much greater sense of urgency to the entire operation."

"What was that about forgeries – you mean fake pictures?" asked the Prime Minister.

"Yes. It seems that one at least of these paintings, one of the ones on loan from your friend Michaelov, Treasurer, was revealed to be a forgery. Somewhat simply, I believe; a matter of anachronicity?"

"Yes, Bill. Only two days ago. And since C's girl, I beg your pardon, operative, was present, I presume she passed this news on to her senior? And he to you, Richard?"

"Via Jennifer, Treasurer."

"Hmm. I got to know Jennifer a bit when I was at Export. Had to rein her in, you know, on occasion."

Richard, sensing a thaw and no longer fearing the Tower, permitted himself a comment, and a twitch of his lips.

"Your encounters are still spoken of in the Service, Treasurer. Jennifer is unaccustomed to contradiction."

"I know this Michaelov, don't I, Jim?" said the PM, "Do you know him, Bill?"

Armstrong answered.

"Yes, we've all met him. He's one of the Kensington oligarchs who've pledged their fortunes to the Gates' foundation. He's a good egg, as far as we know. Of course, some of his mates aren't."

"Does he know his picture's a fake? I only ask out of interest," said the PM.

"We don't know, Prime Minister," said Richard. "We're having a progress meeting at 13.30, at least, the team is, I believe. Shall I report back?"

"To Jim and Bill, I think. Bill, let me know what you decide to do. Jim, before we wind up, any comments?"

"Not really. Obviously Richard's team should carry on with the good work for a while. To find who was priming the journalist, I suppose; in any case Lucy seems to need your *operative* to hold her loom for her, or make scones, or something. Good looking girl. Henry choose her?"

"Jennifer, I believe, Treasurer," replied Richard, who dimly understood that some sort of humour underlay the question. But he was only too pleased that he had not been given a roasting, and that Armstrong seemed positively benign. In fact..."Prime Minister, perhaps I might trouble you, really the finest dram I've taken for many a day..."

Chapter 19

Wednesday August 9   Alan   various police   a criminal

Alan Green had been wrong when he had told Henry that his involvement in the round-up of the Plaistow traffickers would end when the Immigration Service took over. In fact, the commander of the unit detailed to undertake this had been appalled by the instruction, which had, as it were, fluttered down from a desk in the Home Office far too senior for its occupant to understand the dangers involved, and far too senior to be questioned by the unlucky officer upon into whose in-tray it eventually settled. On his own initiative the Immigration Service officer requested assistance from the Metropolitan Armed Police Unit, who were willing to help but only on condition that their superintendent should lead the operation – should become, in their jargon, Gold Commander. This officer, whose admirable criterion for a successful operation was an arrest without a shot being fired, a *very* successful operation being one where no side-arm was even unholstered, insisted upon a painstakingly elaborate briefing, which the Immigration Service handed straight back to SD; to Alan Green. The Armed Police unit had always had a prickly relationship with Special Branch; it seemed likely that Alan, on a higher plane of spookdom, and with a fairly low tolerance of slow-wittedness, might find it very easy to precipitate an antagonism which could imperil the entire operation – get up Goldie's nose good and proper, as Charles put it when he relayed the request.

Alan behaved politely and respectfully in the meeting with the superintendent, and found that his qualities of tolerance were not tested; a junior police officer attended and together they worked out the tactics of the operation. Gold Commander was concerned about the Felixstowe end of the operation, and there was a slight delay while the Immigration Service unit satisfied him that they were competent to carry out what would be a fairly routine round up of a few low value members of the gang – a couple of drivers, the owners of the containers, three corrupted dockers and one customs officer – none of them likely to be more violent than the immigration officers could cope with.

"Now, the two gang leaders, let's have another look at the photos," said the superintendent, "trouble is, there's nothing very distinctive about them; and you said they're armed?" He had been exchanging glances with his deputy, and she added, "As a matter of interest, sir...Mr Green, you're SD, aren't you, we were just told you were Home Office, I really don't know why they don't just tell us straight out – do you need to keep your cover? What I mean is, it would be very helpful if you could..."

"... join in; make sure you know who's who – that's your idea?"

"Obviously," the superintendent said, "that's only if you're allowed to do this sort of thing, if you've got the er skills we require, sorry, that sounds rude, I mean, my men are all fire-arms trained" – he noticed that his inspector was smiling – "Carol, rescue me, say something polite."

"I've met Mr Green before, sir, he was on one of the weapons refresher courses that I ran, two years ago, I think, we all knew he was a spook, sorry, field officer from SD, and he knew it all backwards then. And he never missed his mark."

"And, Mr Green," said the superintendent, "you obviously know your way around the building, these plans you've given us are good, of course, but there's no doubt your presence would be a great help."

So it was settled that Alan would take part, keeping close to the superintendent. They would all be dressed up and unrecognisable; in any case, Alan told them that he would be involved in the interrogation of the gang leader, and that this was almost certainly his last operation for the trafficking sub-Directorate. He was anxious to move on from trafficking to the relatively new section which was being formed, after the bombings in Africa, to counter Middle Eastern terrorism, but that was not something to tell the police.

The operation was in one sense an anticlimax. The warehouse, the temporary home, or prison, of some thirty-five women, girls and boys, sat at the end of a cul-de-sac near Upton Park station. Police, in ordinary uniform, staged a road accident to isolate the street, squads of armed police from the road and railway line surrounded the building, it was entered with the usual battlefield shouts intending, in this case successfully, to disorientate and terrify the targets. All the men in the building were arrested, only one raised a weapon, and since this was a Uzi machine pistol he was shot dead immediately. The gang leader had tried to escape over the roofs, but he slipped and fell before it was necessary to chase him. Alan did not remove his gun from its holster.

The operation was almost completely successful. The death of one of the criminals marred it for the superintendent, not, as he explained to Alan, because he regretted killing a trafficker of twelve year old girls, but because the enquiry by the various authorities would be tedious and time consuming. But the scene inside the warehouse, after the gang members had been removed, was one of the darkest horror. To the police, the prisoners – for that is what they were, caged, separately, in two parallel rows, with divisions of corrugated iron sheets and wire mesh fencing – seemed like animals in a battery, crouching in the far corners, protecting themselves with thin, filthy mattresses pulled up round their shoulders; to the prisoners, young girls in the main, eyes staring and hollow cheeked with fear and hunger, the police in their black padded uniforms and helmets, their faces hidden, appeared quite as terrifying as their former guards. Alan had tried to prepare the police for what they would find within the warehouse, but his words had only been words; the reality was shocking beyond the officers' imaginations.

Bolt cutters were used, social workers and female police arrived, and, as gently as they could, ushered out the imprisoned girls. One, considerably older and less ravaged, hung back, putting some distance between herself and the others. Alan caught the commander's eye, beckoned him over and whispered in his ear. This woman was quickly plucked from the arms of the social worker who was comforting her, handcuffed and arrested, and taken away, now spitting and screaming with rage. The warehouse was soon full again, this time with forensic technicians, photographers, firemen, social workers, even environmental health officers. Alan left, handed over his armour to a policeman in one of the vans, and returned to the police station where the arrested men were detained.

He stood silently, leaning against the wall, relaxed, his arms folded. At the small wooden table in the middle of the room, on a chair which was bolted to the floor, sat the gang leader who had so far said nothing. He was from somewhere in the Balkans, only known as George, he spoke English and was a violent man, a rapist and a murderer. The murders would not be provable, but the rapes and of course the forcible imprisonment of the girls would.

George knew Alan, not of course by his own name, as a low value member of the Felixstowe gang, a labourer unimportant enough to be put from time to time on one of the chicken packing lines in the freezing plant which was their cover. He still did not know Alan's position in the authorities' hierarchy; he was not even completely sure, because he was so accustomed to the interlocking networks of corruption in his native country, that he was, now, in the hands of the police.

In fact, all the other gang members were being dealt with conventionally by the ordinary police. The operation had now been handed over by the Armed Police Unit to a combined team from the Metropolitan and Suffolk forces, based in an unused office of the Essex police in Chelmsford. The logistical problems were enormous, the various lawyers employed by the accused were solicitors whose fees were quite off the legal aid scale, and a covert team of detectives was deployed to investigate the sources of the funds to pay them. These lawyers were not particularly keen on travelling to Chelmsford to babysit ruffians who could hardly speak English, the Suffolk police were not particularly happy with the condescension shown them by their Metropolitan colleagues, social workers were for ever refusing access to their juvenile clients, to the great inconvenience of the police interviewers; all in all the police commander in overall charge suspected that she had been given the job because her male colleagues had bent the Chief Constable's ear on the golf course or at a lodge dinner.

But Alan and George were shut together, in a small room, somewhere else. There was a video camera, of a common type, but George could see that its lead was detached from the socket in the wall. He did not see the concealed camera. Alan had observed George with his men, and seen how short was his temper, and how aggressive his behaviour when he lost it. He thought it likely that George would break the silence, even possible that he would attempt an attack. George was sitting facing the door which Alan had carefully, obviously, left unlocked.

The silence continued. Alan occasionally walked from one wall to the next, always remaining between George and the door. At last, George spoke.

"Who are you? What do you want?"

Alan did not reply. George pointed to the disconnected lead of the video camera. Alan composed his features appropriately.

"I have money. You can have money. How much do you want?"

Alan sat down opposite George. He still didn't speak, but he took a packet of cigarettes from his pocket, a book of matches, a notebook and ballpoint pen, his wallet and mobile phone. He made a neat pile, matches on top, then cigarettes, phone, wallet and notebook. At last he answered.

"I don't think you can get money. I don't think you're important enough. I'm going to take a leak. Don't go away."

This time Alan locked the door behind him. Outside, he walked quickly to a table covered with electronic equipment and sat down by the technician.

"You're sure that the phone will show a good signal?"

"Yes, don't worry, I fixed your phone, it'll show four bars."

"It's better if he sends a text. That's what he usually does. Keep your fingers crossed."

"Yes, sir. Explain to me later?"

"Of course."

The interior of the room was shown on three screens, leaving no point uncovered. They watched as George stared at the neat pile of property which Alan had left on the table; his mouth was open, his eyes darted about the room. He reached out, pushed the cigarettes to one side, grabbed the phone, fiddled with the buttons for a few seconds, then typed in a number, then a text message, then 'send'.

"Got it all, sir."

"And it didn't go anywhere else?"

"No sir." The technician was beginning to look disgruntled. "As you instructed. Exactly."

"I'm sorry, it's trying to look relaxed in there with that bastard, it's made me more edgy than usual. If that makes sense."

"Look at him now."

George had lit one of Alan's cigarettes, then replaced the phone in the exact position in which Alan had left it. The cigarette packet he had thrown carelessly on the table.

"I've got a question, sir, if you don't mind?"

"Fire away. I may not be able to answer it, depends what it's about."

"Well sir, the number and the text he sent are in the phone's memory now, and he must know that they'll also be logged on one of the servers. So he'll know that you can find out what they were. So...oh, I think I see, there'll be a second phone?"

"You've got it. There'll be a cut out; the text message will be relayed – possibly coded, although I doubt if this lot will have got round to that – by some intermediary, on a second phone, to the real recipient. Then the first phone will be thrown away, so since the link, the intermediary, is a person, not a device which would leave a trace, the transmission is safe."

"So *you* are going to send the text, but only after you've found the first phone? Then you'll have your blokes observing, timing the call, that sort of thing?"

"Almost. With a bit of luck we shan't need feet on the ground. I don't fancy knocking on the doors of dozens of upright citizens in the small hours. But it might come to that."

The technician pondered, then understood.

"That's neat! I like it."

Alan was amused by the expression on her face.

"Bit unexpected from the rough and tumblers? Thinking something through like that?"

The technician turned beetroot. She was very young.

Thursday August 10   Henry   Alan   Jennifer, David and Jane (off stage)

"How very ingenious," said Henry, at 0530 the following morning, unshaven, in rough jeans and a helicopter, over coffee from a flask and Penguin biscuits, "but I don't quite see how the, as it were, the second half of the plan worked?"

"Well, it did. Do you really want me to explain? It'll be in the report."

"No, I suppose as long as you've got a result, and my goodness, what a..."

Jennifer's tinny voice interrupted. "I'd like to hear how they did it, if you don't mind, Henry. Turn your microphone up, would you please Alan?"

"OK. Is that better? It took a bit of setting up. We knew the number of the phone which received the text."

"One moment. What did the text say?"

"It was actually in code, just a jumble, that didn't matter."

"Very well."

"... so we could locate it by triangulation. It was pay-as-you-go, of course, and on the Ariel network. But we didn't know what network the second phone would be on – probably Ariel, but we couldn't take any chances. Now, GCHQ had told us that the smallest number of mobile phone calls are made between 0400 and 0415. They liaised with the networks, and asked them to record all messages or conversations originating in that area between 0400 and 0430."

"How big an area? How many phones?"

"It was a suburban area, in the Midlands, about one thousand six hundred phones."

"I wouldn't have the faintest idea how many calls would be made in that half hour by that number of phones."

"Nor did we. But GCHQ did. They said between 18 and 46. So, we got a K branch squad on standby, and sent

George's text at 0406. By 0445 GCHQ were on line with the numbers, and the recordings."

"Good God. How many?"

"Twenty six."

"And? A jackpot?"

"Probably."

"What? Probably!"

"There was one brief call, at 0407, in a language which we imagine to be Slavic. The next two calls were in English, from contract phones. Then nothing until 0421. I asked GCHQ for a translation from the Slavic, and they said that that service was beyond their immediate resources."

"They what?"

"Said they weren't fucking magicians. Sorry, Dame J."

"Right. When is it being translated?"

"When they can get hold of Boris, but we have the address, and we know who it belongs to, so we're taking a chance."

"How have you got the address?"

"The phone was on contract, the bloke owns the biggest house in the area, so he was using it at home. Unless we're very unlucky indeed. We're going through the other calls, but I'll lay twenty to one we've got him."

The day which had started with chocolate biscuits and coffee at six minutes past four ended with a bottle of Teacher's and a jug of water at midnight, in front of Alan's gas fired imitation log burner. It been a very busy one for many people; Alan and his crash team from K branch landed on the drive of a large country house in Leicestershire, just as police cars arrived with the only eight police officers who lived close by and had dressed quickly enough to make the rendezvous in time; but they were enough, and captured four of the five men who had burst out of the house at the sound of the helicopter. Three men, possibly influenced by American films featuring Mel Gibson, appeared to be charging down in a large four track directly at the helicopter, as if it were a pile of empty cardboard boxes, or a balsa wood lorry, then, realising their error, swerved and capsized into the ditch. Possibly, though, they had been encouraged in their exploit, as a means of distracting the police, by the last man to attempt an escape. This man, on his own, did in fact succeed in reaching the public road in a Golf GTi. The local police, however, had laid a stinger across the drive, and the hot hatch drew to a sedate halt as the tyres gently deflated. The occupant turned and raised his hands. He was too old to run away.

"He was also too old to keep his mouth shut," said Henry over the phone to David. "He was a weak link, all right, but he'd started it all, he had the money and he hadn't been pushed aside yet. He doesn't want to spend the rest of his life in gaol. We could hardly stop him talking. Three more outfits; two in East Anglia and, and this is why I've rung you, one in the South West. He doesn't know much about that one, but he does know that they call its boss Dracula. We'll talk more in the morning. My office. Ring Ryan, will you, and get her along too unless she can't swap her shifts; oh, tell her to think of something, I need her here. Then there's a meeting with Jennifer at one thirty."

Jane had caught the last sentence. She leaned over David to hear more, but Henry had finished.

"How will you manage that, then?" she said when Henry had rung off, "Maybe she won't answer her phone? Maybe she's in bed with some fit bloke she picked up in the pub?" She kissed him, and ran her finger down his forearm towards his hand. She was particularly fond of the muscles and sinews and general shape of that part of his body. Then she started to wonder why Henry wanted them both. She would have to ring in sick; it was too late to organise anything else with Danny or Inspector Foster.

Thursday August 10   Bruno   Tall man

Bruno did not like mornings at all. Of early mornings he had known nothing for a good twenty years, but even at eleven o'clock his heavy curtains, lined with black-out fabric, were tightly drawn. He reached for the four soluble aspirins which he always left on his bedside table sometime during the day, ready for the following morning, and dropped them into the remains of last night's final vodka and tonic. Just after eleven his phone rang; it almost always did; his clients knew not to ring him earlier, but by eleven they would be growing impatient. Lack of patience was a characteristic of his clients, who found it frustrating that the sort of painting, or sculpture, which they wanted for the mantelpiece was not immediately available in Harrods. Bruno made a good living from these rich people – he was also paid well by various museums and galleries which had identified gaps in their collections that they needed to fill. But Bruno was greedy, as well as thirsty, and he had on one or two occasions 'found' items for clients which were not of irreproachable provenance. The craftsmanship of the 'Hopkins' which he had placed with Kuznetsov had excited him, and the subsequent proof of its forgery was mortifying. The monetary consequences had also been dire, his cock-eyed decision to make a drunken phone call the previous night to ask Harry Edwards for more money had been stupid and possibly the worst of all had been a garbled threat to spill the beans to Kuznetsov. So he was surprised when the phone call turned out to be, not Harry himself, but some foreigner who said he was Harry's partner, and equally surprised by the emollient tone in which he spoke.

"I've talked over your proposition with my partner, and we can't totally accept the, ah, enhancement of your compensation which you suggested. But we do acknowledge that you have suffered unfairly, so we intend to offer you half what you asked. Please don't think that we will increase this offer. And, let me add, we will consider that your suggestion you might take Mr Kuznetsov into your confidence to have been made in jest. As I'm sure was the case?"

Bruno thought about this offer as quickly as his hangover would allow. Actually, it was better than he expected. Afterwards, when he'd had time to leave a little letter with his solicitor, or in his bank box, as insurance, he might revisit it.

"All right. One third cash, put the rest down as commission on the sale of, God knows, just make it up. Bank cheque, if you don't mind. And soon."

"I am leaving for Buenos Aires at nine tomorrow morning. I will visit with you today at your flat as soon as I have been to the bank."

Perhaps this suggestion made Bruno nervous; perhaps he felt that the arrangements for the handover should be his to control.

"No, not a good idea. There's a pub, near the canal, the Delamere, d'you know it?"

"No. Is that near your flat?"

"Yeah, the other side of the main canal. On Delamere Terrace."

"Good. One o'clock?"

"Jesus. Make it half one."

"Very well. One thirty. I shall see you then."

"How'll I know you?"

"I shall wear a Panama hat with an Old Etonian band."

"Bloody Norah. Are you serious?"

"Yes."

"OK. One o'clock."

The tall man had forgotten that Bruno's street was in Little Venice, close to the canal. He needed to hurry, and had envisaged a simple procedure, in Bruno's flat. But the possibilities opened up by a stretch of water intrigued him.

The obvious route to the pub was along a stagnant backwater, which was more of a scruffy housing estate than a waterway and much resented by the millionaires who lived in the mansions on the Regent's canal itself. The houseboats were jam-packed along the bank, and moored two abreast.

There were very few decorations visible – one or two attempts at gardens in wooden boxes, but no pails or water jugs brightly painted with flowers and fruit in primary colours on a glossy green background, and no potted plants or shrubs. On most boats the curtains were drawn, to conceal the absence, or activities, of the tenants. Perfect, he thought. There was a very convenient diamond shaped area of sludgy water formed by each quartet of barges, between the two prows and the two sterns. The depth wouldn't be great, but it would be sufficient. There were people around, but not too many. In any case, he could always fall back on his first plan if necessary.

At about a quarter to two Bruno emerged from the pub, obviously angry because there had been no sign of a man in an old school hat. As he looked up and down the towpath a beggar, dressed in scruffy cast offs and with blackened teeth, staggered towards him whining something inaudible and thrusting his hand out for coppers. The tall man had always enjoyed acting, otherwise the last fifteen years would not have been nearly such fun. But he had few lines today. The towpath was deserted now except for Bruno who backed away, until they were both standing by one of the larger boats, with a rusty rail surrounding its prow.

After the blow, carefully calculated to stun rather than to kill, he held Bruno's head under the water with his foot until the bubbles stopped, then wiped the smear of blood and tissue from his weapon onto the boat rail. He shuffled off for a couple of hundred yards, then slid the length of metal pipe into the canal. Then he took off his long dirty coat, folded it neatly over his arm, and adjusted his perfectly respectable cotton jacket. What threats remained now? None that he could immediately identify, but, surprisingly, he didn't feel at ease. He frowned, and made for the nearest tube station.

Chapter 20

Friday August 11   David   Jennifer   Jane   Charles   Anthony Henry

"I have asked Jane Ryan, who has been most closely involved in our investigation into the financial affairs of..."

"Let me stop you there, MacMaster," said Jennifer, "our recent operation has been triggered by, listen carefully please, *our concern that attempts have been made to discredit Armstrong by associating him with fraudulent activities.*"

"Of course. Sorry. Well, at any rate, I've asked Jane to give an account of what's happened so far, and to summarise the position as we see it. I think it would be useful if Mr Evans..."

"Yes, certainly. Charles, is there a response from Bucharest? Hurry them up, then. Yes, the Ambassador if necessary. Now, please ask Mr Evans to come in."

Anthony had been waiting, for a short time only, in the ante room. His compliment to Charles upon the prints from the Government Art Collection which he had chosen to hang upon its walls had earned him some coffee and a Penguin biscuit, the chocolaty crumbs from which he was still trying to brush from his shirt front as he entered the inner office. He now knew David well, and Jane, whom he knew as Penny, and was introduced to Henry, although by his Christian name only. He smiled at the woman who must be Dame Jennifer, whom he failed to recognise, either because he hadn't taken much notice of her twenty five years ago, or because he wouldn't have remembered in any case. He wondered whether he dare remind her of their previous meeting, when she had been pretending to be a secretary. No point, really, it was ancient history and she certainly wouldn't remember him.

"You haven't changed much, Mr Evans," she said, "filled out a bit, less hair, quieter tie, what you might expect, really. How do you do?"

Filled out a bit indeed. His waist measurement was just the same as it had always been.

"Mr Evans," said Jane, who had prepared carefully for this meeting, "has featured significantly in our operation. The chain of events which led to our involvement, our suspicion that the Treasurer might be the subject of a plot to discredit him, started with Mr Evans's presence in a sale room where a forged picture purporting to be by a painter called Hopkins was advertised for sale. Mr Armstrong was present also, in a private capacity. This was not as much of a coincidence as it might seem because Mr Armstrong takes an interest in this school of art. The initial investigation was not without certain setbacks, but it became clear, through Mr Evans's involvement and his interest in pictures of the Festival school, that forgeries have been circulating, and that the Treasurer has one such painting hanging on his wall at the moment. It is well known that Mr Armstrong and his wife are very keen on Festival school works, and they have one or two small pieces. They can't afford the major works, like the one hanging there, – except, of course that it is a forgery."

Jane then started to summarise the arrangement that Armstrong had with Michaelov. She described the tea party, and the people who had been there. She then said, doggedly, "We were lucky that the, er, outside art expert involved..."

Henry interrupted, "Jane, everybody in the room knows what you mean by *involved*, so you needn't be so diplomatic. You mean, *the man who disarmed and shot one of our most experienced field officers.*"

Jane looked helplessly at David, who was getting bored with these digs, and showed it. The others smirked, even Jennifer. Jane continued, "We were lucky, I say, that Mr Evans here was *known* to us, has been vetted by IGS on account of work done on projects marked secret or top secret. We saw in Mrs Armstrong's diary that he was going to visit them, and that this visit had been arranged by a Scandinavian man who acted for, or who purported to act for, Mr Michaelov the well-known Russian entrepreneur. During this tea party tour of Armstrong's gallery I observed, I mean I could see, that Mr

Evans was worried about the painting by Hopkins, possibly the most valuable painting there. Perhaps, Mr Evans might …?"

Henry nodded, and gestured towards Anthony, who took up the story.

"One of my close friends, whom I asked to help me while I was fleeing from you lot, and please keep in mind that I thought you were a gang of armed robbers, told me that he had been asked to authenticate – he is a real expert, not an amateur like me – a Hopkins, which he could see was a fake because the date of the car in the picture, a VW Beetle, was later than the date it was supposed to have been painted. That was the only visible clue, but it was enough. I had bought two Bradleys, less important works, of the same school, the 'pictures' of the initial confusion, for what was, for me, a lot of money, and naturally I was worried that one or both of them was a fake too. There had also been a Hopkins in the Dowland's sale – the sale I went to – which was supposed to be one featuring a Morris Minor, but it was actually more like an Auto Union. The VW and Auto Union are of course German cars, which it was possible, but unlikely, that Hopkins would have included in his series, and they weren't recorded anywhere. There's no definitive catalogue of Hopkins' work. Well, the picture in Armstrong's house, with the Beetle in it, was clearly the same picture that my friend Maurice had seen in St Petersburg."

"St Petersburg?" said Jennifer, surprised.

"Yes, Maurice was flown out there. The owner of the picture was called Kuznetsov."

"Really – I don't think I picked that up. Please go on Mr Evans."

"So, after the look round, and it was Axel – I don't know his surname, I lost his card – not Mrs Armstrong who did the talking; not that he was particularly informative, what did you think, Penny?"

"Oh, er, it was useful for me, I mean, I'm not really competent to… and I'm Jane now…" she ended lamely.

"You underestimate yourself, I was very impressed by some of your comments, Jane."

Jennifer and Henry exchanged glances, David looked irritated. "Carry on please," he said.

"Ah, yes. Well, after the bun fight was over, and we were all putting on our coats and things, Axel came up to me and, well, he chatted for a minute or two, then he just offered it to me, said that Michaelov didn't really like it very much, did I, and he named a figure which is about half what I'd expect to pay at auction – if it was genuine, of course. Still far too much for me. I said I'd think about it. I saw him talking to one of the other chaps, he's got a gallery in Cork Street, afterwards. Well, I know him, so I rang him up, but he hadn't made an offer, didn't have that sort of credit line, he said. And that's it, really. I phoned Mr Smith, Mr MacMaster, that is, told him my concerns. I believe, David, that you asked me who else was there? Then you rang back, and asked me to come in. And here I am. I forgot to ask, how's the arm?"

"Much better, thank you. Alan, I think you had a question for Mr Evans?"

"Yes. OK Henry? Good. First, could I mention that when I was on the Somerset Vermeer case, I met Mr Evans's friend, Maurice Symes-Franton, and can confirm that he is considered an expert in this field. But I should like to ask you, Mr Evans, whether you had a conversation with the Romanian Countess, Alison, – we don't know her surname either yet, Charles is finding out for us – at this tea party?"

"No," said Anthony, surprised, "I hardly know her."

"But she's well known in artistic circles?"

"I hadn't come across her before the party in St Ives; I think it must be a fairly recent interest of hers. Apparently she, or her husband, have quite a collection in their big house in Cornwall; well, I think it's a castle, actually, and I believe that it used to belong to the St Aubyns before they moved to the Mount. Only a little castle, a bit like Pendennis but smaller, plus a Victorian wing, apparently."

Something had just struck him; at the Saline Friends party, just before he had left Frieda talking to the Countess about the London, she had said – he could remember the words – 'you know, Henry Edwards' gallery' and then, 'where we got the Hopkins from'. He mentioned this, and explained about her fishy paintings. Everyone seemed more interested in this than he had expected.

"And what can you tell us about her husband, the elusive Count?"

"Nothing at all. I've never met him. I've never seen him at sales, or anything like that."

"Might Mr Symes-Franton know him, do you think?"

"No, he doesn't. I've asked him. He knows there *is* an art collection, but not really *how* he knows. It's sort of common knowledge, he said. Why do you ask?"

"Just dotting some 'i's, you know, trying to tie up some loose ends."

"OK, sorry I can't help there."

Anthony was about to suggest that his friends Christopher and Patricia were a mine of information about who owned, or collected, what, but he decided on the spur of the moment to keep his own counsel. The interest of this group in the Countess and her husband was certainly more than just dotting 'i's or crossing 't's. But there was no point in trying to find out what it really was. Not by asking, at any rate.

Henry stood up, thanked him for coming in, and Jennifer also thanked him, not omitting to remind him of the terms of the Official Secrets Act. After he had left, Henry said, "I don't think there was any need for that, Jennifer," and she replied, "I am never as sanguine as you, Henry, sometimes I feel you are inclined to trust people."

Henry seemed, or pretended, to take offence at this, but Jennifer didn't apologise, just looked at him quizzically. Jane wasn't sure whether Henry thought you should trust some people, or was upset that Jennifer thought he thought you should – and Jane realised that it would be some little time before she understood the way her new colleagues' minds worked, if she ever did. She stole a covert glance at David, his profile conveniently silhouetted against the central light of the Venetian window. Could she trust him? Oh dear, she would so much like to. Yes, of course she could. She saw Charles slip in through the door behind David, holding an envelope between finger and thumb, and tiptoe to Jennifer, miming something to her as he did so. Then he tiptoed out again, while Jennifer opened the envelope and glanced at the slip of paper within.

David spoke then. "If I may, Dame Jennifer, – I am sure that Mr Evans is trustworthy, but I've taken the precaution of having his new car tagged. Just to keep track; as I say, only a precaution, we can take the transponder off in a month or so, perhaps?"

"Excellent. Provided that he doesn't dump it in a load of carrots again."

"He didn't dump it, Jen, it was an accident. And it was spuds." said Henry

"The species of the vegetable is immaterial, Henry. Please don't call me Jen."

"Sorry."

Jennifer read the note which Charles had handed her, then continued.

"I think there are two issues; first, is Armstrong involved in whatever fraud is going on? I think we tend to feel not – I know, Jane, *you* are sure, but you will forgive me if I say that we need more than your subjective certainty."

"Gut feeling," interjected Henry.

"Quite so. And, secondly, our Romanian aristos. The fact that they seem to have recently acquired a painting by Hopkins from a local dealer – and Hopkins is not a St Ives artist, I gather – is significant. As far as we can determine, nothing is known about the Count, neither locally nor in the larger world east of the Tamar. This seems not to be true of his wife, who puts herself about, in charities and what we may loosely term artistic circles. We have no photographs of him. Bucharest confirms – this is an email from Cockburn-Smith – that there is an aristocratic family by the name which Charles has unearthed; a name," she peered at Charles' memo, "which I find it difficult to pronounce, but in Romania they seldom use titles, except occasionally to enhance the attraction of privately owned castles to tourists. Then the title 'Count' is often employed. In any case, many of their records went missing after the Ceausescus were executed. Effectively, they can't help. Nor can Immigration. There are, of course, thousands of Romanians living perfectly legally in the UK, many are British citizens. Any one of them – the men, I mean – could call himself 'Count', just as I believe there is no law preventing me calling myself a Maharani."

At this point, Jennifer swivelled round in her chair to face Jane.

"Ryan. You have read Green's report, it was emailed round first thing this morning?"

"Yes, Dame Jennifer." Christ, what was coming?

"The reason why I asked Green to attend was not his brief acquaintance with the world of art and artists."

"No...?" said Jane, as she tried to recall the short email, which she had only skimmed before hurrying to the meeting.

"No. You *have* read his report?"

Jane twigged. She had, thank goodness, remembered its last sentence. Trying not to act as if she had just solved the last clue in the Times crossword, she said, in tones as matter of fact as she could contrive, "If I were a gangster, and I wanted to give the boss, who was a Romanian Count, a nickname, there is only one which I would choose. Romania is, after all, coterminous with Transylvania." She was quite pleased with coterminous, which she thought was definitely a Dame Jennifer word.

"Good. You are quite right. Now, does this meeting consider that it is worth while investigating the not necessarily shady, but certainly shadowy, Romanian Count, to find out whether he is the Dracula of Alan's report, the leader, that is, of a people trafficking organisation in the South West, and whether he is also connected with a less heinous, but illegal and certainly very profitable activity concerning forged works of art; an activity which impinges, possibly unwittingly, upon the character of the Deputy Prime Minister. Perhaps on the other hand you might think that this is simple coincidence, and a rather absurd flight of fancy on my part?"

Jane had recently received what purported to be an objective questionnaire from the International Coronary Relief Committee, which had ended up by asking her whether she felt it was morally right, for the sake of a mere ten pounds, to allow dozens of old ladies in Bangladesh to continue suffering the agonies of angina. She thought Jennifer's last question fell into much the same category. As she had learned when studying for her Latin GCSE, it was a *num* question. The meeting agreed.

Saturday August 12   Frieda   Anthony   Patricia and Christopher   Maurice

"No," said Frieda, "I haven't. Mind you, I've tried a couple of times, not too obviously, I hope. I invited her round for a drink after the last London meeting, and said bring your husband, and she came herself but he was in Belgium, she said, buying chocolate. In bulk, some deal or other, I don't know. Not truffles or sea shells. Talking of which, didn't she have some sort of joke with Andrew Bond about painting starfish? I can't say I take to him, you know."

It was about seven o'clock, and Anthony and Frieda were drinking whisky at Chris and Patricia's. Maurice was catching up with them later for dinner, after he had finished his afternoon's business, buying or selling paintings in Hackney. Anthony, who had orchestrated the evening, had brought up the subject of the elusive Romanian nobleman and his less elusive wife. He wriggled a little to relocate himself on the meagre cushion which Tricia had offered him as an inadequate barrier between the iron-hard blackwood surface of the Chinese coal scuttle and the ischial tuberosity of his backside. He regretted being quite thin; on the other hand, if he were fatter, more weight would be bearing down. What, he thought, would be the optimal weight at which pain would be minimised? He could, he thought, adjust one of the parameters of the calculation, so he took a large swig of his scotch.

"Oh, I don't know, he's all right," said Christopher, "you don't get anywhere without a bit of nosing up to the players, and the Countess is certainly one of those. Wouldn't you say?" he asked his wife.

"I suppose so, yes, she does talk about her Chagalls, doesn't she? And her early Dutch stuff? Perhaps that's where she got the idea of painting shells, crabs and things? Boring, if you ask me."

"So she never asked you back for a drink, or anything?"

"I don't even know whether they've got a house, or a flat, in town," replied Frieda, "she might just stay in a hotel. Perhaps she's a soroptomist?"

"What?" said Anthony.

"It's a club for professional women. Or business women. Like Rotary. They've got a hotel. And, in any case, why are you so interested in her?"

"No particular reason, we met her, she made quite an impact, – OK, perhaps you didn't, but you can't deny she was striking. However, I wanted to talk a bit about Armstrong's paintings, well, not Armstrong's, his friend Michaelov's. Perhaps we ought to wait until we meet Maurice. Where are we going; Chris, you said you'd book somewhere?"

"There's no need to book. We'll go to the Lotus as usual, we can walk, it's only round the corner in Sheepcote Lane."

"That sounds fun. It's a long time since I used chopsticks."

"We don't use chopsticks, do we, Tricia, they'll give you a spoon and fork if you ask."

"Oh, good."

The Lotus was, in fact, an excellent choice, having been run by the same Hong Kong couple for thirty years, with a clientele, mainly English, who placed more value on satisfied expectations than on novelty. Christopher had brought another bottle of Glen Grant along with him, and immediately poured Mr Li a large glass, which, by the look in his eyes, Mr Li had been expecting. Maurice, Anthony and Frieda ordered the dishes of their teenage Saturday nights – sweet and sour prawns, pork char siu, beef with oyster sauce, Cantonese crispy duck, together with too many dishes of rice. They fumbled with their chopsticks, but persevered. Patricia and Christopher didn't need to order, because Mr Li brought them each a bowl of clear soup and a large plate of noodles mixed with indeterminate delicacies, murmuring 'Lotus special' as he placed them on the table.

After the meal, while the coffee was being served, green tea having been declined, Anthony allowed Maurice a little time to catch up with a couple of whiskies, then he drew the conversation back to the visit which he and Frieda had made to see Armstrong's paintings. Frieda had been captivated by the Laura Knight fairground picture, and she was describing the vivid garments worn by the gypsy girls. Anthony let her finish, then asked her if she would mind describing the Hopkins as well, because he felt sure that Maurice would find that very interesting, especially since it was, apparently, for sale very cheaply.

Patricia and Christopher had put their coffee cups down and were listening intently. They could see that Maurice, who had relaxed considerably during the meal, and had become almost boisterous, had stiffened at the mention of the painter's name, and was staring at Anthony with the sort of exaggerated, pretend-appalled expression which he might have put on if, say, Anthony had suggested a round of cherry brandies and some After Eights, but as Maurice quickly regained control of his features they realised that there had been no pretence involved; he had indeed been momentarily shocked.

Frieda had taken a moment to gather her thoughts, then said that although the Laura Knight had certainly been more to her taste, the Hopkins was also a fine painting, and certainly very valuable.

"I remember it quite well. One of his People's Cars series, although in this case the composition was rather dominated by the bridge and the battleships, don't you think? Still, there it was, not quite bang in the centre, a green-grey Beetle. One of the first post war VWs, I suppose. Interesting that he included a German car so shortly after the war. It was painted obliquely from behind, wasn't it? So you could see the rear window as well as the sloping bonnet. There were the usual Hopkins passers-by, meticulously painted, as always. Is that good enough?"

"Not bad at all. In fact, jolly good for a painting you weren't very interested in. Let me press you a little further. Was there anything in particular you noticed about the car's rear window?"

"No, not at all. A dog with a waggly head?"

"No, of course not. Don't be daft. Did it have a division down the middle?"

"No, I don't think so; no, I would definitely have noticed that. It just looked like an ordinary Beetle. Much the same as you still see now."

"OK, what was the date of the painting?"

"1950. Hopkins always dated his work, even with the month, after his signature. You must know that. So what are you getting at, Anthony?"

Anthony picked up the whisky bottle and filled Maurice's glass.

Then he said, very carefully and deliberately, in order to reassure Maurice that he was not going to mention his trip to see the oligarch Kuznetsov in St Petersburg, "I asked you to come tonight, Maurice, because I wanted you to hear about this painting, which I believe belongs to a Russian called Mickey Michaelov."

Anthony, and probably only Anthony, registered Maurice's surprise, for as far as Maurice knew this was the wrong Russian, "... and is being hung in Armstrong's house, a sort of short term loan. This is an arrangement which has been going on for some time, because Michaelov and the Armstrongs are old friends.

"Now, Maurice, as you know from our undergraduate days, I am, to my own embarrassment, a bit of a sad old car buff, and I noticed that the model Beetle was one which looked just a bit too modern – to cut a long story short..." Anthony knew that he would have to apologise to Maurice later for this undisguised, but he hoped justifiable, plagiarism, and for the use of the derogatory phrase with which he introduced it, "...the model in question was introduced two years after the date of the painting."

"Why on earth should someone change the date?" asked Christopher, incredulously.

"That begs the question doesn't it?" said Frieda, "Perhaps it's not the date that's wrong?"

"Which is one of the reasons why I asked Chris and Tricia to this little meeting," Anthony cut in, "Because if anyone knows any rumours about fake Festival paintings, it'll be you two. As for changing the date – as Chris said, what on earth for?"

"You've just bought two, haven't you, Anthony – Bradleys, I believe?"

"Yes, I have. And yes, of course, that's one of the reasons I'm concerned. But, have you; heard any rumours I mean?"

"Well, Maurice is here, isn't he?" replied Chris, "We know he went to Russia, and we know Kuznetsov has just got rid of a Hopkins. Putting two and two together..."

"You get five," said Maurice, truculently. He also looked crossly at Anthony, who met his eye with an expression which, Anthony hoped, both asked his forgiveness and promised an explanation. "I'm not going to break any confidences, so don't ask me to. Kuznetsov consulted me, yes, that's obvious, and he paid me generously, that's also bloody obvious. So, if you want to play guessing games that's fine by me, but I'm not contributing."

"Very understandable," said Tricia, giving Chris an irritated glance, "Well, Anthony, we've heard about a roomful of Festival paintings down in Cornwall somewhere near St Ives – we thought we'd mentioned it? Maurice? OK, never mind. But we haven't been to see them yet. I rang up Bond at the Saline, but he said he hadn't seen them either, although he was going to. You know what he's like, he went on and on about his new best friend, that Countess woman, and then he started talking about her wretched starfish too, just like you said."

"Yes," said Frieda, "Alison was there when we met Bond in St Ives. And at Armstrong's, as I said. But I don't know anyone who's seen her Chagalls – or, in fact, her husband, the Romanian Count with the Cornish castle. Can it really be a castle?"

"D'you know," said Chris, who had been examining the menu, while not quite surreptitiously enough scratching his shin under the table, "I think I fancy some Chinese Well Cooked Tart. Anyone else? Come on, Maurice, you could manage a slice, I'm sure you could. No? Well I'm going to. Yes, it certainly is a castle. It's right down by Land's End, close to where that thriller writer lives – you know, old black and white film with Richard Burton, something to do with the weather in Berlin, very famous – yes, it's a castle all right. Quite a lot of pretentious Barry type stuff built on, but definitely mediaeval, sorry, early modern I should say, underneath. Very good nick, very warm, pots of money around we thought, didn't we Trish?"

"You mean you've been there? Met the Count?"

"Been there, Frieda, yes, but no, we didn't meet him, just his wife. Last Easter, wasn't it, Trish?"

"Yes, just after. Drop in any time, she said, when we met her at that party at the Saltertons, so that's just what we did, we'd been staying with Bob and Terry in Mousehole and rang her up. Really wanted to see her Chagalls, but they were off being restored. There was still plenty of art around, though, but not really, well..."

"... I mean, Alma-Tadema, Millais, Russell Flint, for God's sake..."

Frieda bridled. "There's nothing wrong with Millais. You can't lump him in with Alma-Tad. And as for Russell..."

Anthony was too interested in Chris and Patricia's visit to Porthguarnon castle (although at the moment he was the only person present who knew that its occupants were persons of interest to the Security Directorate, and he had reminded himself many times that his knowledge was privileged, secret, and must be kept so – at least for the time being) to allow the conversation to deteriorate into a tiresome argument about art and, probably, pornography. There was at least one fact which couldn't be questioned.

"What those three have got in common is value. Festival paintings are Safeway special offers in comparison. Alma-Tad's Moses sold for three million about five years ago, and I'm fairly sure that his Assyrian Cohorts sold privately last year for ten million..."

Knowing this to be incorrect, and despite his resolve to sit silently with his arms folded, Maurice interrupted.

"Fifteen, near as dammit. That bloke in Hangzhou who makes tractors bought it. The colours were right."

"Purple and gold?" asked Frieda.

"Sort of dark crimson and yellow. Not quite as tasteful as John Deeres, but much cheaper, I imagine."

Good, Anthony thought, Maurice seemed to have got over his grump.

"Alison said that she uses Bruno and that St Ives dealer, Edwards, he runs the Red Porpoise, doesn't he?" said Frieda.

Chris had been carefully removing the stones from the lychees which had been perched, as a substitute for the original cherry, on top of his partially defrosted Mr Kipling tart, but suddenly looked up at the mention of the name Bruno. "I knew there was something I had to tell you. It was on the news at seven, I just heard it before you arrived. Bruno was pulled out of the Regent's Canal this morning. His body, that is."

Anthony put his cup down; a little coffee spilt into the saucer. The others sat still for a moment or two, Maurice murmured something sibilant, too quietly to be registered, then Frieda asked whether the police had put out any statement.

"No, too early, I imagine," said Chris, "but I think we all know what they'll find."

The others looked at him, faces blank.

"No, we don't," said Anthony, "tell us."

"Booze, of course."

"He drank? I didn't know."

"Like a fish. Often couldn't even remember where he'd left his car. But he found us that little Corot all right, knew what it was as soon as he spotted it. I wonder how much he made on that? They'll find him full of booze, sure as eggs. I don't think this tart's very Chinese, do you? Hey, Li, what's the Cantonese name for this pudding?"

Mr Li came over to their table, beaming and holding out his glass. Chris refilled it.

"In Kowloon it is called Bakewell Tart with lychees and often with ice cream too. Very popular."

"Well, let's have some ice cream then."

While Chris unwrapped his Cornetto the others sat in silence, pondering death and the various other risks of alcohol addiction.

Why, Frieda found herself wondering, hasn't Anthony mentioned that we've seen the Cornish Hopkinses? Frieda, of course, knew nothing about Mr Smith's, and Fred's, real connection with Anthony; she hadn't given them any thought since they had all left after the party with Bond and the Friends of the Saline. Anthony had kept quiet for no particular reason, just a general reluctance to start a conversation where Smith's name might be brought up, and maybe questions asked about him, questions which he would find tricky to answer.

"Anthony and I have seen the Hopkinses at Boselloe, that's near St Ives, haven't we, Anthony?"

Chris and Patricia, amazed and annoyed, asked with one voice why Anthony had kept this to himself, surely he understood how important it was – how interested they would be – well, of course, if he thought he could...

Frieda continued, "Perhaps I might, just, have been in the market for one, but Anthony wasn't, were you? I don't really know why you were there, to be honest. And what was all that about the Tretyakov?"

But before Anthony could start inventing an answer, she lost interest and said "Oh, never mind, it doesn't matter. The Hopkinses were magnificent, much more to my taste than the one at Armstrong's."

She looked at Chris's plate, at the remnants of pastry and fondant icing lying under the ice cream wrapper. "In fact, both of us liked the Cherry Girl the best, didn't we?"

"Yes. I don't know. The Overseer was wonderful. Mischievous, just like the Cherry Girl. But yes, I think you're right."

"I don't understand this," said Patricia, "the Overseer's in the London, it's been there for twenty years."

Anthony and Frieda exchanged glances; Anthony made a gesture to Frieda, who told them the story of the friendship between Williams' father and Hopkins.

"That fits, you know," said Chris to Patricia. "He was a soldier, and he was in Cyprus. He hated it. And he had a mean streak. But I didn't know anything about painting another Overseer, or about this soldier. Perhaps... "

"It was more than a friendship?" said Anthony.

"He wasn't gay, was he?" asked Patricia.

"No, not really, I don't think so," Chris replied, provoking Anthony to ask, quite loudly, what on earth he meant, *not really*.

"Well, he didn't seem that interested in sex, at all, either way."

"It was the fifties, for goodness' sake," said Anthony, "perhaps he just kept quiet about it?"

"Well, whatever," said Frieda, "there was this picture, and it was good, I tell you."

"What was that other one? What did you call it? Cherry something? What was that?"

Anthony explained this time, describing the painting in some detail.

"You realise that you're describing Destruction Line?" said Chris. "He sold that out of his studio, or at least that's what his executors assumed, they thought it had gone to the States and disappeared like three or four others, sold on probably, it's not recorded. Certainly not auctioned. So he actually gave it away, to this 'friend' of his. Good God. Tricia, you've got your *look*, what are you thinking?"

"It's obvious what she's thinking," said Frieda, "she's thinking that it's a fake. Well, I don't think it is, but it shouldn't be too difficult to tell, should it; I wonder, has Letty got any snaps or sketches of it in her dad's archive?"

"And, if she has, has anyone just happened to borrow them recently?" said Tricia.

"You know Letty?" asked Anthony of Frieda, "I've only met her once, when she was more or less wheeling her father around, at the Gillray dinner last year. Nice sort of person, I thought. So was her dad. Could you ask her?"

"Yes, I don't see why not. But – are we turning detectives or something? Why are we so interested?"

"Come on, Frieda," said Chris, "don't tell me you don't care whether someone was trying to con you out of half a million for a forged Hopkins? And, if it's right, not forged, don't tell me you're not interested. We are, aren't we, Trish?"

"Most certainly."

"Why don't you ring Letty?"

"What, now?"

"Why not, it's not ten yet?"

"Chris, she'll think I'm bonkers. Or drunk. It can wait till tomorrow morning."

"Well, OK, then I'll ring you and we'll arrange something," Chris said to Frieda and Anthony, "and we ought to get down there sharpish, don't you think?"

"Yes," said Maurice, "I can shut up shop for a day or two."

"What about your work?" said Frieda to Tricia.

Tricia laughed. "They can do without us for a couple of days. We just get under their feet, in any case."

Maurice, emboldened by the whisky and wine, asked a question he had often wanted to.

"Who are *they*, Trish, are they cashiers, dealers, is that the word? Is it a bank?"

Chris looked solemnly at Tricia, and placed his index finger in front of his lips.

"She can't tell you, Maurice, we are sworn to secrecy."

"No we're not. But you lot are, now. I'm not really serious," she added, as the other three were looking bemused, "my maiden name is Anderson, my parents are dead and I haven't got any brothers or sisters."

The others stared, still unenlightened.

"Andersons" she said. Then more loudly, "*Andersons*"

Anthony was first to cotton on. "You don't mean *Andersons*, the..."

"Yes, I'm afraid I do. Just me now, and Chris here is sort of in charge, well, he's Chairman, Dad brought him in before he passed over. But there's a CEO, and a board, and all that. I'm not really very interested. So now you know."

"Well," said Frieda, looking rather glum, "I don't stand much of a chance, then, do I, if we both fancy the Cherry Girl, or Destruction Line, I suppose we should call it."

"Not true," said Chris, "We don't pay over the odds, that wouldn't feel right. There wouldn't be any fun, somehow."

Frieda did not look convinced. Nevertheless, they agreed on another visit to Cornwall. Maurice would join them if he could get someone to look after his gallery. Frieda would phone Letty. Anthony would arrange an hotel.

Chapter 21

Monday August 14   Patricia and Christopher   Frieda Maurice   Anthony

"So, oh, it was a good three years ago, this Middle Eastern art history student chappie actually got invited round to Letty's house, well it's Sir Mike's house I suppose, but Letty has been living there for ages, ever since Mike had his first stroke, and she said that he knew all about Mike's work. He brought a girl with him, together they charmed the socks off the old man, so Letty said; he actually quoted from his monograph."

"You mean that first draft thing, that preliminary paper which was going to be the basis of the authorised biography? Of Hopkins?"

"Yes, obviously, what else?"

"Sorry" said Maurice, pronouncing it as if he was going to follow it with the words "I'm sure."

"No, *I'm* sorry, don't take the huff."

"Really, Tricia. Please continue, this is fascinating."

"So, he kept on taking notes, asked all sorts of questions about the way Hopkins worked, his favourite colour palette, very detailed. The girl – his girlfriend, they assumed – took notes as well. Mike couldn't answer very easily, but Letty said she could fill in some of the gaps. Then, he asked Mike to tell him the story of the missing pictures, the ones that the executors sold. Mike couldn't really manage that; he had been very young, and the other executors more or less took control – they're all dead, of course – and in any case, Mike's memory is very unreliable now, as we all know."

"Don't we just," said Chris, sadly, who had known Sir Michael in his prime, when he had been Director of the International.

"Well, this young man, I've forgotten his name, Arab sort of name, I've written it down but it's in my case, in the boot, sorry, at any rate, this student fellow asked if there were any photos of paintings which hadn't been reproduced anywhere, in a book or catalogue. Letty got out her boxes – by the way, he had brought with him a great tray of baklava, you know, those gooey cakes with walnuts and filo pastry and syrup..."

"A whole tray?" asked Maurice, who had been wondering whether Anthony was aiming to stop for coffee, or whether they intended to bat on until lunch, "of baklava? Lucky people!"

"...and they were all tucking in, Mike especially, sticky fingers all over the papers, and she found some pictures, photographs, that is, of quite a few; some of drawings, but two or three, not terribly well reproduced, of the pictures which were sold after his death. Black and white, of course. Apparently the lad was fascinated, and asked if he could have copies, just for his PhD, but there weren't any more copies, and they don't have a scanner, so they said they'd post some on for him."

"Amazing what a tray of cakes will do, isn't it? God, mind that cyclist" said Frieda.

"I can see her," said Anthony, "Don't fuss."

"So," continued Tricia, "he gave them a University address, the Kunstakademie Koblenz, they got on with their tea and cakes, chatted about painting in general, what sort of career he had in mind, how the best graduates work in commercial, not fine, art these days, a well-worn theme, I think. Then Mike asked him about his drawing, that is, had his course involved doing art as well as learning about it? So he took a sketch pad out of his briefcase, and drew Mike's portrait, there and then. It was phenomenal, Letty said, she said it made her want to cry. When he showed it to Mike, the old man just gulped, and his hand was shaking when he gave it back. But the lad left it with them. I wish I'd gone round instead of just phoning."

"Very respectable institution the school at Koblenz," said Chris.

"So it is. And the young man, I wish I could remember his name, studied there all right, until he went missing, that is.

They all knew him, they knew he was brilliant, but one day he just didn't turn up, and that was that. Left all his stuff, some marvellous drawings, even some of his clothes, a leather jacket apparently, very expensive, just hanging on his peg."

"How does Letty know all this? Did she ring the University up or something?" asked Frieda.

"Well, the day after he left Mike's house, Letty was putting all the stuff back in the boxes, trying to get them in some order, and she realised that one of the photographs, the black and whites she'd shown the lad, was missing. It was all a bit higgledy piggledy so she assumed she'd put it in another box. She didn't bother for a couple of days, but then she got annoyed, and went through all the stuff again. It was definitely gone. She was really cross, then, so she rang up Koblenz."

"She speaks German?"

"Of course she does, and they speak English. And that was when she heard the story."

"Did the University get in touch with the German police?" asked Anthony.

"No, vice versa in fact. The police had been all over them apparently and not just the ordinary coppers either, but something called the BKA; like our CID, I think. But they wouldn't give any details."

Anthony was first to ask the question which was in all their minds.

"Was it the photo of Destruction Line?"

"Yes, it certainly was."

By this time they had left the M5 motorway, which they had joined at Bristol, and were driving down the A30 around the northern curve of Dartmoor. They stopped in a layby to look at a map for some indication of where they might find an early lunch. Maurice by now needed output sooner than input, and he climbed from the car to find a handy bush. But he jumped quickly back in, and asked Anthony to drive on to the other end of the layby.

"Don't open your window, there's a dead deer there," he said, and so there was, just starting to expand with the gases of putrefaction. "Let's just go to the next garage, the others can look at the map while you fill up, and I need a pee."

In the end, they decided to find a shop and buy some sandwiches in Okehampton, which was now close. Anthony wasn't particularly pleased with the decision, but in this company couldn't bring himself to make a fuss about crumbs on the back seat; in the end they found a side road which led to open moorland, where they could easily park. A couple of shaggy little ponies with noticing eyes were grazing nearby, possibly waiting, like the rooks in the motorway service area, for discarded crusts, or maybe they just lived there.

Anthony ate his crayfish salad – surprisingly, there had been an upper crust supermarket in the centre of Okehampton – standing up outside the car, to set an example. He was joined by Frieda, Tricia and Chris, but Maurice remained determinedly seated in the comfort of Anthony's brand new e-class Mercedes. Tricia had offered a chauffeured car from Andersons' pool, but they wouldn't have been able to talk so freely, and Anthony's car was big enough for the five of them. Tricia and Chris seemed enchanted by the view, excitedly describing to each other the undulating moors covered with heather, bracken and grasses in every shade of purple and green, the shrub-like oak trees waving frayed grey flags of lichen, the encircling blue sky, even the dear little ponies, with such enthusiasm that Frieda was sure that they were going to compare it with some idealised landscape by an artist she'd never heard of. But this wasn't the case; for once, their aesthetic experience was unmediated.

The hotel which Anthony had booked stood near the coast, only a few miles from Land's End, and took its name, the Dolphin's Fin, from the oddly shaped triangular rock which jutted from the sea at low tide. Various guides had praised it, and Anthony had only been able to reserve four rooms because of a cancellation. The drive from London, especially since Anthony had kept more or less to the speed limits, had taken six hours and they were all tired, Anthony in particular. A nineteen fifties Rolls was parked outside, a grey Silver Dawn, and Anthony drew up next to it. They took their cases into the bar, dumped them on the cement floor and Maurice rang the little brass mermaid whose rocky perch was hollow and concealed her clapper.

"Hello, hello!" shouted a distinguished looking cove sitting at the bar, dressed in Barbour and moleskins and drinking tea. How friendly, they thought; no doubt he was friendly but in fact he was summoning the barman. "Peder, my bill, pronto!" Peder, had he been a merman snoozing full fathom five under the hotel's eponymous rock, instead of hastily finishing off a fag in the scullery, could not have failed to hear this summons. He appeared behind the bar, the distinguished cove paid his bill, found the door and left. The Rolls made its stately exit from the car park, the sound of its engine gradually fading as it drew away towards Land's End.

The barman was thin and his fingers were stained deep ochre to match the ceiling, but he managed four suit cases a time as he showed them their rooms. "I'll bring you a pot of tea straightaway," he said, "and we start dinner at seven, the bar's nicest so I'll keep a table for you until half past, is that OK?" It was.

A small wood fire was lit in the bar, every evening, all year round, Peder the barman told them, partly for the draught and ventilation otherwise damp patches started to show. Their table was laid next to the fire, which was cosy, but meant that Chris and Frieda, who were nearest, had to ease their feet in under the somnolent, woolly and potentially smelly sheep dog which occupied the hearth. When he took their orders, Peder encouraged the dog to move, but over the next hour or so it gradually reinstated itself.

Anthony could see that Chris and Tricia were wondering whether it was worth the mental effort of sorting out a balanced meal with all the complexities of starters and main courses and choices of vegetables, and different drinks before and with and possibly after. When Chris, looking at the bit of the menu which listed different sorts of grilled meat with chips, said, "Why don't we just have ... " Anthony broke in and said that he would definitely like to try the fish soup with home baked bread and aïoli, and then he would probably also have trio of fish for his main as well, this surprising concoction of sole, hake and John Dory. Maurice immediately agreed, and suggested that they should try a lightish wine with the soup, and something a little more robust with the main course. Was Frieda also going to have fish? Would she be happy with his choice of wine? Frieda nodded, but Chris frowned and was about to assert that he would stick to whisky, thank you very much, when Tricia, placing her hand gently on his knee, said that yes, of course they would be happy with wine if Maurice would be sure to choose one with a nice flavour.

"Well, how are we going to play tomorrow, then?" asked Anthony, as their meal drew to a close.

"What do you suggest?" said Chris. "This trip was your idea."

"Was it?"

"Oh, Chris, I don't know about that," said Maurice, who was spooning clotted cream onto the last few crumbs of his treacle tart, "I think it just sort of emerged. We want to look at these pictures that Frieda and Anthony were shown, especially the Cherry Girl, to see if it might be the Destruction Line, and then I suppose, if it is, we have to try and find out how this farmer bloke, Williams, really came by it. Hopkins can't have given it to his father while he was alive, because it was there in his studio after he was dead."

"But how would we know whether it's genuine or not? Don't we think that this student who visited Mike and Letty stole the photo so that he could paint a forgery?" asked Frieda.

"I don't really know. Anthony couldn't tell that Armstrong's Beetle picture was wrong except for the windscreen business. Could you, Anthony?" said Maurice, with a snappish emphasis which only Anthony understood. Maurice was expecting, but had not yet received, an apology from Anthony for the way he had adjusted – stolen – the story of the discovery of the forgery. He knew that Anthony had done this to protect his, Maurice's, confidential relationship with Kuznetsov, nevertheless he was very irritated that this had also had the effect of concealing his own astuteness.

"But surely," said Anthony, "if one of those pictures is wrong, then the others are likely to be wrong as well?"

"That student could have taken the photo for any number of reasons. The actual painting exists somewhere; perhaps he knew someone who it had been offered to for sale, and who wanted to check up on it?" said Chris.

"I think we've just got to go and see them again. I never even considered that they might be fake," said Frieda. "I phoned them last time because I'd heard about the pictures from Hank Edwards, and they were all over us when we went up – I think they wanted to sell one, we got a long story from Williams, and drinks, and to be honest I nearly asked then. But I was a bit put off by that bossy bloke with the bad arm, your friend, Anthony, his name was Smith, wasn't it?"

They agreed that first thing the following morning they would telephone and then all troop up to Boselloe Farm, and ask to see the paintings.

"What if they're not in, or don't want us to see them?" asked Tricia.

"It's a farm, there's always someone in, and I'm sure they'll want us to see them," said Anthony, looking round for support because it had indeed occurred to him that they might just find themselves banging on a locked door for a couple of days. True, it was supposed to be a farm, but he hadn't seen any animals except for the pony, just a tractor and a few fields which could have been farmed by anybody, and how much attention did a field full of turnips really need?

"Come on Trish," said Chris, "time for bed. I'm bushed; Anthony, you must be exhausted, you should have shared the driving."

"Couldn't. Insurance." said Anthony, raising his hands in frustration, "I explained. You're right, I'm for bed." He thought about his recent escapade. He hadn't worried about car insurance then. Had he? He couldn't remember. Had he become normal, law abiding Anthony again? Pity, really.

Tuesday August 15   Frieda   Maurice   Anthony   Patricia and Christopher   Henry (Hank) Edwards   Emily and Peter Williams

The Dolphin's Fin had installed double glazing of the highest modern specification, but Anthony, who occasionally liked a bit of fresh air, had incautiously opened his window before going to sleep. He was woken by the gale and driving rain in the small hours, quickly shut the window and, perhaps because the previous day had been so tiring, managed to drop off again. The others all slept through, and only noticed the change in the weather when they pulled their curtains back in the morning and saw, rather than heard, the torrents sluicing down the window panes.

"Have you got the clothes for this?" Frieda asked Tricia after breakfast.

"I've got a mac. It's hardly enough, is it?"

"I've got my coat," said Chris, "I'll be all right."

"Chris has got a coat," said Tricia, emphasising the indefinite article. "He doesn't like shopping, he'd rather get wet."

"Anthony," said Maurice commandingly, "bring the car up to the door. We'll make a dash for it."

Anthony had little choice; as he had explained, no-one else was insured to drive his nice car.

In the time it took him to fetch it, the others to get themselves ready, kitted out in whatever they thought most waterproof, for them all to climb into the car, and for Anthony to drive the five miles or so to Boselloe, the weather had changed again. The black clouds had been blown away eastwards, the crests of breaking waves sparkled in the sun, the flowering gorse gilded the moors, but the roads were still wet and dirty, and when they parked at Boselloe, and got out of the car, their feet sank into a slurry of decayed granite and manure.

Frieda and Anthony led them into the front garden of the farmhouse. The storm had put paid to the Japanese design in the gravel, and instead of artful swirls it had formed a rough doughnut around a muddy puddle. A dilapidated van, which Anthony recognised, stood at the side of the building with its rear door open, and, as they approached, Hank the cowboy came slowly out of the farmhouse, struggling with a large cardboard box, and making for a side gate close to his van.

"I usually give you a hand, don't I?" Anthony said, taking off his coat and hanging it on a nail in the fence. "What?" said Hank, seeing Chris following the others who had already entered the house. "What the ... oh, it's you again, what are you doing here? No, I don't need any help, thank you... well, you could open the gate for me."

Anthony opened the little wooden gate, and watched while Hank loaded the box.

"Are the Williamses in?" he asked.

"Er, I ... who was that?"

"Collectors, I suppose you might say."

"I just saw a big bloke. Were there others?"

"Yes, they're interested in the Festival School," said Anthony. "That's why I've brought them."

"*You*'ve brought them? Oh. So you've seen the pictures, have you?"

"Of course, that time we met, you remember, I didn't know who you were."

"And now you do?"

"You're Henry Edwards, aren't you, don't you own the Red Porpoise gallery in St Ives?"

Hank paused before he replied. He drew a little bronze box from the pocket of his yellow knitted waistcoat, and took a sizeable pinch of snuff. He offered it to Anthony, who shook his head.

"So you were given the tour? Told the story, how Pete and Emily came by the pictures?"

"Yes."

"But why do you think any might be for sale?"

"Aren't they?"

"Well, I don't know, they might be, I suppose."

It was obvious that Hank was uncertain what to say; *how to play this scene* was the way it appeared to Anthony.

Then Hank said, "The fact is, I've just offered to sell one for them. No, to be honest with you, I've just bought one myself. It was a bargain; I'm not sure they know quite how much they fetch now. Look, it's behind those boxes in the van there. I think I've got a buyer but, if you were interested – or your friends, I mean – for a quick sale, we could go to your bank together? In St Ives? You've got a facility? I could give you a very good price."

Tricia had come back into the yard, beckoning to Anthony. He waved to her and shouted that he wouldn't be a minute.

"Which one is it?"

"I'll show you. Climb in. Where's that screwdriver?"

He heaved a couple of boxes and a tea chest to one side, and revealed a thin plywood crate, carefully secured with screws in each corner. He unscrewed them and prised off the plywood top. The pregnant girl, with her glowing cheeks and dowdy overalls smiled secretly not at, only towards, Anthony, while the foreman stood smugly, proprietorially, behind her.

"It's The Overseer!" said Anthony.

"Yes, it's tremendous, isn't it?"

"It certainly is."

And it was; a marvellous painting. Anthony was suddenly convinced that it was authentic. Hopkins had painted two, there couldn't be any doubt.

He was so excited that he couldn't stop himself.

"How much would you want?"

"Say, two fifty?"

Good God, thought Anthony, two fifty for a Hopkins, and, such a fine one! He might take two twenty five – it must be worth twice, three times, that! He would have to use his firm's account; that would be all right, they were flush at present.

"You say you've bought it; it's your property?"

"We've shaken hands; I'll get a bill of sale. I'll go in and get it now. You stay here and guard the painting."

He jumped down.

By now, all thoughts of forgery had gone, banished by the prospect of owning a Hopkins, and a superb one at that. The sight of the painting had completely put out of his mind the reason for his presence. He had almost forgotten his four friends and their mission, but not the story of Lieutenant Hopkins and Trooper Williams in the hills of Cyprus.

"What an opportunity! And if I can get a provenance ..."

He called out to Edwards, "Can you get him to write a brief note, just a few words, saying how his dad came by the painting?"

"Yes, yes, of course, I might be ten minutes."

Hank disappeared round the back of the house.

A few minutes later, Tricia appeared at the front door again, and, seeing Anthony sitting on the tailgate of the van, she came over to him.

"It's all a bit disorganised in there. Most of the pictures have been taken down and stacked against the wall. They're all over the place. The woman in there is trying to talk about some of them, but she says they're getting ready for an exhibition – at least I think that's what she said – they certainly seem to be packing up. And we hadn't got down to the far end of the room when the husband and a small chap barged in and grabbed one off the wall and made off with it. It's all a bit strange. The pictures look very good, though. I got a quick look at the one that what's-his-name, Williams, took down, it must have been the other Overseer, the one that isn't in the London. From what I could see it looked marvellous."

"What!"

"Yes, definitely. Four or five girls, bloke standing behind looking smug ... I mean, you told us about it yourself, didn't you? You saw it here? Anthony, what's the matter, you look as if you've ..."

"Just now? I mean, in the house, now, not ..."

"Yes, *in the house*, it's there now, they put it face to the wall in the room by the ... the Japanese woman looked quite surprised, but she carried on talking about Hopkins and the

433

army and Williams' father. Another thing that's odd; I didn't mention before, did I, Letty said that the young student's girlfriend was Japanese... are you sure you're OK?"

What he saw of himself then, Anthony did not particularly like.

"Yes, yes, I'm fine, I just, um, remembered something, that's all."

"Oh, sorry, you looked a bit shocked."

"No, um ..." he blinked and shook his head, "no, I'm fine now."

"Well, if you're sure, I ought to get back in, I don't want to seem rude. The girl said that we can see the one she calls the Cherry Girl, it hasn't been packed up yet. Are you coming? They seem to be in such a hurry." She shook her head, noticing that whatever Anthony might have claimed, he still looked far from fine; very shaken, in fact. "I don't know what to make of it all."

Well, I do, said Anthony to himself. What is true of things that are too good to be true?

"In a minute or two; I want to have another word with this character Edwards."

Edwards, also known as Hank the cowboy, emerged a little while later, and came over to the van, waving a piece of paper.

"Here it is. Short and sweet. Look, am I sensing that you'd be interested yourself? Or is it that big bloke and his wife, have they got that Maurice Symes-doodah here to hold their hands? Or that other woman, with her back to us, I think I know her, the one who looks like a lollipop?"

Anthony wondered how on earth a private art gallery, a *shop*, selling items with a status elevated (sometimes only by the proprietor) beyond that of bed linen and cauliflowers, but nevertheless a *shop* reliant upon customers and their cheque books, could survive, in a market economy, where the owner was so grossly ill-mannered? Anthony, although he had often made the attempt, could never quite put aside the Smithian presumption of his economics education, which was that, by and large, for the most part, with the odd exception, competition worked. Perhaps, indeed, it was working now; perhaps the Red Porpoise Gallery was on its uppers, reduced to dodgy deals, or, in this case, the plainly illegal. Yet another new experience for him; well, he'd coped with an armed robber – sort of an armed robber – he shouldn't have any trouble with a crooked art dealer, especially a small one.

"So, how would you want me to pay?"

"Oh, it is you, then. We could both go to your bank, St Ives is nearest."

"No-one has two hundred and fifty thousand pounds in their current account."

"Transfer it, get a loan, I don't care how you do it. But payment today would mean, well, I can't tell you how much it would mean. And, you know what a bargain you'll be getting."

Anthony had not thought as far forward as he might have done, as he certainly would have done if he had been, for example, analysing the probable costs and benefits of a new leisure centre in Liverpool. Once again his adrenals were pumping away, and they spurred him on to confront the fraudulent dealer in dramatic style. He climbed into the van, followed by Edwards, looking for all the world like a little pixie as he clambered aboard, with his tight green corduroy trousers, pointed shoes and bright yellow knitted waistcoat. Anthony made a large gesture, encompassing the entire contents of the van; numerous flat cartons including the half opened packing case which contained the Overseer.

"Two Overseers my friends and I could swallow, Mr Edwards, but three seem somewhat excessive. No doubt these other cases contain Overseers numbers ..."

He momentarily stopped in order to count how many sealed cartons were leaning up against the side of the van. He didn't notice the change in Edwards' expression, nor the knife which he had drawn from his back pocket.

"Good gracious, your friend's leaving in a hurry, Mr Williams," said Frieda, as she saw the battered white van driving through the farm gate, spreading arcs of mud and manure as it turned abruptly onto the lane and sped away.

"Oh, he always drives like that," he replied, "Like a ... like a ..." but the simile escaped him, because he was too shocked by Edwards' sudden departure. Edwards had arrived early in the morning, with instructions to close down the operation. All the paintings were to be packed up and loaded into his van, and he would drive away with them to a destination which was, as always, kept secret from Peter and Emily, who were to lock up the farmhouse and disappear until summoned again to take part in another 'project'. They were used to this by now, it was all part of the operation, they thought of it almost as a business; they had even been supplied with a credit card, in the name of what seemed to be a carpet shop in Cheshire, to cover their expenses. Edwards always phoned after a while and would tell them the next location, and what research to do. But on this occasion everything seemed too hurried – he was sure that they could place at least another two, possibly three, paintings; they had been told to expect a visit from the egregious Andrew Bond from the Saline, and since Bond would probably be escorting the glamorous and talkative Countess they would have spread the word all right. Especially since he would be allowed to promise Bond a rake-off. Not the Countess, of course. Countess indeed! He didn't know anybody down here who'd actually met the Count. Some Mid-European financier, they said, more often in Vienna than London. Emily had done a brilliant job on Hopkins, digging this soldier-farmer friend out of a pile of crap in the Courtauld archives. And she said that the paintings that Hank brought them were the best that Rembrandt had ever done. He was Lebanese, apparently, so Hank had let drop once. Although, knowing Hank, that probably meant that he was an Eskimo. But where the hell was Hank off to now; half the paintings were still hanging up, they had to get rid of these London people before they could get on with the packing, and they had to be out by the evening. He saw that that big fellow Chris was chatting to Emily, oh God, why does Emily keep on talking, why doesn't she just do her smiling inscrutable thing?

"So you weren't actually at the Courtauld?" Chris was asking her.

"No," she replied, "I just used to go there to see Ivor, he helped me with ... some work on Poussin I was doing for the sale room. Catalogue entries, you know, that sort of thing."

"So which art school did you go to?"

"Oh, none in England."

"Ah, I see. So where ..."

Peter had joined them, and took hold of Emily's arm.

"Look, I'm really sorry to break up this chat, but we've got a lot to do, Emily, before this evening. We've still got to pack up ..." he looked round the room, "the Cherry Girl and, um, that Welsh footbridge one ..."

"Aberhafesp" said Chris.

"Bless you" said Peter, absent-mindedly. "Come on Emmie, I'm really sorry, I've got to drag you away, I'm sure Mr er um will understand. Thank you so much for coming to see my pictures," he said to Chris, "I'm always delighted to show people my Dad's paintings, and tell them the story. But now, we really must..."

Chris was not a sensitive person, otherwise he would have found his role as Chairman of a large company very trying, but even he was able to infer that the tour was over, and that their departure would be welcomed. Nevertheless, he glanced round towards Frieda and Tricia, who were cooing over the Cherry Girl, and registered a minute, momentary, fluttering of Tricia's eyelids, and a slight nod of her head.

They thanked their hosts and gathered themselves up to leave.

"Where's Anthony?" asked Frieda.

"Last I saw of him he was chatting to that picturesque character, Edwards, isn't it, Frieda, just by his van. Wasn't he going to help him with a packing case?" said Chris.

"I saw him after that," said Tricia, "He looked upset, worried or something. But he said he was all right."

"He wouldn't just go wandering off," said Maurice, "he was too interested in the pictures. Is he unwell? Maybe ..." he addressed Emily, "is there an outside lavatory? One used by the campers?"

"No, we don't have campers any more – there was one, and Mr Evans must have used it when he came earlier, in June, but the wall fell in, it was rotten. Perhaps he went there and – perhaps he's had a...?" Peter was already half way through the door, with Chris close behind him. But neither Anthony nor Anthony's body were found, not in the lavatory, not in the barn, not in the fields or garden. What Frieda did find was Anthony's mobile phone, ground into the mud near the garden gate, close to where Edwards' white van had been parked.

"Jesus, what's happened? The phone's been crushed, look!" said Maurice, at the same time as Emily ran up to Peter and whispered something into his ear.

They all thought of the van, and the violent way it was driven, and the expression which passed across Peter Williams' face when he saw Edwards leave." He must have gone with that man, in the van!" exclaimed Tricia, "What was he doing, do you know? You looked as shocked as us."

"Yes, I was; and no, no I don't know what he was doing, I really don't." His voice rose as he emphasised these last few words. It was true that he, too, had looked upset when the van had accelerated noisily away, upset and angry, Maurice had thought, and they were convinced that he had been taken completely by surprise. Now he looked distraught. Then they all, except Frieda, started shouting themselves, demanding once again to know what Edwards was doing, where he was going, why he was there; all questions to which the answer was either obvious, or impossible to give. When she could get a word in, Frieda said, "He works in St Ives. Does he live there?"

"Yes, he does, over his gallery," Peter replied, "I don't think he's got anywhere else."

"Where's his gallery?"
"Do you know St Ives?"
"No."
"Take us with you and I'll show you where to park."

"Take you with us? Why? And how?"

"Because he's gone off with our paintings as well as your friend. God knows what he's up to. But if we don't get him quick he'll disappear, I know he will."

"What do you mean, disappear? What about his gallery, all the stuff in it?"

"It's not his, it's all sale or return, and it's tourist rubbish in any case."

"Emily, lock it up again, set the alarm!" shouted Peter.

But she had already done this. She had also spotted Anthony's coat which was still hanging on the fence, and searching its pockets found his keys. Now she started the car, executed an efficient three point turn, and drew up by the little knot of people who were blocking the farm gate and arguing about what to do next. She leaned over the passenger seat and opened the door. "Peter, get in the front, quickly." But her plan of escape was unwittingly frustrated by Chris who was nearer the front of the car and who immediately opened the door and heaved himself in. The others piled in the back, Frieda ending up on Maurice's knee.

The large car purred off down the drive and onto the road, quite as fast as Edwards' rusty old Transit, but, owing to Emily's competence and the numerous electronic devices ensuring the Mercedes' adhesion to whatever surface it encountered, with much less fuss and spray.

They soon joined the coast road along which Frieda had driven a fortnight before.

"Beautiful scenery, isn't the sea a wonderful colour, d'you know, Trish, I can only think of Matisse who painted a finer depth of blue?"

"I can't see from here, Chris, Frieda's head is in the way. I hope you're quite comfortable in the front?"

"Yes dear, very, thank you, this is an excellent vehicle."

Emily drove down the Stennack into St Ives, past the sign which lamely forbade all except 'authorised' traffic, through a narrow combe lined with featureless pebble-dashed terraces, between a nondescript cinema and a dauntingly oppressive Methodist chapel which was being used as a theatre, to a narrow cross roads where the Victorian library faced a night club and a burger cafe. Over the cross roads the buildings became a little more quaint, if not particularly interesting. In front of the Guildhall, itself undistinguished, stood a massive bronze by Barbara Hepworth, and the road was lined with small galleries and second hand book shops. Emily slid the large car through a narrow chicane, and drew to a halt in front of a low door with a slate tablet set into the stone beside it. This was the entrance to a gallery, discreet and with a certain air of refinement; it was called the Labyrinth, the words cut into the slate in lettering of an unusual design, which Maurice thought owed something to the style of Eric Gill. The Red Porpoise was a less prosperous looking affair, a short way up an alley leading back from the sea

They got out of the car, and found they were only yards from the waves, which were breaking gently against the sea wall, the other side of a sturdy granite parapet. An actor, resting for the summer, was dressed up like Captain Hook and entertaining a group of children with terrible tales of shipwreck and piracy. They followed Peter and Emily into the Red Porpoise.

The paintings, drawings and prints on the walls, the sculptures and pots on the shelves and in glass cases, were a very mixed bag. Maurice immediately recognised the markets at which this collection was aimed; he had started off with the same ideas, and, thankfully, had made enough money to move on to art which he himself enjoyed. Williams had implied that it was all junk; it wasn't, a few pieces showed talent and originality. But most didn't, and some were hideous. The guardian of this miscellany was the usual languid girl, dressed in black, who might conceivably acknowledge a customer's – no, the word customer might imply that she was a shop girl, quel horreur, – a *visitor's* presence if he or she were very well dressed and spent some time looking at the more expensive pieces. This girl spoke, not actually to them, more into the air which surrounded them.

"You can't park there, you know, the warden'll be on to you like a shot."

"We don't care about that, has Hank come back?" asked Peter.

"Oh it's you. No, I'm afraid Mr Edwards is still out. I think he's gone to a sale."

"We'll go up to his flat then, and wait for him."

"You can't just go up to his flat!"

"Yes I can, he gave me a key. Look. Wait for me there, he said. I've brought some important clients with me."

Chris had absented himself during this interchange, and was minutely examining a little drawing.

"This is nice. Look, Trish," he lowered his voice, "it's an early Horace Blundell, I'm sure. What do you think? It's just signed with an H, he did that sometimes."

"Chris," she said, without opening her mouth much, "we're looking for Anthony, not for some bargain in a gallery."

"Well, I think it is. How much do they want for it? Good Lord, we can't miss this."

"I'll have this one," he said to the girl in black, interrupting her argument with Peter. "Could you put some bubble wrap round it for me, please?"

"Pardon? Oh, you want to *buy* it, er yes, of course. I'll just, um, how would you like to pay?"

Peter said to the others, "This way. Up these stairs. He opened a door marked 'Cloakroom', revealing some pegs, a drum of floor polish, a bicycle pump, a door with a picture of a lavatory bowl on it, and a door marked 'Private', which he pushed open. A flight of stairs led to another door. Peter stood by this door, Emily seemed to have left, Chris was sorting out credit cards, the girl in black was taping up bubble wrap, the other three climbed the stairs and crowded together on the little landing.

"What are you waiting for?" asked Frieda, "why don't you unlock it?"

"Because I haven't got a key," he replied.

"But ..."

"That was my front door key."

Emily then appeared at the bottom of the stairs, ran up them and took some sort of large screwdriver from her shoulder bag. She handed it to Peter and ran down the stairs again, calling back as she went, "It's all I could find. You'll have to shove it as well." Peter inserted the flattened end between the door and the jamb, by the lock.

"On three!" he shouted down. Emily held the bottom door open.

"One, two, three!"

As he shouted 'three', he wrenched the screwdriver back, the door jamb splintered, and he shouldered it open.

At the same time, Emily slammed the bottom door shut, with a bit of luck masking the sound of the destruction upstairs. The girl heard the door slam, but was intent upon her sale. Chris had quite forgotten about Anthony in his delight at encountering an undervalued drawing, an incautious delight considering the purpose of their expedition.

The flat was quite small, and a couple of minutes' search revealed no paintings, and no hiding places. Williams said to Frieda, "Why don't you go and ask the girl if she knows anywhere else he keeps his stock – a warehouse unit, perhaps, anything with a bit of security? I don't know of anywhere, but he could easily have been keeping it secret from me. Emily, are you sure you've never heard him mention anything?"

"Yes, of course I'm sure. Try to keep calm, Peter."

Peter bit his lip and clenched his fists, but did not otherwise respond.

Maurice, meanwhile, was searching through the papers which were lying in bundles on a table in the living room. There was also a small roll-top desk, and Maurice was quite prepared to break this open if they found nothing useful on the table.

Frieda had gone back downstairs, and Tricia had decided to go with her. They saw Chris chatting with considerable liveliness to the girl in black, who no longer seemed quite so languid and even seemed to know something about art and the work of local artists. She had the vocabulary, at least. Tricia caught Frieda's eye, and rolled her own upwards. Frieda grinned.

"What's the time, darling?" Tricia asked Chris who, slightly puzzled, looked at his watch and told her. Frieda saw that the girl automatically registered Chris's gold Rolex, and her manner became almost animated.

"Yes, I do actually," she said to Chris, hardly acknowledging the approach of the two women, "I've taken some classes at Penwith and I make, just simple things, you know, bangles and necklaces. Mainly out of acrylic, but sometimes silver, I have to call it white metal, of course, but everyone knows what that means, don't they?" Tricia wanted to respond that it means that you can't afford to have them hall-marked, but the girl had just remembered the Penwith class on marketing, where the fairly unreconstructed lecturer in business studies had reminded them of the fact, obvious to him, that women have got to be made to want jewellery so that men will buy it for them. So she beamed and immediately concentrated all her charm upon Tricia, who stopped feeling irritated with Chris and quickly thawed. However, the girl knew of no storage facility used by her employer – 'the owner' she called him, leaving their relationship, and the terms of her presence there, somewhat hazy. On second thoughts, he did have a phone call once about some pictures he was going to collect, and maybe there was somewhere he hadn't told her about? She remembered the phone call because when he put the phone down he had just clicked his tongue and said 'Bloody Dracula'; he didn't say it exactly *to* her, more to himself, you know what I mean?

"Dracula? Well, isn't that strange?" said Frieda, "Mr Edwards did say that he would have two or three paintings – the Festival School, do you know it? – for us to look at. Perhaps we should give him a few more minutes now; we can always come back tomorrow."

The girl looked surprised.

"The Festival School? That's way beyond ... yes, of course I know of it, but it's um not an area of great interest to Mr Edwards at the moment ..."

Frieda helped her out, "I expect he buys and sells a few works privately – perhaps acts as an agent sometimes?"

"Perhaps; I don't know. Possibly." The girl was starting to look unhappy, maybe, Frieda thought, she was worrying about the visitors who had remained upstairs.

"I say, Tricia," she said brightly, hoping to distract the girl, "look at these delightful little studies of starfish and sea anemones and, er, whelks?"

Tricia looked at the terrible daubs, then understood why Frieda had started talking about them. Once again the girl was taken aback; the gentleman had chosen a very nice little drawing, but these, she didn't know why Hank could bear to have them in the gallery. Well, she did know, it was because they were painted by that Countess woman, and he was knocking her off, wasn't he? No-one who appreciated Festival paintings could possibly like those travesties. Frieda had guessed right; the girl had become worried about the people who had gone up into her boss's flat. Her quandary was that she wasn't supposed to leave the gallery unattended – she couldn't just run upstairs and see what was going on – nothing, she hoped. With relief, she heard the sound of footsteps on the creaky uncarpeted stairs, the banging of doors and the chatter of Hank's unheralded guests as they returned to the showroom. She looked round the gallery and counted heads; six, that was right, thank goodness.

When they left she quickly ran through the cloakroom to the foot of the stairs, and peered up. Yes, they had shut the door behind them, she didn't need to go upstairs herself. A couple of tourists had come in, looking for a nice souvenir. She followed them round, watched every step they took, was indeed about to break her own rule and enquire whether she could be of any assistance, when, embarrassed, they fled – which was a pity, because they had earlier seen, and had at home an ideal gap to hang, between the wall mounted central heating boiler and the cupboard with the Waterford sherry glasses, a spiny lobster badly painted by the gallery owner's aristocratic but untalented paramour.

Upstairs, Maurice, Emily and Peter had searched the flat for anything which might give them some sort of clue where Edwards had taken Anthony – by force, they had assumed; why otherwise would he leave so abruptly? Maurice and Peter looked in all the drawers and cubby holes of the desk, and among the papers on the table, Emily searched the bedroom, bathroom and kitchen. They found nothing, and Emily joined the two men in the living room.

"Did you look under the bed?" Peter asked Emily.

Gazing at the mess of papers on the living room floor, she made no reply, and gathered them up, first arranging them in a tidy pile on the desk, then, when each had yielded no clue, placing it neatly on the table. In between the two stapled pages of a price list for paintings at an exhibition in another local gallery she found a handwritten note.

"Did you see this?" she asked.

Peter looked shiftily at Maurice.

"Did you, Maurice?"

"No, I don't believe so; you didn't?"

"No; sorry Emily. What does it say, please?"

Emily read it.

"One-two-three out, I've got the goods for you here. And some cockles and mussels, hard luck! xx A" and at the top it says 'Totleigh Towers.' It's a woman's writing, I'm sure. No date."

They all stared at it.

"Totleigh Towers rings a bell," said Maurice. "Give me a minute or two."

Emily found nothing else that the men had overlooked.

"We'll take that note with us. I think we should get out now, that girl might come up any time," said Peter, "she's a bit of a worrier. Nice, though."

Emily shook her head at this pointless remark. Peter was also a bit of a worrier, she knew that well.

"Come on then, try and make the door look shut, please," she said.

Outside, the car had, amazingly, escaped the attention of the traffic warden. They squeezed in and Emily drove to the outskirts of the town where they found a small industrial estate where they could park, between a wholesale fishmonger and a tool hire depot. They tried to make sense of the handwritten note. Maurice was squirming around, annoying Frieda who opened the car door, slid off his knee, and stood on the pavement. She had memorized the note. Maurice kept saying, "I know it, it's on the tip of ..." Peter kept reciting, "One two three out", Emily sat quietly. Chris said, "We should have asked the girl if she knew anybody who was allergic to shellfish, you know, cockles and mussels" but as soon as he had said the word "shell fish" Frieda and Tricia knew the answer to that part of the puzzle.

"Those awful paintings!" "Those hopeless pictures!" they said simultaneously.

At more or less the same time, Maurice remembered where he had heard of Totleigh Towers.

"It's Wodehouse! Sir something or other Basset's pile. There was a telly series, you know, it was filmed at Highclere Castle. It's Barry, like the Houses of Parliament."

"Peter, please stop counting" said Emily.

"What?" said Peter.

"You're counting, out loud," she said.

"I'm what?"

"Counting" she replied, raising her voice, as much as she ever did.

"That's it!" he shouted, "it's a nickname, 'One-two-three' it's the Count! And it's her pictures ..."

"What about the 'out'? Of course, she's telling him, the Count's out! Not in, away from home. And 'xx' well that's obvious, and she's Alison, isn't she, so that's the A" said Chris.

"So Totleigh Towers is ..."

"Porthguarnon Castle," said Chris.

"And what are 'the goods'; Hopkinses? What were the others, before the Hopkinses; Wallises?" said Frieda. Then she, too, had a sudden inspiration.

"Bloody Dracula. The girl told us, Edwards said it under his breath, 'Bloody Dracula'. The Count."

"So what's the ... oh my goodness, of course, he's Romanian, he's a Transylvanian Count!"

They had, apparently, parked in such a way as to impede the access to the fish warehouse's back entrance. A small shiny white van, with a whiting making a meal of its own tail painted on the side, had drawn up beside them, and honked its horn. The driver gesticulated then, since Emily gave no indication that she understood, he got out of his van and came over to the Mercedes, waving his arm and looking cross.

Emily and Peter exchanged glances; Maurice saw them do so. Somehow, up to this very moment, he had thought of the six of them as a group, jointly engaged in whatever it was they were jointly engaged in. Emily and Peter had been as much in the dark as the other four; they were just as outraged by Edwards' departure, his abduction, if that's what it was, of Anthony, and they didn't know about Bloody Dracula. But they weren't really a group, with the same aims, were they? The Williamses were part of the fraud, they knew that the paintings they were so cleverly and elaborately marketing were forgeries, even if they didn't know who was painting them, or where, or who was organising the whole network. Who was behind it all; who was the mastermind? They were still criminals, even the delicate, appealing and competent Emily, whom Maurice was now observing intently.

Peter and Emily opened their doors simultaneously. Emily reached for the ignition key, but Maurice had forestalled her, had leaned over and pulled it from its lock. When he was praised for this by his friends afterwards he couldn't claim for sure that he knew what her intentions were; that she meant to deprive them of the ability to follow; it was, he explained, a sort of general feeling that she should be stopped.

Within seconds, Emily and Peter were driving away in the fish van. The van driver ran futilely after them, giving Maurice time to jump out of the front passenger seat of the

Mercedes, push Frieda back into the rear seat which he had just vacated, slide himself into the driver's, start the engine and lay down rubber, leaving the flabbergasted fishmonger to his rage and gesticulations.

The road from the industrial estate joined the road into and out of St Ives which they had followed before – the only road leading west. This must be the direction to take, if the castle is somewhere near Land's End, thought Maurice. Unfortunately, after about a quarter of a mile the road bifurcated. Straight on was the same road they had come down this morning; left was signposted Penzance. Maurice tried to picture in his mind the crooked foot of Cornwall; should he try to find the main A30 near Penzance, or should he carry on along the road which followed the fractured northern coastline, and perhaps cut across south further down? He couldn't decide, they would have to look at the map.

There was no doubt that the southern route around Penzance was the quicker way. It was shorter, and the route, from Penzance at least, lay along a main trunk road. Maurice thrust the map at Chris, told him to navigate, and set off again driving as fast as he could. "We must get there before the other two, mustn't we?" he said. He wasn't used to driving fast in a big car, and the road twisted up and down the hillsides. Cars coming towards him were often forced to squeeze into the hedge as they could see that he appreciated neither how narrow was the road, nor how wide his car. Tricia, who had taken the map from her husband when she saw that he was staring without obvious understanding at the Falmouth page, said, as mildly as she could, "I don't think you'll be able to overtake them, Maurice, she knows the roads better than you. And she was a very good ..."

"All right, there's no need to shout," he replied, braking so hard on a bend that one of the electronic devices corrected the car's trajectory with what seemed to be a series of sledgehammer blows to the wheels.

"Christ Almighty!" Chris exclaimed. Frieda was staring rigidly out of her window; she had been trying to think hard about the last time she had had sex, but without much success.

Maurice was now driving a little more calmly, and Frieda repeated what Tricia had said. Then she added, "We haven't actually decided what we're going to do. When we get there, I mean. Surely, if those two arrive before us ..."

"We don't know that's where they're going, do we? Not for sure," said Chris.

"No, you're right, not for sure. But Edwards has got Anthony, hasn't he? For God's sake, it's our only lead. We ought to make some sort of a plan. We can't just knock on the door and ask to see Mr Evans."

"Well," said Tricia, with a note of doubt in her voice, "Alison did say, drop in at any time, didn't she, Chris? We could say we wondered whether the Chagalls had come back from the restorers."

"I suppose we could," Chris replied, "it might seem a bit rude, it's nearly lunch time, she might think we were just after a free meal."

"Oh gosh yes," said Maurice, "we must remember our manners. It wouldn't be the thing at all."

"There's a pub in this village, look," said Chris, "perhaps we ..."

"It's a joke, Chris," said Tricia, "It doesn't matter if Alison thinks we've come to service the Aga as long as she lets us in. Verstehen?"

"And then, well, we tell her about Armstrong's fake Hopkins. We tell her that Edwards has driven off in a stolen van with a load of the Williamses' pictures. We say that we know she's having an affair ..."

"No Frieda, we don't really know that," said Tricia.

"Of course we do. All that about the Count being out? Why else would she tell him that?"

"All right. Couldn't we just say 'very friendly'?"

"For goodness sake. Then we say that we think their Hopkinses are fake, too. And we see what she says."

"But if the Williamses are already there ..."

"We shall just have to play it by ear. Will they have phoned her?" asked Maurice.

"No, I don't think so. They'll want to surprise her; they're chasing Edwards too, don't forget."

Chris had noticed a filling station on the A30 which they had joined after Maurice had, to his passengers' considerable disquiet, negotiated his way through two narrow gullies and avoided a family of white peacocks which had fluttered down from the high granite wall of an old farmhouse close to the road. Nobody remarked on this because, in the circumstances, it was just the sort of thing they might have expected. The petrol gauge was getting low – this was the sort of thing Chris noticed – but not so low, he thought, as to make it worthwhile risking another rebuke from his wife. But what he saw on the forecourt was certainly something to mention.

"That was the fish van at the pumps there, you know," he said, "they must have been out of diesel. It was definitely them."

"Well, what a bit of luck!" said Frieda, after the chorus of noisy relief had died down.

"Yes, well done for noticing that, darling," said Tricia, squeezing his hand. "About seven or eight miles now, I should think."

Chapter 22

Tuesday August 15   Jane   David   All the politicians and senior civil servants

"How do you like your porridge?" Jane called to David, who was in the shower. She was just following the microwave instructions to the letter, and she realised that whatever he replied, what he was actually going to get was predetermined. She had bought the oats, which came in a packet apparently dedicated to a religious sect, because she thought it was a sort of cooking compromise between cornflakes and the bacon eggs and sausage thing which she did not feel up to.

"Porridge? Oh, anyhow is fine. With some honey?"

Damn.

"What about marmalade?"

"Possibly sugar?"

"Great."

Over breakfast, at seven in the morning, with the sun streaming in over her table and more good strong coffee in her new large cafetière, Jane felt as happy as she could remember. She looked round her room with satisfaction. She was pleased with the changes she had made; the new pictures, the brightly coloured throw on the settee, the re-arrangement of the furniture so that it was possible to see her view – the various roads, far below, and the corner of the wall of the entrance to the garden of Buckingham Palace. This was, in truth, merely a glimpse, and a glimpse of what was only a symbol, but at that moment it seemed important to her. The main change however, and the change without which all the others would have meant very little that morning as she prepared for work, was that the dining chair opposite was not unoccupied. It was occupied by David MacMaster, who was her boyfriend. She shut her eyes, told herself to grow up. But what other word was there? Her last relationship hadn't been at all satisfactory; he'd turned out to be a bit of a wet. Not like

David. The man in Munich, of course, had been different again. Well, there was no point in going there; he had been dead for over a year. And he had been wicked. She looked at David again, who smiled at her.

"You look happy. Why are you so cheerful today?"

There were many replies which she could have made, but she just smiled back.

"What's he doing today, then?"

"PM early morning; I go with, and come back, then collect. Afternoon; the House, go with, come back, collect. Off at six."

"In-between time? Tea and chat with Lucy?"

"Richards will be there most of the day, I'll be running through schedules and reports and that sort of stuff some of the time. But yes, I've no doubt tea and chat will occur, and, it is to be hoped, jam tarts."

"Bakes a good jaytee does she?"

"Pastry's a tiny bit too thick, perhaps. But very acceptable. What have you got on?"

"This and that, you know."

"No, I don't know, do I?"

"Ah now, there's something I ought to tell you. Charles has been giving me old-fashioned looks for a few days now and yesterday he gave me these. He asked me to pass one on to you."

He handed Jane a slip of paper, and put his own on the table in front of him. Jane looked at hers. It was headed with what Jane recognised as her own HR number and the letters ASC. Underneath the heading it was blank. She looked questioningly at David, who said, "You've got to write down my name, my department, and the date our, um, friendship started. Then you've got to sign it."

"You're joking!"

"No, I'm not. I can see the point, can't you?"

"What does ASC stand for?"

"Acknowledged Service Connection. Look, if we don't write it down, then Charles will. And since Charles knows, everybody else does too."

"It just seems a bit cold, somehow. OK, wilco." She filled in the form and handed it back to David. "Will you give it to Charles when you go in?"

"Sure."

"Don't you mind? Just a bit?"

"No, not at all. Why should I?"

Jane considered it for a moment, and realised that she had thought a secret relationship to be somehow more romantic than an Acknowledged Connection. But it wasn't, and she was pleased that David was happy to do his Acknowledging too.

Lucy hadn't been baking jam tarts, but had been trying her hand at a sort of pastry bun which she said they used to have for tea in her home town of Preston. She couldn't remember whether or not her mother had baked them herself; she suspected they had been bought from the shop on the main road. These buns consisted of thick greasy pastry, slightly flaky on the outside, wrapped round a glutinous plug of syrupy currants, and Jane thought that the inhabitants of Eccles must have worked long and hard at tiring manual jobs to justify, or even make it possible to consume, such calorie intensive stodge.

While they were drinking their early morning coffee, and pushing bits of uneaten Eccles cake around their plates, Jane decided that the Acknowledgement allowed her to tell Lucy about her new boyfriend, who she said was an officer in the foreign service, slightly senior to herself. Yes, he was good looking, a bit older than herself, no, not Public School, had been to Oxford (she stopped herself saying 'too'), was witty: and much else besides. She was surprised at the pleasure she derived from being able to do this, and it also made her realise how friendly she and Lucy had become. It was only later on in the morning, as she was mentally compiling her report – not her Protection Officer report, but the secret report to the SD – that she started to feel uneasy about how close their friendship was becoming. But she argued to herself that this friendship was genuine, and reciprocal, and it hadn't been contrived deceitfully. This seemed to make a difference, but she still hoped Lucy didn't mention anything in confidence, maybe something quite personal, which she, Jane, had then to decide whether to report or not. Somewhere in the back of her mind a thought was developing, which at the moment she tried to suppress, that this would not be an issue at all for most field agents. What would David say? If only she could ask him, but of course she couldn't.

Just after ten o'clock, Alice drove up in the armoured Jaguar, and they set off for Downing Street to pick up Armstrong. Jane got a friendly wave from the young constable on duty, who had gone out of his way to chat to her on a number of occasions, and was, in fact, trying to pluck up the courage to ask her out for a drink. They didn't have to wait long for Armstrong, and they were back home soon after eleven.

"So," Armstrong said to Jane as he hung up his jacket, "what do you think of the Hopkins?"

He gestured towards the room where the paintings were hung and walked down the hall to its door, obviously expecting her to follow. There had been an edge to his voice which made Jane uneasy.

"It's not ours, of course," he added, pausing and turning round, "it's Mickey's. Axel brought it, you've met him, haven't you?"

"Yes, once or twice now – the first time, I thought his Bentley was the most beautiful car I'd ever seen. But it's actually Mr Michaelov's, isn't it?" She was aiming to divert the conversation from the topic of the painting; she was surprised that he had suddenly brought it up, and hesitant about replying.

Armstrong laughed. "Oh, that car! We took it on holiday once, Lucy and me, you know, a few days in East Anglia. We visited Waddesdon in it as well; it seemed very appropriate. Yes, Axel brought it round for us occasionally, before I had to have you lot around, and armour plate, and all that nonsense."

Jane was about to ask him about Waddesdon which she'd read about but never visited, but he carried on,

"However, I would really like to have your opinion of the Hopkins; I'd like to talk to you about it. I believe you were on duty when Axel had one of his, well Lucy and me, we call them viewings? We know that Mickey sometimes discreetly sells some of them on – well, probably Axel does that for him – but it suits us, we'd never have such paintings around otherwise."

He opened the gallery room door and went in, beckoning her to follow. She had hardly moved when she heard his shout.

"What the ... Jane, the painting's gone, who's ... Lucy! Lucy!"

Martin Richards, the Protection Unit constable whose shift overlapped with Jane's, came rushing out of their little room. Armstrong turned to him.

"The picture, it's gone, do you ..."

"Yes sir, your wife took it, just before you got back. Said she might be a while, left without telling me where she was going. There was a phone call, she said, it might have been a text, I can't remember which, and I think she said from Axel, but then she just dashed off. I've just been logging it, she's not supposed ..."

There was a short silence.

"Yes, of course, I should have remembered," said Armstrong, calm again. "We made an arrangement with a gallery, I had temporarily forgotten. You're quite right, she should have explained it to you in advance, and allowed you to arrange her transport. I'm sure she'll apologise to you when she returns. Thank you for explaining your concern to me."

Armstrong's first alarmed cry came back into Jane's head. *Jane, the painting's gone.* Perhaps it was her memory, playing tricks. No, it wasn't. He had called her *Jane.* He knew who she was.

She must report this, immediately. She must tell David as quickly as she could. Then, as she reached for her phone, the obvious possibility struck her. She felt the attack of despair; a cold, dead feeling, a gap where her heart had been, quite different from physical fear. *David knew already.* She was immediately as sure of this as she had been sure of his trust and love. But why had he needed to deceive her? Why had he – or they – built up this fiction? And if he could deceive her in this, then he could have deceived her in what was so much more important to her. Why had he needed their relationship to be anything but simply professional? She was suddenly, irrationally, desperate. There were so many other explanations, but none of them entered her mind. And, did Armstrong know that he'd called her Jane? She looked at him. Yes, he did.

When Richards had retreated to complete his report, Armstrong beckoned Jane into the kitchen, where he filled the kettle.

"Tea?" he said. She shook her head.

"Yeah, right," he said, in an accent more of his youth than his parliamentary years, and fetched a bottle of gin from the dresser and some tonic from the fridge. He poured two drinks and pushed one over to her.

"What's happening, Jane?" he said, "Just a quick drink, then I think it's you and me to Henry. Or Jennifer. Or both, I don't know. Jennifer's man MacMaster's your boss, isn't he? Could you ring them now, please. Use your SD phone."

"They're sending the fire engine," she said, after she had made the call. "There's a meeting; they're all coming on here – no, they didn't say. David, sorry, MacMaster's liaising with PU. They'll be here in forty minutes. In the meantime... " she paused, unsure how to continue, "could you, that is, would it be possible for you to tell me ... " she broke off, realising that she had no personal rights in this matter, that her own distress, her stab of dismay at Armstrong's use of David's name, were issues for her and for no-one else, and in any case Armstrong's own problems were now much greater than hers. Her sudden grief had made her forget her sense of proportion as well as her place. Jane, who only twelve hours previously had been happier than she could remember, now felt as if the foolish edifice of her self-deception was crumbling round her feet.

But Armstrong had seen the shock in her eyes when he had let drop Henry's name, and Jennifer's, and the way in which it had turned into pain, and her complexion had changed, when he had spoken MacMaster's. He liked Jane, and saw no reason to leave her in unnecessary distress, because he had guessed what had caused it.

"I only knew anything about it a couple of days ago; and it was only this morning that I was told how serious it was. You know, you've obviously heard of, Sir William Buoy-Dodd? He told me, the PM got him in first thing this morning. The PM stayed. Buoy-Dodd dropped his po-faced look; I've never seen him so worried in my life before. They tried to pretend – oh, that doesn't matter, it's water under – I don't really blame them. But now, apparently, they think that there's another threat, a connection with something much worse. Look, you've got to know Lucy quite well, haven't you? It wasn't just pretence, was it, just a front you were putting on, just doing your job?"

Jane shook her head, and was going to answer, but Armstrong continued.

"No, I didn't think it was. You seemed too nice for that." He paused. "Was the idea that I ... did they think that I ...?"

She found herself unable to pretend that she didn't know what he was talking about.

"No, no, I just had to ... fit in? Be friendly. I don't think you were ... I don't know, I don't really know what Dame Jennifer planned."

"No, well, – about Lucy; has she said anything to you about the pictures? The one picture, I suppose, the Hopkins which they all say is a fake? You know it's a fake, don't you?"

Jane nodded.

"Did Lucy suspect anything?"

"Not this morning, I'm sure. We had quite a long talk; she'd made Eccles cakes. We talked about cooking."

"What else?"

"A friend of mine," she said, miserably.

"She didn't say anything? No clue why she might have gone off so suddenly?"

"No, honestly, no clue. The transport will be here in five minutes, I'll have to go and log off. Would you excuse me?"

"Of course."

Jane returned to the PU room, where Richards was waiting impatiently. She didn't think that he liked her very much.

"Had a quick drink with the boss, then? Make sure you enter it."

She stared him down and leaned over to log off. She saw that Richards had made an entry much earlier:

"Frederick Smith phoned; Penny North to return call when convenient. She knows the number."

At the time the call had been made she was in the car with Alice and Armstrong; Danny was also there. Frederick Smith was David; 'when convenient' meant when in private.

She hurried to the cloakroom, and shut herself in the lavatory, but David's calls had been rerouted, and when Charles answered she ended the call without saying a word.

For fifteen seconds or so she had been subconsciously aware of an approaching emergency vehicle; she realised this only when the bell and klaxon stopped. She should tell Armstrong that his transport would arrive within a minute; the din was always switched off well before the vehicle stopped. She wondered whether he knew what to expect; perhaps he thought that 'fire engine' was SD slang. The interior had been refitted somewhat in the manner of a police command post, with rather more sophisticated electronics and better padded seats, but on the outside it was a fire engine, pillar box red and decked about with ladders and hosepipes. On this occasion it was delivering, not collecting. If Martin Richards was surprised when a fire engine drew up outside, he was amazed to see a number of middle aged men and women, smartly and fairly formally dressed in civilian clothes, jump from the vehicle, followed by a member of PU staff, whom he recognised, and his amazement turned to consternation when he recognised the last man to emerge.

They sat round Lucy's dining table, after Jane had hurriedly removed the boxes and baskets of coloured yarn, and unclamped the loom. Henry sat at one end, Jennifer at the other. David sat on Jennifer's left, and had signalled Jane to sit next to him. She tried to indicate soundlessly that she had returned his call, but she thought that he probably failed to interpret her gestures, constrained as she was by the presence of what seemed to her to be the entire British establishment, assembled in Lucy Armstrong's dining room. On Jane's left was a woman only slightly older than herself, who offered her a minimal smile, which Jane returned. On this woman's left sat a man unknown to Jane, and on the right of Henry at the other end of the table, sat C, taller than the others, partly on account of his height, partly his ram-rod bearing. On Henry's left sat Sir William Buoy-Dodd, the frankly terrifying Cabinet Secretary, on his left another unknown woman, on her left, Armstrong. The last two to arrive sat in the two remaining chairs; another young woman, with the same confident bearing of the woman sitting next to Jane. She sat next to Jennifer, leaving the seat opposite Jane for the Prime Minister. Amazingly to Jane, although not to most of the others, who knew how carefully he was briefed for meetings, he leaned across to her and said, "I enjoyed your mother's Wife of Bath. Hit just the right note, I thought." Then he nodded to the woman who had come in with him, who glanced once at her laptop and started speaking.

Jane listened intently to this woman's summary of the reasons for the meeting, its background and the problem it was meant to resolve. She explained why the disappearance of Armstrong's wife had led to such apparently disproportionate activity. Jane quickly inferred that the speaker was the civil servant who held the Western Africa desk – Foreign Office jargon meaning that she was in charge of British relations with countries in that part of the world. It was, apparently, common knowledge around this table – and Jane had learned by now to give no indication that this was the first she had heard about it – that an important deal, a bilateral treaty, was about to be negotiated with the President of Campa Fidela, by means of which the British Government would obtain access to all sorts of minerals, including, of course oil, in return for help building an infrastructure, an education system, a health system and a working democracy. At this point of the Foreign Office woman's report, when she paused, Jane could see that raised eyebrows, a ripple of movement, a shuffle of papers gave an indication that, perhaps, she had a little more to say on the issue. "And an army, of course," she continued, and the ripple subsided. The British negotiating team would be led by Armstrong, and the president of Campa Fidela was, not to put too fine a point on it, desperate to make a deal. The Prime Minister interrupted.

"He's scared shitless that they're going to be invaded by West Kasai. And he's not a bad bloke, all things considered. And this agreement isn't just 'important', it would certainly hasten the end of our economic woe."

"Yes, Prime Minister. I believe a modest task force – Gerry?"

"First planes two days, Marines four days, first main wave ten days, second fourteen, Prime Minister."

Gerry was the man two to Jane's left. She leaned forward to adjust her jacket, and glanced at him. She hadn't recognised him previously, because she had only seen him once before, and he had been in uniform. He was the Chief of Defence Staff, an Air Chief Marshall. She tried to look calm, and possibly succeeded, but it was very, very difficult.

The Foreign Office woman continued.

"The Director General of SD," she inclined her head towards C, who nodded stiffly, remembering that he had been a brigadier on the Falkland Islands when Bumpers had been a flight lieutenant trying to blag his way onto one of the Vulcans, "the Director General of SD has made this group aware that efforts have been made to discredit the Treasurer, who has carefully built up a position of trust vis-a-vis President Tsafeeto."

She carried on, explaining why this attack on the person of Armstrong was being made, and in whose interests.

This woman's exposition, Jane thought, was excellent, and the logical way in which it was delivered equally commendable. But she had an irritating way of pausing after making an important point, raising her eyebrows, looking around the room and saying "D'you see?" and pronouncing the word 'see' as if it had the syllable 'ah' as a suffix. This reminded Jane of a lecturer at Oxford, who had also taken his glasses off and waved them as he reached the final phoneme. She found that her concentration was in danger of veering towards this mannerism, waiting for it to happen rather than taking in the content of the speech, and, each time it did, surprised that the Prime Minister wasn't annoyed that the speaker was in effect asking him if he grasped what she was saying. Despite this distraction, however, Jane understood that there were 'powerful international interests' who stood to gain by the collapse of the Campa Fidela regime; multinational companies, even countries, well known for the ruthless methods which they were quite willing to use; bribery, blackmail, the employment of mercenaries, even murder – this preferably, but not exclusively, within Africa itself. Stories could be planted in newspapers, some of which were, in any case, owned by companies where interlocking directorships and shareholdings, or the circles of acquaintance of some employees, meant that there were few degrees of separation between the respectable and the nefarious.

During this report, as the Foreign Office woman droned on – Jane used this term in her mind, but was aware that it was unjustly pejorative – she watched the Prime Minister who, she realised, seemed intent upon its effect on his friend, Armstrong. The person whose disappearance had brought this issue to a head was, after all, Armstrong's wife, not some stranger about whom they might feel concern, but only in a distant, objective sort of way. And, clearly, Armstrong was distressed. In any other circumstances he might show it more; but in other circumstances, without his knowledge of the possible reasons for her disappearance, would he actually be distressed? Leaving the house carrying a picture, with her phone switched off, for about an hour might be unusual, uncharacteristic, but it hardly counted as vanishing.

When this report ended, Buoy-Dodd spoke for a minute or two, confirming the importance of the talks so carefully orchestrated by Armstrong, and his opinion that no other British politician than Armstrong would be trusted in the same way. He also outlined some of the threats which had been neutralised, and he mentioned the opportune death in a road accident of one of the journalists trying to dig up dirt.

"Opportune?" asked one of the Foreign Office women.

"Yes, Felicity, a drunken driver in a stolen car, also killed." Henry then explained that there was a real risk that a people-trafficking operation, involving, as such operations usually do, prostitution and abuse, could also be linked. The merest hint of a connection to such activities would mean the end of any political career, and with this particular career the Campa Fidela treaty also.

"Could you enlarge on that please, Henry, what link?" asked Felicity.

Henry explained about the forged paintings; that the owner of the genuine paintings, Armstrong's friend Michaelov, had only very briefly fallen under suspicion, but that now it was believed that a certain shadowy Romanian, possibly, but probably not, the holder of some title or other, was behind both the forgery fraud and the trafficking operation. They surmised that Mrs Armstrong had been asked, or ordered, to return a picture which the Security Directorate believed to be a counterfeit. The Service did not know whether this had been part of a systematic plot to discredit Armstrong, or a simple fraud for gain.

He ended by speaking directly to Armstrong.

"We all understand, sir, the distress which you must be feeling. We have nothing but admiration for the stoicism which you are showing," he looked round the table, and everyone nodded or murmured their agreement, "and we shall pull out all the stops to end this affair and end it with your wife safely back home."

Armstrong blinked two or three times, nodded and said thank you.

"Which is why," the Prime Minister said to Jennifer, "I am treating this affair as an absolute priority."

The Air Chief Marshall let slip a fairly obvious stage cough.

"Yes, OK Gerry," said the PM, "not an absolute priority like salads for school children or a breakwater for Bognor. I mean, an *absolute priority*. Keep your task force ready; Condition Red, ladies and gentlemen."

Chapter 23

Tuesday August 15   David   Jane   Alan   Armstrong   various Senior Persons

David was as anxious to tell Jane that he had not been party to concealing anything from her, had not *used* her in any way, as she was to hear it, but he had to wait a little while until he was able to do this. Their helicopter had landed in the surprisingly extensive grounds of Beckton sewage treatment plant in Newham, and they had been taken as pillion passengers on motorbikes the short distance to City Airport. Alan Green was already sitting in the Cessna Citation, which whisked them to the little used Predannack airfield on the Lizard. There they transferred to one of the search-and-rescue Sea King helicopters which were always on patrol, or on training exercises, along the Cornish coast, and provoked no curiosity among the fishermen and farmers. It hadn't been possible during the flights for Jane and David to talk privately at all, either because of the extraordinary clatter the helicopters made, or because Alan Green was sitting between them. They were deposited by the Sea King in a field near Land's End; the cheery pilot, a naval Lieutenant, had offered to winch them down from a hundred feet, just for fun. Jane had wanted to, but David had decided it would be self-indulgent. The meeting in Victoria Park had ended at two o'clock; by six they were sharing a tussocky, windswept field near Land's End with some shaggy long horned cattle, which had looked up with no great interest at the helicopter, and then resumed their grazing. David, Jane and Alan were sensibly dressed in the naval ratings' overalls which the helicopter pilot had given them; two medium and one small, she said, no gender differentiation, she had had to go and get them herself from the stores at RNAS Culdrose and sign a special chitty. Anyone would have thought she was going to take them home to do the gardening in.

"Well, we do, don't we?" said the co-pilot. "Speak for yourself," she replied, and (to the three passengers) "here are some pasties for your lunch. And what's this? Irn-bru? Not sure what that tastes like."

"Steel gurrduz," said the co-pilot.

The pasties were good, the Irn-bru novel, and Jane's overalls tight, which she didn't mind at all, although the effect was partly spoiled by the Kevlar waistcoat . The helicopter took off and carried on around the cape, as if on a routine patrol. Alan excused himself temporarily and made for the cover of blackthorn, gorse and small dogged oak trees at the edge of the field. This was the first opportunity which Jane and David had to talk, but it wasn't really necessary any more; David had obviously been as surprised by the turn of events as she; the decision to come clean to Armstrong had been taken by C, Buoy-Dodd and then the PM himself, and had happened before the flight, if such it was, of Lucy Armstrong. Jane and David touched hands, and snatched a quick smile at each other, then Alan returned, struggling with the brand new metal zip.

Charles, as a matter of routine, had checked with K Branch ops control on mobile phone coverage along the South Cornwall coastline. They had told him that it was classed from Patchy to Non-existent, so he had asked the navy at Culdrose to supply the team with the two way radios which they found worked best in the granite landscape of West Penwith. David and Alan buttoned up their collars against the wind, and set off uphill towards the coast road, only a few hundred metres north. Jane took the cliff path west. They would communicate when each was in position.

*****

Fifteen seconds after the Prime Minister had uttered his decisive *'absolute priority'* at a quarter to two in the afternoon, Sir William Buoy-Dodd had telephoned the Commissioner of Metropolitan Police. Sir Richard had telephoned the Director of GCHQ, and within thirty minutes almost the entire surveillance capacity of the realm was devoted to the task of locating Lucy Armstrong. Her name, and various other keys such as 'Dracula' and 'Hopkins' were fed into the word recognition software, and the virtual switch of the SD computers monitoring the British communications network was thrown to 'Comprehensive', a procedure so momentous that Parliament had made it dependent upon authorisation by three Law Lords (or two Law Lords and the Master of the Rolls). Luckily, GCHQ was able to bypass this legal obligation by asking the resident officer of the USA National Security Agency to enter the new keywords and loop its feed back into the British system.

It took eighteen minutes to establish that Lucy's credit card had been used at Paddington Station, another four to identify the train, coach and seat. The train was the five past two o'clock to Penzance, arriving at half past seven. Detectives reached the station in six minutes, and had confirmed almost immediately that a lady carrying a large rectangular parcel had boarded the train at five minutes to two. She had bought a through ticket to Penzance, but every station on its route would have to be monitored. The train had left on time, which meant that it would already have made its first stop, at Reading, at twenty five minutes past two. It was now nearly ten to three, and the train's next stop was Taunton, at eleven minutes to four.

By this time the Prime Minister, the Foreign Office and the Defence staff had returned to Whitehall, leaving Armstrong, Sir William and Sir Richard, Dame Jennifer, Henry, and the two junior officers, David and Jane.

"I want one person running this," the PM had said as he left, "to report directly to the Cabinet Secretary. Bill, you must consult Richard over who it should be. I'm having a teleconference with Jacques Santer and Gerhard Schröder about various payments which we mustn't call agricultural subsidies. I can't get out of it, but you can interrupt. Jim, go and get some food down you, stop worrying, we shall sort this. Bill, keep the Treasurer in the loop."

Sir William looked at Sir Richard, who in turn looked at Jennifer and Henry.

Henry spoke first. "I don't want to pass the buck, C, but we might have to cut some corners here ..."

Sir William indicated an urgent need for something he had left in another room, and said that he would be back in a minute or two. He beckoned Armstrong to accompany him.

"... and if anything is a ticklish issue ..." Henry continued, C nodded, and Jennifer indicated her agreement.

"Henry, I should value your liaison skills. Your networks. Are you happy with this?"

"Of course."

Sir William returned, and C told him that he would recommend Jennifer as head of the operation.

"Very well. I shall return to more mundane duties. In the absence of the Treasurer I have to preside over a duel between the Chancellor and the Home Secretary."

"A duel à l'outrance, I trust?" replied Sir Richard, grasping him by the elbow and steering him towards the door. The Cabinet Secretary chuckled.

"Possibly. I have already arranged with the Home Secretary's second that his powder should be damp." Before C, who was anxious to leave Jennifer to get on with things, could edge Buoy-Dodd out of the room, he turned and said to Jennifer, "Keep me up to speed, won't you, Jennifer. Every two hours or so?"

David and Jane had remained silent as the great people had conferred, but it was to David's mobile that the information about Lucy's train journey was sent. Jennifer had already logged him as executive head of Stoker, her choice of name for the operation which she had been the first to suggest at the meeting Anthony had attended. Stoker would be the basis for any new plan, which would have to incorporate the 'rescue', as they decided to term it, of Lucy Armstrong. Jane was convinced that this was an appropriate word; the others had more open minds. Armstrong himself had not returned to the dining room; when Jennifer, Henry, David and Jane were the only four left in the room, and before they could start restructuring Stoker, Jane said that she would go quickly and check that Armstrong was 'all right'.

"Of course he's not all right" said Jennifer sharply. "But yes, go and see what he's doing."

Armstrong was sitting on his own at the kitchen table. He must have put the kettle on, because it was steaming away on the hot plate of the range. He said hello to Jane, stood up and took two old and stained mugs from the draining board. They were made from some light weight material like melamine and were decorated with silhouettes of children on horseback.

"Do you want that cup of tea now?" he asked. He picked up a small jug, which didn't look like a milk jug to Jane, more like a gravy boat, and opened the door of the fridge. She didn't know how to reply.

"Actually I'd love one, but Dame Jennifer and the Deputy Director are still here, I'm not sure ..."

Armstrong hesitated, and looked round him, as if there was someone else there who would tell him how to handle this.

"All right, I'll make a pot. Maria doesn't seem to be around. Would they like biscuits, do you think?"

In the two hours or so which had elapsed since he had first shown how shocked he was by Lucy's sudden departure, Jane watched Armstrong's qualities of leadership dissipating as his character became something much more ordinary, that of a man in distress needing help and comfort. This made her feel sad to start with; she had been attracted by his strength, but then, if he hadn't shown his feelings in these circumstances he would have been a different, less humane person. He was, for sure, a man who could cope easily with political adversity, who could deal with 'events'; but threats to his family were different.

"I'll go and ask them. You make the tea?"

"Yes of course, the tea. I think there's some sugar in this cupboard, we don't usually take it, not many people do these days, do they? Will you go and ask them if they want any sugar?" After he had spoken these words Jane could see him frown, and he shook his head as if to scatter all such trivialities. In something approaching his old manner he said, "I would be grateful if you would ask Jennifer if they could check up on Caroline. My daughter. As a matter of urgency."

Jane returned quickly to the dining room.

"He's very upset. Struggling. Dame Jennifer, he asked if you could, 'check up on Caroline', he said."

Henry answered, "No need for that, she's always well protected, and I did check, as soon as his wife went missing. Caroline's fine, she's on a campsite near Bordeaux, with her boyfriend, his mate and his mate's girlfriend. The girlfriend is quite sound, and she keeps in touch with us."

"Good, I'll tell him she's safe. Also," with a little trepidation, "would you like some tea? And do you take sugar and would you like a biscuit?"

"Yes, no and yes." Jennifer replied immediately, "Is he making it? Good, gives him something to do. Ryan, go and help him, find a tray or a doily or something. You're leaving with MacMaster in fifteen minutes, so you won't have time for any yourself. The Deputy Director and I will stay and take care of things here. Tell the Treasurer we'll join him in five minutes. Who's the other PU here? Fetch him into the kitchen, get him talking to Armstrong about football or something."

Jane went back to the kitchen first, and found Armstrong standing at the sink, resting his hands on the draining board and looking out of the window. He had found a packet of biscuits, dark chocolate digestives, but hadn't got round to opening it. There was a crumpled tea towel on the work surface near his left hand, and when he turned round towards Jane he said, "I was just drying these mugs. They're pony club, you can see, can't you?" He showed her the motifs on the mugs, which she had already noticed. "The three of us, we used to go away to gymkhanas on Saturdays. Caroline was in the team, and Lucy was one of the mums who helped. We'd never been horsey, but the other parents were very good, they showed us what to do. I wasn't in Parliament then, of course, just the local council" ...a fleeting smile ..."and I had some weekends off. On the whole they kept quiet about politics, social issues; just a few comments about gypsies and welfare scroungers."

What was it about him that was different, Jane thought; it wasn't particularly what he said – he had often chatted about fairly mundane topics – and she didn't think it was the way he said it. Perhaps it was pheromonal, perhaps he was discharging different chemicals and she had subconsciously registered the change? Or perhaps it was her own position which had altered, since whatever happened next would be down to the team that she was in, not to Armstrong or his; she no longer had to pretend to be some sort of junior security trainee, well down the pecking order. Not that her perch was particularly high in the hen house even now. But still.

"Why do you think Lucy is taking this bloody painting to Cornwall?" he asked her. "What's the connection? Do you think she knows it's a fake? Did you tell her?"

"No, of course not," Jane answered with as much emphasis as she could. "Certainly none of us. But perhaps someone else did. Did that man who works for the Russians find out?"

"Axel? I don't see how, it was only luck, wasn't it? It had fooled a lot of people, hadn't it? Experts, I mean. I suppose she might have found out somehow? What about those other people who were here last week? The fellow that Henry told me took your chap MacMaster's gun off him? Unbelievable. And all the others? Frieda Semperdine? I've met her before. Perhaps that's why Lucy's rushing off with it. She might be taking it, getting rid of it, back to Axel perhaps; to protect me, well, both of us, of course, if the wretched thing's a fake, and apparently there's something else going on too, something much more dangerous. It could be that, couldn't it?"

He brightened up again. "Yes, that's probably the answer. I understand you're going to be chasing the train. Your lot will be getting on at Taunton, presumably?"

"Detectives, sir, Taunton police. There are Special Branch officers at Portishead near Bristol and they're already on their way, but it's unlikely they'll get there in time, nor can anyone from SD, our lot, that is. But the CID have a photo and full description. They'll be perfectly competent to identify her."

"But what will they do then? She won't take kindly to being ordered around by two blokes, especially if they're in civvies."

"They'll have been properly briefed, sir."

If only she could be confident that that was true.

She added, "They're not stupid, they know whose wife she is. And they won't be blokes, they'll be women."

"I don't want her going anywhere without at least two of you – that is, of course, you're not really PU, I mean at least two people who can protect her. And it goes without saying, nowhere near this dealer, gallery owner, Axel uses, what's he called?"

"Edwards, sir."

"That's right. He's a possible link to, I'm not sure that I believe this, Dracula, isn't he?"

Armstrong seemed to have recovered some of his authority.

"In fact, I just want her home. As soon as anyone reaches her, make sure she rings me."

"MacMaster's the operational leader, sir, I'll tell him, of course."

"Do that. I'll tell the Deputy Director."

There were only five minutes left before Jane had to leave with David, and it wasn't particularly easy for her to persuade Martin Richards to alter his routine, which at the moment involved logging, with conscientious – the word Jane used to herself was pedantic – accuracy, the unusual events of the last two hours. Important visitors he was used to, but they didn't often arrive together, unannounced, in a fire engine. He didn't at first take kindly to being asked by Jane to go and chat to the Treasurer because he regarded her as his junior, which, in PU terms, was certainly true. She had to say that one of the big-wigs had especially asked that he should do this, because in the circumstances (which she did not specify) Armstrong needed close monitoring and he was much more experienced than she was. So he agreed, asking her to complete the computer-work. She was sure that Constable Richards would be interested in football, a subject about which no politician – especially one from Liverpool – dared remain ignorant, and there was a burning issue over the ownership of Prescot United, which had been grabbed in a dawn raid by the Sultan of Q'mquot.

Soon she found herself jogging with David from the house on Wetherell Road into Victoria Park and towards a point between the fountain and the bandstand, where a tiny red helicopter was waiting. Jane thought at first it was an air ambulance, because her mind was running along the lines of phoney emergency vehicles, such as the fire engine, but in fact it was one of the helicopters used by the National Grid to make sure that there were no problems with the overhead lines, and that no-one was using a digger near an underground cable. They squeezed in and it whirred away, heading east.

August 15 Afternoon   Lucy   Axel   Johnson

"Madam, I must ask you to place your large package in the racks provided at the end of the carriage."

The fat lady sitting next to Lucy in the aircraft-like seats of the two o'clock to Penzance nodded her vigorous agreement. And this was not unreasonable, because although Lucy was doing her best to hold the disputed Hopkins at the angle which least inconvenienced her neighbour, although this meant that it dug painfully into her own right leg just above the kneecap, it still protruded into the space in front, and only slightly to the left of this lady's head, a lady who was already uncomfortably jammed, by virtue of her girth, into a seat which had been designed for the average. Just as Anthony had wanted to say, ten days previously, "I can't because my gun's in it", but obviously couldn't, so Lucy wanted to say, "I can't because it's worth a million pounds," and, again, obviously couldn't.

The ticket inspector sighed.   Once upon a time conductors – guards, they had been called – of railway trains had been respected members of the official classes. They had worn tailored uniforms of three piece dark blue serge with a watch chain and silver whistle looped over their stomachs. They had metal badges, polished like the insignia of the Blues and Royals. Now, she wore a skirt and blouse of humdrum design and fabric. Mind you, she was quite well paid, after her year's training. And so she should be; she couldn't imagine that there was anywhere better designed than a railway carriage to encourage bad temper and arguments between cramped and disgruntled travellers, especially if the train was running late. She was expected to remain calm yet authoritative. In fact, her job depended on it.

"Madam, you must place your large package in the racks provided at the end of the carriage."

Lucy was travelling Standard class.   It just hadn't occurred to her to buy a First class ticket; she never did when travelling on her own, despite the entreaties of the bodyguard who usually accompanied her.

"Would there be more room in First?" she asked. "Maybe I could find a seat with an empty one next to it?"

The conductor was surprised, but relieved.

"There are some at the moment, yes Madam, but it may still be a problem if the train fills up; but I don't expect it will, not many Firsts get on at Taunton, more leave usually. But ..." she hesitated, she could see that if she didn't find a solution the fat woman was going to give her stick, she was already snorting and wobbling her chins about, "... it should really go in the rack, it's a safety regulation." But she could see why the passenger didn't want to put it on the rack, it was very clumsily wrapped, it looked like a picture which could easily be damaged by the corner of a suitcase. "You'll have to pay to upgrade, it's a lot extra. Well, perhaps I could do a cheap one, I suppose, I could just ... look, come with me and I'll find you somewhere, somewhere suitable."

Lucy struggled off to follow the conductor, being forced to squeeze past the bulbous knees of her neighbour who was certainly not going to make the effort to unwedge herself and rise for Lucy's convenience. The conductor found her a temporary seat in the corner of the buffet compartment, where she could prop the painting up on the floor against the side of the carriage.

"What about your other luggage?" asked the conductor.

"I haven't got any," she replied. The conductor realised that she wasn't even carrying a handbag.

"It's all right, I've got my purse in my pocket, I never carry a bag."

Girls with rucksacks, off camping or to a festival, maybe; the conductor had never before encountered a middle aged lady, wearing ordinary but definitely not chain store clothes, travelling with neither handbag nor shoulder bag. And she had said as they were looking for a suitable seat that she was quite prepared to pay a First class fare. All very odd. She had an idea.

"I think I should just check your ticket, madam, if you don't mind, I'm sure you understand." Lucy was now beyond understanding anything, so she just nodded and fumbled out her ticket.

"I see it was bought on a card, madam." That was a shot in the dark, but who paid cash for a ticket costing sixty pounds? "So might I just check it?"

She memorised the name, and handed the card back. The name was vaguely familiar, but she didn't bother to try and make any connection. Later, she wrote it down in her little log book.

Without taking her eyes off the painting, Lucy bought herself a cup of tea and a chocolate biscuit.

There were four uniformed police officers and a detective at Taunton station, waiting for the London – Penzance train to make its scheduled stop. Their job was to ensure that if Lucy left the train at Taunton they should meet her and escort her to the police van waiting outside, where they would ask her to telephone her husband. Two of the police were very sceptical about the practicality of this plan.

"Look, Karen," said one to the other, "if they've had a domestic, and she's scarpered with a valuable bit of their stuff – their joint property, perhaps it's just her property – then she's not going to ring him up and say 'OK darling I'll come straight home,' is she? And what are we going to do? We can't just arrest her. Typical man. Who does he think he is?"

"Well, he's the Deputy Prime Minister. But I know what you mean, it might be quite difficult."

"Quite difficult! And d'you know what that tosser from HQ said?"

"I can guess. God's gift, he thinks he is. Has he come on to you yet?"

"I'd like to see him try. Just *look* at the way he walks. Strutting up and down like ... here's the train."

Lucy did not leave the train, and the four uniformed officers returned to their van. The detective was the last person to board the train, just before it left. His job was to find her, try and persuade her to leave the train with him and return by police car to London, and if she refused, to radio in and report directly to Henry, who would make arrangements

475

which did not concern the police force. He should have had a partner with him, but this woman hadn't answered her radio; she had two other tricky cases on the go, and could have been anywhere.

The next two stations, Tiverton and Exeter, would also have uniformed police on the platforms, but the train arrived at the following station, Newton Abbot, three quarters of an hour after leaving Taunton, and it had been judged that either Lucy would have been located by then, even if she were trying to hide, or the detective would have made certain that she was not on the train, in which case she must have alighted at Reading, the stop before Taunton. Station staff at Reading were already being interviewed, and it seemed unlikely that she had left the train there; no-one interviewed yet had seen a woman carrying a very large flat package.

The train left Taunton with the detective standing just inside one of the carriage doors, wondering which end of the train to start. He was wearing too many clothes; he had put on a quilted leather jacket that morning, because he was thin, and wearing jeans, and his wife said that it suited him, but the weather had turned hotter than he had expected, and he hadn't reckoned on the day's emergency activities. He was thirsty already, and hadn't had time that morning to fill his plastic flask from their tap at home. Perhaps it would be a good idea, he thought, to find the guard first, or inspector, or whatever they were called. Where, come to that, were the transport police? Almost certainly they didn't have a CID presence at Taunton.

He was fairly new to the area; it was a damn sight nicer than Leicester, he and his wife had a new semi quite near the centre of the town, but you could get into the countryside quickly, even by walking. They were going to try for their first baby soon. He saw the woman in the brown uniform; she was in the next carriage, talking to a passenger, and seemed to be pointing to a notebook and explaining something. He didn't know how to address her; she was bound to have a badge or a neck strap with a card on it, but he disliked peering at badges on women, it seemed so rude. He decided; he would quickly tell her what he had to do, then he would go to the buffet, show them his warrant card and ask for a glass of water. He hated wasting money, especially on artificial-tasting, fizzy drinks, because they were saving hard for the baby. Then he would go quickly to the rear of the train, and work his way forward systematically. Perhaps he could ask the guard lady to check the toilets, to see if any of them were locked for any length of time. The train had reached a high speed now, and he found that he had to clutch the little knobs on the tops of the seats as he made his way down the carriage.

The guard – he saw, actually, from her conspicuous badge, that she was Eileen and her job was called 'conductor' – was still talking to the passenger, who turned out to be a clergyman, thin like Ives and even taller, but much older. He was nodding at what she said, and repeating some of it, with the expression of someone doing his very best to understand, but also someone who expected his interlocutor to give him her full attention and not to expect him to hurry.

"I see, I think," he was saying as Ives approached, "this ticket, which purports to allow me to travel to Penzance without changing at Plymouth, is in fact invalid for that purpose. Had I taken a later train, or indeed one of a number of earlier trains, the regulations would ..."

"It's not really a matter of regulations," the conductor replied, "more of the contract between ..." she looked up at Ives, who was now standing quite close, and had eased his warrant card a centimetre or two out of his top pocket, enough for her to guess what it was. "If you return to your seat, sir, I'll come and find you and tell you about the later trains you can get from Plymouth or the excess charge; but if you don't mind I should speak to this other gentleman now."

"Now why would that be?" asked the clergyman, peering hard at the detective over the top of old fashioned gold rimmed half spectacles, "would it not be more sensible to finish your explanation to me first? Surely now this gentleman has not been waiting very long?"

There seemed to be a very slight Irish lilt in the clergyman's voice. His clothes were rather blacker and more formal than those of most C of E clergymen the detective had encountered; he was even wearing black gloves and as he bent over Eileen, presumably the better to hear her, socks of a rather surprising magenta were revealed, a colour which immediately reminded him of the flowers, like little ballet dancers, which covered the hedgerows surrounding the campsite in Cornwall where he and Margaret, and hopefully soon James or Catherine, spent their summer holidays. "Look", Margaret had said in delight, "they've got purple knickers and red skirts!" He didn't want to interrupt, especially since he thought that Eileen might have to go through the whole rigmarole again with this vicar if she didn't finish it now. There was no great hurry; he would quickly locate a woman (whose emailed picture was in his pocket) accompanying a large flat rectangular package, if she were, in fact, on the train. He signalled his willingness to wait by shaking his head and tucking the warrant card back in his top pocket. His reward for this act of self-denial was a smile which he decided might be classed as gracious from the clergyman himself, and a positive beam from Eileen, who had been thinking along the same lines. In fact, the vicar soon understood the point Eileen was making, and he left them to return to his seat, again smiling, the detective even wondering whether he was going to offer them a little blessing. But the monsignor had decided that would be a step too far.

Eileen of course recognised the lady in the photo with the square package, and told the detective that she would probably be in one of the First Class carriages by now, with the package in the next seat.

Ives slowly made his way to the First Class section, scanning the Standard Class carriages as he passed through. There was, as Eileen had suggested, no sign of Lucy, and he decided that before searching First Class he would return to Eileen and ask her to monitor the toilets for him. There were, it seems, six functioning toilets, and although the task would keep her quite busy she told this nice, young, quite fanciable policeman that a change was as good as a rest, which wasn't strictly true. She passed the clergyman, who was reading a magazine called the Tablet, which he lowered and then beckoned her over. His ascetic features were marred, she now noticed, by a network of visible capillaries on his nose, which was almost the same colour, if not quite the same shade, as his socks.

"Would you be telling me now," he asked, and oh yes, he was definitely Irish, "whether the canteen is forrard or aft?"

She pointed back, in the direction of the buffet car. He dropped his ecclesiastical air for a moment and whispered, "And would they be selling a nice drop of brandy, do you think?"

She assured him that they stocked every type of spirit, and moved on before he might ask her if she would be joining him in a wee dram – no – well, whatever the Irish called their boozing.

In the buffet car, which was almost empty, the monsignor was all affability, chatting away to the bartender, remarking upon what a kind and helpful lady was their conductor, and would she be travelling all the way to Penzance, to her no doubt fine upstanding husband and her quiverful of children? The bartender thought that Eileen had two children, but didn't know anything about her husband. And she lived in Maida Vale, so got off at Tiverton, crossed to the other platform, and carried on her job with the next London bound train.

"Off at Tiverton; well isn't she the lucky one?" said the priest and, buying a miniature of brandy, returned to his seat.

As the train was pulling out of Tiverton where only a few passengers had alighted, and the police who had lined the platform had returned disappointed to their other duties, the detective went in search of the new conductor, hoping that he or she would be as friendly and helpful as Eileen.

Before, however, he could locate this person, and explain the help he needed, he encountered the priest, staggering from his seat into the short passage linking that compartment to the next. It wasn't very easy to stand there, because the floors of the two carriages were overlapped and moving independently, and the priest, who looked pale and ill, seemed to be in danger of collapsing.

"For the love of God, help me into the toilet, I need to sit down, I need a drink of water ..." his speech deteriorated into an incoherent mumble. His accent was very strong. The toilet door was just behind him, so without hesitating the detective seized him by the arm, managed to push the door open, and helped him onto the seat. It suddenly occurred to him that perhaps the problem was simple; perhaps the priest was horribly drunk. He leaned over him to smell his breath. The priest grasped him for support, with surprising strength. There was indeed a strong smell, but not alcohol – or, perhaps, some obscure alcohol? Tequila? Surely not, the Irish don't ... what was that stuff, the stuff in a bottle with a little pad Margaret used for getting spots off the settee? ... and now he smelt it no longer, because it was chloroform. The priest removed the tissues from the detective's face and flushed them down the toilet bowl, then carefully, even gently, found a vein and injected 2.5mg of Propofol slowly over the next minute. He propped the detective up as best he could, removed his warrant card, and made sure that he was unlikely to slide down in a way which might obstruct his breathing. The priest took a wallet from his own pocket and exchanged it for that of the detective, then sprinkled the miniature of Courvoisier over his T-shirt.

The next compartment was marked First Class, and Lucy, who was snoozing there, her hand carefully inserted between the package and the string tied round it, woke up to see her friend Axel leaning over her.

"Axel! What are you doing on the train? When did you get on?"

"At Reading. I just made it in time. Now, my dear, I'm afraid we have a change of plan forced upon us. We need to get this wretched painting to Mickey – and I can't tell you how sorry I am, I'll never forgive myself, really I won't, but if it were to get out that you and Jim – I've never known Mickey so furious, I assure you I haven't."

Axel seemed agitated, even flustered; it showed in his complexion which was blotched pink in places. She had never before seen him even marginally disconcerted. He collected himself and continued,

"The painting. We've got to get it to him in Dartmouth – yes, of course he's got a yacht, has he never told you? So we must leave the train at Newton Abbot."

"When's that? What's the time?"

"In a couple of minutes, you must get your bags, is there anything in the rack?" He looked above her head.

"No, nothing, I haven't got anything except the painting, I didn't have time after your call."

"Yes, I'm sorry I didn't pick up your text right away. I think there must be more to this than we're aware of. Mickey was so furious ..."

"Yes, so you said."

"Maybe he's just worried about the effect on Jim if the news about it came out; they're very good friends, after all, and no-one likes to see his friend in trouble. Yes, I expect it's just that. He's worried about Jim."

"Axel, you don't have to tell me what it would mean for Jim. You can just see the headlines in the Shield."

"Of course, Lucy, I'm so sorry."

"So where's this boat, then?"

"Near the Naval College, he said, Drum Moorings, any taxi driver would know."

As the train approached Newton Abbot they made their way to the end of the compartment, where a knot of people was forming around the open door of the toilet. Someone was saying, "No, he's breathing all right," and someone else said, "Smell the drink on him!" Now the conductor was pushing his way through, and as the train slid to a halt at the platform, and Axel stepped out, turning round to help Lucy with the picture, they heard the conductor say "He's called Mackenzie, his driving licence says he's from Glasgow."

As they crossed the railway line, by means of the cast iron bridge which led to the up platform and the station exit, Axel, to Lucy's surprise, said that he had missed his lunch, and must have a bite to eat or would start to feel unwell. He suffered, apparently, from mild diabetes; this was the first Lucy had heard of it. She suggested a sandwich in the station buffet, but Axel turned up his nose at this and led her some distance up the High Street to a tavern that called itself the King Henry Hotel, but was really just a fairly run down boozer.

"We've just got time for a snack," he said, "before the car comes for us."

They ate a couple of dismal sausage rolls, and in twenty minutes or so a burly man came in and tapped Axel on the shoulder.

"Car's here."

They put the picture in the back of the car, an old, capacious, Volvo Estate. The burly man, whom Axel addressed as Johnson, drove, and Axel sat next to him. Lucy shared the back with a number of worn cardboard boxes, piled on the floor and seat, and had to push one aside to find the end of her safety belt. There were also boxes in the luggage area behind the back seat, on top of which Axel had placed the picture. Some were fastened with brown parcel tape, but some had merely been folded shut. They all seemed originally to have contained food or cigarettes, tins of rice pudding, cheap luncheon meat, baked beans, and bratwurst. One box was labelled in what Lucy thought was Polish; the illustration showed jars of pickled cucumbers. The cigarettes were all high strength: Capstan, Gauloises, Navy Cut and various foreign brands of rolling tobacco.

Almost as soon as they set off Axel asked Lucy to hand him her mobile phone. He pulled it open and removed the battery. She was very surprised, and showed it, and he explained that this was to prevent the police tracing and following her. She couldn't understand this at all.

"The police? They wouldn't, surely? I mean, they're not involved? The whole point is to get this painting back to

Mickey before, well, I'm not sure why it's so urgent but you said he's ..."

"Listen to me. You're married to the Deputy Prime Minister, of course if you go missing everyone's going to be looking for you, picture or no picture."

Axel's mood had changed, he had become taciturn and distant and unwilling to explain anything more to her. She had never seen him like this before – he had always seemed like an ally, helping her develop her scheme to open a gallery of her own, persuading his employer to let her hang in her own house paintings which she couldn't possibly have afforded to purchase, offering her real friendship in a life otherwise dominated by superficial, fleeting contact with her husband's colleagues or acquaintances. How many real friends did she have? They had had real friends in the early days, up North, but as Jim's career, and status, had advanced, these had been left behind. How many people did she know whom, for example, she could ring up on the spur of the moment and ask round for coffee and a chat, or go to a film with, or even share confidences? She couldn't think of any. There was the new Foreign Office girl, Penny, the one seconded to the Protection Unit for some reason or other. She was young, of course, but she did seem genuinely friendly, and interested in the same sort of things as herself. *Sympathique*, that was the term. Yes, she could imagine asking her if she would like to, maybe, visit an exhibition, or do something quite ordinary together, like a morning's window shopping in the West End. But how many older friends like that were there now? She couldn't think of any.

She had only a vague notion of the local geography, and no idea of the route they should follow from Newton Abbot, but when she noticed that they were skirting Plymouth, and about to cross the Tamar Bridge into Cornwall, she realised that they could not possibly be heading for Dartmouth. At first she just felt puzzled, then, when she realized what this must mean, her disquiet was replaced by something closer to consternation.

"Where are we going? This can't be the way to Dartmouth!"

She directed the question at Axel, but when he neither replied nor even acknowledged her question, she repeated it, more loudly, to the driver. He, too, ignored her.

"I asked you a question! Answer me, will you," she asked again, then when it still remained unanswered she leaned over and grasped Axel's shoulder, wrenching him round and shouting in his face.

"That's enough," said the driver, flatly. This was the first time he had spoken. He pulled into a layby on the dual carriageway, just before the bridge, turned the engine off and was about to open his door when Axel grasped him by the arm.

"Wait. CCTV everywhere. Over the bridge; wait until we're through Saltash."

What did he mean, thought Lucy, wait for what?

Axel turned to her. He smiled, apologetically, but unconvincingly so. This bulky, taciturn man, Johnson, must presumably be an emissary of their friend Mickey. Perhaps he was a bodyguard, one of the cold-eyed minders kept by billionaires; not that she had ever noticed such people around Mickey when they had met in the past. But he certainly seemed to be worrying Axel.

"I'm sorry, Lucy, we seem to be getting very confused instructions. Johnson has been told to drive us to Mickey's house in Cornwall; apparently he left his yacht yesterday. We'll stop in a couple of miles where it's quieter, and I'll phone to make sure he's there."

"He'll be there all right. Why don't you just cut the crap?" said Johnson.

They drove on, over the bridge, into Cornwall.

"I never knew Mickey had a house in Cornwall. Whereabouts?" Lucy asked, after they had regained the dual carriageway.

There was no point, Axel thought, in concealing their destination. He had got her off the train in time by concocting a story about a yacht in Dartmouth – now, the fewer surprises en route the better.

"Very near Land's End. A place called Porthguarnon. He's got houses all over the world. New York, Italy, you name it. This one used to be a castle, a long time ago – it's small for a castle, but quite large for a house."

The unusual name 'Porthguarnon' rang a bell; where had she heard that before? She couldn't remember immediately; it would come back to her, she was sure.

It did indeed come to her, as they were nearing Liskeard.

"Porthguarnon – that's where that Count and his wife live, isn't it? Alison was at our house, Axel, you remember of course you do, last week, when you were all round looking at the pictures, and this wretched fake Hopkins was still hanging up?"

"Yes, naturally she was there, I brought her. Mr Michaelov's house is very close now."

The road from Plymouth joined the A30 south of Bodmin Moor, and Johnson drove on, very fast between the speed cameras whose location he obviously knew, slowing down once when he spotted a dark blue BMW in his mirror, and not speeding up until it had turned off. This was because he also knew the unmarked cars which the Devon and Cornwall police used to patrol the road, the only decent dual carriageway in Cornwall. There was very little attractive scenery for Lucy to admire; Bodmin Moor was behind them, and even that can be a disappointment to romantically inclined readers of Daphne du Maurier. Johnson could not drive fast along the narrow stretch through the flat scrub and sedge of precious Goss Moor, its flora and fauna of great excitement to scientists with magnifying glasses to their eyes and the incurious sky to their bottoms; the waste heaps from the clay quarries around St Austell were ugly on the horizon; closer to the road the scattered settlements and crumbling mine works around Camborne and Redruth were equally cheerless. Lucy had travelled this road before, but had forgotten what a depressing journey had to be endured to achieve the drama of the coastline. She glimpsed St Michael's Mount as they came down the hill towards Penzance, shut her eyes to blot out the ribbon of fast food joints, supermarkets and derelict train sheds, and dozed as the car turned off the A30 towards St Buryan.

Porthguarnon Castle was approached from the road along a gated drive which had been carved into the east face of the great granite cleft which led down to Guarnon cove. It had been a simple early sixteenth century keep, built upon an outcrop and more or less impregnable upon the seaward side. Its functions had never really been tested; it was too small to hold much of a garrison, and the sally rovers merely gave it a wide berth as they rowed up the coast in search of infidels to enslave. It had been bought for her husband by a whimsical nineteenth century lady whose father had left her a fortune derived from the manufacture and sale of a patent medicine derived from cedar wood oil. Her husband had given up his country doctor's practice, and devoted himself to renovating and enlarging the castle, employing first an architect from Bristol whose plans were too simple, then, at great expense, Sir Charles Barry himself, then, when Sir Charles refused to incorporate an Italianate tower into a gothic revival scheme, an architect from Truro who was quite prepared to compromise any aesthetic principles he might have held for the sake of the enormous fees he would earn.

So the castle became a hotchpotch, but the keep remained, presenting a semi-cylindrical granite face to the sea, pierced by the original arrow slits, and broken only by the narrow outwork of the privy chute, at the base of which grew a magnificent Chilean rhubarb, thrusting forth its outrageous flower spikes, fertilised by four centuries of aristocratic excrement.

The Italianate tower had been reduced in the final scheme to a stubby four storey affair, looking rather like one of the disguised water cisterns sometimes seen on the stable blocks of grand houses, or next to the central hall of a Victorian asylum. Visitors' rooms, Lucy was told, were in the top floor of the tower, and Axel took her up in a modern lift while Johnson went to find their employer. The picture, still wrapped up, was left in the hall, guarded by a suit of armour and a stuffed badger. The room into which he showed her was surprisingly ordinary; the furniture looked like post war utility pieces, and the bed itself was metal framed.

"When you're ready, come down for some tea. Press the button for the lift, then 'G'. Mickey will be relieved to see you, and no doubt will wish to discuss this, ah, unfortunate affair."

A single window, large enough overall to light the room well, but divided by stone mullions and transoms into small rectangles, some glazed with fragments of mediaeval glass, gave a view of the sea, the sky, and a few yards of the rocky headland to the west. There was a wash hand basin, with a bar of soap and a towel; the towel was clean, but the soap was not new.

Lucy washed, then tried the door of what she presumed was a toilet, but was just an empty cupboard. She went out onto the landing. There were two solid oak doors, but both were locked. Back in her room she saw that the bedside table was the sort which had a small square cupboard; before she had opened it she knew what she would find; there it was, something she hadn't used since she was two years old. Well, she wasn't going to use it now. How could Mickey expect this of his guests? Or indeed, of his domestic staff? Of course, she knew little of his background. She walked across the landing to the lift, and summoned it. For thirty seconds she waited, staring at the little light, listening for the ping, then decided it would be quicker to go down the stairs. She turned away from the lift. She had not noticed before; there were no stairs. Returning to her room, she shut the door, sat on the bed and decided to wait five minutes for the lift to come free then try again. But after two or three minutes she heard the ping of the lift arriving, and got up to go to the door. Before she reached it she heard the scrape of a key; she tried the door; it was locked.

August 15   Axel   Edwards   Rembrandt

Some forty feet below the window in Lucy's room, French windows opened from the dining room on to a terrace which ran roughly north to south, overlooking the valley down which the Porthguarnon stream flowed into the sea. Below the dining room, towards and eventually hewn into the hillside, ran a gloomy windowless tube, the kitchen corridor. The butler's pantry, then the kitchen itself, were the first rooms off the corridor, then came the still room, the dairy, the bakery, the pastry room, the vegetable room, the butchery, the game room, the dry store room and two or three others whose functions had been forgotten. These rooms were built along a ledge of the cliff, excavated explosively by a gang of tin miners drafted in for the purpose, and a narrow drive along the ledge also provided access to the castle for servants and delivery men. The whole elaborate arrangement so impressed local County families that one of the most prominent Cornish landowners, Thomas Robartes of Lanhydrock, asked his architect to visit the Castle before redesigning the Lanhydrock kitchens.

It was to the kitchen itself that Axel directed his steps after he left Lucy, imprisoned like so many other virtuous ladies in the topmost room of a castle tower. Johnson had not reappeared, so Axel went and collected the picture from the hall, kicking the badger as he passed. The badger accepted this customary affront, and slid sideways towards the knight in armour. Axel had made a number of decisions in the last few hours, and even he found it difficult to accept with total equanimity what he now saw as inevitable. But where many people might have felt the stroke of doom, Axel felt only mildly out of sorts. He wondered whether he could arrange for the Bentley to be shipped directly to Valparaiso in the few days left before his own departure. They were both fond of the Bentley, and the Chilean climate would suit its bodywork reasonably well. But it probably wasn't worth the effort; his alter ego in Santiago had never shown any interest in vintage cars, and it would be an unnecessary link between his two lives; a small link, nevertheless, a link. They would do without the Bentley. He would not have denied, if the question had ever arisen, that the lives of others presumably held a value. It was just that the value he placed on his own life, and his own fortune, was much higher. Infinitely so. He would not punish, but he would not hesitate to do what was necessary to ensure his own safety. He hoped that his future, in South America for at least five years, would be shared with Alison. He did not need to forgive her for her affair with the absurd Edwards, because neither forgiveness nor a desire for revenge were emotions he ever felt. His only love was for himself, and as far as he could tell Alison's behaviour with him, in bed or out of it, had not changed after she had started screwing the art dealer. And as for revenge, he just couldn't see the point. In any case, Edwards was a loose end, and would soon have to be tied off. He hoped Alison would accept this sensibly.

It was Axel who had borrowed Michaelov's Hopkins to act as an exemplar, a template, for Rembrandt to base his paintings on; that had been a good idea and had led to five or six successful sales. The error which had led to the discovery that the 'people's car' pictures were counterfeit was probably down to Edwards' Japanese girl; either she had provided Rembrandt with the wrong photographs, or marked up the wrong pages in a book – something like that. Or perhaps Edwards hadn't explained clearly enough what was needed; whatever the reason, the question of who was to blame was now immaterial. Axel slid back the iron bolt and pushed the kitchen door open.

Rich Victorians built their kitchens like gothic chapels, with steep roofs and elaborate ridges pointing up to heaven, purportedly for ventilation and the comfort of the turnspits, but really because they worshipped their stomachs as much as their god. The heavenly host may have expected hymns of praise through the open windows of the clerestory; what drifted up to the angels was the Old Testament scent of burnt offerings as well as the more delicate vapours of pies, pastries and stews.

The windows and skylights on the south of the kitchen had been painted over with whitewash, and most of the light now came from the north. The accoutrements of the kitchen had been piled up in the grate, except for the assortment of basins, bowls and tinned copper saucepans in which Rembrandt mixed his paints. Rembrandt himself was stepping back to judge whether he had painted the cross on Archbishop Fernando's pallium in a sufficiently impressionistic style, the style used for decorations on costume by Velazquez in his later years.

Rembrandt was young, with features which suggested a mixed origin, probably Middle Eastern and European. He had only seen Axel once before, in the distance, at night, and in the dark, but in circumstances which linked the tall man unequivocally to a chain of crimes which included trafficking, slavery and murder; for the art frauds his dealings had been only with the pixie man, the man called Edwards.

Rembrandt was an artist, a fine artist but one with little flair for advertising his talents, and no luck in attracting the attention of the marketing men who determine whether an artist, however brilliant, shall be rich and famous, or poor and unknown. He had fled war torn Beirut for Germany, and persuaded the faculty at Koblenz to admit him; they didn't need much persuading, in fact, because his portfolio was outstanding. He had no money, and his course was full time – in any case, his only interest was painting. So he took a few trips around the art galleries, to see what was selling, and quickly turned out two commonplace but possibly saleable pictures, following the style of a recently dead artist, fairly well known in Germany, but not internationally. Eventually, after being shown the doors of numerous galleries, usually politely, always unequivocally, he found one in Grünstraße which offered to take his paintings, demanding, of course, 'in the circumstances' an outrageous mark-up – meaning, Rembrandt himself would only receive a pittance. Tired, footsore and anxious to buy a decent meal, a bottle of schnapps and some more tubes of paint, Rembrandt agreed to these terms, begged a small advance, left the pictures and returned to his bedsit. Within a week he had spent his advance, much of it on a new Italian jacket which looked in the mirror as sexy as the shopkeeper had promised, and had decided optimistically to go and see how his paintings were selling. The girl in the gallery was non-committal, nor did she give any immediate signs that she had mistaken him for a pop idol. The owner, however, seemed delighted to see him, told him that the paintings had sold – in only a week! – and that he would happily stock some more. He would give Rembrandt a higher percentage; indeed, he would go fifty fifty, which Rembrandt should understand was very unusual for such an inexperienced and unknown artist. Rembrandt was delighted, wondered whether he should try and extract an even better deal, but decided against it. They chatted a little, and Rembrandt promised to deliver three more canvases before the month was out. He had tied up none of his artistic capital in this enterprise, he had not compromised his aesthetic integrity and he firmly told himself that he was doing it for the money only. He was quite sorry that he had given the dealer his real name; still, he hadn't signed the paintings. Perhaps he could sign the next batch, maybe using a pseudonym? The dealer thought not; many very well-known artists never signed their work, he said, and perhaps the clients – for the time being, not in the future of course when you're famous, he said with a confiding smile – would prefer their guests to wonder a little about the identity of the artist who had produced such beautiful work! Which made little sense, but Rembrandt was by now quite under the spell of this mellifluous entrepreneur and his promise of a continuous stream of riches. They talked about modern European artists, trends in colour and form, the difficulties of conveying meaning. How strange it is, said the dealer, that there should be fashion in colour! He rummaged under his desk, found a fairly recent sale catalogue, and thumbed through it.

"Take, for example, these artists." He pointed at three or four pictures, abstracts, similar only in their generous use of a bright impasto yellow. "They have realised how the use of a particular yellow attracts patrons from Asia. Extraordinary, is it not? But true. And, the wealth of the Chinese – unglaublich!

The story of Rembrandt unfolded sadly with the predictability of a soap opera plotline. Of course, the dealer was attaching false signatures to Rembrandt's yellow paintings and selling them for tens of thousands of euros. Of course, when Rembrandt found out, the dealer threatened to claim that Rembrandt was complicit, even the instigator of the fraud. And of course Rembrandt was then persuaded to direct his talents to producing forgeries of internationally renowned artists. The fifty fifty split became a reality.

It would have been sensible for Rembrandt to pay more attention to the way he disposed of his new wealth – as he had promised his crooked partner – but he was still really only interested in drawing and painting. While forging new masterpieces by old artists he found it difficult to develop a painting style of his own, but this stricture didn't seem to apply to drawings. When he was fed up with the formulaic distortions of a cubist nude, or the neurotic detail of a Flemish breakfast, he would draw; contemporary café life while sitting over a Bock and a slice or two of wurst and pumpernickel; reflective scenes drawn from his memories of a Lebanon before the cataclysm; a portrait of his parents sitting each side of a window overlooking the Mediterranean, his father reading the paper, his mother pouring ink-black coffee.

He opened an account in the Deutsche Mineral und Land Bank, and poured all his euros into it, month by month. The sale of a Cézanne, to an Indonesian billionaire, yielded, after the enormous costs of its stealthy marketing, well over a million euros. The German authorities were not, then, so alert to the dangers of money laundering as were, for example, the fraud police in the UK. However, a deposit by a foreigner with a student's visa of such a large amount into a simple current account caused something of a stir behind the counter of the DMLB; the Einhaltungdirektor was consulted, and a reluctant reference was made to the Geldwäscherei desk of the German financial control agency. It only took a single visit from a fairly mild mannered member of the financial police to throw Rembrandt into a complete panic; he knew how police behaved, he was from the Middle East. He took as much cash from his bank account as the Geldautomat would let him, and fled.

He bought his way to Britain, eventually taking the fishermen's route from Douarnenez to Newlyn, making two changes in the Channel where he was thrown from dinghy to dinghy by men who did not particularly care whether or not he slipped and drowned. He found himself, in the middle of the night, standing shivering upon a rocky shore with a steep climb in front of him to the coast road where he had been told to turn right and walk; Newlyn was only a kilometre away, he could see its lights. He had an address and a name, and had been told that he would be expected to work, probably in the fields, and, to start with, for no pay beyond his board. He only lasted two days cutting broccoli; weeping with fatigue, and excoriated contemptuously by the country-bred workers from the Baltic States, he sought out the supervisor and begged to be put to the work which he knew; but his English was so bad that he could not explain his talent. The supervisor knew only one way to deal with malingerers or troublemakers, and that a crude one, but the field where they were working had no privacy; it was near both the road to Penzance and the farmyard, where the farmer's daughter was tacking up her pony. In a desperate attempt to explain, Rembrandt seized the paper pad and pencil, used to record the weights of vegetables cut by each field hand, and within a few seconds had sketched a likeness of the supervisor.

"Draw! Paint! Anything, me!" he shouted, starting another drawing, of the girl and her pony.

The supervisor was a local man from Penzance; this was a holiday area, and he knew that much more money was made from tourism than from farming, and that growing broccoli was in any case not much better than an excuse to claim subsidies from the European Union. If this wuss could set up his easel on the harbour at St Ives, and draw portraits so quickly – well, he could make a fortune. No, *they* could make a fortune. But did he dare?

Reluctantly he had decided that he didn't dare. Not off his own bat. The best he might expect would be a few quid from the boss if the scheme came off. In any case, the gang master wasn't the real boss. There were others, he'd seen them; he never really knew who was in charge. And there was someone he'd never met, someone they were all scared of. And it'd take more than some local yobbo to scare the gang master. What was it they called him? Dracula, that was it.

As Rembrandt and Axel looked at each other among the pots and pans, easels and canvases, it was obvious that Axel had been recognised immediately; Rembrandt never forgot a face, even one seen fleetingly in the dusk.

So, thought Axel regretfully, there's no mileage in the "I've come to rescue you from this den of thieves" plan. What a memory the man must have! It had been dark. He had been wearing a hat, too, pulled well down. But surely Axel's own imagination, the powers of invention of which he was so proud, would be up to devising some other scheme. Perhaps it would just come down to money? Rembrandt had been promised half the proceeds of their fraud, after three years, and then they would release him from his obligation to them. He had accepted this promise, although Axel and Johnson had no intention of honouring it, but seemed to have become less and less interested in the future, less and less querulous about his physical surroundings, while his obsession with his art increased.

He hadn't started off as a prisoner; when he needed to do research Miyu – Emily as she was called in England – had accompanied him, to galleries and archives, to private houses such as that of the de Cragnanmorts. But as time passed he became more demanding, more mercurial. In the end he refused to leave his studio to waste his time 'on trips'. Miyu should do his research for him. He had insisted that the billionaire Russian, mentioned occasionally by Edwards, should supply him with examples for his forgeries, and

Edwards had brought paintings to the castle. He examined them minutely for days on end, photographed them from every angle and in some cases removed them from their frames and stretchers to measure the thickness of the paint. When Edwards remonstrated, he had threatened to call in the guards and have him thrown out; in fact, in his own little suite of rooms, he had turned the tables on his captors.

The Velazquez archbishop, on which he was now working, had taxed Emily's powers of research to the limit – Rembrandt had invented a scenario where the dead prelate's family, dissatisfied with the grim death mask portrait in which he appeared swathed and biretted in black, had commissioned a further painting, in which he would be shown in the full fig of his archiepiscopal splendour. She had found contemporary portraits of archbishops, pages from ancient books showing Catholic regalia, and had been sent off to the Prado to take photographs of dresses and lace in as many pictures by Velazquez, and as close up, as possible. Why could you not, Rembrandt had demanded of Edwards, have brought me a painting by this artist? Does the Russian not possess one? Can he not borrow one from a viscount or a bayonet? He knows all these people, for sure.

Rembrandt found out that the National Trust owned a cardinal, by Velazquez himself, not a studio of, nor a school of; it was hanging in a stately home in Dorset. He peremptorily sent Edwards off to borrow it. Of course they could not possibly lend it out; the very idea was absurd. Why couldn't the student, whoever he was, join the Trust and come to see it in situ? The mention of Michaelov's name, and a substantial donation, had cut no ice with the incredulous curator. This, at least, was the story Edwards told Rembrandt.

Axel, although he had had no interest at all in art before Edwards had told him about Rembrandt, had learned a lot in the last three years. He looked round the castle kitchen, Rembrandt's studio, which he had only entered once or twice before, while the painter was out, taking exercise in the castle grounds. It was the usual jumble of canvases, rags, half empty cans of turpentine, unidentifiable liquids in all sorts of bottles, brushes, unused, wedged in jam jars, or caked with old paint and abandoned on old newspapers. Anything served as a palette, roof slates and chopping boards especially, and when the paint hardened the palette was thrown into one of the Bristol sinks. Two or three easels held work in progress, including the Velazquez archbishop; there was a Stanley Spencer – Emily had taken a day trip to Cookham and brought back dozens of photographs, and Michaelov owned a Spencer 'Money Changers' set in the porch of Holy Trinity church, which they brought down for a few days – and a Courbet of a woman washing her feet and showing her bottom. Axel had been dubious about the archbishop; the 'discovery' of a new Velazquez would be inordinately difficult to organise; not because the style or execution of the painting would be a problem – arguing over the authenticity of paintings by Velazquez was an accepted pastime of Spanish art historians and critics – but because any sort of scientific examination would prove that it had not been painted in the seventeenth century. So, he would either have to find a buyer who would take it on trust, or, more likely, a laboratory expert who could be bribed or blackmailed. These things were difficult, they took time, which was why Axel sometimes wished that Rembrandt would stick to relatively modern work. On the other hand, contriving the back stories for the frauds was a challenge which Axel usually enjoyed meeting, especially if it gave him the opportunity of developing a new disguise and a new personality.

He still wondered whether he should simply offer Rembrandt a pile of money – he would be able to have Johnson's share, not, of course, that Johnson was aware of this – and promise him all the facilities he might need in beautiful Santiago? He had abandoned the notion that he could just leave him, along with the guards, gangsters from Romania and Albania. The brute who ran 'Mainline', the straightforward slavery side of the business, would carry on without him, and, of course, without Johnson, and was so mired in wickedness himself that he would gain no advantage from turning informer. In any case, the man knew hardly anything about him.

Axel had half formulated a different plan, to pretend a rescue and fly the young man out to Chile where he might once again practise his talents, but this plan would only have worked if Rembrandt had failed to recognize him. Only two of the guards who patrolled the corridors and cellars had ever seen Axel, who was very careful to leave the control and distribution of his human inventory to his partner Johnson. Axel never entered the cellars, nor did he procure the food nor any drugs which were needed. Johnson had always insisted that Axel took his turn in the disposal of the bodies of those whose illnesses had not responded to medicine, but this was not often and did not, in its nature, compromise his anonymity. He was surprised, in fact, how infrequently people became ill; young men and women, especially the women, seemed able to survive extraordinary privations.

"I have been expecting you," Rembrandt said before Axel could speak. Unusually, he looked frightened. His eyes betrayed him, darting from Axel to the door, as if he were afraid someone else might be coming, then to the table, then back to Axel. What had he been told? Had he been threatened? "I have been expecting you ever since the fool Edwards brought the wrong photographs. I had no way of knowing. Look, this is what he brought."

He scrabbled nervously through a pile of papers on the table, but before he could locate the right ones Axel walked up to him and laid his hand gently on the painter's arm. The gesture was friendly, but Rembrandt tautened with fear. This fear was justified; his life was truly in the balance.

"It doesn't matter now," said Axel calmly. "We must look to the future. We can start again. But not here, not even in this country. We shall start again. We can choose where, you and I. Do not forget that you are rich now."

He continued in this vein, speaking quietly, repeating himself, using short sentences, keeping his hand in light contact with Rembrandt's arm. After a while the hypnotic repetition had the soothing effect he intended.

"What do you mean," said Rembrandt, "that I am rich?"

"I mean that we will pay you what you have earned; we have done well, it is a pity that we could not continue here, but we must not, ah, tempt fate, you understand, I am sure. And I am certain that in, let us say, some South American country there will be a way to unlock your account in Germany; do not forget your wealth in the German bank. You have never been convicted of any crime in Germany, and your dealer in Germany never betrayed you."

The complementary concepts of great wealth and life in South America were more than Rembrandt's fragile mental state could encompass. His mind fastened upon the first, and excluded the second. He was now in a great panic, unsure whether he was to be freed, unsure even whether he wanted to be freed, but certain that he would not countenance another migration. His protestations, unthinking and violent, cast a decisive weight into the scales of his future. Axel wasted no time now; removing his hand from Rembrandt's arm he turned away abruptly and left the studio, bolting the door shut. He made his way to the small kitchen yard, took a satellite phone from his pocket and made a brief call.

A sudden commotion at the castle door distracted him from his search for the less humane of the two ruffians guarding the corridor. Johnson, thunderously angry, had hurled a man to the floor; it was Edwards, crouching in terror under the raised steel gauntlet of the faceless knight. Propped up on the patient badger was another picture, its carton half open; one of Rembrandt's Overseers. Lying in the doorway was another man, trussed all over and gagged with gaffer tape. It took Axel a couple of seconds to recognise this partly mummified figure, and in those two seconds the mummy also recognised him.

Edwards' arrival, although it had obviously infuriated Johnson, was extraordinarily fortunate. Moreover, the swaddled prisoner was one of the loose ends which Axel had decided would not be worth the trouble to tie off; but since the opportunity was now presented to him, as it were pre-prepared, he could hardly ignore it. He asked Johnson to attend to Rembrandt for him and told Edwards to help him drag Anthony through to the dining room. The explanation, the excuses, which Edwards had started when they had dumped Anthony by the dining room fireplace were interrupted by the peal of the old fashioned bell, and the hammering of the huge lion's head door knocker. Axel was not expecting visitors. He swore, under his breath, violently. He heard the sound of quick, sharp footsteps crossing the hall, the creak of the old elm floorboards, and the sound of the door being pulled open.

Johnson, meanwhile, had hurried to the kitchen where Rembrandt was waiting, apprehensive, indeed more than apprehensive, after the abrupt end of his encounter with Axel. Johnson stood for a moment in the corridor, drew and racked his pistol, pulled back the heavy door bolt and entered, letting his right arm hang by his side with the hand holding the gun concealed behind his back.

Among the preparations Rembrandt had made to paint a counterfeit Velazquez was the importation of a number of mirrors to reproduce the effects seen in some of the Spanish master's work; this idea had come to nothing, but the mirrors remained, some hanging, some propped up against the wall. So Rembrandt immediately saw the hand with the gun, reflected and re-reflected; the room was full of guns, held in right and left hands alternately. Johnson also saw that he saw, and Johnson himself, temporarily disorientated, also saw multiple Rembrandts, staring at all points of the room. As Johnson hesitated, Rembrandt seized a copper sauteuse, full of a congealing mixture of glue and chalk which he had intended to use to prepare a canvas, and hurled it at Johnson. In the same moment Johnson fired, and the bullet hit the frying pan in mid air. The room was suddenly full of the most shocking noise, as the heavy pan crashed into the nearest mirror. Rembrandt dodged to one side, taking cover behind an easel, but the canvas fell to the ground leaving him exposed and defenceless. Johnson aimed carefully, but as he did so Rembrandt saw, in one of the mirrors propped up in the wall behind Johnson, another hand, holding another gun, a revolver. Johnson's eyes lifted, and he began to change his aim, raising his gun higher. But Johnson was too late. Two bullets hit him in the chest, his body jerked back and he fell. The figure with the revolver, perched on the sill of a clerestory window, let a rope down and slid to the floor. She walked to the body which had been Johnson; the blood was pooling but it was no longer pumping from his wounds. It was running now in the grouting channels of the floor tiles; it flowed round the encrusted paint to create an artwork of inestimable value. The body lay still. Unlike Anthony, aeons ago, she followed the correct procedure, bending down and feeling for a pulse in the neck. There was none. She turned to the young man, who was sitting silently, but trembling as he breathed, in a throne modelled on that of Pope Innocent the Tenth.

August 15   David   Alan   Jane

Maurice had reached the twin stone pillars which marked the turning down to Porthguarnon. The castle was not visible, and it was unclear whether the narrow road which presumably led to castle and coast was public or private. He pulled onto the verge. The Mercedes was not completely undamaged; Maurice had been unaware of the behaviour of Cornish hedges, which sneak out surreptitiously at their base when cars with expensive alloy wheels take left handed bends; and, of course, the word hedge is itself deceptive, meaning a granite wall in Cornwall. But no incident had occurred which had necessitated a stop, nor caused significant harm to the bodywork, even down the narrow lane from St Buryan, which he took in error because it was signposted to a hamlet which he had noticed on the map, but which was actually some distance to the east of Porthguarnon. He had, it is true, just driven quite dangerously close to two blue-overalled workmen, who had probably had to jump into the ditch, but he had certainly not hit them as he passed.

Maurice and his three passengers, Frieda, Patricia and Christopher, all got out of the car. The workmen, back on the road now, stopped walking, and one of them took a small pair of binoculars from his pocket.

"That's Maurice Symes-Franton," Alan said to David, "what the bloody hell's he doing here?"

"Can't be a coincidence. Who are the others?"

"Not sure. I've seen the man; it must have been when I was on the Vermeer business. Some art connection. See if you know any of them."

David took the binoculars.

"The woman, the taller one, she's called Frieda something. She's the one I met at the farmhouse. She's art, too. They're getting back in the car."

The Mercedes pulled off the verge, and swung down the drive, gathered speed and disappeared from view.

David called Jane on his radio; she answered immediately. She was two hundred metres west of the castle, having skirted it on the coast path, which crossed the castle grounds on the landward side. To the south of the coast path, the side of the castle and the sea, there was a considerable fence with a metal gate where the approach road crossed, and as Jane spoke the Mercedes drew up at this gate. The driver got out; Jane could clearly see that it was Maurice. She couldn't make out the passengers in the seats on the left hand side of the car, but she could see the woman in the back.

"One of the passengers is called Patricia. I met her with Armstrong. We talked a bit. She was with her husband; it was at Armstrong's visit to the auctioneers in Bond Street."

"Yes, that fits. Are they driving through the gate?"

"No, there's a lock on it with a number pad. Wait – they've left the car – climbing the gate; Franton's stumbled, he's fallen flat, he's up now – yes, the other man's Patricia's husband, Chris, I think, and the other woman's Frieda Semperdine. Ah, you know her, of course."

"Have they seen you?"

"Maybe, but I've got a map in front of my face and a beanie on. And overalls. Yes, I know, but they haven't seen me in my police uniform, just in my Mary Quant. Yes, I'll be very careful near the house. Castle. Yes, you *know* that I'm wearing my Kevlar. David love, stop worrying, I'm wonder woman, remember?"

David told her to try and see if there were any obvious entry points, although this was unlikely if the castle was being used as a hostel for illegal immigrants or a warehouse – a prison – for slave workers. He and Alan would approach from the east, and try to cut off Franton's party.

"What if they're involved in it too? No, of course, they'd have known the entry code for the gate. What will you tell them to do?"

"Go straight home, of course. Then I'll call again. Let's get on with it."

"Wilco. You be careful too."

But David and Alan were delayed. They had decided that after dealing somehow with Franton's interloping group they would separate, David approaching the east facade of the castle – with the cliffs and sea on his left – looking for points of entry, and then working his way round the south side, climbing along the cliff if necessary. He would then join up with Jane on the west side of the castle tower. Alan would bang on the front door and pretend to be a lost foreigner on a climbing holiday. They were carrying rucksacks and ropes; the deception was not intended to be more than temporary.

The castle itself was still hidden from them by copses of blackthorn and pittosporum; they intended to meet Franton's party where the track dipped slightly and was probably not in full sight of the castle. They had no real expectation that there would be any sort of guard; indeed, at this stage they were not even certain that Lucy was in the castle, nor, if she were, whether she was a prisoner or a guest. That the owner of the castle was a criminal they had no doubt – it was certain that he traded in human beings – but although a castle presumably had dungeons and thick walls, they had no guarantee that his stock in trade was not stored elsewhere. Nevertheless they moved forward with caution and now in silence. It was as well that they did, because as they approached a field gate in single file, using the hedge as cover, David, in the lead, saw a man standing at the gate, apparently speaking very quietly to someone the other side of the opening who was obscured by the granite gatepost. David indicated this by sign to Alan, and they both squeezed closer to the hedge and stood completely still. The second man moved into view; they were both dressed in camouflage, with military style forage caps, and various items in cases strapped across their chests. David and Alan exchanged puzzled glances; was this a uniform? Then Alan's expression suddenly cleared. As the men turned round, and discovery was inevitable, he moved forward and, also speaking quietly, asked, "Have you had any luck?"

The first man pursed his lips, shook his head, and replied, "Not even a glimpse. We think a peregrine must have had it."

"Or the harrier?" said Alan.

"Possibly. At any rate, we haven't seen it."

"Well, cheers mate, good luck."

Alan turned away to re-join David, but the man continued to speak.

"Are you climbers?"

"Yes; we thought we would try the cliffs by the castle. Haven't even seen them yet."

"I shouldn't, if I were you. The cliffs can be crumbly round here. Why not go over to the north coast. You must know Bosigran?"

"Done it too often, mate. Thought we'd try something new."

"And it's all private here; not National Trust or anything. Blokes at the castle aren't friendly. I'd give it a miss if I were you. I really mean that. By the way, where are your helmets?"

"In our packs. What's it to you?"

"Oh, nothing, just wondered."

David was looking impatient now. Clearly he thought they should bid farewell to the twitchers. Then he sneezed, and reached into his deep right pocket for a handkerchief. The atmosphere surrounding the little group had changed; the twitchers had started to look unsettled, suspicious. One of them pulled at the strap of his binoculars case, which was an odd shape for binoculars, and at the same time David drew his hand from his pocket and pointed his revolver at the man's heart.

"Stand completely still, both of you. Alan, draw your weapon."

Within a second, the two twitchers were covered. Within thirty seconds they were disarmed. They were carrying an assortment of hardware; guns, tasers and short wave radios. One of them had rebelled in the process, and he was now lying on the grass, clasping his hands to his stomach and gasping in an attempt to get his breath back. David stood guard while Alan secured them, gagging them efficiently and safely.

"We'll drag them into the bushes. It's far enough from the cliff path; shouldn't be any walkers. We can send someone for them afterwards."

David's radio crackled.

"David, why the delay? Symes-Franton's lot have reached the front door. Christopher is banging away at the knocker, I can hear it where I am."

"Small problem, dealt with. On our way now. Is there any access?"

"Can't see one. Just making my way round the tower, where it joins the cliff. They're in; all of them now; door's shut."

"Have you seen any birdwatchers?"

"What? Well, yes, I did. Near the path."

"And?"

"I said hello, quietly, he said have a nice walk, where are you going, I said thanks, Lamorna, he said cheers."

"Did he follow you?"

"No, hang on, let me just ... I can still see him, wandering about by the path. Stupid place for a birdwatcher. Oh, I understand."

"Keep an eye on him. He'll have a taser and a Taurus 45."

"Heavy gear."

"They take themselves seriously, this lot. Don't get too worried, ours were dressed to kill but they were pretty useless. Still, you be careful"

"For goodness sake, David. Call again when you're round the back of the tower?"

"Roger that."

The east face of the castle was part of the original building, at the south eastern corner of which the cylindrical tower rose, dominating the rocky beach which lay fifty metres below. The tower walls were merely a vertical extension of the greater granite ramparts of the cliff itself; the tower, unnecessarily impregnable, was as much a lookout post as a fortress. But impregnable it was; slit windows half way up, larger windows only at the top. No protrusions, and granite blocks laid with hardly any gap. Perhaps gibbons could manage it, not humans. Fifteen metres of convex impossibility. David looked down; worse; superficially smooth granite, but weathered and dangerous. He looked up; he saw the only way. Where the tower's wall curved out sharply from the main block, which had been added later as the castle changed its nature from stronghold to mansion, the walls of the building were of rusticated construction; and there was a drainpipe. The valley between tower wall and sloping roof was lead; steep, but not excessively so. No windows overlooked this route, and within thirty seconds David had scaled the roof, swung over the ridge, and would have slid down the valley the other side had there not appeared immediately in front of him another roof, again fairly steeply pitched, but with the ridge well below him. The building was rather like a lady chapel, attached or close to a great church or cathedral. There was a row of windows high in its eaves; most of them seemed to have been white-washed, and some of them were open. He eased his way down to the leads which divided the two buildings, and, crawling along the wide flat gutter, reached the nearest open window. At that moment Jane's voice came, crackly, over his radio.

"David, Lucy *is* here. I have seen her in the top window of the tower. Not the old round one, the square one by the door. I think she was trying to open it. We can't get her out that way, the window's too small."

"I can't see from here. I'm on the roof, between the main block and this chapel affair. I'm in the valley, you can't see me. But there's a way in, three windows are open here. Can you get up?" He explained where he was.

"I don't know. Give me a second. OK, I'm at the corner of the chapel wall; but it's not the same this side, not how you said it was where you were. I don't see how I can get up here. There's no drainpipe."

"It doesn't matter, I'll drop a rope over. Can you see it? There's a big stone knob thing I can belay it to – there, how's that?"

"Perfect."

And in thirty seconds she was crouching by him.

"David, there's someone inside, I can hear him moving."

Gingerly they crept closer to the window, and peered carefully over the edge. They saw the pictures, the mirrors, the discarded tins and brushes, the floor a kaleidoscope of spilt and hardened paints, the easels encrusted with the scabs of oozing or congealed pigment, the systematic chaos of a painter's studio. They saw a young man, darting from easel to easel, adding colour to paintings from a tarnished copper saucepan, which he was swinging about in time with some grand music, possibly a Beethoven overture, on a CD player. Jane quietly tied the end of her rope to the stone finial, and arranged the rest in a coil on the window ledge.

"Sorry Jane, me first," said David. Jane shrugged, but then, almost simultaneously, the young man switched the music off and they heard a scraping noise, the sound of the door bolt being withdrawn. Jane saw a big man enter and she also saw, reflected in a mirror propped up by the door, his hand, behind his back, holding a pistol. David had not seen this; she had no time to tell him. She drew her gun and cocked it as the man below fired his first shot. Almost as soon as the bullet hit the saucepan she knew that he had seen her. He raised his gun to fire, but she shot first, two shots, perfectly aimed. Pushing the hank of rope over the window ledge, Jane slid down to the floor.

Chapter 24

August 15   The Cast, excepting only the Great People in London

Shrewishly, Maurice pushed aside Chris' solicitous hand.

"I can manage on my own, thank you," he said, dabbing with his handkerchief at the mud on his knees and the arm of his jacket. "Let's get on with it, let's get down to this damned castle."

The drive crossed a large field, with cows in the distance, then wound through an area of shrubbery, largely taken over by invasive foreign rhododendrons. The great door of the castle, solid oak, pointed, gothic, looked to Frieda and Maurice too forbidding to be the customary entrance; they looked for a wicket in it but there was none. A path led along the eastern side of the building, down some steps to a lower level where they thought there might be a more ordinary door, but instead there was just a row of small windows, barred securely and glazed with opaque glass. As they retraced their steps, Maurice found to his surprise that Frieda had clutched his arm, her fingers biting astonishingly hard into his flesh. She pointed to one of the windows; the old opaque, wired, glass had been replaced with a new pane, which merely distorted rather than concealing, and pressed against the glass was a small face and the palms of two small hands. The eyes were wide, the mouth was open, the person was speaking, calling, but the glazing was soundproof. Another arm appeared, a large blurred figure loomed, and the child disappeared.

Frieda and Maurice stared at each other, their minds a whirl of possibilities. But they had no time to consider, or discuss them. Chris had walked straight up to the great door, yanked the dangling handle of the ancient doorbell, and beaten a tattoo upon the huge door knocker. The door was opening, and they were all ushered in.

Alison had opened the door to them herself. Christopher and Patricia she of course remembered, and her damnably unguarded invitation to them to pop in any time they were around – she had always known that Chris was a bit odd, *on the spectrum* was a phrase coming into vogue, but Patricia should surely have known that such an invitation was a matter of form only? Frieda and Maurice she remembered when they had reminded her of their various meetings.

What could she show them? Most had been sold, or packed up for sale and sent off to auction houses, or returned to their various owners. Mickey's own paintings were long gone. Those that were left – she hardly remembered which were genuine – hardly any, she thought – well, did that matter now?

The library; there was a Claude in the library, a Monet and, she thought, a Constable. Then she remembered the furore over the Eastwich Constable but, she reminded herself, it didn't matter, now. She would give these annoying visitors a quick look round, a gin or a scotch or something – what was the time? – and hasten them on their way. Who could bring up some drinks? Nicholls had just gone charging off to the basement, there had been some cock up, one of the children had got into the guards' rooms. She would have to get the drinks herself. And biscuits; or crisps; where were they kept? As these and various other thoughts of random levels of importance were passing through her mind she was politely ushering her guests to the library, when the door which led from the kitchen corridor opened abruptly, and Axel entered the hall.

Alison turned to him and beamed.

"Darling, we have guests; let me introduce you," she said, "Patricia, Christopher, and um..." – she waved in the direction of Frieda and Maurice, "allow me to introduce my husband, the Count. Axel."

None of those present were looking at Frieda, because they were busy shaking hands and murmuring platitudes about how much they'd heard, how nice to meet at last – and if they had been they would not have seen her jaw drop, nor her eyes open wide, nor her eyebrows vanish under her fringe, because she was not the type to signal her emotions that way, but they would have noticed a change in her expression, a momentary look of amazement.

None, that is, apart from Axel, the Count, no doubt other names as well. He was staring at her; clearly, she thought, trying to place her, trying to remember where they had met. It had only been a brief meeting, one or two words exchanged at Lucy Armstrong's tea party, but he had in fact recognised her immediately, and his look was not due to his uncertainty about their acquaintance. He was, in fact, trying to work out what to do with her. She was not attached to the gay in the bow tie, that was obvious. The two others, man and wife, he knew by reputation; very rich and quite eccentric. Alison and he had marked them some time ago, and they had visited the castle, but Alison had worried that they might be too knowledgeable, and too careful, to be deceived even by Rembrandt.

His heart sank. Why had Alison answered the door? Wouldn't they just have gone away? Perhaps not. Well, the only solution now was sadly clear. Johnson would have dealt with Rembrandt by now; a stupid man, Johnson had no qualms about killing the innocent, the unconnected. He was, Axel had always thought, a naturally callous person. So Johnson could also deal with this woman, whose name he forgot. Johnson was going to fall down the cliff afterwards, in any case; the number of crimes he was supposed to be escaping from was already large; one or two more would make little difference.

How, then, could he detach her from the other three, who would presumably be shown a few pictures, given a drink, and shown the door? Before he forgot:

"Sweetheart, don't forget the dining room is in a hell of a mess, the men moved the pictures out to the morning room; there are paint tins everywhere, I wouldn't want our guests to stumble over anything."

She nodded and smiled. "Why don't you lock it, darling, we don't want the staff in there either."

"Jolly good idea. Oh, by the way, darling, Hilda," he turned to the visitors and explained, "one of our cleaning ladies, said she felt a bit faint and is having a little rest, up in the tower room; so later on, perhaps you could go and see how she is? Maybe you could take her a glass of sherry, or something?"

Axel had been thinking hard about the party at Lucy Armstrong's, where he had encountered Frieda. She had said something about the paintings, something which revealed her taste; what was it? He remembered, and her name. He went up to her, more or less turning his back on the rest of the company. The slight sing song intonation returned to his voice.

"Frieda, isn't it? We've met, of course, at the Armstrong's; Alison and I, sometimes we play a little game; I don't call myself a Count in town, I used to once, but the British aristocracy can be quite derisive, you know, quite good at the put down. However, to come to the point, I remember what you said, that you liked the paintings of Laura Knight and Alfred Munnings – well, let me show you something, just down here, in my study. Alison and the others can start in the, ah, library, and we can join them in a minute."

There didn't seem to be a painting by Knight, nor one by Munnings in the room off the corridor where he led her. Nor did it seem particularly studious; no desk, very few books. A notice board hung on the wall with what appeared to be some sort of duty rota, and a tyre firm's calendar, last year's and showing the October page which was illustrated by a startling nude.

Frieda had little time to feel her surprise, and no time to express it. Dizzy with the effects of chloroform, unable to stand without support, incapable of speech, she was helped, stumbling, back into the hall by Axel.

"Frieda's been taken ill. It was sudden, I think it might be a stroke. Help me get her into a chair," he said to Maurice, who was nearest. "Alison, ring for an ambulance, straight away please."

The telephone was in the passageway, in a mahogany booth constructed when it had been installed a hundred years or so previously, to emphasise its novelty and provide privacy, and Alison ran to it. After a few minutes she returned and reported that the air ambulance was on its way; there would be no room for any passengers, so if any of the group wanted to see her in the hospital, they should leave now and drive directly to Truro. Alison herself had some St John's Ambulance training, and would look after her in the meantime. It was a clever scheme, and devised with extraordinary speed; but it failed. Patricia asked Christopher and Maurice to lay Frieda upon the rug; she raised Frieda's feet and rested them on the badger.

"We'll wait. There's no point us going to the hospital. I don't think she's had a stroke. There's a really strong smell; I think it's chloroform."

Patricia continued to cradle Frieda's head, and looked from the Axel and Alison to Maurice, and then her husband, and said, "Chris, I think you should phone the police now. And the ambulance." He reached into his pocket and she reminded him impatiently that there was no mobile signal, then indicated the telephone cabinet, still keeping her eyes on the Count and Countess.

Axel and Alison – whatever their names really were, whether or not they were married – exchanged glances. There was no time left for a neat and tidy departure, no time to lay the false trails which they had planned, no time to sew up all the loose ends which Axel so hated to leave unravelled, no time for anything but escape.

Alison spoke first.

"I don't want any of you to move now. Just keep perfectly still. My husband will explain what is going to happen."

Maurice and Chris were, to start with, puzzled. How was she to enforce this peremptory instruction? Then they saw, in the doorway to the passage, a large man, dressed in overalls, holding the sort of gun which police carry at airports, and they understood that he, not the ambulance, had been summoned on the corridor phone. The gun was not held in the way patrolling policemen hold guns, it was pointed directly at them.

"Axel," she continued, "keep this lot quiet and I'll go and tell Johnson to get the RIB ready straight away. Nicholls, are you ready, can you take over now? How many have we got in the corridor?"

"Not many. Two men, three women, two kids. But the next lot arrive on Tuesday. Lee and Parkes will be back by then, so that's OK. But," he pointed at the four visitors, "what about them? Two of them" – he indicated Maurice and Frieda – "saw the Algerian kid at the window before I got to him. What are you going to do about that?"

"They're going to come with us," said Axel, "for a short way, at least."

"The Denmark shaft?"

"As far as the blocked adit, yes."

The conversation made no sense to the visitors, who knew next to nothing about Cornish mines.

Alison went to find Johnson; she knew that he had had business with Rembrandt. Axel heard her footsteps, quick and heavy, as she returned. Why was she running? He saw the pallor under her heavy make-up, she was not quite trembling, but her breath came fast and shallow.

"Nicholls," she said, "Have you ..." she looked at Axel, "did you tell Nicholls to ...?"

"What?" they replied, simultaneously.

"It's Johnson. He's been shot. He's dead."

Maurice was aware that he was not the figure in the room that Alison and Axel would consider the most threatening. He had always wondered how he would behave in a situation where his, or someone else's, life were put in peril. At exactly the moment Alison was saying, "He's dead" he found himself walking smartly to a door, located in the middle of the side wall, which he had noticed was slightly ajar. It was lined with green baize, which was wrapped half way round the door edges and was clearly the entrance to the servants' quarters; there would be narrow corridors and back stairs, up to the main part of the house, and down to store rooms and sculleries. Down, in fact, to the rooms through the windows of one of which he had seen the pale, blurred face of the calling child. Before Nicholls could react, he was through the door, which he closed behind himself – unfortunately, there was neither lock nor bolt.

"Nicholls?" said Axel.

"Meredith's down at the back door, the area door. He'll deal with him."

But Maurice was not making for the door, he was making for the room with the child. It would, he calculated, be down about six stairs, then about two or three rooms from the corner of the building. He found the staircase almost immediately on his left and dived down it. The man Meredith only caught a glimpse of his vanishing back, and hesitated; should he investigate, or stay, as he had been instructed, by the door?

Maurice saw three doors which could, he thought, have been the doors to the room in which he had seen the child. They were all heavy, all bolted, but there were no locks. He unbolted and entered the middle room, which was empty. It had a concrete floor, and there were two hand basins and two lavatory pans. This was the room he had seen; one of the opaque window panes, behind bars set in cement, had been replaced by clear glass. He went quickly to the next room, unbolted the door. He had found the child.

*****

When Henry asked Maurice and Patricia, and Dame Jennifer asked Christopher, to explain what happened in the next ten minutes – Frieda was spared the ordeal of this debriefing, because she had still been all but unconscious – and then compared notes, and listened to the recordings of the interviews, they found that it was almost impossible to work out the exact sequence of events. Anthony, David, Jane and Alan contributed, but their views had only been partial.

Alan, working round the north of the castle, had decided to enter by a third storey window of the square Victorian tower; the climb was, for him, very easy, and he thought it unlikely that third storey windows would be alarmed. Inside he found himself, although he did not know it, in a room directly below that in which Lucy was imprisoned. Systematic searches of buildings were supposed to start at the bottom and work upwards, but since he was near the top, and since he was looking for someone to rescue, not a target in hiding, he decided to go up to the top floor first. There was a lift, and stairs, but after running up the stairs he found a solid unpanelled door blocking the way onto the fourth floor landing. The door was fastened by means of a modern three point locking system with a flush fitting security cylinder; it would be impossible to break down or lever open with the light tools in his pack. But this unusual security measure must be serving a purpose and made him determined to get up to the top floor. He went down the stairs to the third floor again; he could either go out of the window and climb up to the room above, or attempt the lift shaft. The lift shaft would in fact be easier, and certainly less visible. It did occur to him to try the lift button first, but he was not surprised when pressing it had no effect. Lift doors are not often closed particularly firmly, and by a combination of levering and wedging he opened these enough to squeeze through. The lift was at the bottom – he would have had to retreat had it been parked at the floor above – and he climbed up to the doors for the fourth floor. These were easy to open, because he could get to the fastening mechanism, and he swung himself through onto the fourth floor landing.

The floor and walls of the square landing appeared to be carpeted and painted in a spangled blur of crude, vivid colours, with a preponderance of scarlet. There were three heavy doors, solid oak. The window was in the west wall, and the late afternoon sun, shining through a clumsy representation of some panoplied hero ripping the arm off an ogre and releasing a cascade of gore, provided the lurid illumination which had startled Alan. Faintly, through the cracks in the lead strips between the stained glass panels, he could hear the waves upon the beach far below. Then, surely, the unmistakeable sound of a bullet fired and hitting metal, then two further shots. Someone in one of the rooms had heard the shots also, because he heard a scream, a cry for help, then, on the door in front of him there came a violent banging.

"Who are you?" he shouted, as loud as he could, through the weighty door. "Call your name out!"

"Lucy Armstrong" he heard, and quickly replied, "are you alone?"

"Yes, yes, who are you?"

"Security Directorate; my name's Green. Stand away from the door!" he shouted, then, when no reply came "Did you hear me? Please answer!"

"Wait – tell me – tell me the name of the girl, I mean, my female protection officer."

"Jane. You probably still know her as Penny. She's here too. Downstairs."

And, he thought, I hope to God she – or David – was on the right end of the gun firing those rounds.

"All right, I'm standing back."

The door, although it looked strong, was not protected by all the modern security fittings of the stairs door, nevertheless there were two large mortice deadlocks, spaced correctly, about 600mm apart. There was no heavy furniture on the landing which he could use as a ram. If he could not kick the door open at the lock side, which he was afraid would be the case, he would have to attack the hinges. His fear was correct. The locks would not yield to his feet, even after flying kicks followed by painful landings. He would have to try the hinges; pray they hadn't fitted hinge bolts.

"Listen now; can you see the hinges?"

"Yes."

"How many?"

"Two."

That was some small relief. "How far are they from the top and bottom?"

"About eighteen inches."

Forty five centimetres. "Right. Bottom one first. Stand back again."

He stood with his back to the door, and kicked backwards, like an angry pony. After five or six kicks the screws started to pull, from the door, not the jamb. After about a dozen the foot of the door was pushed back about an inch; he could see where in the wood the screws were fixed. His ankle, and knee, and probably his hip felt as if he'd done them serious damage. But now, at least he could talk to Lucy without shouting.

"Is there a bed in there?"

"What? Yes."

"Look at it. Can you tip it up, can you crouch down, get it, the mattress, between you and the door?"

"Yes."

"Do so now."

In a moment he heard her voice, strained but fainter.

"Done it!"

He drew his Glock, and fired diagonally at the door, exactly where the screws entered the stile. After he had fired four shots, the four screws were exposed. The bullets had bitten deep into the oak, and remained in the wood. There had been neither splinter nor ricochet. He kicked the door back once more, and it pivoted on the top hinge, enough for Lucy to grab it on the inside. They pushed, and pulled, and the oak at last splintered at the top hinge and the door first swung open on the tenons, then toppled into the bedroom. Lucy fell back out of its way at the very last minute.

"Thank you, thank you. What's happening? I mean, is it just the two of you, you and Penny? I don't know how many of them there are – there's Axel – our friend, I thought – and another bloke, big fat man. I can't remember his name. And they said Michaelov was here – they pretended I was his guest – what's going on? Why did Michaelov need that picture?"

"There are three of us, at the moment. Others are coming, but your rescue was the first priority. We'll explain it all later, but we think these people are criminals, I mean, serious criminals. Not just to do with pictures."

"But – I only knew I was a prisoner an hour or two ago; what do you mean, serious criminals? Axel is our friend! So's Michaelov. And what's Penny doing here? She's only a ..."

"Penny, her name's Jane actually, is also SD, and she's extremely good at her job. And Michaelov isn't here. We know that; he's in Seattle. He was never involved. He knew nothing."

"Will someone explain all this later? Does my husband know what's going on?"

"Of course he does. I think he's coming too. But we had no time to lose."

"I see. You mean, they're – they were – going to use me as a hostage?"

"Possibly. We don't know, yet. But now, I've got to keep you safe until the cavalry arrives."

"What are we going to do?"

"It depends on David and Jane. I need to speak to them."

He took out his radio, and looked round at the thick granite walls. He smashed the window pane with his gun, and rammed his elbow through to widen the opening.

"Fingers crossed," he said and pushed the hand holding the radio, his arm and one shoulder, then his head, through the casement. Lucy could only make out his side of the conversation.

"Johnson, you said? What? I can't ... that's better. Are you sure? Yes, then he was a mercenary in Africa. That's right, the interviews after the Upton Park raid. Where are you both? With who? Say again? Good God. Yes, we can try. She looks quite fit."

He pulled himself back into the room. The remnants of the glass had cut his ear, and blood ran down over his collar. Then he ran out onto the landing, over to the window, and pushed at one of the points where three stained glass panels met. The window quivered.

He turned back and spoke to Lucy.

"There's no longer any threat from outside. But we don't know how many men are in the house, and how many of them are armed. And there are four more potential hostages, they arrived just as we did, God knows why they turned up. So we've got to get you out. It's safe outside now."

"How do we get out? The stairs – the lift – it goes down right to the middle of the house. What are you doing?"

Alan had grabbed one of the bedroom chairs, and now he ran with it to the stained glass window on the landing, and in four or five shattering blows Grendel and his nemesis lay in glittering fragments on the grass at the foot of the tower. A long way down; four storeys, forty feet at least.

"We do it the other way round in training," said Alan, "now, have you got a good head for heights?"

"I can't climb down there!" said Lucy, peering over the ledge.

"You don't have to," said Alan, "I shall lower you down. Unless you've got a real phobia? I mean, we've got a choice. Either out of the window, or I can try and keep them off. But there are more of them, and I don't know how they're armed. Probably machine guns."

"You might drop the rope. I'm a bit fat. Oh God."

Alan had already dragged the bedstead to the window, and was arranging his rope, passing it twice round the metal frame.

"Look, this makes it easier to control. And, as you say, you're not very fat, I can easily lift you." He seized her round the waist with his hands alone, and swung her into the air. "So there's really no problem. Just keep yourself off the wall with this. He handed her a pillow, then tied the rope in what a sailor, or a scout, would have recognised as a bowline on a bight. He helped her into this makeshift cradle, and before she could gather breath to demur – and later on she couldn't remember whether or not she was going to demur – she was swinging down the side of the building, laddering her tights and scratching her legs on the first windowsill, pushing herself off the wall using the pillow as a fender, avoiding the next two windowsills, and landing with a crunch, breathless, bleeding a little but safe, upon the shards of Beowulf. Alan secured the rope to the bedstead and followed her quickly, sliding down the rope like Jack Aubrey down a forestay. Lucy saw police cars parked near the distant fence, and four officers in uniform running towards them.

"Off you go, they'll look after you, your husband will be here soon. I've got ..." he waved vaguely towards the interior of the building, peered quickly through the ground floor window, smashed it open and disappeared. She ran as fast as she could to meet the policemen, and fell into the arms of the nearest. The others drew their guns and formed a protective screen around her as they all retreated to the cars, where she was offered the ritual comforts of blanket and sweet tea, and assured that she would be able to speak to Armstrong over the radio as soon as they had reported in.

"You did very well indeed madam," said the sergeant reassuringly, "for a ..." he intercepted a look from the inspector, and continued, " ...short while, we wondered what was going on; that's the third window the SAS bloke's smashed while we've been here, isn't it, Charlie?"

By now, Lucy had recovered enough to speak, but she was naturally still in shock. She smiled at the sergeant. "And all for a painting by Hopkins! You wouldn't believe it, would you? I'm not *very* fat, am I?" The policemen had been given few details, and exchanged glances. One of the young constables offered her some more tea.

The room into which Alan had burst was empty, except for some filing cabinets and cases of corned beef. His fibrescope showed a passage the other side of the door; it, too, was empty. There was an old-fashioned telephone cabinet to his left, opposite that a door, slightly ajar, then the passage gave on to a larger space, almost certainly the entrance hall. He left the room, and edged towards the hall. At least two, probably three people were shouting; they must have heard his shots in the tower, he heard the name Johnson, someone, a female, spoke of the sound of splintering glass.

His steady progress towards the hall was brought to a halt by an extraordinary sight which became only partly visible as he passed the open door opposite the telephone. Within the room, by the fireplace, a woman with a knife was kneeling beside a large sausage shaped bundle, swathed in silver tape; she was about to plunge the knife downwards. But before he could react physically, the scene resolved and he saw Jane Ryan releasing a figure, a man, from the bands of gaffer tape which imprisoned him. Ryan saw him, and beckoned him in to help. Anthony, freed from his bonds, could not stand unaided; he sank to the floor again, trying to restore strength and circulation to his limbs.

"Is David safe? Where is he? And who's that?" asked Alan, who had seen a small outlandishly dressed figure, immobilised more conventionally than Anthony had been, but gagged in the same manner.

"Yes, David's safe, he's in the next room, it's got its own door into the hall. I don't know who the pixie is, he was supposed to be guarding Evans."

Recumbent but attentive, Anthony quickly told them who Edwards was, and why, and how, Anthony had been transported to the castle. Normally, Anthony's language was fairly free from obscenity. "The little bugger pulled a knife on me, then he hit me with a spanner, then he trussed me up like fucking King Tut. May I kick him a bit?"

"Certainly not. Unless he tries to escape." Alan asked, "Jane, who's where?"

Jane told him the situation in the hall, as far as she knew; there was Nicholls by the wall, with a sub-machine gun, Axel, now revealed as the Count, certainly armed as well, his partner or wife Alison, probably armed. One man who had come to the kitchen to kill Rembrandt was himself dead – those were the shots which Alan had heard – yes, she had fired two of them – but there might be others. The visitors, possible hostages, were four in number, all known to him except Frieda.

"What did you do with the man in the kitchen? Rembrandt?"

"We restrained him and left him there. He can't go anywhere."

"David and I will deal with the situation in the hall. Can you locate any other targets? Don't take risks, just recce. Remember, the main job's done, Mrs Armstrong's safe."

Jane retreated down the corridor, and, finding the back stairs to the area passage, worked her way along it, first to the back door which had been guarded, until a few moments previously, by the man Parker, then, retracing her steps, to some doors at the other end which stood open and let in a little daylight to supplement the gloom of the scanty, bare, underpowered light bulbs. The first room, a stinking washroom, was empty, but a sound, a strange sound, which she could not immediately identify, came from the next. The door was only half open, and she pushed it gently with her foot. A large man, in overalls, with a machine gun, was holding at bay a group of men and women, and a child. The child was suppressing sobs, and drawing her breath in a series of jerks – this was the sound Jane had heard. One of the men was Maurice, who stared at her with absolute astonishment. Jane levelled her gun at the man in overalls, who had seen the expression on Maurice's face, had tensed, and then spun round. To Jane's dismay, two of the women, one of them pulling along with her the weeping child, had sidled around, behind the gunman, leaving him in a direct line between themselves and Jane. If she missed him ... she would not miss him ... she *could* not miss him ... but as he turned the muzzle of his gun towards her, his eyes widened, his mouth opened, his knees buckled and he fell to the floor. The hilt of a knife – a bread knife, kitchen knife, something of that sort – protruded from his neck, angled down in such a way that the blade itself must have been driven upwards into his cranium. There was little blood. Which of the women had done it? It was impossible to tell.

*****

Rembrandt was sitting comfortably but immobile, his hands and feet secured with plastic ties to the arms and legs of the velvet Papal throne, when he saw, for the second time, a female face at the clerestory window. The last face had been, he remembered, remarkably beautiful. He thought of her in artistic terms, even, or especially, when she was strapping him, quite kindly but securely, to the armchair. He remembered every feature. One day, he thought, he would paint her portrait; in his own style, which he knew he would find soon. He knew that she had saved his life, although he was a little unclear about the order of events, and the purpose of her arrival.

The new face was very familiar. It belonged to the woman whom he had been taken to meet many times by the pixie; the woman who had once accompanied him to an old man's house in London; who had found him books and papers and pictures; all that he asked for. They had met in strange places, the pixie man had said that the castle must remain secret. She was pretty, in the way in which many Japanese women seem pretty to Western eyes, and he hoped that she had come to release him, but his mental focus remained upon the face of the woman who had tied him up. His attitude, his preoccupation, was not as strange as it might seem; he had adapted to a life where only art brought rewards, mainly as an end in itself, but also as a means to the few luxuries which he enjoyed.

The second young woman did release him. Maybe she was surprised to find a rope so conveniently to hand; maybe she had seen the other two come in that way. At any rate, the only difficult part of his escape was climbing up the rope. In the end they piled furniture up, and knotted the rope, so that he only had a short distance to climb, and knots to prevent him slipping. This time he had no demands to make, no requests for pictures or information. He never questioned her authority.

They crept around the foot of the cliff and waited in the mouth of an adit for dusk to fall. Whenever Rembrandt made as if to speak the Japanese girl put her fingers to her lips; neither of them so much as whispered during the entire escape. When it was nearly dark they continued, carefully avoiding two men, probably police, who were rustling the bracken and even talking in undertones, until they came to the stream. There they joined the cliff path which they could safely follow in the dim light of the clouded moon. Eventually they came to a small village where they turned inland, found the road, and made their rendezvous.

*****

Anthony had recovered, had rubbed life back into his pinioned limbs and felt exposed and bored standing around staring at the little rat Edwards, although he derived some satisfaction from the look of apprehension upon the face of the little rat, who had presumably heard Anthony's suggestion to Alan. As he peered around the corner of the door, and when the prospect of imminent sudden death in a hail of sub-machine gun bullets should have tempered his curiosity, but did not, he saw that it was possible to edge some way along the corridor towards the sound of voices from the hall without becoming visible to its occupants. So that is what he did, but he miscalculated the distance which he could traverse undetected, and he too was confronted by a tableau, a more complicated one, as if a motion picture had been abruptly stilled. He puzzled to interpret it. Some of the characters on the screen noticed him; some did not. To the left stood his friends, Frieda clinging to Patricia. Maurice was missing, replaced by – wearing? – a suit of armour. A badger lay dead at Frieda's feet. Axel and Alison stood together by the fireplace straight ahead of him, a darkened rectangle of wallpaper showing where a picture had been recently removed. David Smith – MacMaster – stood at their side. His gun was half-raised and he was preparing to speak. On the other side of the passage door, only a few feet away from Anthony, stood a man with a sub-machine gun. At this point, the screen unfroze and the motion picture resumed. However, his interpretation was in error; movies are only watched but he was involved in participation theatre.

As David, who had only that moment entered, levelled his gun at Axel, Anthony heard a shout of "Police, drop your weapon!" from the doorway on the right hand side of the room. The man with the machine gun responded by turning his gun towards the sound, but was immediately felled by two shots, one from David's gun and one from the gun of the man who had shouted, who now burst into the hall. The machine gun fell to the floor, by Anthony's feet. Anthony's eyes were fixed upon Axel and Alison. Axel held a gun – but so, now, did Alison. The man who had shouted, one of MacMaster's men, Anthony presumed, was staring at Axel's gun, but as far as Anthony could tell no-one had seen Alison's. She started to turn to MacMaster, and clicked something upon her pistol, bringing it up to aim at him. Anthony stooped, seized the gun at his feet, and raised it to point at Alison. The trigger of the last gun he had held had needed force to pull, but this was a different sort of weapon and as he lifted it his finger touched its trigger.

Only – a month? – ago, he had been staggered by the sound of a single shot. Before he could release the trigger this time, some twenty bullets had been sprayed around the room, most of them very high, bursting chandeliers, shattering windows, destroying entire collections of ginger jars and Dresden statuettes. The noise was extraordinary and masked the shot with which Alan dealt with the threat from Axel. Alison had been unnerved by the noise and destruction, and at the same time had been tackled and thrown to the floor by David, who had at the last minute noticed the pistol in her hand. He does not know whether he would have achieved this without Anthony's startling intervention.

Not all the shots which Anthony fired missed human targets. When David stood up after Green had secured the fake Count and his fake Countess he was clutching his left upper arm with his right hand. A drop of blood splashed to the floor, then another. David looked down at his sleeve, and to the red stains on his shirt cuff. He moved his gaze to Anthony who appeared both defiant and embarrassed. Like Anthony, David did not swear a lot, so all he said was "Please don't do it again."

The following year

The appalling events which marked the first few years of the new millennium prevented Jane and David from enjoying any sort of lengthy holiday together; they had made many different plans for their honeymoon, but had to put them all in abeyance. David had been promoted, and, since his Arabic was now good, was running agents in the Middle East. Jane had a complicated brief, liaising with the Americans concerning dangers posed by the various violent organisations which had proliferated since the invasion of Afghanistan. The operation upon which they first met, the protection of a British politician from threats to his good character and its exciting, but parochial, conclusion, seemed utterly trivial in comparison with the present threats to the peace of the entire world, threats which, they both thought, certainly included the hypocritically named, and crudely implemented 'war on terror'.

They did, however, manage to take just enough leave together for a brief holiday, hardly a honeymoon, because they had now been married for over a year. They visited Jane's mother and were entertained to dinner at high table where the wine was excellent and the food, to Jane's surprise, prepared in the modern manner. A slightly off-putting incident occurred; a youngish don, also a guest, whom Jane vaguely remembered bumping into once on her Mama's staircase, looked intently at David after a conversation about the policies of the West towards the Arab states, a conversation to which neither Jane nor David contributed more than uninterpretable murmurs, and said that he was quite disenchanted, *quite disenchanted*, like many of his friends, and he would be more than happy for David to mention that to his colleagues in the Foreign Office, *or elsewhere*. David's expression hardly changed, but Jane understood that he had been given a message, and knew it.

Then they spent a week by the sea in Suffolk, walking along gentle duck boarded paths in the soft grey light, threading their way through dunes and marram grass, looking at birds and flowers, and holding hands. Jane's professionally acquired interest in art had blossomed into real enthusiasm, and in the last couple of years they had bought pictures and sculptures at various auctions – usually taking advice from Anthony or Frieda, who had both become friends. There was a small gallery in the high street of a pretty pink and cream village quite close to Lavenham, where they had had a pub lunch on the last day of their holiday, so Jane, as usual, pulled David in to see if there was anything she thought they couldn't live without. The gallery was surprisingly crowded, and a tray of glasses with white wine was standing on a side table, together with bowls of nuts and crisps. It was a private view – in Jane's experience such privacy was only notional – and they attached themselves to a group of people standing round a man wearing a bow tie who was addressing them.

"...we're not often privileged to offer the works of so well-known an artist," he was saying, "especially ones which have never before been on the market. In this case, however, there's quite a family connection. He and my grandfather were art students together at the Slade at the beginning of the last century – they were quite a notable crowd, you know, Nash, Nevinson, Spencer – but my grandfather wasn't nearly as good as Sunny, he never kept up his painting, nevertheless they remained great friends. The two of them went on holiday once, a boating holiday on Lake Windermere it was, and one afternoon, in beautiful weather with a light breeze, when they'd just rowed a couple of hundred yards from the jetty at Bowness, they decided to raise the sail. The boat didn't have a very tall mast, of course, and there was no jib, just a mainsail. My grandad was the only one of them who knew how to sail a boat – he'd lived in Porchester, just over the water from Horsea Island, and kept a little boat there for fishing. Sunny had no idea – everybody called him Sunny, you know, because he was always such an optimist – and since the weather was so nice, and the wind so gentle, he asked Grandad to give him a sailing lesson. Well, perhaps he should have refused, certainly we would say that now, but in those days people didn't bother so much about life jackets and all that rigmarole, and Sunny was quite set on it. It's not really too difficult to get the hang of sailing a small dinghy..."

A weather beaten man in a Guernsey and faded rust coloured cotton trousers was rather taken aback by this, and looked as if he might interrupt. David's eye was caught by a small picture, a portrait, which was hanging in a different part of the gallery, partly shielded and now revealed by the movement of the dissenting sailor. This painting was not one of those in the exhibition area, and it was painted in a totally different style. David took Jane's arm, and steered her away from the exhibition, towards the wall where the portrait hung. There was a young man there, sitting at a desk and typing away at a word processor, who looked up as they approached. He smiled at them with the faint, schooled smile of the courteous gallery owner, his eyes flicking cursorily over them before returning to his keyboard. Then his expression changed. He appeared to force his eyes up again, to drag them back to look at Jane. His gaze remained fixed upon her, the rest of his body as rigid as his stare.

Jane was looking at the painting, the portrait, as was David. She had only seen the young man once before, but she immediately recognised him. David, who had only seen him fleetingly, did not. But they had both recognised the subject of the portrait, the wonderful portrait, full of life and vigour and beauty, so different from the anodyne, if competent and valuable, paintings in the exhibition.

"How are you? Are you doing well now?" Jane asked, and he nodded. He tried to speak, but could find no words.

"Is the portrait for sale?" David asked.

Again he nodded. Then he found his words, but spoke to Jane.

"For you, no, no, of course. It is a gift. You saved my life. I shall never forget. I shall paint another, for myself alone..."

Over in the exhibition area, the man with the bow tie, whom David, but not Jane, had now recognised, was continuing his tale.

"...when one of those sudden gusts of wind – you know how treacherous the weather can be on Windermere – took Sunny by surprise just as he was attempting to gybe; they were quite off balance, and capsized in a second, just like that, they were both splashing about in the water. Well, it turned out that he couldn't swim! My grandfather was a strong swimmer, and within a matter of minutes ...."

At that point the girl who had been looking after the tray of drinks moved over to David and Jane, turned and offered them glasses of wine. She was a very demure Japanese lady, not a girl at all; she glanced at David, and he looked at her. She looked steadily back; he smiled. He held up his hand to decline the drinks.

"We must go now, I think," Jane said, and, taking David's hand, led him out into the street. He spoke first.

"It's a beautiful painting, surely there would be no harm..."

"David, David, you know that we can't."

"Yes, I suppose that you're right. Of course you're right."

"I'm afraid you'll just have to make do with the original; tell you what, I'll get Anthony to take some nice pictures, he's quite good at it now."

"I think you mean photographs, don't you?"

"Tea and a cream bun?"

They crossed the street to the Copper Kettle and, resisting the temptation to speculate about what the future might hold for Rembrandt and his little team, started to plan the next few weeks of their complicated life.

Acknowledgements

I am profoundly grateful to Hilary Richings for her help and suggestions, and for proof reading. Philippa Stilwell has been indefatigable in support; to her my thanks. My thanks also to Roy Phillips and Rob Donovan for their comments and encouragement.

The cover was designed by Heather Allen, the photography was by Lothar Spurzem.

Printed in Great Britain
by Amazon.co.uk, Ltd.,
Marston Gate.